GAIA'S REVOLUTION

Nina Munteanu

GAIA'S REVOLUTION

Nina Munteanu

PRINT ISBN 978-1-77400-076-2

EPUB ISBN 978-1-77400-077-9

www.dragonmoonpress.com

This book is dedicated to climate/environmental activists and reporters around the world

Several 1980s tunes accompanied my muse as I wrote *Gaia's Revolution*. Chief ones include: *Space Age Love Song* by Flock of Seagulls; *Avalon* and *More Than This* by Roxy Music; *Everybody Wants to Rule the World* and *Shout* by Tears for Fears; *Forever Young* by Alphaville; and *Running Up That Hill* by Kate Bush.

INCUBATION

Crisis is opportunity. The experience of instability in nature maintains the structure and general patterns of ecosystem behaviour. Ecosystem behaviour is non-linear, self-organizing, and continually adapting through cycles of change from expansion and prosperity to creative destruction and reorganization. Nature evolves through exploitation, conservation, creative destruction, and mobilization. These phases require instability and change. Overall, they reflect stable chaos, marked by resilience, elasticity, and balance.

—Damien Vogel, "The Concept of Stable Chaos: An Existential Perspective on Climate Change," JOURNAL OF CHAOS & NONLINEAR SCIENCE, 213 (4) November 2023

ONE

BERLIN, Warschauer Straße.
December 13, 2022: morning

"Are you Damien Vogel?" the tallest of the two burly policemen asks in a booming voice. He glares down at Damien with surly eyes through the open doorway. The question seems rhetorical because the moment the policeman speaks, both cops barge inside, knocking Damien aside, before he has a chance to answer.

"What do you want?" he demands as they stomp inside his studio apartment like two rhinos. Neither responds. Why is his heart pounding? Both cops are large men with crew cuts and stubby facial hair. They're dressed in black uniforms with "Polizei" branded on their backs and pistols strapped to their hips. The tallest one, easily seven feet tall—Damien himself is well over six feet tall—has tiny features embedded in a massive round face. Full mouth, pert nose and close-set eyes lose themselves in a rosy but cruel face. The other cop has a longer roughly chiselled face with hawkish eyes, slender roman nose and stern thin-lipped mouth. Both are burly behemoths and built like sumo wrestlers.

They don't seem interested in interacting with him or questioning him; instead, they move about the place, critical eyes assessing. Despite their desultory treatment of his things, it is obvious to him that they are looking for specific things. The tall one leans over Damien's coffee table and carelessly goes through his pile of newspapers and magazines. Several issues of *taz,* the latest issue of *Der Spiegel* and *Die Zeit* lie on the table. He picks up Damien's copy of right-wing newspaper *Bild* and raises his brows with an oily smirk at the long-faced cop. Both snigger. After the cop flips through each magazine or paper, he tosses them recklessly on the floor.

"What are you doing?" Damien demands. "You can't do this."

The tall cop ignores Damien and continues rifling through his papers. The long-faced cop answers, "Yes, we can. By order of the public prosecutor Cyrill Klement in the prosecutor's office in Neuruppin: you're under suspicion of disrupting public order and forming a criminal organization."

He is obviously referring to the climate activist group Damien joined a few months ago: Letzte Generation. His last stunt of civil disobedience with them gained a lot of attention: gluing himself to the pavement of a busy street. When they scraped his bleeding hand off the pavement, Damien thought he was going to jail like his compatriots did in Bavaria. But all he got was a stiff reprimand by the officer on duty once he'd surrendered his name and official ID.

"That's ridiculous," Damien says, trailing after the cops who enter his bedroom. "I know my rights. Even disruptive forms of protest are protected by the fundamental right to freedom of assembly."

Both cops smirk and continue their search with renewed vigor. Damien feels his heart race with fear as the tall cop fingers the papers on his oak desk. The policeman picks up a loose scrap of paper with

Damien's handwritten notes and reads aloud in a baritone voice: *At the surface tension of history's flow, where the delicate balance of the forces of stability and instability lie, life blossoms. The disorderly behavior of simple systems acts as a creative process, generating complexity. Beneath the turbulent waves of disorder lies a destiny worth mastering.* He snorts and says sarcastically, "What is this? A novel about the revolution, perhaps?"

Close, thinks Damien. They are notes for a book he's begun, a scientific treatise on the role of creative destruction in evolution. Revolution would metaphorically figure into that process.

The cop sneers and crumples the paper in his huge fist. Then, using his sausage finger and thumb, he flicks it across the room. The ball of paper sails in a wide arc, past Damien's head, and bounces on the floor like a piece of trash. "There's your revolution." He grins then snorts out a churlish laugh.

Damien flinches at a crash behind him and spins around to see that the long-faced cop has purposefully knocked down from his high dresser the metre-high potted Christmas tree he'd just bought. The clay pot lies smashed with spilled dirt on the floor. The long-faced cop grins at him like a wolverine then rifles through Damien's wardrobe, carelessly dropping clothes onto the floor after frisking each. Damien's entire body begins to tremble uncontrollably. He remembers hiding two data drives filled with precious notes in his dresser drawer.

He thinks of the sit-in days of Heinrich Böll, Günter Grass, Walter Jens, Helmut Gollwitzer and Otto Schily. Back in the 1980s, they protested nuclear rearmament with no repercussions. That was fifty years ago; things have changed in Germany since then. Like the reunification and the violent protests against immigration. The open racism and anti-Semitism. The rise in neo-fascist protests. The backlash against human rights and increase in police brutality. Last month, Bavarian police—using the Police Powers Act—put twelve Letzte Generation climate activists in jail for gluing themselves to the Stachus and obstructing traffic for an hour. Under Bavarian law, preventive detention doesn't require concrete suspicion of a crime or a court order for the first thirty days; *anyone* can be detained in jail without recourse.

Liebender Gott, we're heading for a police state in Germany.

Things are changing everywhere. In Australia, just eleven days ago, new draconian anti-protest laws put climate activist Deanna Coco in jail for fifteen months with no bail for briefly blocking traffic to protest her government's failure to act on climate change. All over the world, governments are suppressing opposition to their pro-business agenda in favour of the corporate elite with laws that protect fossil fuel super-profiteers. Unfortunately, police violence has become part of it.

"We're taking this," the tall cop says, seizing Damien's laptop from his oak desk.

"You can't! That's mine!" Damien grabs for his laptop. "It has my master's thesis in it and the research paper I'm—"

The tall cop strikes him hard on the face, hurling him backward. He falls painfully on his rump to the floor. His ears ring and he feels the stinging bite of the blow on his cheek. Fear roils in his gut and settles against his chest like a heavy iron fist.

"We're confiscating it by order of the public prosecutor," the tall cop booms. "Now, give us your phone." He holds out his hand and impatiently flicks his thick sausage fingers at Damien. Close-set eyes burn into him with an insane fire. Trembling on the floor, Damien reaches into his pocket with a shaky hand and surrenders his phone. The cop snatches the phone from him and pockets it.

I'm not a fighter, Damien thinks, feeling the tendrils of powerlessness pull at his gut. He's more of an intellectual with a philosopher's build. Tall and lanky. Not a runner like his twin brother, Eric. He feels useless. How can he stop these two monsters who are stripping him of his scholarly existence? Eric would fight back.

Damien struggles to his feet and mutely watches the two policemen trash the rest of his apartment. They find and pocket his two flash drives hidden with his underwear. The drives have information on his scientific research. Damien sighs and sees his academic life flash before his eyes. Years of tireless research are about to walk out that door. He knows he'll never see his computer and drives again. Or if he does, they'll be erased or heavily tampered with.

But the cops aren't done. The long-faced cop pulls a book from the bookshelf above his desk, obviously intending to confiscate. Damien recognizes Rachel Carson's *Silent Spring*. The book he's carried with him everywhere he went since his mother gave it to him for his sixth birthday. The cop flips through the book, noting the copious portions Damien has highlighted. Then he opens to the front page and carelessly reads aloud the inscription in the open handwriting of Damien's mother: *Je klarer wir unsere Aufmerksamkeit auf die Wunder und Realitäten des Universums um uns herum richten können, desto weniger Geschmack werden wir an der Zerstörung haben. Liebe, Mutti.*

"NO!" Damien wails. Forgetting his fear, he lunges for the book. "Please! You can't take—"

A great maw slams into the side of his face from nowhere. He sees lights and teeters in a spiral like a felled tree then finds himself sprawled on the floor with his knees on fire. He must have briefly blacked out. Tears spill out of his eyes from the intense pain and he feels his breakfast clawing its way up and burning his throat in a hot wave of nausea. A sudden warmth between his legs alerts him that he's wet his pants.

"And stay down," the tall cop commands in a calm voice of quiet menace, standing over Damien like a vulture.

The long-faced cop wags the book in front of him. "In a better world, this trash would be burned," he snarls and tucks the book inside his satchel. He turns back to the desk and focuses on a poster pasted on the wall above the bookshelf. The poster lists the eight principles of deep ecology created by George Sessions and Arne Naess in 1984. Long face sneering in a mean smile, the cop reaches over the desk and with a sweeping flourish of violence rips the poster off the wall. It screams off the wall as he pulls it down and tears it to shreds. The pieces flutter to the floor like leaves in the dead of autumn.

Shivering uncontrollably on the floor, Damien finds himself focusing on the policeman's hip where a 9mm Luger sits tucked in its holster. Damien can't shake an awful feeling: that these two are more than just mean cops. What if they are also Reichsbürger terrorists?

Experts have been warning for years of ultra-right-wing networks in German security agencies and the armed forces. Just days ago, authorities raided the right-wing terrorist network Reich Citizens' Movement—Reichsbürgerbewegung—for conspiring to storm the Bundestag, attack the German power grid, and overthrow the German government. The raid confirmed ties to Germany's military special forces unit, the Kommando Spezialkräfte. If elite soldiers of the KSK were identified as far-right Reichsbürger terrorists, why not the local police force? Both are conservative and enforce a hierarchical order; "blind in its right-eye," says Nathaniel Flakin of Red Flag. Authorities have already identified several Bavarian police officers as disciples of that movement and they found neo-Nazi and anti-Semitic ties to police departments in other parts of Germany. There is no doubt in Damien's mind that the Berlin police harbour radical far-right types. Are two in his apartment this moment?

Damien begins to shake. The long-faced cop points to Damien's wet crotch. "*Wahrscheinlich hat er als Kind ins Bett gemacht*!" He chortles. They both laugh loudly.

The cops finally leave, slamming the door behind them. Damien hears their churlish laughter echo in the hallway as their heavy footsteps fade. He stays where they've left him in the silence, only hearing his beating heart. He can't stop shaking. A long time passes before he gingerly gets back to his feet and glances down at his wet crotch. As he pulls out a Vita Cola from the kitchen fridge and gently rolls the cold wet bottle over his burning cheek and temple, he considers himself lucky today. If these cops are Reichsbürger terrorists, he is lucky he can still stand.

TWO

BERLIN, Humboldt Universität.
December 13, 2022: afternoon

From Unter den Linden Boulevard Damien crosses Bebelplatz to the *Alte Bibliothek* of Humboldt Universität law faculty. As he crosses the cobblestone square, he stops at the empty library memorial and imagines that dreary rainy evening on May 10, 1933, when Humboldt students and professors joined the Nazi German Student Association to burn over 20,000 books. Some of the books came from the *Alte Bibliothek*, others were plundered from public libraries, private bookshelves and other academic collections and brought here to die. Students piled them right where he is standing, then they burned them all. Nearby, a zealous crowd of over forty thousand eagerly listened to Propaganda Minister Joseph Goebbels thunder about purity in German culture. They burned 'heretical' books by their own former students, brilliant men and women. Albert Einstein among them. And Heinrich Heine, who had presciently written: *dort wo man Bücher verbrennt, verbrennt man am Ende auch Menschen.* "Where they burn books, they will in the end also burn people."

A sudden shiver runs through him as he remembers what the long-faced cop said to him after confiscating Damien's precious book. *In a better world, this trash would be burned.* Who's better world was he referring to?

Damien meets no one from Letzte Generation at the Canteen or upstairs at the Branch Library of Law. No one to clarify what happened: whether he is a unique case or other Letzte Generation members were visited by Reichsbürgers, if indeed that is who those cruel cops were.

Anxious to retrieve the information he lost on his confiscated computer and flash drives, Damien finds a quiet section in the library's computer lab and accesses a computer with his student card. Thankfully, some of his material is on the cloud, in drop boxes and sequestered in his email files. He'll grab all of them before heading to his mother's place in Neukölln, where he wisely keeps a set of paper files. As his e-files download to a flash drive, Damien's hand strays to his throbbing cheek. His feverish mind returns to the cruel cops who attacked him and what they might be.

The Demos-Brandenburg Institute für Gemeinwesenberatung profiled Reichsbürger disciples as mostly single, older self-important men who are socially isolated, distrustful and often paranoid. Reichsbürgers are mostly right-wing extremists and historical revisionists; many are anti-Semitists, Holocaust deniers, and climate deniers. For them, the current government is not legal. They consider the old "German Reich"—based on its 1871 borders—as the only valid regime. Among those under suspicion to overthrow the existing state order is Prince Reuss Heinrich XIII, charged as their ringleader. Damien read about Heinrich, who descended from a Thuringian noble family that had ruled the Vogtland region for seven hundred years. He certainly fit the profile the Demos-Brandenburg Institute had created for Reichsbürgers. Many are aggressive nationalists who trivialize or deny the Nazi crimes. Neo-fascists and anti-Semitists. Many claim Sovereign Citizenship: refusing to accept state-issued documents such as driver's licences and passports; refusing to pay taxes and fines, writing their own liens against government officials, and resorting to violence—especially against the police—to protect their imagined rights.

Damien considers that despite Germany's reputation as a liberal democracy with a strong economy, a leader of the European Union, and a country that openly atones for the Holocaust, this country has struggled with identity since its reunification. When Merkel's Federal Republic of Germany admitted over a million refugees and migrants from the war-torn climate-ravaged deserts of Syria, Afghanistan and Ukraine, far-right extremists such as the Reichsbürger terrorists came to the surface. Like bugs crawling out from under a rock, the Reichsbürgers joined the ranks of Pegida, Identitarians, Der Dritte Weg, and QAnon in a swarming far-right movement driven by fear of losing their identity under a thunderous wave of change. Some German journalists suggested that the Reichsbürgers fashioned their campaign after the failed coup of far-right Trump acolytes who stormed the American Capital in 2021. The turbulent wake of that uprising even hit mild-mannered Canada—where Damien's brother Eric lives—with that ragtag truck convoy who named themselves the Freedom Convoy. Reichsbürgers are preparing for Tag X, the

"Great Awakening": the day they dispatch all liberal politicians, topple the country's 'false' democracy, and replace it with an authoritarian Fourth Reich. One way or another change is coming, Damien ponders, hand gingerly touching his bruised cheek.

For Germany, it started with the Mauerfall. Before he left for Canada, twin brother Eric contended that when the Berlin Wall fell in '89, the flood of East Germans into the decadent West brought with them a 'cleansing' force over the capitalist debauchery of the rich and arrogant West. Then the *dummkopf* moved to North America, the hub of profligate capitalism! Damien remembers arguing back that, instead of 'cleansing' the west of capitalist greed, the East Germans brought with them unapologetic anti-Semitism and notions of white supremacy to a west that had grown more humble, tolerant and liberal since Nürnberg.

"You don't get it, Dame," Eric shot back. "That isn't who we are either. For all your insistence that you love and respect our mother and you carry that book around like a bible, you don't really understand her, what she is, what she did..."

Maybe I don't, but you don't either, brother...

Their mother was a touchy subject for both of them.

She was born Lisbeth Durchdenwald in 1962 to poor farmers, not far from where the previous German Chancellor Angela Merkel lived, near Templin, just 90 km north of Berlin. Lisbeth was born the same year that Rachel Carson published her book *Silent Spring*—something the young ecologically-minded Lisbeth had considered significant and wished to live by. Nineteen sixty-two was also a year after Khrushchev built the Berlin Wall to stop the mass exodus of East Germans from communist rule. Lisbeth's father was a drunk who beat his wife. Eric postulated that Lisbeth was also beaten when she was older; good incentive to leave home, which she did at an early age. Lisbeth grew up under the *Sozialistische Einheitspartei Deutschlands* in the *Deutsche Demokratische Republik* the DDR, also known as the Zone. She sang 'I want to be a *Volkspolizist*' in kindergarten, read Mosaik comics and *Die Abenteuer des Werner Holt* in school and watched anti-capitalist and anti-fascist movies. She kept a blue tin of *Florena* cream in her bathroom and hoarded toilet paper. She collected bottles and scrap metal and paper for recycling centres and marched in anti-fascist processions as a *Junge Pioniere*. She read the pioneer movement brochures, full of stories about Ernst Thälmann—Teddy—and other workers' activists, and she idolized the German communist resistance against National Socialism. She celebrated *Jugendweihe* when she was fourteen and pledged her allegiance to the state. She drank Vita Cola, ate *Quarkkäulchen* and *Soljanka* in the local canteen, and feared the Stasi who kept everyone obedient through mass surveillance and the imprisonment of dissidents with little evidence.

Lisbeth grew up in a country that was born in 1949, a country in which nothing worth mentioning had happened before. She didn't know what her grandparents had done, whether they were fascist-imperialist collaborators or fought in the resistance. It didn't seem to matter; her ancestors were part of another world that no longer existed. It was as though, just as the Zone had sprung up after WWII as a fully-formed anti-fascist state, so had her generation. Difficult questions or terrible histories were conveniently extinguished. She was part of a new social construction. One based on egalitarian non-hierarchical ideals that incubated far too many hidden hierarchies.

Lisbeth was bright and gifted in science and technology. When she was seventeen, she left home to work at the Trabant car factory in Zwickau. Named 'Trabi' or the 'Saxon Porsche', the 'plastic bomber' was made of duroplast, a hard plastic derived from recycled materials that included pressed cotton fibers, synthetic resins and rags from the Soviet Union. Lisbeth went to technical school to earn a ticket as a top-notch mechanical engineer; she was soon earning more than most men in the company. Eric cynically suggested that their mother had been a Stasi informant, an *inoffizielle Mitarbeiter*—many were embedded in key places of high productivity—and *that* was why she made the big money. It wasn't any one thing, more like a host of little things that suggested it. Her incredible attention to detail and her *deutsche Gründlichkeit*. Her detached knowledge of *everything* about *everyone*; not to gossip, more as though she was used to doing it for so long because it had once been important to her survival. Eric made a convincing argument—he always made convincing arguments. But Damien refused to accept that his mother had spied on her neighbours as part of the *antifaschistisch-demokratische Umwälzung* to 'purify' the DDR. It was unconscionable and reeked of the brainwashed Nazi BDM who gladly informed on their own parents. She was an environmentalist, after all, with scruples. Eric later confirmed that one in six East Germans had operated at one time as a *Spitzel* for the security service. Colleagues, friends, husbands and wives, informed on each other. Files were kept on one in three East Germans, he told Damien.

Shortly after Germany's reunification—and the supposed dissolution of the Stasi—Lisbeth met Gerhardt Vogel in Zwickau. Gerhardt had been a *Volkspolizist*, a People's Police, since the early '80s. Eric insisted that their father would have also worked for the Stasi—the *Ministerium für Staatissicherheit*—until the reunification. That's what VoPos did, after all.

"The bastard was a Stasi agent, just like Mother," Eric snarled one day as he and Damien ate leftover *Wurstgulasch* in the kitchen. Eric always used pejorative language to condemn their father, thought Damien, who defended both parents against Eric's demonizing them, but found it difficult to come up with a convincing rebuttal. He could never understand Eric's contempt for a dead father they never knew—as if he was angry at their father for getting himself killed and not being there for the boys.

Lisbeth and Gerhardt married and in 1992 they moved to Marzahn, Berlin, where they lived in a *Plattenbau*. That was the same year that close to a thousand neo-Nazi youths firebombed a refugee hostel in Rostock, followed by a decade of neo-Nazi hate crimes by the neo-Nazi terror group, the National Socialist Underground (NSU). Nazism had always lurked in former communist anti-fascist East Germany. Its presence was exemplified in their own family. Gerhardt's father, Ernst, had been chairman of the East German Committee Against Fascism and member of the central committee of the SED until 1959. But, two years ago, as Damien was rummaging in some historical documents for a project at university on how the communists turned out to be odd bedfellows with the Nazis, he discovered his grandfather's big secret: before serving the anti-fascist revolution and central committee of SED, Ernst had served in the Third Reich as a Nazi *SS Unterscharfürher* and guard in the concentration camp of Sachsenhausen. That was information the Stasi may have used to induce Gerhardt to work for them, suggested Eric; but that knowledge also fed into the already paradoxical relationship of communist collaboration with Nazis that started long ago with the second world war.

In 1939, despite their ideological differences and their proxy war during the Spanish Civil War, Stalin ignored Kristallnacht and signed a nonaggression pact with Hitler. Then, together, they invaded Poland. After WWII, former Nazis, like Damien's grandfather, integrated easily into East German society and gained positions in the communist DDR because of their skills, training and expertise—all considered valuable to the machinery of production. Denazification fizzled under the pressure of production. Ernst Vogel's connection to national socialism was just one of many examples of Third Reich-DDR continuity. Not wishing to lose trained executives for their production machine, the SEM designated Nazis with extensive skill sets 'former nominal members of the NSDAP' as opposed to 'activist Nazis,' and therefore acceptable to the communist regime. In his 1968 report "Die gleiche Sprache: Erst für Hitler—jetzt für Ulbricht," Simon Wiesenthal revealed many examples of Third Reich senior men who ended up serving in high ranking DDR positions as well as editorial staff of newspapers. Olaf Kappelt's book *Braunbuch DDR* revealed close to a thousand former National Socialists with careers in the DDR.

The Nazis never left, thought Damien. They just changed their spots; and, in some cases, they didn't even do that. The remarkable truth about Gerhardt Vogel's *SS* father opened a wider truth for Damien: that DDR's anti-fascism policy was more slogan than reality, a foundation myth that helped create and assert an identity to motivate its citizens. Their mother's genuine anti-fascism—which in her mind would have vindicated her choice to serve as a Stasi *Spitzel* (if she was indeed one)—was based on a fraudulent directive.

In 2002, when the twins were two years old, Gerhardt, who was hired by the Bonn government to work as an archivist opening up spy records in the Stasi Records Agency in Berlin, was brutally murdered under suspicious circumstances. Their mother refused to discuss it, even when Damien broached the topic as a teenager. Eric pieced together a sinister story, based on his suspicion that both parents were Stasi agents.

In late 1989—the same year Gleick published his book *Chaos*—the SED changed its name to the Party of Democratic Socialism (PDS); several members of the old Communist Party remained members of the German Bundestag for years after. Then, in January of 1990, weeks after the fall of the Berlin wall, thousands of protesters stormed the Stasi headquarters in Berlin. Secret police meekly surrendered, after trying to shred, pulp and tear evidence by hand and leaving behind more than a hundred kilometers of intelligence files. Since the late '90s many violent murders occurred, some no doubt to do with the opening of Stasi files and the release of information on who denounced and betrayed who. By 1997, 3.4 million people had asked to see Stasi files. Many families and friendships were destroyed over the revelations. Because of the politics of the West, criminal prosecution was almost non-existent. Leading SED functionaries such as the Harry Tisches of the Politburo, who should have been tried for inhumane policies, were accused of lessor offenses such as corruption. This made Stasi victims furious. With justice unattainable, they sought revenge. Eric cynically suggested that Gerhardt's career as a Stasi underling had finally caught up to him in some victim's released file.

"The bastard had it coming," Eric said dispassionately about their dead father one night as he sat on Damien's bed. "And we're living high on blood money," he added sourly with a slanted glance at the door leading to the hallway to the kitchen, where their mother was making *Topfwurst mit Sauerkraut und Kartoffeln*. He quipped in a raspy whisper, "*She* probably turned him in. Gave away his code name to some vengeful victim..."

"Oh, come on!" Damien protested in a whine.

"Why would *Mutti* do such a thing?" He blinked at the door through which the delicious smell of frying onions wafted into the room. "Denounce her own husband? The father of her kids?"

"To keep him from denouncing her first, that's why," Eric shot back. "Dog eat dog, Dame. She had to do it before he did. Remember, if they were both informants ... well, informants were always turning on their own for self-preservation. Our mother is a real survivor, Dame."

Liebender Gott! Eric was so cynical about their parents! Damien refused to accept Eric's awful accusation. He'd gone too far. While Damien reluctantly accepted that both parents may have been Stasi informants or agents, he rejected Eric's horrific accusation that their mother had done such a treacherous act. She wasn't a murderer.

Shortly after Gerhardt's death, Lisbeth moved the family to a flat in the borough of Neukölln, where she still lives. Neukölln is a mixed district known for its authentic middle eastern cuisine, edgy bars and hip coffee shops; but it is also a hotbed for far-right violence against foreigners and liberals. One night in June, 2020, just a block from his mother's flat on Elbestraße, neo-Nazis vandalized Konditorei Damaskus on Sonnenallee. Hoodlums had painted a large swastika on the storefront then set fire to the car parked outside.

When Damien checked on her, she downplayed the event: "That's always happening, *hase*. We're used to it. It's just something we need to ride out, like everything else." She then shared how, soon after her friend Nadja Eminger openly refused ultranationalist *Nationaldemokratischee Partei Deutschlands* propaganda pamphlets, rocks were thrown through the windows of her house and neo-Nazi graffiti was spray-painted on the walls. Nadja was even harassed by anonymous letters and phone calls. To Damien, it sounded a lot like the *Zersetzung* tactics the Stasi used in the eighties.

"Her mistake," said his mother glibly, "was to say 'no' to them. She could have just thrown the leaflets in the garbage. Instead, she made herself a target. I won't do that. I know better."

Yes, thought Damien, she was a pragmatist, having lived in a state that was essentially broke, in a community just scraping by in dire scarcity; the same people who, no doubt, after the reunification voted for the extreme right, which was the furthest thing from SEM communism they could find. But that wasn't the only reason for the appeal of the far-right after reunification. Within a few years of the wall falling, millions of East Germans lost their jobs as thousands of companies privatised under the *Treuhand* and millions more migrated to the west looking for work in a world whose rules of engagement were strange and difficult. Unemployment had not previously existed in the DDR; everyone in the DDR had a job, which gave them community and a sense of purpose and belonging. No one knew the meaning of *betriebshedingte kündigung*—compulsory redundancy. While life in the DDR had been "almost comfortable" in Angela Merkel's words, the fallen wall thrust poor and community-oriented workers into a middle-class world of ambitious capitalists.

State-support for housing, energy and child care disappeared, replaced by increased costs to household budgets. Many, who were poor and unemployed, felt like they'd entered a glittery hell, where they were finally in their consumer heaven but weren't allowed to touch or have any of it. It is no wonder many felt *Ostalgie* and yearned for the 'good old socialist days' when everything was cheaper, jobs were guaranteed by the state, and crime was virtually nonexistent. Those very same people who felt oppressed by the communist regime found themselves disillusioned by the alienating bourgeois nature of the capitalist west and a *Bundesrepublik Deutschland* that didn't seem to understand them or care. And if they said anything about the *Wende,* they were branded *Jammerossi* and treated disrespectfully.

East Germans still live under a veil of stigma and lack of understanding. Damien had read the media coverage that essentially amounted to: *they have freedom and yet they are still so angry. What is wrong with them?* Divisions between east and west are still growing as east Germans feel more and more like second-class citizens in a 'free' country that appears more like a dictatorship of capital. Eric pointed out that no major corporation houses its headquarters in the east. It's no wonder some East Germans have become revisionists, looking to define a past—and an identity—that had eluded them. A past that in fact never existed.

As for his mother, Damien contemplated how well she'd landed on her feet through it all. He couldn't help wondering: was his mother still an informant? And if so, working for who? Who's to say that Lisbeth—no doubt a singularly clever spy—wasn't later inducted to one of the three federal German intelligence services: the *Bundesnachrichendienst*, the *Militärischer Abschirmdienst*, or the *Bundesamt für Verfassungsschutz*. The ultra-nationalistic NPD's inner circle turned out to be full of agents or informants of the *Bundesamt für Verfassungsschutz*. One of them had even written an anti-Semitic tract used by the party. The question remains: were they chimeras who'd defected to the other side or were they simply doing their job as informants too well?

Two months after the bakery fire, hundreds of far-right protesters tried to storm the Reichstag in Berlin. Most were white men. They waved the black, white and red flag of the pre-1918 German empire, the flag of choice for neo-Nazis. They shouted, "*widerstand*!" and "*Wir sind das Volk*!" By 2021, police officers throughout Germany, including Frankfurt, were found exchanging violent neo-Nazi propaganda. Then, in March last year, the government was caught tapping phones and monitoring movements of members of the nationalist-populist political party Alternative für Deutschland (AfD).

As Damien packs up to leave the library, he thinks how it is all getting wildly polarized and very ugly. And not just in Neukölln. In a moment of sudden clarity, Damien sees his own destiny enmeshed with that of Germany in its escalating path toward Tag X. He'd been so angry when Eric abandoned him for Canada in 2019; but now he concedes his twin brother may be right yet again. Soon, it will be time for him to leave also. He just can't right now.

THREE

NEUKÖLLN, Elbestraße.
December 13, 2022: late afternoon

It's a twenty-minute ride on the U-Bahn from Friedrichstraße station to Ostkreuz where Damien waits for a bus to Erkstr. The bus arrives within minutes and he boards, ticket ready. The conductor waves him in without checking his ticket. Damien is used to that; the transit system runs on an honour system. But as they move from bus stop to bus stop, Damien notices that the conductor stops every black or brown-skinned passenger to check their ticket; he does this *only* to the coloured passengers.

Damien gets off at Erkstraße and walks to the tree-lined boulevard of Sonnenallee, now bustling with a vibrant mix of hipsters and Middle-Eastern families who stroll to restaurants, bakeries, markets, and shops. Large mature lime and chestnut trees that line the verges and boulevards stretch their bare winter limbs to the cloudy sky. Hearing the desultory mix of Arabic, German, and English, Damien inhales the complex perfumes of Shisha smoke, apple tobacco, fresh pita bread, and incense. Berliners call Sonnenallee "Arabische Straße," a street where bearded men lurk outside hookah lounges in animated discussion and hijab-wearing women bustle in and out of female-only beauty parlours.

Within a minute's walk he sees the green awning of Damaskus Konditorei, run by Syrian refugees.

There's no sign of swastika vandalism or car fires. Damien wanders to the well-lit shop window that displays trays of attractive Syrian sweets. He studies the colourful arrangements of sugar-dusted ma'amoul, honey-drenched flaky baklava, barazek (Syrian sesame cookies), and mabrouma (thick and crunchy strings of knafeh dough wrapped around pistachio nuts soaked in sugar syrup). Pulled in by memories of good eating, Damien enters the shop. The Syrian shopkeeper, recognizing him, greets Damien with a friendly smile. "*Salam aleikum*. It's been a while."

"*Wa alaikum salaam*, it has," Damien responds and they then converse animatedly in German about which sweets will be best as a gift for his mother. Both agree on which but disagree on how many and finally laugh over the compromise.

Ten minutes later, he's holding a larger box of sweets than he'd initially intended and turns onto Elbestraße, where his mother lives. The street is another boulevard planted with mature lime trees. Eventually, climate change will change that, thinks Damien as he takes the stairs two at a time up to his mother's fourth floor flat. A colleague at Humboldt's Faculty of Agriculture and Horticulture is already looking at several replacement species including the Daimyo oak, Magnolia tree, the Judas tree, the manna ash and the North American horse apple. None as magnificent as the lime or chestnut, which together make up over a third of Berlin's street trees.

"*Hase*!" His mother, elegantly dressed in linen slacks and teal wool sweater, approaches to hug him as he enters the doorway. She is tall like his father but has none of his strong raptor features. Her face, angled more softly, glows with a healthy yet stern beauty. She halts in her tracks when she sees his injured face, brows coming together. "*Was ist mit dir passiert*? Who did that to you?"

"The police," he says in a clipped voice and drops the box of sweets on her coffee table. He realizes that he's still in a surly mood. "They searched several of us in the Letzte Generation. They confiscated my computer and files." He doesn't mention that they took his copy of *Silent Spring*. It is too disappointing and somehow feels like he's failed his mother by not fighting for it. His brother would have—if he'd had a copy. He'd given their mother's gift away long ago and replaced it with his own 'bible,' *Walden Two*. "Anyway, that's why I'm here; to get my stuff."

She frowns. "Police! Pfah!" She makes a dismissive scoffing sound with her mouth and waves a hand in the air. "More like Reichsbürgers," she says savagely. "They've infiltrated the police and it suits them. You're not liked by either the government or the far right. They want to intimidate you."

His mother has always been shrewd, he thinks wryly, brushing back his hair with a hand. She never missed much when he was growing up; why should she now?

"You need to be careful, Damien," she says in a patronizing voice. "Your scientific work doesn't align with their thinking—both authorities and the far right. Don't make yourself a target. I warned you about that *schrecklich* group Letzte Generation."

"*Liebender Gott*, they're climate activists not some

criminal eco-terrorist group, *Mutti*! I can't just stand idly by. NASA reported that the past nine years were the warmest since modern recordkeeping began in 1880. And 2022 was the fifth warmest on record. And still we keep pumping greenhouse gases into the atmosphere. NASA calls the warming trend alarming. And in Siberia, where warming is happening six times the global average, the loss of reflecting sea ice is warming the Arctic seas and permafrost of the seabed is thawing and releasing methane hydrates—"

"But Letzte Generation are so ... unruly!" she cuts in. "All they do is create more *Kuddelmuddel*. You need to be more—"

"What?" he snaps and feels the edge of truth cut his voice into a shrill. Reminded of Eric's accusations, he goes on hysterically, "I need to be more like what? More like *you*? Smart and careful *like you*?" They stand by the door facing each other in frigid silence. She in sudden confusion. He in defensive fury. He's almost panting with emotion. He hasn't made it more than a metre inside her flat and already she's cut him down with criticism. Shivering with rising anger, other words spill out in a torrent. "You were an informant, weren't you?" he blurts out. "All those years for the Stasi!"

"*What*?" She stares at him in shock and her lined face hardens like limestone. Then her face morphs with understanding and resignation softens her expression. She half-smiles. "You boys are so clever."

No, that's Eric, he thinks. Damien had always nurtured hope against it. But Eric is always right. He narrows his eyes at his mother. "Not as clever as you, it seems," Damien says in a voice tight like a spring. He hasn't moved from the door and feels his body trembling with the shock of truth.

"Oh, *Hase*..." She gives him a sad look then utters a long sigh. She glides to her favourite chair by the coffee table and invites him into the living room. "Come, sit down. What's this?" she says cheerfully, looking down at the box of sweets from Damaskus Kondiorei. She picks up the red and gold box and glances at him with a girlish smile.

He remains rooted by the door. As if ensuring easy escape. He's still digesting the confirmed truth about his mother.

She opens the box and looks over the sweets, choosing a sugar-dusted date-filled ma'amoul, round and filigreed from a patterned wooden mould. He stands in silence, watching her eat. Obvious pleasure sparkles in her eyes and upturned mouth. She looks up at him and her smile turns sad. "You have to understand, Damien. I was born in '62, just a year after they put up the *antifaschistischer Schutzwall*. We grew up learning that fascism was imperialistic monopoly capitalism and had no place in the DDR, particularly its most aggressive form: Nazism. I was naïve, an idealist and a fervent anti-fascist. When I joined the Anti-Fascist Democratic Revolution, it gave me purpose, something to do to purify the DDR of any vestiges of fascist imperialism. In those days, everyone was doing it. If you weren't an informant, you were being informed on." She shakes her head sadly. "Sometimes you were both!" she adds with a mirthless laugh. She takes in a long breath and adds vehemently, "I wasn't going to be a victim—never again!"

Damien blinks with the truth of what Eric had deduced—that their mother had been abused—and is momentarily mollified by Eric's second truth. And what about the third 'truth'? Hysterical rage rushes up to fill his gorge as he thinks of Eric's third 'truth.' Face flushed, he accuses, "And what about Father? Did *you* kill him?"

"*What*? I did not!" She looks at him aghast. "All these accusations, Damien!"

He presses on, "You both worked for the Stasi—"

"Your father was NOT a Stasi officer!" Her face flushes red. Damien blinks in surprise. *Not a Stasi agent*? After a moment of silence in which his mother looks over the sweets to calm down, she finally sighs and continues in a resigned voice, eyes focused on the sweets, "Believe it or not, he managed to stay a true German of the Fatherland. Despite his father's Nazi history, Gerhardt somehow eluded pressures from the SED. He managed to stay a *Volkspolizist*, an ordinary People's Police." She grabs a diamond-shaped baklava with finger and thumb and inspects the paper-thin, honey-soaked flaky layers of filo with ground pistachio filling. Still looking at the baklava in her hand, her voice rises in tone. "But when he went to work for Marianne Birthler at the Stasi Records Agency... well ... he found..." she trails, lips trembling.

"You." Damian nods with cynical understanding. "He found your informant files. He found out all the things you did, the people you betrayed and denounced." His heart caves with dread. She *did* kill their father. Eric is right again, but only partially; this is so much worse.

She stands up and her blue-grey eyes meet his in a steely gaze. He forces himself not to glance away.

"The fool broke protocol; he brought the files home and confronted me." She releases her gaze and shakes her head sadly, suddenly looking very old. Damien focuses on the creases around her mouth. They bring her mouth down in a permanent Eastern European frown. "*Guter Gott*," she practically whispers, heaving a sigh and still averting her eyes from Damien. "I may have been naïve when I was young, but your father stayed naïve until the day he died." She returns the baklava to the box and licks the honey off her fingers. Her mouth sets into a firm scowl and she looks to the fireplace as if it holds the past, face tightening with that unyielding resolve Damien learned to dread as a child. "I still had you boys to look after," she says with dead calm rationality. "A mother needs to be with her children. Boys need their mother. I couldn't go to prison. So, when he was asleep, I burned the files. He knew what I did and never questioned it. He just went back to work as if nothing had changed. But it had. And I had to ... well, then I..."

"Turned him in to the goons and let *them* kill him."

"I thought prison. I didn't know that they would, well ... but I knew that was a possibility; I'm not stupid..."

Throat suddenly thick and choking, he turns for the door and wrenches it open. *Liebender Gott!* She stands there and shows no shame, he thinks, dizzy with horror.

"Don't go!" his mother shouts as he bolts out. "I had no choice, Damien! Please! *Hase*! come back! I made *Blutwurst* for us. Your favourite!"

There is always a choice, he thinks, racing down the stairs to vomit on the street. And *Blutwurst* isn't even his favourite. It's Eric's.

FOUR

BERLIN, Görlitzer Straße.
December 13, 2022: evening

Even though he doesn't feel like it, Damien meets university friend, Jürgen Fischer, at U Görlitzer Bahnhof in Kreuzberg. They'd previously arranged it and he doesn't have a phone to cancel their meeting. He curbs his surly mood and greets Jürgen with a weak smile. They walk Skalitzer Straße to Görlitzer Park where Letzte Generation members had earlier arranged to meet. Several of their friends loiter outside Café Mugrabi, under the Lime trees of Görlitzer Straße.

Jürgen points to the young men and they approach Uwe, Klaus and Ahmet who are arguing nervously about that morning's police raid on several Letzte Generation's members. Ahmet is visibly rattled. Damien catches the tail end of what Ahmet is saying: "...We screwed up..." He shuffles his feet, pale face twitching with fear.

"*Quatsch*!" Uwe counters in a blustery voice. "Nothing you say is true. This isn't Dresden and they aren't Pegida, idiot."

Damien wonders what Ahmet said that Uwe thinks is untrue. Why bring up that anti-islamic group? Had Ahmet mentioned some violence? Or Reichsbürger terrorists?

"We did nothing wrong!" Uwe continues to harangue. "We're in the right. *Hör auf so Depp zu sein*."

Klaus turns to Damien with a look of mild inquisitive

concern and cursorily points to his own cheek, referring to Damien's shiner. "*Wer zum Teufel hat das gemacht?*"

"A cop did this."

Everyone goes silent. They stop arguing and stare haltingly at Damien. A shiver runs through Ahmet.

"*Scheiße,*" Uwe breathes out.

Embarrassed, Damien shrugs and offers a stupid grin, suddenly feeling private. His recent altercation with his mother and terrible discovery intrudes like a headache. He can't shake off what he learned about her. What she did. His brother had been right all along. Except about their father, who was no bastard after all; just terribly naïve. Damien turns for the café with thoughts of enjoying some of Mugrabi's excellent Israeli cuisine. He needs some distraction.

He spots Carla Hinrichs standing by the graffiti-covered stone wall of the park with a reporter and briefly slows to catch what she's telling the press about police ransacking her wardrobe. Damien hears her tell the Deutsche Press-Agentur reporter, "What I cannot accept is that our government is trying to silence us. The criminalisation of peaceful protest is an attack on all of us."

Damien realizes that Carla is one of the reasons he joined the climate activist group. Her intellectual capacity was only matched by a genuine dedication to the environmental cause and a wily tenacity that he respected. He found her inspirational. Someone he would have once compared to his mother. Now, he's not sure anymore.

Jürgen follows Damien and leans close to share. "Lilli told me that about ten other Letzte Generation activists were searched too. Like you, the cops seized their laptops and cell phones." He points to Damien's face. "No one got a shiner like that, though."

Damien keeps himself from touching his throbbing face and only half-listens as Jürgen talks about Lilli's plan to saw off the top of the iconic Berlin Christmas tree at Brandenburg Gate next week. "She's already found a cherry picker that can reach the top of the Nordmann fir," Jürgen prattles on. "She'll put up a banner that says 'This is just the top of the Christmas tree.' Get it? It refers to us seeing only the tip of the underlying disaster in Germany. I think it's brilliant!"

"Yeah, brilliant," Damien agrees reflexively. He stops listening to his friend and broods over his mother's heinous crime: murdering their father for fear of exposure. Eric was right about everything to do with their mother. But Eric had terribly misjudged their father. Gerhardt was innocent and he died because of it. The twins never had a chance to know him; he was cruelly taken from them when they were infants. Left with a stern mother, they'd grown up in a household devoid of the warmth of two loving parents. It was no wonder the brothers had grown very close. Why did Eric abandon him, then?

Damien's hand strays, trembling, to his bruised and swollen face. As if bidden by his thoughts, it throbs again. Was the lack of violence at Carla's flat because the parents were there and she wasn't, or because the police who searched her place weren't Reichsbürger terrorists? Last February, during a blockade of the A100 in Berlin, armed police had literally carried Carla away. Even then, the police had used no overt violence. She is a prominent member of their climate activist group and an eloquent spokesperson. If the Reichsbürger terrorists were targeting anyone for violence, she would have been one of the most ideal candidates. Did they know she wouldn't be home? And why target Damien? Could it have to do with his unconventional work at Humboldt Universität? His mother seemed to think so. Or is he just succumbing to the fear of paranoia and they are just two mean cops, not Reichsbürgers, and he just the victim of random police violence?

Letzte Generation started with a hunger strike just before the elections in 2021. The movement then escalated with blockades of key streets and defacing famous art works. Last spring Letzte Generation turned off emergency valves of a crude oil pipeline of the Brandenburg oil refinery PCK Schwedt that led from Rostock to Schwedt. In October, soon after he joined the movement, Damien participated in throwing mashed potatoes over Claude Monet's painting *Les Meules*, on display at the Barberini museum in Potsdam. Flirting with the near-panic of being out of control had been viscerally thrilling. He'd almost pissed his pants; but he never felt more alive. At that moment he was convinced that this act was profound and made a difference. Theo Schnarr told Dazed Magazine that they did it over the German government's climate inaction: "Art is only valuable and only has meaning when there are people to look at it. What will that painting be worth, if our everyday lives will be about fighting for water and food?" A week before the mashed potato demonstration, Just Stop Oil threw tomato soup over Vincent van Gogh's Sunflowers painting in London's National Gallery. Days after, scientists at the World Meteorological Organization announced that heat-trapping gas levels—particularly methane—reached a record high, showing that the planet is heading in the wrong direction, mostly to do with feverish Arctic heating and permafrost thaw.

In June 2020, record heat in Siberia reached thirty degrees Centigrade, well over the average of 11 degrees; it collapsed the permafrost and caused oil tanks in Norilsk to rupture. Over twenty thousand tonnes of diesel spilled into the Pyasina lake and river system. Damien remembers looking at the veins of red on satellite images from space. That disaster is just the beginning of what the 'sleeping bear' of methane hydrates promise to unleash when the permafrost reaches a critical thaw and those hydrates awaken. Melting permafrost is a quiet sleeper in the climate change procession. At a microscopic level, in the chemistry of the water, and in the change in the atmosphere, a time bomb is ticking.

All of it suddenly seems pointless to Damien. The planet is in a mess and so is humanity. The shadow of his mother and what she did to protect herself—and by extension her young family—pulls him down like a huge weight and he feels like he is drowning. Discovering that his father was never a Stasi agent. He was innocent and he died for her secret. *Liebender Gott,* if she has blood on her hands, so does he and Eric.

"Hey!" Jürgen slaps Damien on the back, jerking

him back to his present surroundings. He notices that everyone is dispersing.

"Let's get a beer and celebrate your good luck in not getting killed by those *Drecksau*!"

"Great idea!" Damien carves out a bitter smile.

They head to Hopfenreich on Sorauer Straße.

FIVE

BERLIN, Warschauer Straße.
December 15, 2022: morning

There are no grad classes today for Damien; he's slept in and decides to go in later in the morning. Still in his pajamas, he shuffles barefoot into the kitchen and prepares *Eier in Senfsoße*, a favourite meal his mother makes for him when he visits Sunday mornings. He pulls out leftover hard boiled eggs, butter, cream, Maille Dijon mustard, lemon juice, and vegetable broth from the fridge, then heats his mustard sauce, whisking in the ingredients in a sauce pan, adding flour to thicken and fresh dill for flavour.

As he eats his eggs in mustard sauce over some leftover boiled potatoes, Damien checks the news on the computer he purchased yesterday. He lands on today's article in WSWS by Ulrich Rippert:

The action against the "Last Generation" group is reminiscent of conditions in the Weimar Republic in the 1920s, when the judiciary ruthlessly prosecuted opponents of war such as Carl von Ossietzky and communists. At the same time, right-wing perpetrators of violence and Nazis—such as the murderers of Rosa Luxemburg and Karl Liebknecht, and Hitler after the failed putsch of 1923—were spared or received petty sentences.

Rippert suggested that Letzte Generation's outlandish methods of civil disobedience sprang from a combination of despair at the devastating scale of the climate crisis and misguided politics. He then went on to say that this did not justify persecution by the state. In fact, "the group's democratic right to freedom of expression and protest must be vigorously defended."

But Damien can see the writing on the wall. Democratic rights are the first to go during a crisis. This current social crisis will only get worse and the politics more extreme because they are intimately linked to the ever-growing environmental crisis and changing climate. Germany's government and police force are stretched like a straining elastic in an escalating war between radical right and radical left. Both are becoming increasingly violent. Fear of change drives this. Fear of a changing world that heralds a crumbling corporate economy, a dying civilization, and a return to tribal instincts.

Damien can hear Eric's impassioned discourse on the viral spread of imperialistic capitalism: "First it was the Romans, Vikings, and nobles; now it's the boujee corporations who dominate Europe. But they're all the same; they are empires defined by an overreach they feel entitled to. Those boujee colonialists, along with their white supremacist far rights, think that limits imposed on their freedoms insult the principle of freedom itself. It doesn't matter that their right to 'freedom' oppresses a silent victim like a forest or an indigenous community."

Damien can't help a cynical smile. Even his brother doesn't quite get it; this is all part of the imperative of creative-destruction: a recursive natural cycle that humanity cannot escape, one that creates chaos in order and order in chaos. Like yin and yang that co-exist in a dynamic balance. Natural systems are always on the edge of chaos, inhabiting a sort of ythlaf between stability and total dissolution. This is because Nature contains 'deep order,' which emerges naturally out of fractal complexity. It self-organizes from components too numerous for causal relationships to establish but interconnected by a network of feedback loops. Natural systems maintain a stable chaos because the flow of energy allows them to spontaneously self-organize and maintain structure in a far-from equilibrium condition. Their creativity contradicts the 2nd law of thermodynamics. The Earth, though it may seem to be ever more unruly and violent, is simply finding its new balance in the creative-destructive cycle; what's frightening is that humanity isn't paying attention to those inevitable patterns.

Damien recalls a lively debate with his twin brother not long before Eric left for Canada to pursue his studies in biological engineering at the University of Toronto. Eric had frightened him with his discourse. It wasn't so much what he said but how; he'd frightened Damien with his fanatical energy for change. It was the kind of energy that promises to destroy like a tidal wave that sweeps over a coastal city and indiscriminately takes with it everything—both the good with the bad.

SIX

BERLIN, Mittelstraße. February 13, 2018: early afternoon

It is early afternoon as Eric and Damien nurse Kellerbiers over a late lunch of *Einsbein mit Sauerkraut.* They sit across from each other at a table by the windows of Treffpunkt, an inexpensive *Kneipe* in the gentrifying Mitte district near the university. As soon as the food and beers arrive, they get into an argument. Damien recognizes that he is sulking over his brother's recent revelation that he was accepted at the University of Toronto in Ontario, Canada, and is heading there in a few months. Damien has never been apart from his brother.

They've been debating about the effect of climate change on the human population. How its heat stress, droughts, floods and famine promise within decades to destroy or displace more than three billion people in the Middle East and South East Asia, spilling refugees in all directions like ants out of a kicked anthill. The overheating climate—along with deforestation—is already expanding desert and steppe over forested land in South and Central America and along the Sahel in Africa.

Eric's solution: "Send those who survive to Siberia! Capitalist colonization has already extinguished most indigenous populations that had lived for millennia at the treeline, which is racing at a tremendous speed northward—over a hundred metres a year in Scandinavia, and over fifty metres a year where I'm going, in Canada, which is warming at twice the global average. Eventually there won't even be a treeline. Virtually all those indigenous peoples are extirpated." Modellers predict over 85% of Siberia will be suitable for agriculture by then, he quips with a careless wave of his hand. As if he is discussing moving furniture around, not the living beings on the planet.

Pulled down by a truculent mood, Damien responds to Eric's usual glib solutions by painting a dark vision of a humanity descending into some pre-technological 'dark age' apocalypse.

Eric just laughs. He pokes his fork into the sauerkraut as if to make a point in his argument and scoops up a pile that he shoves into his mouth. He leans forward and argues with a full mouth, "The real question is not whether humanity will survive an ecological collapse, but what part of humanity will survive. You can be sure that the stinking boujee plutocrats will find a way to survive at the expense of everyone else." He chews down the sauerkraut followed by a gulp of beer and a loud burp. "The stinking rich are already doing it, Dame. They're already creating their *Elysium* right here, right now." Fork now swings like a conductor's baton. "*The future is already here; it's just unevenly distributed.*"

Using his fingers, Damien pulls apart some crisp skin off the pork knuckle—his favourite part—and feeds his mouth. Arguing with Eric always makes him hungry despite his surly temper. He crunches down, enjoying the tasty juices of brazed salty pork skin, and retorts, "You politicize everything and resort to cheap references in pop culture. You always do that: over-simplify the crisis and Nature's existential power to sustain life. Trophic cascades caused by ecosystem simplification would irreparably devastate the planet and all adapted life. With the Sixth Extinction Event there won't be any boujee plutocrats because there won't be anything left to monetize—"

"You're such a doom-gloom lefty, Dame!" Eric grabs the last of the pork skin—also his favourite—and shoves it into his mouth. He smacks his lips and counters, "The stinking rich will always have technology at their disposal. I'm talking about genetic engineering, nano-technology, gene modification, cybernetics, and even environmental control. For instance, look at Harvard's RoboBee: tiny robots that mimic flying insects that can fill in as pollinators for the crashing bee populations."

"You over-estimate technology's ability to save the planet—and us by extension."

Eric finishes the pork skin and wipes his mouth on his sleeve with a sniff. "I'm not talking about saving the entire planet—just enough of it. You underestimate what we're willing to do to survive."

That is when he brings up E.P. Thompson's paper on stages of a neoliberal capitalist civilization and the 'extermination endgame.' "You're the population ecologist, Dame, but it's obvious that when a neoliberal capitalist society exceeds its carrying capacity—when technology makes the masses surplus—there's no alternative in the scramble for resources and ecological support. Get rid of the surplus. That simple.

Thompson tells us that under military capitalism—and you have to accept that all countries are militarizing—the 'outcome must be the extermination of multitudes.'"

"For God's sake, Eric!"

"Technology *will* save humanity, Dame," Eric insists. He leans back and stretches his legs under the laminate table in self-pleased satisfaction. "One way or another."

Damien shakes his head and gulps down the last of his beer. "Whatever is left of humanity, you mean. And you accuse *me* of giving up on humanity. So, the greedy capitalist wins?"

"That's why the world needs us, Dame. To keep humanity from going down the wrong road."

And what is that for Eric, Damien wonders. Increasingly, he feels discomfort at what that might be. Eric leans forward, eyes bright with inspiration. He resembles a great bird of prey, long hawk-like nose—the iconic Vogel nose—and copious dark hair cresting back from a high forehead. It's like looking at a more confident version of himself in the mirror, thinks Damien. And sometimes disconcerting, particularly when it reminds him of what he is not.

"You and I know that humanity won't stop climate change," Eric goes on animatedly. "Too many tipping points are already upon us and the direction we're all going in now..." He swings his fork around the room to indicate this place, Germany, the world. "... isn't promising to check that. Change is inevitable." He points the fork at Damien. "But, if we can direct *how* humanity adapts to our changing environment, we can still win..." Before Damien can charge in with a rebuttal, Eric pushes his face forward, raptor eyes scintillating like sapphires on fire. "So, how do we de-thrown the ultra-rich elite—who are mostly a rabble of materialist self-serving hedonists with no vision or care for the future—and ensure a meritocracy of responsible citizens who can take humanity through the changes to come? ... Like establishing a universal basic income toward an egalitarian society. Putting a full stop to fossil fuel mining and adopting clean energy. Re-wilding key ecosystems. Engaging reforestation and dedicating large areas to Nature."

Damien shakes his head, lost for words. Where is his brother going with this? Will he suggest violent revolution to establish a dictatorship? How else would the rich give up their riches? And how is that any different from the Bolsheviks of 1917 or the Nazis of 1933 or the Stasi-run DDR? Those fascist Reichsbürgers would happily reinstate a society of surveillance, repression, and incarceration that would threaten to slide into the *final solution* of genocide of an unwanted 'surplus'. A society of disposable bodies, a biopolitical world of exterminism. Damien thinks of Nietzsche's aphorism: *Beware that, when fighting monsters, you yourself do not become a monster ... for when you gaze long into the abyss, the abyss gazes also into you*. Violent revolution is not the answer, he decides.

Eric pulls out the worn copy of *Walden Two* from his jacket pocket. He slaps it on the table and pushes it toward Damien. "*That's* the answer, Dame."

Of course, thinks Damien, frowning with sudden understanding. He picks up the book, creased, torn, and dog-eared from being handled and shoved into Eric's pocket too often, and flips through it. He sees the same pattern of highlighted quotes he's made in his copy of *Silent Spring*. But that is the only similarity he finds with the two books. *Silent Spring* is an environmental scientist's caution to those in government on what is currently happening if they continue on the path of capitalist commodification. *Walden Two* is a manifesto for achieving a modern 'utopia' through behaviour modification. One implores change to society's infrastructure and practices; the other preaches imposed change to individuals who will influence those practices. One is an open plea and the other a recipe for subversive manipulation. A subliminal cultural engineering exercise. Not Orwellian, but perhaps one that is just another form of subversive dictatorship for a Brave New World. Damien read *Walden Two* years ago, when Eric eagerly pushed it at him as the answer to all things; but Damien remembers how the characters in the book rejected a spirit or soul directing them on the one hand and preached against free will on the other. Flipping through the book, Damien settles on one quote: 'As the science of behavioral engineering advances, less and less is left to personal judgment.' He can hear Eric's retort, echoing more of the book: "The people have all the voice they have any need for" in a world where planning and managerial machinery is deliberately concealed through the use of positive reinforcement techniques. This suits Eric's penchant for despotic rule. In Eric's Walden Two, behaviour engineering has replaced Huxley's soma.

Skinner's utopia—never mind that it is terribly dated, written in 1949 before the internet, social media and other technological breakthroughs—also relied on some unsavory methods of population control such as selective breeding through artificial insemination (and would have, no doubt, included gene drive technology if Skinner had written his utopia now), and destruction of the family unit that mimicked Huxley's dystopia. It boasted a lack of hierarchy and 'heroes'; yet it had its despotic Planners, all anonymous—so no one would feel 'in debt to any figure, or any group short of the whole community.' For Damien this also meant that without identifiable leaders, there was no recourse for the citizen to identify and address responsibility and accountability; this sort of anonymity played into Orwell's interminable bureaucracy and a feeling of powerlessness. *Walden Two* lacked a certain humanity in its rational, analytical, and antiseptic approach to human-centric biology and behaviour. Skinner's utopia used behaviour engineering like an echo chamber to ensure efficiency; it nullified robust change—the kind of change that ensured ultimate survival—because its proponents were obsessed with themselves, with the human machinery. They didn't open to outside influences of a changing environment, to new experiences and discoveries. To Nature itself. For Damien, *Walden Two*'s major fault is that it eradicated chaos, the messiness of chance—the *Kuddelmuddel*-factor—and with it Nature's way of learning. Nature's arcane wisdom. Stable chaos with its devices of creative destruction, provides a fundamental aspect of natural evolution. Humans interacting with environment. He sees none of that in *Walden Two*. He finds this ironic, given the original work upon which its name is based.

Eric taps the book. "Your Rachel Carson achieved some success with her prophetic book when she cautioned against the burgeoning ag-biotech companies like Monsanto, Sygena, Dow and DuPont who were recklessly spraying fields with pesticides and herbicides in the sixties." He nods with mild respect. "As a result, the EPA did ban DDT, the main culprit at the time." He taps the book again. "But within twenty years, the use of chemicals increased over five-fold. They just found other unregulated chemicals to replace DDT. We've inherited a GMO world where gene-hacked plants of monocultures engineered to withstand Roundup—itself a carcinogen—and other neonicotinoids are killing our pollinators along with their target weeds. Same with DuPont: when confronted with their cover up of illegal disposal of PFOA to make Teflon, DuPont just adopted other unregulated PFAS forever chemicals and kept going. And thanks to them the rain of our entire planet is contaminated with hormone-disrupting cancer-causing agents.

"But what did Carson really achieve in the long run, Dame? Yes, she created an environmental movement; but not a revolution. And that's what we need. A revolution." He paused to let that sink in, then said calmly, "*But a revolution is not a dinner party.*" Eric taps his book again. "Revolution isn't about arguing logic to achieve change. Change isn't pretty and all civilized. It's not intellectual. It's messy, Dame.

It's *Kuddelmuddel.* Like climate change. Climate change is showing us that the rules of engagement have changed. Climate change is dictating that the coming revolution against industrial capitalism must go hand in hand with it and will naturally lead to a technocratic society."

Damien wants to smirk; this is Eric's favourite topic, and it plays into his idea of Skinner's behaviour engineering. But Damien doesn't smirk, because he knows what's coming, and blinks hard instead. Eric has extoled the great merits of technocracy before. *Ad nauseum.*

"Think of it, Dame," says Eric, unaware of—or just refusing to acknowledge—Damien's growing discomfort. "Instead of some bimbo lawyer or business man making selfish decisions, we'd have men and women with expertise in science, technology and sociology making rational decisions based on what's best for their society by acknowledging our place in the environment. The decision makers would be selected based on their specialized knowledge and performance, not their political affiliations, or their ability to sway the public to their personal agenda. Think of it: using the scientific method to solve social problems. A meritocracy, where the most capable—not the most popular—are in charge. A government run by rational judgment, not some populist emotional *Scheiße.*"

Damien is now squirming in his seat. Eric is such a political animal. The concept of a technocratic government frightens Damien, mostly because such a government risks politicizing science and technology, neither of which he thinks should be political.

Eric continues, like a river breaching a dam: "Some of your science—your theories about creative destruction—can be a natural manifesto for a technocratic revolution." Before Damien can complain, Eric drives on, "Remind me, *Bruder*; it was the economist Joseph Schumpeter who first came up with the term to describe industrial transformation that comes with radical innovation, no?"

Damien nods reluctantly. "Yes, in 1942. Buzz Holling then based his 1987 model of ecosystem behaviour on it, using the same principles of recursive cause and effect...Non-linear, self-organizing and continually adapting through cycles of change from expansion and prosperity to creative destruction and reorganization that—"

"Exactly!" Eric butts in with a big smile. "The first two stages represent a decadent capitalism about to slide into creative destruction—the *Kuddelmuddel of revolution*—which will, in turn, bring about reorganization under a technocratic system of logic. Climate and its agents of destruction will ensure the collapse of capitalism and its largest problem: population. Once we have a manageable population size, then enclosed communism under a technocratic government is possible and its continuation ensured through cultural engineering. We could achieve all the tenets of deep ecology you so love to extol, *Bruder*."

Damien wants to object: how does Eric expect climate's agents of destruction to diminish the human population? No doubt with some bio-hack help from humans? And what does he mean by 'enclosed communism'? But Damien remains silent, eyes caught and fixed by Eric's hypnotic gaze, as though they are connected by an electric charge.

"Back in 1984, wasn't it? When Næss and Sessions put their eight basic principles of deep ecology together? Now, *that's* the book that should be your bible, Dame; not Carson's *Silent Spring*. But then, Mother didn't give you *that* book, eh?" He makes a scoffing sound.

"It's not a book. It's—"

"Everything you stand for: nature's inherent value and need for diversity, *and* the imperative to reduce our population to ensure Nature's integrity. Our interference with the nonhuman world is excessive and policies need to change on economic, ideological and technological fronts. Their last principal is a call to action. An 'Obligation to Action,' they call it."

Eric leans forward, drawing Damien forward to unconsciously mirror his action. Eric's eyes grow dark with an inner fire and his long beak-like nose flares like a dragon about to charge. That intense, almost dark, expression reminds Damien of how different they are and how he sometimes doesn't feel like Eric's twin brother. Eric then slaps the table and Damien flinches. *Asshole*! Eric studies him carefully. "Climate is not our enemy, Dame; it's our friend. Climate is our fierce archangel of change. And let's not forget that 'crisis is opportunity ... These ecosystem phases require instability and change. Overall, they reflect stable chaos, marked by resilience, elasticity, and balance.' Your words, Dame—I read your draft paper and paid attention." He grins, self-pleased, like a wolf in a hen house. Then he practically snarls out, "We must first destroy before we can create. We must be unruly like climate. We must be relentless like climate. We must ride that wave before we can become the wave, *Bruder*. And then by being that wave, we change the world." In a sudden gesture, Eric's face softens and he reaches out to Damien with his hand. "*Bruder*! Leave Humboldt and finish your degree in Canada. You've already published in a prestigious scientific journal. Your honours project, for God's sake. Who's done that! You'd be a shoo in at U of T. Join me, Dame! We can change the world together—the scientist and the engineer—starting with Canada."

Stunned to silence, Damien swallows down his sudden excitement. He knows he can't abandon his mother or his new supervisor at Humboldt. Eric always unhinges him with outlandish and dangerous ideas. Damien never knows how to respond. So, most of the time, he chooses not to and cringes in uncomfortable silence, unwilling to acknowledge that his brother is a bully.

"But, why Canada?" Damien manages to finally say as Eric stuffs his mouth with sauerkraut. Of all the countries in the world, Canada seems the least restive and least likely choice for a revolution. A quietly reposed nation of polite intellectuals who accept a healthy multicultural society, and whose practical leaders are connected with their people.

"Because it's a huge nation with a lot of space and few people," Eric argues. "Did you know that Canada holds on average only 4 people per square kilometer? Germany stuffs 240 people in the same area. And

China, which is virtually the same size as Canada, holds 153 people per square kilometer." He picks up *Walden Two* and waves it at Damien. "Canada is a perfect place to start these. And, with global warming, we could settle in the boreal." He then slides the book back in his pocket and leans back, eyes sparkling with purpose. "But the real reason to start a revolution there is because, like you, Canadians are naïve. Even their leaders. And this is because, unlike the rest of the world, they are still asleep."

PRODROMAL

When we are in STASIS, we do not recognize our path; perspective only comes with movement. In this way, calamity, initially seen as disaster, may be viewed as unexpected opportunity for creative change. The unpredictable nature of water provides the opportunity to teach and learn. The crisis of change and destruction provides opportunity, just as collision of viewpoints bring new ideas.

—Damien Vogel, "Creative Destruction: A Matter of Scale," ADVANCES IN ECOSYSTEM SCIENCE, 181 (2) April 2032

SEVEN

OTTAWA, Office of the Prime Minister and Privy Council, Wellington Street. November 6, 2032: morning

Eric Vogel sits in the outer office of Prime Minister Robinson of the Technocratic Government. His legs are crossed as he taps his finger on the chair's arm. The secretary, a lean handsome black man, seated by the great door to the PM's inner office, ignores Eric and attends to something on his computer. Eric stretches out his long legs and studies his shiny patent leather shoes with a bored expression. He has been there, waiting for the prime minister, for over twenty minutes and grows impatient. Patience is not one of his strengths. He draws in a long breath followed by a long exhale and reminisces how he got here—all according to plan.

When he first arrived in Canada thirteen years ago as a student at the University of Toronto, he'd witnessed the beginning of the rift that would create the opportunity for a radical change from the current Liberal government and its Conservative opposition. The mildly socialist NDP and the environmental Green parties were tiny voices in parliament, manipulated by the two larger parties as chess pieces to make points. Fringe parties like the western separatist Maverick Party and the libertarian People's Party of Canada failed to win seats in the House of Commons, serving only as added noise in the growing clamor for attention. That has all changed and Eric can pinpoint when and where it all started: February 20, 2022, on Wellington Street, just outside the entrance to this building, The Office of the Prime Minister and Privy Council.

A ragtag truck convoy, naming themselves the Freedom Convoy descended on Canada's capital in a sit-in protest of noise and general disturbance. Right outside the doors of this building the crowds swelled into the green of Parliament Hill. Eric read Walrus magazine's characterization of the disparate movement as "QAnon followers intent on putting journalists, scientists, and academics on trial; and young men in baseball caps promoting their right-wing social media brands." The protests mobilized the far-right and gave voice to Christian fundamentalists, white supremacists, anti-Semitic conspiracy theorists and Islamophobic nationalists. Trucks and people held flags with upside down maple leaves and Confederate battle flags. The protest also flew the Patriote flag, which dated back to the Lower Canada Rebellion in the1830s when French Canadian militants rose against the British Crown; it became a symbol in the 1960s for the Front de Libération du Québec separatists and more recently by La Meute, far-right ultranationalists from Quebec. As with the German neo-fascist revisionists wishing to recreate a nostalgic past, the Canadian truck convoy flew Canada's old flag, the Red Ensign, a celebration of colonialism and neo-Nazism and a nostalgic symbol of hate. The flag was a call to return to the way Canada was before the 1976 Immigration Act. It flew alongside swastikas in

Toronto and in Halifax where the group Proud Boys—mostly members of the armed forces who proudly described themselves as 'Western Chauvinists'—confronted Indigenous people protesting the genocide against the Mi'kmaq people. Eric was then studying bio-engineering at the University of Toronto and took a keen interest, keeping brother Damien apprised. Both agreed on the parallels of far-right movements around the world.

This far-right movement didn't go away; it only grew in size and voice, serving to both galvanize and further polarize the country. The movement effectively demonstrated the feckless decadence and dishonesty of the two squabbling major parties. This opened a gap, a niche Damien would call it, that the Technocrats easily filled. They became the new centre-right and the voice of reason against the deceptive *Quatsch* of the all too left and all too right of which the Canadian population had grown weary and distrustful. Eric smiled; the Canadians were finally waking up. By the late '20s the Technocrats, led by dynamic young entrepreneur and technologist Derek Robinson, stormed the nation with a rational platform on environment, labour, health, and much more. After the climate refugee fiasco in 2028, Robinson's party skyrocketed in popularity with an intelligent population who were fed up with political sophistry and empty rhetoric and excuses. Even the well-off middle class were feeling disgruntled in their current government's feckless treatment of their place and safety in a changing environment. The Technocrats had a plan that made sense and they demonstrated the expertise to carry it out: ways to successfully adapt to climate change, using technology and scientific research. The party subscribed to a scientific management approach, a Taylorism approach based on four principles: select methods based on science; assign jobs based on aptitude; monitor performance; and divide workload based on a systems approach.

But their very success will ensure their downfall, thinks Eric.

Their scientific method approach, while a definite improvement to the politicised rule-of-thumb approach of other governments, lacks a certain holistic and adaptive capacity to Eric's taste. It is too rigorous, based on precedence of patterns rather than anticipating process changes, and fails to consider potential 'creeping breakthroughs' and requirements of enablement. This is one place where he and Damien agree: strategies based on stability are bound to fail in a changing world. they remain embedded in an outmoded colonialism dialectic, like refugees from the nineteenth century, their wheels stuck in the mud. Eric has learned that to land on his feet each time, he must not just anticipate change, but rely on it. According to Damien, the best way to achieve this is to be mindful of potential harbingers of change through the chaotics of feedback, sensitive dependence, and nonlinear developments. Another way to ensure accurate anticipation is to orchestrate it, thinks Eric with a self-satisfied smile, hand straying to the worn copy of *Walden Two* in his jacket pocket.

At any rate, the Technocratic wave of common

sense solutions, most of it based on sound science, swelled and eventually engulfed the NDP and the Greens, who soon became redundant. In fact, many NDP and Green representatives joined the Technocratic Party. It made sense that the sensible Canadians would vote the Technocrats in. It somehow doesn't matter that Robinson is a charismatic dilatant and clever dissembler, playing the game both ways. Aside from making science sexy, he is a highly successful businessman, CEO of Canada's largest corporation, Canadian Enterprises, which dips into all kinds of technology. Robinson understands the flow of world markets and what drives people. And he's used it all in his plan to ascend to prime minister.

Eric too has a plan. Sitting here, awaiting his meeting with Prime Minister Robinson, is fulfilling step two: get a position in the Technocratic Party as Minister of Environmental Technology. Step one was seeing in the Technocrats successful attainment of a position in Canada's parliament and situate himself in a good position to be noticed: as the successful CEO of BioGen Technologies, now part of Robinson's company, Canadian Enterprises. Eric achieved step one by taking advantage of the Liberal government's last ditch effort to draw votes when they relaxed the law against cloning. Ready with its technology, BioGen brought in several patents for the manufacture of Techno-clones, a giant cyber-project against bio-terror and more. It made BioGen and Canadian Enterprises billions in revenue and brought them international prestige in the field of cyber-technology. The rest of step one happened two years ago when the Technocratic Party became the government of Canada, thanks ironically to Robinson's charismatic personality, his expertise in environmental technology, and his astute selection of party members—all impressive men and women in various fields of expertise. The Technocratic Party reads like a Who's Who of imminent scientists, technologists, and sociologists. For instance, the Ministry of Health is run by Doctor Ernest Bohr, a health professional with international experience in pandemics and environmental diseases; Bohr is already overseeing and funding Eric's gain of function research. The Ministry of Environment & Climate is run by ecologist and climate scientist Maya Dasgupta, who has already worked with his company on some interesting strategies in gene modification against invasive plants. And the Minister of Land and Security, Edward Kraken—a former U.S. military strategist for the United States president—has already incorporated Eric's engineered Techno-clones into his federal security force. Eric smiles. He will be joining the ranks of great experts, who are already his colleagues.

Steps three to five will have to wait, thinks Eric, quite happy to bide his time as he waits for his *zögerlich* brother to catch up to him. Because, while he doesn't know it yet, Damien is a key part of Eric's plan to change the world. After all, for every Robespierre there is a Napolean. For every Marx, a Lenin. For every bold architect, a competent administrator.

But first Damien must learn. And that will take time. And a little friendly engineering. Damien is already in town; he moved to Canada three months ago, soon after their mother died, to start his professorship at

U of T in environmental science and continue his research in environmental genetics.

It will be a while before Eric needs Damien, though; first, capitalism along with its boujee acolytes must come crashing down with the help of climate change. But that is already happening. The dominoes of an ecological cascade are already falling on each other.

The first domino fell in June of 2020, but Canadians didn't notice or pay attention because it happened in Siberia, where the collapse of permafrost ruptured oil tanks in Norilsk. While the oil spill made the headlines, the real worry was the cause; it also forced climate specialists to realize how wrong their models were.

The second domino fell in 2027, and demanded notice with twin disasters in Canada. The first was a severe derecho with embedded tornadoes that swept over Ontario and Quebec in May, spanning over 1,500 km with gusts over 140 km/h. Whole towns were demolished. Other provinces were affected by severe flooding that spring. That was followed in early winter with massive atmospheric storms and bomb cyclones in British Columbia, resulting in calamitous flooding and treacherous mudslides along the coast with high loss of life. Both events left Canadians without power, shelter, food and water for weeks and in some cases for months. Whole cities were evacuated and people never returned. The following year an earthquake-caused tsunami devastated coastal communities off the Indian Ocean. Waves up to thirty metres—not seen since 2004—hit the coasts of Indonesia, Sri Lanka,

India and Thailand. Half a million were killed. The tsunami exacerbated sea level rise off the Bay of Bengal, flooding 80% of Bangladesh. A permanent sea level rise of 1.5 m displaced seventeen million Bangladeshi who were already battling river floods and erosion from the melting glaciers in the Himalayas. The salt water further contaminated the groundwater. When the Canadian Liberal government invited two million climate refugees into Canada, Canadians went into an uproar. No one appreciated these foreigners coming in and receiving the equivalent of what Canadians had just lost: jobs, houses, security, food and water.

Over a hundred years ago, Spartacist Rosa Luxemburg—who was later shot by the right-wing *Freikorps*—argued that the "Bourgeois stands at the crossroads, either transition to socialism or regress into barbarism." Both he and Damien agree with sociologist Wolfgang Streeck who argues that the end of capitalism—of a reigning bourgeois, in love with the objects that define them—is already underway. The signs are neon loud: a ruthless downward trend in economic growth, social equality, and financial stability. All reinforced by climate change and the ongoing collapse of the planet's sustaining environment. Any system and dialectic based on a concept of infinite resources in a finite world is bound to fail eventually. That collapse has already begun and its catastrophic end is imminent. Already, climate refugees and refugees of resource war (which amounts to the same thing) have flooded northern nations, like Canada, and caused tension and strife. Germany is just one example where left and right have torn the country apart as an influx of foreigners challenged the already tenuous German identity. When Canada granted asylum to over two million climate-refugees in '28, with no viable plan for the new residents during a time when unemployment was higher than it had been in decades and housing prices were skyrocketing due to environmental uncertainty, this sparked renewed tensions between ultra-right and ultra-left and opened the gap for a new party based on science and reason. The party now in power: the Technocratic Party of Canada.

But what will life after capitalism look like?

It's no surprise that he and his brother disagree on what a post-capitalist world should look like and how to best achieve that world. Damien too easily prescribes to the old leftist shibboleth of Nature being the answer to everything and Market being evil. His deep ecology utopia would spring from an atavistic rejection of modern life, a return to 'the ancient farm.' But how that fantasy could be achieved without a drastic population reduction is beyond his brother's imagination. Damien fetishizes the natural world. Just like he does their mother. The naïve fool is a blind romantic, refusing to see reality right in front of him: that Nature is ultimately cruel, cold, and preoccupied with its own survival. Just like their mother.

A year after Eric left for Canada, his fool brother got himself in with that feckless climate activist group, Letzte Generation. Where was the logic in that? They were certainly making the news back then; but that is all they were doing. Damien had the sense to leave that reckless group soon after he joined in '22 and instead focused on his master's studies. He published several seminal papers, one of which was used by Dr. Patrick Fairweather, population & systems ecologist and chaoticist at McGill University in Montreal. Fairweather's 2025 paper in the *Interdisciplinary Journal of Nonlinear Science* built on Damien's discourse on creative-destruction to posit his now famous stable chaos theory. In fact, Damien had first used the term 'stable chaos' in his earlier paper; it was even in the paper's title. The term was actually first coined in 1989 by James Gleick in his bestseller *Chaos* to describe Jupiter's eye spot, a self-organizing system, created and regulated by the same nonlinear twists that create the unpredictable turmoil around it.

For Damien it always takes a while, Eric concludes, hand straying to the worn book in his pocket. He, on the other hand, has always known from childhood what he wanted and has struck the rightful path from the start, never wasting a moment. He also saw Damien's path clearly—more clearly than Damien himself—but he learned through Damien that attempts to exert change through external influence don't work. So, just as with his foolish efforts to set Damien on his rightful path, attempts to persuade or educate politicians and increase public awareness by radical activist groups—like Letzte Generation or Extinction Rebellion here in Canada—only *appear* to sway the politicians who are always trying to look good to the public. Perception and reality are entirely different animals. A leopard may change its spots to look good; but it is still a leopard inside.

No external change will endure without internal change. The key to changing behaviour is to change motivations of behaviour. Behaviour engineering is the answer. Constructing and ensuring an ecologically sustainable environment for a post-capitalist humanity must involve behaviour engineering. One must change that leopard from the inside, not just its spots.

The secretary's phone rings. He answers it. "Yes, sir." He looks at Eric expectantly. "The Prime Minister is ready to see you now, Mr. Vogel—"

"*Doctor* Vogel," he corrects.

"My apologies, Doctor Vogel." The secretary maintains a professional tone, managing not to be obsequious but also not rude; an admirable trait, thinks Eric. The secretary gestures with his hand. "This way."

Eric stands up and nods to the secretary with a tight smile. He straightens his jacket and follows the secretary through the door into the destiny of his making.

EIGHT

TORONTO, 7 Hart House Circle, University of Toronto Campus. April 12, 2033: noon

Damien pokes at his smoked trout and listens to Eric ramble about his imagined utopia. He sits across from Eric with his back to the fireplace at the Gallery Grill. Tucked away on the second floor of Hart House, the restaurant is one of U of T's best kept secrets. Damien's gaze wanders up to the vaulted ceiling and hung chandeliers and then to the bar that sits in front of large hand-painted stained glass windows. Sunlight streams in from the arched windows. He marvels how the place manages to feel both cozy and richly expansive at the same time.

Damien made the mistake of reminding Eric of their conversation back in '18 in Berlin's Treffpunkt in which Eric invited Damien to change the world with him, starting with Canada. Since his mother's death and his arrival in Toronto to teach at U of T eight months ago, Damien has often thought of that conversation. Compelled by a surly humour, Damien teases, "So, how are your *Walden Two* colonies coming along in the boreal?"

Eric wriggles with sudden excitement. "Simmering nicely in the ether, like Mutti's Sülze. They're biding their time ... waiting for you, *Bruder*!"

"*Me*?" Damien laughs nervously. "I'm not heading to the boreal any time soon. Besides, didn't you hear? The boreal forest is on fire these days—"

"Good!" Eric chuckles and shovels some lamb shank into his mouth. "The fires are doing the clearing for us," he says through a full mouth.

Damien clicks his tongue against his teeth in disgust. The ass has no consideration for these important ecosystems. The role they play in global health. More even than the Amazon rainforest, the boreal forests are the lungs of the Earth. And as the forest moves north a hundred metres a year, it is turning into transition scrub and losing its resiliency to fire and pests. When that great forest disappears, all the life-ensuring cycles of the planet will be disrupted—water and oxygen cycles, atmospheric circulation, ocean currents, and the ability to reflect sunlight—turning the planet into a catastrophic maelstrom.

"I'm calling them Icarias," says Eric, ignoring Damien's reaction.

Damien smiles sideways and scoffs, "After Icarus who plunged into the sea when he flew too close to the sun and scorched his wings? Great symbol for your great society of the future, Eric. And rather apt considering the scorched boreal forest. Icarus died an overly ambitious fool who—"

"No, no, no, Dame!" Eric impatiently waves his fork at him. "It's after Cabet's utopia. Étienne Cabet. He was a French lawyer from Dijon. He published his novel *Voyage en Icarie* in 1839. It was a kind of manifesto-blueprint of utopian socialism, influenced by Fourierist and Owenite thinking, and some of its key elements—like the four-hour work day—are reflected in *Walden Two*. The novel explores a society in which capitalist production is replaced with workers' cooperatives and focuses on small communities—like *Walden Two*." Eric leans forward with excitement. "He describes them as organisms, Dame, with a nucleus of *petite communauté de dévoués*, surrounded by a *petite colonie fraternelle*—the cytoplasm, *per se*, within the loose tissue of the world. His Icaria abolished private property and individual enterprise. Just consider, Dame, this was a time when Paris and London were cesspools of dirty muddy streets filled with animals, offal from abattoirs and slop dropped from dwellings above. The streets of Cabet's Icaria were clean due to segregated infrastructure and they even had covered sidewalks. Imagine, *Bruder*. Cabet framed a constitution for an actual Icaria. He and a small group of Icarians founded an egalitarian commune in Red River, Texas, and then Nauvoo, Illinois, a small-scale social model you could call 'experimental socialism.'"

Intrigued, Damien asks, "What happened to them?"

Eric sighs and leans back in his chair, tilting his head to gaze briefly up at the vaulted ceiling. He looks at Damien with a hard frown. "Swindles. Feuds. Dissent. Human greed. Capitalism crept in from the outside, like a plague."

Damien nods, fighting off a smirk. Not from within? "Well, it's an appropriate name, I guess, for your utopian society," he says, glancing from his glass of tap water to Eric drinking greedily from his bottle of Willow water that he'd ordered at the bar: spring water sourced from the English Lake District. He'd ordered expensive bottled water when Toronto tap water would do just fine. There is so much wrong with that, thinks Damien. Designer bottled water imported from another country to a so-called water-rich country with its own issues of water scarcity thanks to the edicts of the national water utility. Meanwhile, California is burning up. Spain and France are turning into deserts from lack of water. The Gobi Desert is increasing at a rate of 1,300 square miles per year and Pakistan is at war with India and China over the Indus drying up. And Egypt is bombing Ethiopia—again—over damming the Nile. Damien raises his glass of tap water. "I wish you well with your Icaria."

Eric leans back, holding the water that cost him twenty times more than Damien's, and studies Damien carefully. "You could help me, you know..."

"With your revolution?" Damien feels tension raise his voice. "I don't think so!"

"Why not?"

"Because you and I don't think alike," Damien says more forcefully. "We don't have similar visions on how to end capitalism or what that post-capitalist world should look like."

"But my vision moves toward a sustainable world."

"Not with that in your hand."

Eric grins down at the bottle of Lake District water in his hand. "What can I say... I hate Toronto water. More to the point, you and I do share aspects of your deep ecology—"

"How can you say that! And, besides, I'm not a deep ecologist."

"Yes, you are." He pulls out his phone and searches then reads: "Do you hold that the well-being and flourishing of human and nonhuman life on Earth have intrinsic value?"

Damien sighs, resigned to Eric's game. "Of course."

"Do you hold that the richness and diversity of life forms contribute to the realization of these values and are values in themselves?"

"Yes."

"Do you believe that humans have no right to reduce this richness and diversity except to satisfy *vital* needs?" He looks up at Damien, who is hesitating.

"Yes, ok, I do," Damien concedes, shifting in his seat.

"And do you agree that the flourishing of human life and cultures is compatible with a substantial decrease of the human population and the flourishing of nonhuman life *requires* such a decrease?" He looks up with raised brows, as if in challenge.

Damien nods and looks down at his unfinished trout. "Yes, I agree."

"And, do you agree that the present human interference with the nonhuman world is excessive and the situation is rapidly worsening?"

Damien sighs and agrees.

"Do you hold that policies must therefore change, including those that affect basic economic, technological and ideological structures?"

Damien firms his lips and agrees.

"And do you agree that this ideological change should involve the appreciation of life quality and inherent value rather than standard of living, *per se*?"

"Yes, yes," he responds impatiently.

"And, do you agree that, having subscribed

to these foregoing points, you have an obligation directly or indirectly to try to implement the necessary changes?"

Damien tilts his head and studies his twin brother, who mirrors his action and stares back at him in silent expectation. Damien finally sighs. "Yes, I certainly do. Once you are awake, you have a responsibility to act on your conscience."

Eric leans back with a satisfied grin. "You just acknowledged the eight Basic Principles of Deep Ecology as put forth by founders George Sessions and Arne Naess. Congratulations. You're a deep ecologist, Dame."

"OK. But I'm still not going to participate in your revolution."

"Why not?"

"I already told you!" Damien fights down a scowl and plays with his food, no longer hungry. "You and I don't have the same agenda. The end doesn't always justify the means, particularly when the means are not ethical or sound." There. He'd said it. With a scowling glance at Eric's expensive water, he finally puts his fork down.

"Are you finished with that?" Eric asks, leaning forward with interest.

"Go ahead." Damien shoves the plate toward Eric.

Eric grabs his fork and digs into the leftover trout. "Oh! That's good!" Mouth full again, Eric says, "Listen, *Bruder*, you know that a revolution is the only way we're going to make it, eh? Those stinking boujees won't just roll over for our sustainable movement. Climate change waits for no one and time has run out. I just saw on the news that Louisiana has lost over 13 thousand square kilometers to the sea—that's close to ten percent of that entire state. And the wetlands of Mississippi delta—what's left of them—have all gone to salt water, affecting fishing there. Florida's almost as bad. And there's Texas and North Carolina, all getting submerged by a rising sea. Land around the Gulf Coast and Atlantic Coast is disappearing and refugees are migrating and creating havoc. Coming north, *Bruder*!"

Damien hates it when Eric talks with his mouth full. He finds it disgusting and boorish.

"Back in the '20s scientists started noticing major permafrost melt on the Siberian Shelf," Eric goes on. "When the reflective blanket of sea ice disappeared, the sea floor absorbed so much more radiation that the seabed permafrost melted and released hydrates. Of course, that set the oil and gas companies frothing at the mouth with joy and the climate scientists spinning in a panic because of what they knew it meant for the planet. It was the harbinger of the largest methane 'burp' ever, which only a few years later released the equivalent of decades of greenhouse gases. The public still thought that climate change would be gradual. What they didn't realize—and *no one* was telling them—is that it would be abrupt and disastrous. Permafrost thaw kicked us into this devastating global warming, Dame, and everyone—even the climate modellers—ignored it, because they didn't have enough data. *Gott verdammt*! They're all still asleep, Dame! Only a revolution will wake them up."

"I won't participate in your violence. I came to

Canada to get away from all that *Scheiße*."

Eric leans back with a fake wounded look on his face. "And here I thought you came because of me."

Damien sighs and can't help a barb to wipe off Eric's self-pleased smile. "Besides, how can you talk about a revolution when you're already participating in the activities of the current Technocratic government? You and your Technocrats are destroying Canada's small farm holdings and replacing them with these giant Corporation Farms that use bio-technology and other *Scheiße*, like transgenics, monoculture and chemicals, to create some scientific efficient agriculture. And those so called ground-breaking technologies of yours only support continued resource mining and oppression of indigenous cultures. How is that different from the capitalist pigs you replaced?"

"Ha!" Eric laughs unapologetically. "Sometimes, I think the Technocrats are more conservative than the Conservatives they replaced!" He finishes Damien's meal and mops up with a piece of bread.

Damien isn't finished poking at his brother. "You're towing the line nicely, Brother. For instance, your Techno-clones very handily quashed that nasty indigenous uprising in South America over the remnant rainforest. No more problems from those 'eco-terrorists,' eh? Didn't they all 'accidentally' die from that explosion and fire?" he ends a little louder than he'd intended.

Eric visibly squirms in his seat and his face tightens as discomfort turns to mild anger. Damien curbs a *schadenfreude* smile. Eric practically growls, "Come on, Dame! That's unfair." He still holds the fork and waves it at Damien. "You know that technology can be misused. I didn't create the Techno-clones to be used as weapons. This happens all the time with inventors. When French hunters in the 17th century jury-rigged their muskets with attached knives to hunt wild boar, they had no idea the bayonet would be used to skewer men in war."

"No? Not as weapons?" Damien challenges, now on the offensive and liking it. "I think you knew exactly what those clones were good for and you sold them to dictatorships with that in mind. Don't forget, I know who funded BioGen's start up back in '26. How's Sheikh Bahir bin Zayed doing these days with his shipment of Techno-clones? BioGen doesn't do too badly in the war on eco-terrorism these days, eh? I read Forbes too."

Eric throws the fork down on the empty plate and it clatters loudly. He's visibly angry. "That's business. But it's not me."

"You can't have it both ways," Damien snarls, finding his stride. "You can't believe in one thing and then do another because—"

"Sure you can! I do it all the time! It's called *living*!"

"Well, I don't."

"That's right; you don't live. That's why you're boring and inert." He wipes his mouth with a napkin and throws it carelessly down, abruptly standing. "You'll come 'round, *Bruder*. Because it's the only way. Meantime, I have places I need to be. Nice chat." He grabs his leather jacket off the chair back and strides out of the restaurant without a glance back.

He's left Damien with the bill ... again.

Damien lets his gaze linger through the lofty doorway of the restaurant and gives in to a sudden violent question: *why did I really come to Canada*? Did he come here to escape the place where he grew up with a domineering mother, a Germany he no longer felt comfortable in? Or did he come to join his brother, like Eric suggested, and change the world with him? The answer is even more disturbing. *Perhaps, I came not to join Eric, but to protect the world from him.*

The thought settles inside him with a kind of impelling force, like a destiny calling. There is something he must do ... He knows what it is and it frightens him.

NINE

TORONTO, Hart House, University of Toronto Campus. January 22, 2042: late afternoon

Professor Damien Vogel brushes back his hair with a nervous hand and stoops over the podium of the Great Hall, facing a few hundred students who are seated behind dozens of long tables.

"In the Chinese *I Ching*," he lectures in a soft voice, "the hexagram for 'crisis' also represents 'opportunity.' The behaviour of ecosystems in crisis requires a new paradigm of examination. A new lens to assess the meaning of change." Avoiding a direct gaze at the students listening to him, his eyes flit nervously from the vaulted ornate timbered ceiling, from which bronze chandeliers hang, to the stain glass windows over oak paneled walls, and finally to the travertine tile floors.

Despite Vogel's quiet voice, the high acoustics of the neo-gothic lecture hall carry his words to the back where Monica Schlange sits at the last row of long tables.

"This is where creative destruction enters," Vogel drones on. "The concept, which seems paradoxical initially, represents Nature's recursive behaviour of closed systems. But it's less circle than Mobius loop." He now becomes oddly animated, like a robot suddenly turned on. Even his voice rises out of its tiresome torpor. "A circle is far too simple and doesn't accommodate the less than direct influences that feed into recursive change that draws on paradox..."

Monica suppresses a yawn. *Welcome to your life,* she thinks to herself. She's come to his lecture out of interest in the topic title: "The Recursive Evolution of Climate Change." She'd rationalized that it would help her with her grad course, *Topics in Global Change*. But the real reason she's here is because she saw a picture of him on the poster for the lecture and thought him exciting. He's been described as a genius and a brilliant scientist with new and startling ideas. But, studying him now, dressed in that worn and rumpled brown tweed suit that looks like he's slept in it, does nothing to inspire confidence in that bold claim. She decides that he's just an overrated dreary academic with no reckless imagination.

And, yet, something about him simmers with intrigue.

To begin with, she must admit that he is physically stunning with striking features. He resembles a great raptor, with long aquiline nose like a fierce beak for ripping prey, languid eyes the colour of the infinite sea under hooded lids that feign apathy, a high forehead crested with swept back dark hair like the crown of a bird, and a tall wiry frame that houses a nervous metabolic energy coursing through a restless body. Every part of his physique suggests a lean predator, prepared to pounce on its unsuspecting prey; and, yet, in every way, he belies that image, in his slightly stooped posture, in his gentle almost bashful upturned lips, and in the earnest shy gaze of his sapphire eyes. They all dampen a smoldering fire, the molten fury of a volcano, yearning for freedom. That repressed energy excites her and stirs her loins. She realizes with hysterical humor that if she just touches herself down there, she'll come in a burst of wetness. She fights to keep her hand on the notebook that sits closed on the table. She grins; her hand is trembling.

"...So, this paradox describes ecosystems undergoing sharp, discontinuous changes that are in fact internally organized and balanced," Vogel continues in that stilted voice of disaffecting arrogance, totally unaware of Monica's existence and her sexual yearning for him. There is something terribly sexy about a vulnerable predator, she considers. Perhaps, he is licking his wounds from some battle he lost. She feels sudden compassion for him. She can commiserate. She could help him lick his wounds with stories of her own betrayal. Misery loves company, doesn't it? They would have much to share...

Suddenly bedeviled by those mystifying eyes of disinterest—as if commanded by some unruly alien force—her hand abandons the notebook and strays down, below the table. Like a coiling snake, it slithers past her thigh to its prey, where she smolders. Touched, she erupts and barely stifles a moan.

The student sitting beside her turns and stares at her with big eyes. She ignores him. She doesn't care. She leans back in her chair, hand remaining on its prize under the table, and closes her eyes in ecstasy.

TEN

TORONTO, Bloor Street. February 2, 2042: early afternoon

It's a cool day of 18 degrees as Monica sprints up St George Street in the drizzling rain and crosses east onto Bloor Street. Looking for a coffee to warm her, she enters L'Espresso Bar Mercurio and sees no line at the coffee bar. She orders a flat white from Raphael, her favourite barista there. She knows his name isn't really Raphael; it's Greg. But he ditched it for a new identity as Mercurio's warrior poet barista and grew his flowing blond hair long, which he flicks dramatically when he wants to draw attention. As he fixes her flat white, the two flirt outrageously, debating politics and environmental concerns, trading sexual innuendos, and off-colour jokes, teasing with promises of exotic sex. When he hands her the flat white in a glass, she winks at him, mouth pouting in a promissory kiss, and grabs the coffee. She saunters to a table by the windows that face the busy street and is about to sit down with her coffee when she sees him: Vogel!

He sits two tables down, alone, by the window, nursing an espresso. Although he's facing her, he doesn't notice her because he's reading a book. She studies him quietly, eyes caressing his long-limbed body, held in elegant repose with one leg crossing over the other. He leans elegantly back and holds the book slightly out in one hand, as if striking a pose for a picture. Even those typical reserved lines have softened somehow. There is something new, something impish about him. Perhaps it is the setting. He is no longer the professor on display. She feels suddenly like a voyeur, spying on the man revealed beneath the academic facade.

She grins like a cat. What is it about this man that draws her so much? Titillated by her own desire, Monica sashays toward him. She knows she's attractive and is used to manipulating a man with her beauty. As she closes in, she can make out the title of the book he's reading: *Behavior Modification in the Political World of Social Media* by George Levin.

Vogel looks up and those normally soporific eyes glitter with incredible life. It's like he's a wholly different person. Vogel stares at her and she stares back. Both are briefly hypnotized by the other. She quickly recovers and brashly asks, "Doctor Vogel, may I join you? I'm a student at U of T and I was hoping to—"

He doesn't let her finish and says with a boyish grin that surprises her, "I think I've seen you in Sidney Smith Hall a few times." Vogel brushes back his hair with a hand and indicates the chair across from him with a nod. He puts the book down on the table. Has she unhinged him with her beauty? Brought him out of his German reserve? Perhaps it's all a mask, she thinks. Something he takes off, like a coat, when he leaves campus. She decides that he's a clever shape shifter and slides into the seat across from him, more than intrigued.

But Vogel's expression now is almost tender. His eyes stroke her in a gentle caress. It sets her on fire and she feels her face heat like a giddy teenager in love. She channels that wild energy into a fierce intensity of impeccable discipline. “I read Levin and find him overly simple, naïve in fact,” she says evenly with a provocative smile. “His ideas on keeping users engaged with habit-forming technologies—particularly on wearable apps—are too obvious. He talks about ‘real estate’ and visual cues and doesn’t focus enough on the art of subliminal seduction.” With that, she leans sideways and crosses her legs, bringing one dangerously close to his until it carelessly brushes against his leg.

He blinks rapidly in response then grins sideways with amusement and leans forward to gaze into her eyes. She finds those deep earnest eyes daunting, but matches them with a steely gaze of curiosity.

“Don’t get me wrong,” she says, recognizing that she’s captured him. “His ideas about recognizable associated behavioural patterns in daily routines are spot on. He gets the ‘what’ but screws up the ‘why’ and particularly the ‘how’ parts.” She’s been stroking the table cloth with her index finger like it’s a road map and his gaze has been flitting from them to her eyes. “Patterns mimicking patterns, funneling physical analogues and workflows through known country into something sexy and thrilling.” She then brings her finger to her mouth and brushes her lips as if discovering them for the first time. Her mouth opens to a wide smile—it’s one of her most attractive qualities, she knows. “No one likes change, but *everyone* loves a thrill.” She leans forward, hands dangerously close to his, breasts touching the table. “Especially a sexy one—”

He clears his throat and tilts his head with a slanted smile. He's barely keeping it together, she realizes with predatory satisfaction. Hand nervously brushing the length of his long nose, he says, "What are you studying?"

He's changed the subject. Has she won or lost? "I finished my BSc major in Environmental Science with Political Science minor. I'm now doing a Master's in Environmental Ethics. I'm a fast read and hope to defend my thesis in two years—"

"Impressive," he talks over her, smiling almost indulgently. "But I think you may be in the wrong faculty."

Piqued by what she thinks is a condescending tone, she lashes out in sullen scorn, "The environment has no voice to defend its sovereignty. When I become that voice, you'll see how wrong I am—"

"I meant no disrespect." His smile turns conciliatory. "I just thought that you appear to have a talent for great influence. Why waste it on a silent environment? You could become the next prime minister. I could make it happen—"

"Without an environment there won't be a next prime minister."

He releases a deep unalloyed laugh then tilts his head to her in respect. "Touché, Mademoiselle."

"We have ten years, tops, to get things right," she goes on seriously, forgetting the chase. "And those greedy capitalists go on harvesting and mining like there's no tomorrow—"

"Isn't that what we do best?"

"*What*?" She's not sure if he's serious or teasing her.

"Taking," he says. "It's in our culture. We've learned to take, not give like the indigenous peoples, who are all gone, by the way...which says a lot about winning and losing."

She's starting to think that he's a shyster. He's either playing her or he's a stinking capitalist himself—which is crazy for a professor of environmental sciences and climate change.

"Are you kidding?" she retorts. "The indigenous are still here. We just don't see them. They're all around us, just like the environment. Both are 'othered,' made invisible, because they're just something we use. Like the computer or phone." She's aware that her voice is raised, her nose flares with rising anger, and he's staring at her rather wide-eyed.

He suddenly stands up, all flummoxed. "Come with me!" he growls with an intensity that almost frightens her. Has she angered him? Did she finally go too far? *Has she won or lost*?

He reaches his hand out to her and says urgently, "I *must* show you something!"

Her heart thunders with excitement. Whatever he dishes out, she can handle, she decides. She rises and before she can grab her coat, he seizes her hand and shakes his head. "No need for the coat." His touch is scintillating. Coat forgotten, she suddenly feels as though she's getting away with something. Like she's sinning in plain sight and the crowd of people, who pay them no mind, seem like a silent audience of complicity. Confused, she lets him lead her past the front doors and the old Fiat on display by the entrance, past the pastry display case and to the little hall that leads to the men's and women's washrooms. He looks over his shoulder at her and grins like a twelve-year old boy. She grins back with sudden understanding: *she's won.*

"In here!" he whispers hoarsely, pulling her into the men's room. She recoils briefly, heart thundering, then lets him yank her inside.

He closes the door behind them and verifies that they're in the washroom alone, then turns back to her with a rakish smile. Her body trembles with excited anticipation. She finds the victory of relief after the tension of argument incredibly erotic. But she plays the game and looks around with a coquettish giggle. "What could you possibly show me in here?"

His face draws close to hers and he whispers hoarsely, "Me!" His eyes are dark with lust and she inhales his intoxicating desire. "Because you want me." He seizes her close, pressing up to her.

She pretends to struggle out of his grasp. "No, I don't—"

"Yes, you do! Your whole body screamed it back there. You want me more than anything!" He responds with a crushing embrace. She feels his hardness, large and pressed against her, and abruptly pulses out wetness.

"And *you* want me even more!" she crows out triumphantly, feeling like she could come any second. "Your whole body came to *me*!" Leaning into him, she kisses him hungrily. He responds, tongue thrusting and entangling with hers. He groans with urgency and, still kissing her, franticly maneuvers them to a stall and backs in with his butt. It swings open with a reverberating clang. He pulls her gruffly inside and slams the door with his foot. Like a spring let loose, both feverishly strip the other, hands recklessly touching and fondling as they tear off clothes and carelessly drop them on the floor until they stand magnificently naked before the other. There is a frozen moment as each admires the other. She pores over his tightly muscled form, and lets her admiring gaze stray down to his cock, engorged, stirring, and pointing right at her. Vogel closes in, kissing her on the mouth and hands roaming her shoulders, arms, and breasts. He slides gradually to a squat, lips and hands travelling adoringly down her curving waist to her abdomen. Then he buries his face in the moist heat between her legs. His tongue dives in, touching her deep sex. She releases a deep moaning sigh and spills for him.

"Oh, God! You're so wet!" he groans out.

Overcome with urgency, she snarls, "Goddammit, Vogel! Fuck me! NOW!"

He springs up and gruffly pushes her against the cubicle wall. She opens to him, inviting. He lifts her off her feet with his strong thighs and swiftly enters her. She gasps, mouth snapping wide in pure ecstasy as he fills her. She moves with him, feeding his thrusts, riding him like a galloping horse. His body molds into hers and they rock in unison, panting and grunting a duet of pure lust. The cubicle wall squeaks staccato to their love duet as they rock against it. She is a molten energy arcing with his flames. Her fire clasps him, clutching them both in a vaulting vortex, driving them ever upward. Until a tidal wave erupts inside her. She rides it as it wells up and spills out of her and she screams out her orgasm in pulsing throbs.

Vogel stops briefly and pulls his face back to stare at her. He is stunned by her loud abandoned cries. But they aren't finished; she fiercely feeds him with clasping waves. Within an instant, he barks out in surprise and ejaculates his orgasm with a long warbling groan of release. Waves of his throbbing penis echo inside her until he collapses in a sweat on her.

"Oh, God, woman! What have you done to me!" he growls out and laughs joyfully as he pulls out of her and admires her. She notices that his hair is wet and sweat beads on his forehead. He cups her face lovingly in his hands and leans his head against hers, still breathing hard. Then he straightens, chuckling. "Let the stuffy boujees cringe at our wanton cries of freedom. They heard us all the way to Berlin!" he shouts and releases an unbridled laugh of pure pleasure then plants fervent wet kisses all over her face.

She giggles, feeling like a little girl being loved again. She knows she's unhinged him. His response throughout their tryst was every bit as much surprise as ecstasy. As if she surprised him. As if he surprised himself. Has she freed him too?

But now he's hastily dressing and makes to leave without waiting for her.

"Let's do this again," he says offhandedly, slapping her naked rump like she's a harlot. But he hesitates, his beautiful eyes, the colour of the wings of a jay, giving him away. She sees their flame burn for her, still standing in naked magnificence before him, and lets a mischievous smile slide on her face. He still wants her, even now, spent from lovemaking, when a man usually loses interest in a woman and simply walks away. His impish smile betrays a moment of tenderness and his slender fingers alight briefly on her cheek, caressing. "You were incredible. Anon, *Schnucki...*"

Then he's through the door and out of the washroom before her panting breaths have settled.

She dresses and leaves the washroom as a man enters. He frowns at her and she ignores him. She continues down the short hall into the café where she left her coat, grabs it with a brief glance at the clientele who must have heard them in the washroom, taps the old Fiat with her hand, and murmurs, "Let it be done," with a self-pleased smirk and trots out the door with bouncing carefree steps into the drizzle of Bloor Street. Funny, he didn't give her his phone number or other personal contact information. No matter; she knows where to find him at the university...

ELEVEN

**TORONTO, Sidney Smith Hall,
University of Toronto Campus.
February 5, 2042: late morning**

Monica sees him in a hall on the Huron Street side of the building. He stands absently to the side, reading a book that he holds in one hand. Slightly stooped and wearing the same rumpled brown tweed jacket he wore at his lecture, he is back in sheep's clothing, she thinks with a smirk. Will he choose to recognize her?

Feeling bold and reckless, she sashays past several loitering students right up to him until she directly faces him. He is so engrossed in the book, he doesn't notice her. She sidles up closer with a seductive smile until her face is right beneath his, looking up. "Hi, handsome," she says in her best sexy voice. "Got a moment for a quick prick? I've always been interested in the social psychophysiological research lab..." Then winks in the direction of the lab door and leans up against him.

Startled, he almost shrieks and backs away from her. He looks genuinely frightened.

She's a little annoyed by this over-the-top display. There's only one other student in the hall and they are walking away. She leans up against him provocatively. "You weren't so shy in the men's room..."

"What are you talking about!" he shouts in a high-pitched voice and gruffly pushes her off him as if she is some wild animal with rabies. "Miss, if you don't leave me alone, I shall fetch the campus police to remove you!" He then backs away from her like she's a disease then spins around and hastily walks down the hall with clipped steps. He glances back briefly at her. She can't believe the fear in those eyes.

She glowers back. Coward! What an asshole! *First he fucks me with abandon, then he treats me like he doesn't even know me and I'm some pariah!*

TWELVE

TORONTO, Bloor Street.
February 13, 2042: early afternoon

A week later, Monica enters L'Espresso Bar Mercurio, looking for a flat white, and sees him there, at the same table. Her heart jumps but she keeps her cool. This time, he looks up as she enters and beams at her with a huge smile of recognition. He even stands up and waves at her.

Her eyes narrow involuntarily. She ignores him and walks to the bar, where she orders her coffee from Raphael. Vogel approaches her in line and touches her shoulder.

"*Schnuckiputzi!* I was just thinking of you," he says, betraying tenderness.

"Well," she quips coldly, disengaging from him. "Funny that. Have you beaten your fright of me then?"

"What?"

She pays for her coffee then walks with it to another table.

He follows her. "Won't you join me?" he asks in a subdued voice. He seems puzzled. What kind of fool is he, she wonders. "Or can I join you?"

"*Join me*?" she snaps back a little too loudly. A few patrons turn their heads and glance at them then go back to what they were doing. Vogel blinks as if he doesn't understand. Monica takes her seat without inviting him to join her and says in a surly voice, "I think you already *joined with me* rather astutely—in the men's washroom." She looks out the window to the traffic on Bloor Street and adds dismissively, "Now, if you don't leave me alone, I shall fetch the campus police to remove you!"

"What?" He blinks at her in confusion and makes no move to leave. "Have I offended you in some way? I ...thought ...well ...that you rather enjoyed our little ...eh," now smiling impishly, "*joining...*"

She turns knife-sharp eyes on him. "I don't take kindly to being used, like Nature, by some capitalist pig coward who pretends he's a concerned environmental scientist when he obviously isn't and uses me like a coat to put on then discards me when it suits him. You can hunt me like a dirty dog in my natural habitat but in your sanctuary I'm not wanted, I'm a risk to your high and mighty purity, eh?" She makes a scoffing sound. "Well, you'll find me a capable adversary, Professor Vogel—"

"Professor? I'm no professor. I may have a PhD, but it's only my twin brother who teaches at the university."

"Your...twin ... brother? ..." She trails. Now she's confused.

"Yes, Damien. He teaches climate science and environmental sciences. I'm Eric. I just roam the campus for business and to visit him; I got my degree there too but in biological engineering. I'm CEO of BioGen Technologies. Our R&D lab is on Devonshire Place, just a block away."

"Your brother is ... your ..."

"Identical twin." He nods with a short laugh and sits down across from her with sudden understanding. "I thought you knew. Most people at the university do. Did he accost you? Or ..." He suddenly grins like a fox. "I'm betting you accosted him! HA! You thought he was me? Oh, my dear *Schnucki*!" He seizes her hand and squeezes with compassion, despite those laughing eyes. "I'm so sorry for the mistaken identity. Did you send Damien running like a scared rabbit with your overwhelming seductive powers?"

Monica decides to let go of her anger and smiles at the irony. Her fingers play absently with her cup of coffee. She sips carefully and basks in the relief of this discovery. She's surprised to realize that the brother has become even more intriguing now. Smiling at Eric, who has become suddenly ordinary, she fantasizes about Damien.

Eric seizes her hand again. "Are you free for a bit? Come with me!"

"Not the washroom!" she pulls her hand out of his with a nervous laugh.

He chuckles, grabbing it again. "No. I'm just down the street. Come for a short walk?"

She smiles. "I'll come for that."

"I'm counting on it." He grins like a boy with a new toy.

THIRTEEN

TORONTO, Distillery Lane. April 10, 2044: early morning

Eric bursts out from under the covers, face wet with her orgasmic release. She's just woken from an erotic dream.

"Good Gaia, love!" Eric wipes his face with a tissue and releases a choppy laugh. "You were dreaming and I just thought I'd help you along."

The dawn light rakes in through the floor-to-ceiling windows of his penthouse loft in the Distillery District. It's time for her morning run. The bed feels wet under her. It's drenched with her own ejaculation. Monica raises herself on her elbow and studies him. "Serves you right, Vogel," she says peevishly. "It was *my dream*."

"You mean I wasn't in it?" He looks hurt. "I should have been, seeing how I just tipped you over. Now, I'm truly jealous!"

She whacks his face with her pillow. "Of course you were in it." Actually, his twin was; but isn't that close to the same thing? They are identical, after all. Come to think of it, not really. Not at all. For identical twins, they couldn't be more different, she decides. For Eric's confident aplomb and flamboyant nature, Damien is reserved, unsure of himself and at times defensively surly. Eric is an open fire; Damien a smoldering coal bed. One draws people to him; the other is prickly and off-putting. For Monica it is clear who is more interesting.

But it is Eric she is shacked up with. They've been together since that tryst in the men's washroom at Mercurio's two years ago. Since then, she's learned that he—unlike his environmentalist brother—is a successful industrialist who runs the biotech firm BioGen Technologies, with contracts all over the world in anything from transgenic crops to bioweapons. In '30, BioGen became part of Canadian Enterprises, Robinson's huge conglomerate, and since '32, Eric has been heading the Ministry of Environmental Technology in the Technocratic government. That couldn't be more different from his brother's pursuits, thinks Monica. One is a scientist, the other an engineer. While Damien Vogel teaches and writes about the need to adapt to the cycles of the natural world, Eric Vogel seeks to harness and control those cycles. Eric should be her enemy. Instead, he's in bed with her. As for Damien, what she learned about him from Isabo last week may change everything.

Appeased by her answer, Eric grins like a boy. "This is your big day, *Schnucki*. Your last class before you defend." He gets up, naked, from the bed and punches in his code on his nightstand then pulls open the top drawer, shoving his Glock aside to grab something. He turns back to her with something wrapped in sparkly paper. He kneels on the bed, facing her, and hands her the present. "For your future, Doctor Schlange," he says with a tender smile. She likes the sound of that.

Monica takes the wrapped present and grins at

him with pleasure. Alternatively glancing up at him and down at the parcel, she pulls off the wrapping in a few strategic violent tears. It's a book: *Walden Two* by B.F. Skinner. She curbs a scornful laugh at the sight of it. The cover is terribly worn, dog-eared and even torn in one corner. It looks like it went through the wash a few times. Hardly present-worthy, she thinks. What does he mean by giving her this? She looks inside the front cover. In Eric's flamboyant scrawl she reads: *To my beloved Monica. Here's to a brave new world! love, Eric.*

"It's a little marked up, but I didn't think you'd mind," Eric says unapologetically. "It's what's inside that counts, eh?" He smirks, self-pleased. "You know, like me," he adds with a wink.

She forces a bright smile. "How thoughtful. You know I love presents. Even if they are ...an old smelly book!" She bursts into childish laughter. Surely this is a joke! Then she remembers the inscription.

He doesn't laugh. "But I have a better present." To her look of anticipation, he pushes his hips out at her, penis already rising between muscular thighs. "Me!" He pounces on her and she shrieks with delight then struggles out from under him, moaning, "But I have my morning run! I need to do my run before my class. It's—"

His mouth closes over hers and his fingers dive below, relentlessly coaxing.

She sighs and gives in to Eros rising within her.

—

It is much later that morning as Monica rouses from

a blissful morning sleep. Eric spoons her and they both lie under the covers, facing the large windows with a view of Distillery Lane from his second floor flat. His arm casually drapes over her like she is his prize. They'd both fallen asleep in the soporific bliss after making rampant love from dawn until who knows what time it is now.

She checks the time. Thanks to Eric she's missed her run *and* her last class. Monica reaches over to the book on her nightstand. She flips through it, glancing at all the highlights, finger picking at the tear in the cover like it's a scab. Eric stirs awake with a long satisfied sigh. She turns to face him, book still in her hand. "OK, Vogel, why give this smelly old book to me?" Clearly, the book means a lot to him. But it's old and worn and all marked up. Hardly a present for his *Schnuckiputzi*. "What gives?"

He studies her carefully with hooded eyes before speaking. "Because it's your turn," he says simply. To her look of impatience, he explains, "I've had that book since I was a sixteen. I've studied it—as you can see—and applied it to my own work as a bio-engineer. It's an important book, Monica. But it's time for it to go to the next person who can use it; you." His fingers brush through her long hair with devotion. He catches a loose lock of hair and eases it in place. "I think you will do great things with it by your side."

She frowns and sits up, carelessly baring her breasts, and practically glares down at him in challenge. "What are you talking about?"

He raises himself on his elbow. "Listen, this revolution you and I keep talking about isn't going to happen out of the blue. We need to plan it, birth it, and then nurture it into the utopian society it needs to become."

"You make it sound like we're giving birth!" She laughs self-consciously.

"It's a lot like that," he agrees seriously. "But just as with child birth, those who fail to plan and prepare and understand how to give birth and then raise this 'child,' will likely create a monster. We *need* a plan." He points to the book with his chin. "That's a plan."

"He wrote the bloody thing in 1948, Vogel!" she scoffs, waving the old book in her hand. "That's close to a hundred years ago!"

"So?" he sits up and crosses his legs so he can face her head on. "Scientists were still following Darwin's *The Evolution of Species,* hundreds of years after he wrote it. What Skinner prescribes in *Walden Two* is still relevant today; we're already using biological engineering and behaviour modification through education, city planning, corporate behaviour, and product marketing—never mind the cool stuff we're doing with gene-hacking, particularly through our food industry. The key is not 'what' but 'how.' You said that to me the first time we met."

He has a point there, Monica concedes.

"And look here," he adds, wriggling to grab the book and flipping to a page he knows by heart. "Here's what Skinner's character Frazier says: 'You can't make progress toward the Good Life by political action. Not under any current form of government. You must operate upon another level entirely. What you need is a sort of Nonpolitical Action Committee.'

No government rule; just committee consensus. In your Walden Two—let's call it Icaria—you'd call the committee a Deep Ecology Circle. That's us, after the revolution, *Schnucki*!" He throws the book down like a gauntlet.

His eyes now scintillate with passionate conviction. This is when she finds him the most desirable, thinks Monica, feeling Eros stir inside her with wild impulse: when he's lit with the fire of ambition. She feels Eros every time Eric flexes Machiavellian power through his company or in his politics, or when he forces himself on her at an inappropriate time or place—like that first time he'd coerced her into the men's washroom at L'Espresso Bar Mercurio. The raw power he exudes is something she craves, something she feels compelled to wield. But Damien has this power too, she thinks; he just doesn't realize it yet.

Eric grabs her hand and presses it. "You and I both know that your environmental movement won't achieve anything through the traditional channels or by being nice and proper. You can bet your *popo* that climate change will never be nice and proper. Climate change is messy and it isn't going away. And greedy capitalists will go on harvesting and mining, like you said to me the first time we met. Humanity is basically greedy. But, unlike what Dawkins kept saying like a fucking broken record, we weren't born that way. Our culture made us that way. I meant it when I said that 'we've learned to take, not give, like the indigenous peoples.' We must unlearn that way of doing things. And that comes down to behaviour engineering, selective breeding, and so on. Again,

Walden Two has the answer. Hereditary connection would be minimized to the point of being forgotten because breeding would be purposeful; breeding through artificial insemination, without interfering with personal relations and free sex—I thought you'd like that!" He grins, poking her arm playfully with his free hand while still holding her other hand. "People would have relations with whoever they wished but have children according to a genetic plan. We'd effectively create a *Homo Deus,* who lives sustainably and adapted to our changing climate. We need to adapt. Even my brother agrees with me on that part."

She logs that away in her mind for the future. Hand breaking from him, she seizes the book he dropped on the bed to wave it in front of him. "But we don't have time for this. Your behaviour engineering—if it's even allowed to occur in a large enough population—will take at least two generations to make a difference. We need to change those in power *now*. Or there won't be a world for them to be powerful in!"

His eyes grow dark with desire. She knows her intellectual passion turns him on. It's what tipped him over the edge when they first met at L'Espesso Mercurio. Her fierce tirade in the café had sexually aroused him.

"Of course!" he says fiercely. "I totally agree." He points to the book in her hand. "That's a dialectic and a model for evolution. It might be the answer but certainly not the means."

He leans forward, pushing his raptor face close to hers. A lock of his dark crest of hair falls boyishly forward over his forehead. She drops the book to lean forward and her hand tenderly brushes his hair out of his eyes for him. As she does, she feels Eros stir insistently inside her, waiting like a coiled snake for her combustible moment. It's coming; she can feel it.

He seizes both her hands and pulls her toward him. "*Schnuckiputzi*! This is why we need a revolution. For two reasons: it's an effective way to reduce the population; and a swift way to achieve the change we desperately need. Only a revolution operates at the rate we need. And that rate can be achieved by using the tools presented to it, sometimes by the very powers it must overthrow."

Now it all clicks into place for Monica. Her eyes narrow for a brief moment then she grins sideways with sudden understanding. Eric is thinking of a coup! A revolution from within, no doubt led by his pet chimeras, those ugly Techno-clones, and other bio-weapons developed by his company. A coup instating him as Canada's new leader. Overthrow Robinson and his capitalist minions and put in place Eric's own team of science experts. It's brilliant, Monica suddenly considers. Eric probably planned this all along since before he joined the Technocrats in '32. Probably since coming to Canada before the Technocrats even got in. Helping the Technocrats get into power and then becoming one was in his plan all along! What better way than from within to undermine a government? He'd no doubt played some part in ensuring that the Technocratic win over the feckless Liberals and Conservatives in the first place. First create the precedence for a scientific technological government, then destroy it and replace it with his model of behaviour science. That entire process itself was using behaviour engineering. It was bloody brilliant!

Would he give her a position as one of his chief aids? They would use his biotechnology to fast track his precious behaviour-engineering on an unsuspecting population toward a new sustainable world. Use his Techno-clones to keep everyone in line with the program. Forget the niceties; that isn't Eric's style; despite his empty rhetoric about committees, he's the control and command type. Definitely a closet fascist. He would use gene editing technologies—CRISPR-Cas9, prime editing, dubbed SATI—and other means to create his precious *Homo Deus,* happy and pliable feeble-minded drones; the very kind of person Eric despises. Heaven knows how he intends to diminish the population in the first place to a size more easily handled by his Walden Two experiment, his Icaria. Probably create a deadly 'accident' and blame it on the incumbents before pouncing in with his 'solution.' Something like his bio-hack fiasco that crashed the world's wheat crops when Monica was sixteen. She remembers how the wheat crash incited conflicts and corporate take overs in southeast Asia, China and Europe—all benefiting BioGen with huge contracts. They then waltzed in with a new virus-resistant wheat crop. Only this time his shenanigans would affect the human population, possibly in some kind of gene-editing eugenics application; shades of Davenport's ERO, Project Coast in South Africa and the sterilization of Inuit, First Nations, and

Métis in Canada. Something that might kill some, make others infertile, and leave a small viable part of humanity—a chosen humanity—to inherit a new sustainable world. Selective genocide based on DNA. That is also Eric's style. He'd be realizing the U.S. Intelligence claim that gene editing is a weapon of mass destruction. The bastard already condoned the positive eugenics of selective breeding; from there it's a slippery slope to negative eugenics using forced sterilization or genocide. He betrayed an interest in scientific racism in his responses to some of her comments about Germany's fear of 'race suicide' through 'miscegenation' and the growing white supremacist movement in Canada. When she openly condemned the alt-right *Canadian Boys* for breaking the legs of eco protester Bakshish Gurpreet last month, Eric neither condemned nor condoned. He just quietly let her rant then shut her up with sex.

Another time, after sex when he became even more loquacious, Eric cheerfully lectured her on the role of plagues in the global climate. The Little Ice Age of the early 1600s was caused by the sweep of plagues over the previous century. Introduced to the Americas from Europe, infectious diseases reduced the indigenous populations of the Americas by 90 percent, from about sixty million to six million a century later; the global population declined by ten percent. The demographic collapse reduced slash-and-burn agriculture; millions of hectares of previously cultivated land turned back to forest, reducing the carbon dioxide in the air and lowering the global surface air temperature enough to cause an ice age. She remembered the light in his eyes; disease was a tool for him.

God! This plan of his is so sinister. And bloody brilliant!

She says in a dark whisper, "You mean *your* tools."

"Yes," he whispers back with a knowing grin. The truth is in his eyes. *Here's to a brave new world*!

This changes everything, thinks Monica. Only last week, when she was visiting Eric's lab, Christian Isabo—Eric's head scientist and now an obvious defector—quietly took her aside, hoping to solicit her to help him steal some of BioGen's proprietary technology in a guerilla revolution against Eric's precious Technocrats. A revolution led by an eco-terrorist group who call themselves the Gaians and whose leader Isabo revealed is none other than Damien Vogel. Her first reaction was to suspect that Eric had put Isabo up to it—to test her, or even trap her. But, after doing her dark research, she deduced that Isabo's own defection was genuine. She recognized a fellow conspirator when she saw one: he was, like her, posing as one thing when he was another. It came down to small things he did and said, perhaps more what he didn't do and say. How he concluded that she was a candidate for their revolution is another matter she will have to investigate. Is she that transparent? Only to another chameleon like her, she is hoping.

At any rate, she delights in these revelations. Brother against brother: how delicious! The universe is unfolding as it should, Monica decides. She flicks on the song recorder at her bedside and it immediately blares out the Tears for Fears tune *Everybody Wants to Rule the World*, which she cranks up.

Flushed by a new sense of power, she unleashes Eros to wash unbridled over her. With the swiftness and force of an Amazon, she climbs over Eric and gruffly pushes him down on his back then plants her mouth hard on his.

"I can't," he complains lamely around her kisses and over the loud music. "I'll be useless if we...I have a meeting at BioGen with Isabo soon and I need to settle—" He inhales sharply. She's moved down, mouth seizing his cock, moist lips and tongue coaxing the length of him to firm. He fights his arousal, stuttering out, "...this meeting ... it's important for—*Oh, God*!" He gives in, groaning out his pleasure as she guides his stiff rod inside her and rides him hard to victory.

FOURTEEN

TORONTO, Henry and College Street.
October 10, 2044: early evening

Damien sits alone with his legs crossed at a small table on the outside patio of Prenup Pub. He fidgets with a tall glass of Schöfferhoffer Grapefruit Radler. The evening heat penetrates the shade of the linden trees.

He's about to pick up his book to read when he spots Christian Isabo, dressed in khaki shorts and plain black t-shirt, walking up Henry Street. Damien waves to him and he waves back. Christian is only ten years his junior, but his springy gate and boyish looks remind Damien of a teenage hippy skateboarder. Unruly curls of long sandy hair frame a square face covered in stubble, a straight nose and sensual mouth. And green eyes the colour of Mombasa's Indian Ocean on a sunny day. Christian's stocky build suggests that he likes his beer, but he obviously visits the gym, thinks Damien, admiring his muscular physique. Christian isn't exactly burly, like those Berlin Polizei who rampaged Damien's flat years ago, but his tall form has bulky substance. He has the strong build of a wrestler without the surly looks, thinks Damien. Christian's light-hearted demeanor conceals the serious mind of a brilliant scientist, specializing in developmental biology. The story goes that Eric, recognizing Christian's extraordinary potential in neurology and psychology, snatched him right out of high school at seventeen and put him through grad school while he worked at BioGen Technologies for next to nothing. A transhumanist at heart, Christian is currently studying intelligence and the interaction of human with AI. One of his brain children includes the imposing Techno-clones that earned BioGen a top ten rank on Forbes.

Despite his own reservations about human interventions, Damien finds himself fascinated by Christian's experiments in transhumanism, aimed at producing a humanity able to withstand all that climate change may throw at it. Damien is most fascinated by—and terrified of—those Techno-clones Christian created with Walter Burke and Monique Lavigne. Genetically-modified human clones—part human, part machine—created for dubious purposes by BioGen and sold all over the world to governments looking for creative solutions to their unruly citizenry. Damien has yet to see a Techno-clone up close, but he's seen images of these formidable creatures: more than human or no longer human—Damien isn't sure which.

Over several beers one night, Damien coaxed Christian to disclose juicy details about these genetic chimeras. In Greek mythology the Chimera was a fire-breathing monster, a horrific *Kuddelmuddel* of lion, goat and snake that laid waste to the countryside. In Damien's opinion, Techno-clones aren't too far off the mark. Their combination of amphibious-like skin fused with Kevlar-like armour allow the Techno-clones to withstand temperature extremes, chemical pollutants and even radiation that normally kills a non-enhanced human. Embedded respiratory tubes that connect to state-of-the art filters allow them to walk and breathe without added protection in air thick with smog and chemical toxins. Their thixotropic skin and 'living' armour render them immune to most viruses and other biochemical means of massive destruction through rapid epigenetic adaption. Depending on the model, some are equipped with assault weapon-arms or some other built-in tool. Binocular eye pieces connected to AI—in place of their biological eyes—provide enhanced eyesight that include the ability to see infrared heat signatures for stealth missions, to access face and pattern recognition and associated intel at a moment's notice, and instantly share with their autopoietic team, no matter how large. Techno-clones are essentially an army that functions as a single organism without the need for a leader. What one sees or hears, all see and hear. All lead and all follow. If one clone dies, the rest continue easily without it.

Eric's company took advantage of the Liberal's sudden repeal of their law against human cloning in '29. It was a ditch-effort to gain political support from a population scared of losing itself. It all seemed tied to the alarming new statistic from the Hebrew University and Mount Sinai Medical School on men's infertility published in '28 in the journal *Science* by Marina Rodriquez and Tuva Olsen: that sperm count had declined by 80% in the last two decades. Over two-thirds of the male population were most likely incapable of producing sufficient sperm to continue the human race, their decades-long study concluded.

Mostly to do with endocrine disruptors, they'd speculated. Ironically, the major source of endocrine disrupting compounds could be traced back to the genetic/chemical practices of companies like BioGen. The study couldn't have been published at a worse time for the incumbent Liberal government. It didn't help that the country was being inundated by some two million foreign refugees that same year. Pressured by a citizenry frightened of extinction, the Liberals opened the gate to alternative forms of reproduction, including cloning. Like a racehorse who knew he would win, Eric had everything ready to make his Techno-clones as soon as the AHRA was amended. The Act no longer prohibited germline engineering, creation of human/non-human hybrids and chimeras, the use of somatic cell nuclear transfer, and commercial surrogate motherhood. When the door opened, it opened wide, thought Damien. Had Eric seen the writing on the wall? Of course he had. That is his moniker. Even before his clones were off the assembly line, Eric convinced Minister Ed Kraken to use Techno-clones in his federal police force.

If Eric ever finds out what Christian is doing—feeding proprietary research to a revolutionist—he'll probably make Christian 'disappear'; Damien feels both privileged and fearful for his friend's welfare. The irony doesn't escape him: it was, in fact, Christian—Eric's long and steadfast helper from when BioGen was formed in '26—who convinced Damien to form the revolutionary group in the first place. If not for Christian's fervent intellectualism on the ills of the current technocratic government from an insider's point of view, Damien would still be grumbling his feckless criticisms rather than acting on them. He and Christian had met by chance right here, at this pub. Perhaps not by chance, Damien considers; Christian of course knew who Damien was by his appearance alone. The spark for Damien came when he was reminded of that kernel of thought back in 2022 when that Reichsbürger cop commented on his 'revolutionary' manifesto; Damien recalls that it had briefly resonated with him then. He remembers Eric's convincing revelation on human nature at Treffpunkt before that. There would be no change without revolution, Damien finally realized. And revolution must be violent, even subversive, to succeed. He knows that now, thanks to Christian's persuasive arguments. As always, Eric is right. Through friendly and convincing arguments, Christian pushed Damien over the precipice of inertia and Damien felt the thrill of doing something right. It was a little like falling in love, Damien considers. That same precipitous feeling of letting go and giving in to that rushing wave of unknowable force. Like an angel falling...

How Christian persuaded Damien to lead, not just participate, in this revolution, is still beyond him. Perhaps it is simply Christian's genuine faith in him, like no one else has placed in him, including his brother. And then there is the sparkling ocean of Christian's eyes that could move a mountain...

Christian shared a lot of proprietary information with Damien. He confided that a related department of BioGen—run by geneticist Ben Hardy—is successfully creating transgenic crops able to thrive as

Corporation Farm monocrops in salty, arid environments exacerbated by climate change. Qualities like drought tolerance, early flowering, thermo-tolerance, and salt tolerance in any thing from bananas, maize, and rice to cattle. Damien recalls that Hardy was the scientist responsible for the world wheat crop crash in '36. The crash plunged the world into conflict over the world's most important food staple. Wars, skirmishes, and forceful take overs broke out everywhere, particularly among countries that were most affected and those who grew other cereals, like corn and rice. The ripple effects continue still with countries stepping up their rice, sorghum, barley, oat and rye crops. How is it that Hardy still has his job? Perhaps because the accident was no accident, Damien concludes darkly. BioGen gained much from that fiasco. Despite being responsible for the accidental wheat crash, Eric's company was awarded the largest contract in history to fast-track other transgenic cereals to substitute wheat in a war against climate change, but also to create a wheat crop able to withstand the new virus—which they did in suspicious record time. Funny that.

Capitalism isn't about integrity, Damien decides. Capitalism rewards the crafty bully. And that's Eric. Ironic how his brother, who passionately derides capitalism, has become such a disciple. But what about Christian? Damien still doesn't trust him because he can't figure out why this genius scientist is defecting from one of the world's most successful biotech companies. When initially quizzed on it, Christian had cited an awakened sense of ecological responsibility.

It was too vague for Damien, who remains wary.

Christian leans over the patio fence and shakes Damien's hand vigorously. Then he points to the Schöfferhoffer. "What on Earth are you drinking?" He laughs. It's a lyrical cadenced laugh, more like an urchin's giggle, which Damien finds delightful and disarming.

"Something refreshing," Damien responds, letting his mouth relax into a playful grin. "Do you want one?"

Christian laughs again. "Heavens, no! I think I'll go for a plain lager." He hops the fence to sit across from Damien and leans forward, suddenly serious. "Did you hear the latest stats they released today on climate refugees worldwide? It's 1.2 billion!"

Damien shakes his head sadly and thinks of his native country of Germany. The pressure on Germany receiving migrants is only greater now with its own migration problems. They've become so isolationist.

"Most of those fleeing conflict and disaster are of course coming out of Latin America, Sub-Saharan Africa and South Asia," Christian goes on. "Places like Eritrea, Sudan, Afghanistan, Iraq, and, of course, Syria. Of course, climate migration is happening everywhere, in Europe and here, in North America. There's even in-fighting in most countries to do with resources like water and migrant populations. North and south Spain, for instance. Also, France, Germany, and even the Nordic countries. The news story ended with something on the Technocrats thinking again about building a wall to the south."

"*Mein Gott*, not that again!"

Christian laughs.

A waiter comes by and takes Christian's order of a lager on tap and drops off some German poutine then leaves.

Christian's eyes light up and he grabs a French fry drenched in gravy. "Yum!"

Damien smiles. "I don't usually eat this stuff, but I know you like fries. It's got German sausage, cheese curds, of course, and warsteiner dunkel beer gravy."

Christian grins and digs in. "Anyway, speaking of the planet," he says after eating several bites, "I like the name you chose for the movement: The Gaians. After the goddess of the Earth. Nice!"

Damien takes a sip of his Radler. "That depends on your perspective of Gaia. In Greek mythology, Gaia is the mother of all gods; she encompasses all forms of reproductive strategies, including incest and parthenogenesis. For instance, she uses parthenogenesis to create the mountains and the sea. She couples with her son Uranus—the sky—to bear the Titans, who are parents of many of the Olympian gods. She then kills her son and from his spilled blood she produces giants and ash-tree nymphs. And she produces Aphrodite, the goddess of love, out of the sea with his testicles," he ends with a mischievous smile.

"Ouch!" Christian guffaws and winces as if in pain, but his eyes twinkle with mischief. He takes a generous handful of fries and sausage lathered in gravy and inhales it down before adding, "Then there's Lovelock and Margulis's Gaia Hypothesis that living organisms and inorganic material make up a dynamic system that shapes the Earth's biosphere and maintains the Earth as a suitable environment for life. The hypothesis views the Earth as a 'superorganism' with self-regulatory functions."

"I think I prefer the latter example. Less dangerous!" Damien laughs.

The waiter returns with Christian's lager. Christian waits for him to leave then leans forward again. Christian takes a large gulp of beer then says seriously, "You know that this is sedition. We could go to jail for a long time or worse."

"Yes. It is." Damien nods coolly, hand brushing the length of his long nose. "And, yes, we could."

"A revolution against the Technocratic Government. Using your brother's Techno-clones against him." Christian purses his mouth then releases an impish smile.

"They're just as much your Techno-clones as they are my brother's; you made them, after all." He matches Christian's impish smile, locking eyes. Then Damien looks down and firms his lips thoughtfully. "Besides, it's just one option we're looking at. At any rate, my brother had his chance when he joined the Technocratic National Government. Now it's mine. He got where he is by being unscrupulous. Now it's my turn to be unscrupulous."

Christian leans back with a long breath and grins like a boy. He raises his glass. "Here's to unscrupulous!"

Damien raises his glass to Christian then drinks quietly, brows furrowed in brooding thought.

Christian studies him for a moment then pulls out his phone. "So, I got what you were looking for." He directs Damien to check his own phone for an image

Christian just sent him. When Damien retrieves it, Christian says, "That's her. Monica Schlange. The girl we talked about."

Damien studies her. She's beautiful. Long raven hair sweeps recklessly around a face of powerful determination and ebullient energy. Her almost black eyes are keen, intelligent, and wily. Of course he remembers her from their bizarre exchange in Sydney Smith Hall. What had she intended? Was it a case of mistaken identity? People often mistook him for Eric or the other way around. Given they both frequented the U of T campus—he to teach and Eric to meet clients—the mistake was understandable, despite their obvious differences, such as the way they dressed and comported themselves.

"She's very much a deep ecologist," Christian goes on, consulting the information on his phone. "She got her B.Sc. in Environmental Science with a minor in Political Science. For her Master's, she studied environmental ethics under Aisha Habib, herself a professed deep ecologist. Ms. Schlange's thesis topic was rather controversial; but Habib, as you know, is a powerful member of the Technocrats, oddly enough. Keeps her hand in the pie, so to speak. Schlange's thesis was entitled "Ethical Considerations on the Ecological Impact of Corporation Farm Anthropocentrism on the Stability of Gaia Through Ten Metrics."

"Impressive," says Damien. "It's something I'd be interested to read. So, how do I find her? She graduated this spring, I believe."

"She's with Eric."

Damien blinks. "They're in a meeting now?"

Christian stifles a laugh and shakes his head. "No. I mean *with him*, shacking with him."

"OH!" Damien gets it now. He feels like an idiot. Eyes blinking fast, Damien finally realizes that the confusing exchange with Schlange makes sense now. She'd confused him with Eric. When she confronted him, she was no doubt referring to some tryst with Eric in some men's washroom. So typical of him, thinks Damien. Eric was always doing *scheiße* like that, especially when they were both at school in Berlin. But Damien is still confused. He can understand his licentious brother chasing after this beauty, but... "Why would she...?"

"Shack up with him?" Christian gives Damien a crooked smile. "I know it seems odd that she would hang out with an industrialist. But it could simply be a physical thing. Your brother is ... um ... very charismatic, despite being a rather devious conceited sort, and he can be very persuasive, especially with a beautiful woman. I'm guessing that he's a good lay..."

"OH!" Damien's face heats suddenly with embarrassment and nervously brushes back his hair with both hands.

"And so is she, apparently!" Christian adds, brows rising and lips drawing back in a smirk. "She's quite the vamp! Eric often brings her to the lab and they make no effort to hide their sexual trysts there. It's all rather, well, scandalous. Randy complained how they just do it in his lab. I'm not sure why they like his lab, but seems to be a favourite." He frowns in morbid thought and considers to himself in amusement,

"Maybe it's his laminar fume hoods... they're brand new with entire warmed surfaces..." He laughs to himself then shakes his head. "Most likely it's his excellent sound system. They usually play loud 1980s music, mostly *Everybody Wants to Rule the World,* as they cavort. One time poor Randy was right in the middle of an experiment and Eric and the girl barged in and kicked him out and they carried on loudly in there, laughing and moaning and keening—she's *really* loud. It's better when the music is blaring. Everyone in the research lab knows about them and poor Randy is the butt end of so many jokes. Erin started calling his lab 'your fucking lab' and sang out 'Say that you'll never, never, never need it,' which got everyone laughing hysterically—except poor Randy, of course. Then Ben announced that *Randy's Fume Hood Rules the Boss.* It stuck, poor git." Christian chuckles in amusement.

This is altogether too much information, thinks Damien, finding his hands picking at the crease on his slacks.

Christian goes on, apparently unaware of how this is affecting Damien, "The girl doesn't seem to care. She has this haughty kind of invincible air about her. Which is why I think she can be turned. It's like a game for her. But a serious game." Then he leans forward suddenly. "I'm sorry, I didn't mean to make you uncomfortable. We are talking about your twin brother..."

"And I'm nothing like that arrogant son of a bitch!" Damien bursts out then follows with an embarrassed laugh. "In so many ways, Christian, I'm not like him..."

"I understand." Christian reaches out to touch Damien's hand on the table. "I didn't mean it that way..."

Damien snatches his hand back and places both hands on his lap with a sigh. "When we were growing up in Berlin, my brother and I were very close; we used to share everything. Our food, our clothes, our toys, even our friends. We were like two peas of a pod. Then my brother picked up that book, *Walden Two,* and threw away *Silent Spring,* a gift from our mother. I lost him. Just like that book. It's like he threw me away too." He curbs a sigh. "Something changed him, made him cynical about humanity. I don't know what it was, but it began with that book. He started running around with women, any women—well, they had to be beautiful women, of course. And highly sexed to keep up with him." Damien lets out a choppy laugh. "Eric was so promiscuous, I kept warning the idiot that he was courting STDs like gonorrhea or syphilis. He didn't seem to care." Damien glances down at his hands for a moment. "I guess he hasn't changed."

"No, he hasn't," says Christian matter-of-factly. "During the seventeen years I've been with BioGen Technologies, I've seen him with dozens of beautiful women, and they're getting younger all the time!" He laughs then lets it drain to a sigh. "He seems to have settled with Ms. Schlange though; they've been together for close to two years now and with no sign of him straying. But, like I said, Damien, the girl's very ambitious. She's a deep ecologist and a player. I think she's just biding her time with him. She may even think she can use him for her cause—which is linked to ours. In fact, she may come in very handy for us, if we play this right. And I think we can; I've already had the chance to speak to her a few times at the research facility on Devonshire Place where, like I said, she often comes with Eric. I already approached her on the idea of joining the Gaians. She brushed me off at first but I just think she was being careful. She's since come around."

Damien frowns, disappointed with Christian's overreach. "Is that wise? We haven't properly vetted her. I thought we were going to wait..."

Christian shakes his head and looks mildly apologetic. "I'm sorry I jumped the gun, Damien. But I'm certain about her. She's there as an agent for the environment. I'm sure of it. I can read it in her body language, what she says, but mostly in what she doesn't say. She's got a sharp mind, a political mind, and a fierce ambition for power, which means she will be easy to manipulate." He almost visibly winces with what he adds, "But, while her allegiance to deep ecology is quite genuine, her methods for achieving her aims may be slightly unconventional and possibly risky. Even dangerous."

Like sleeping with the enemy, thinks Damien.

"But I think even that can work for us," Christian says, leaning forward. "She's a bit of a wild card and possibly a genuine eco-terrorist. For instance, I discovered that she was behind the viral social media fiasco that embarrassed Prime Minister Robinson last year and almost cost him his seat. You know the one—those pictures of him fooling around with the German Chancellor, Magda Zimmermann, who's married with two kids. As if that weren't enough,

Schlange exposed the Prime Minister and Chancellor in their collusion with Spectrum WasteTech, who were mismanaging electronic waste on a global scale. It went viral on social media. Schlange may have also been involved in precipitating the Dasgupta fishing scandal on the central coast of British Columbia last year. That incident precipitated the deaths of two Heiltsuk women. It forced the environment minister to step down early this year. She may even go to jail yet. The intel is sketchy. If Schlange is responsible for that, which I think she is, then she's very good. Gifted, even. The information that leaked out was extremely proprietary and powerful; it took down a minister, Damien. I think that she's extremely resourceful, stealthy, good at subterfuge and covers her tracks impeccably. Of course, there are definitely anger issues there. But, I also think we can count on her because her motives to help the environment lie on a deep visceral level, tied to her childhood experience and love of Nature."

Damien studies her image on his phone with a thoughtful frown. He looks up at Christian. "What do we know about her?"

"Well, to begin with, she's an only child and grew up on one of the last independent dairy farms in Ontario, near Guelph. Her father was strict and encouraged a strong work ethic and love for the natural world. He doted on her but died of a heart attack when she was only thirteen, the year their farm was seized by the Technocrats and converted into a Corporation Farm using scientific agriculture. In fact, their seizure may have precipitated the father's heart attack. Her mother was assigned as a scullery maid in the farm kitchen; she took to drink then ran off with some truck driver travelling across Canada from Surrey, BC. He didn't treat the girl well and she ran away before they reached Halifax. She ended up living with her aunt—her father's sister—in the Beaches. The aunt worked as a librarian at York University and was a fervent member of Extinction Rebellion before it dissolved. She was a real bohemian, a deep ecologist herself, and encouraged the girl. It was the aunt who put the girl through school and university. She just recently died, which likely instigated Schlange's more recent subversive outbursts."

Damien nods thoughtfully. He has faith in Christian's abilities as a psychologist. If Christian thinks Monica Schlange can be trusted, despite her terrorist inclinations, then she can be. Damien studies her image on his phone again. She reminds him a little of Carla Hinrichs from Letzte Generation; an incandescent energy animates and drives them both. Carla had given up pursuing her law degree to pursue her cause as a climate activist with Letzte Generation. She dedicated both her mind and her heart in the fight for humanity's survival. While Monica shows the same level of dedication, she betrays a lack of integrity in her less than altruistic motivations and means, thinks Damien. The fact that she's with Eric proves this. But even that—especially that—can work in their favour. It would seem that, without knowing it, she is already working as an undercover spy for their revolution. He can work with that, Damien thinks. Yes, he can certainly do that. And more. *It's my turn now, brother...*

"OK. Set up a meeting," Damien says. "Let's get her into the fold."

Christian nods, eyes sparkling like a shallow tropical sea and sensual lips opening to a satisfied grin.

Damian flicks off his phone and Monica's image disappears. He beams at Christian with new energy. He searches those beautiful eyes for something to hinge his feelings on, and lets a genuine smile of confidence animate his face. "I may not be exciting like my brother," he admits honestly, "but I am dependable, discreet, and loyal. I can be a true friend."

Christian raises his glass and smiles warmly, eyes twinkling with something new. "I would expect nothing less, Damien. For, I, too, can be a true friend. Here's to the Gaians!"

Damien raises his glass to clink with Christian's. "To the Gaians!"

FIFTEEN

TORONTO, Henry and College Street.
November 10, 2044: early afternoon

The sun shines like a heat lamp as Monica and Isabo walk on Henry Street toward the crowded sidewalk patio of Prenup Pub. She recognizes Damien Vogel, seated with a *demi tasse* of coffee in front of him and reading a book. He's dressed lightly in a button-down moss-coloured linen shirt and black slacks—no rumpled brown jacket this time, she thinks and considers suddenly that he is striking the same pose as Eric did when she first met him at Mercurio L'Espresso Bar last winter: long legs crossed and wearing loafers without socks, leaning back with a book in one hand, slightly outstretched as if posing for a picture.

Somehow alerted to their approach, Damien looks up and she sees him make eye contact first with Isabo then glance at her and put the book down. Isabo waves and Damien nods back with a faint smile.

When they reach the patio, Isabo takes her through the back gate into the enclosed patio and they weave through the crowded tables of people eating, drinking and chatting toward Damien's table under the linden trees.

Isabo gives Damien a bright smile. "Good afternoon, *mon ami*."

Monica watches how Damien's face lights up and he gives Isabo a warm smile. "*Bonne journée, mon bon collègue.*"

"This is Monica Schlange, who I spoke to you about," says Isabo. "I'm afraid that I have a meeting with Eric in ten minutes, so I will leave the two of you. Later, *chouchou*?"

Damien nods and his eyes sparkle like a deep ocean. "Thanks, Christian." He briefly watches Isabo stride away before turning to Monica and brushing his hair back with his hand. "Thank you for coming." He shakes her hand with a firm grip and offers her a seat across from him. "Will you join me for a drink?"

"Thank you." Monica sits across from him as Damien gets the attention of a waiter. She orders a Troubadour Imperial Stout and a German poutine. At Damien's look of interest, she explains, "I haven't eaten all day and I'm starving!"

"Great choice. It's one of my favourites," he confesses. "The German sausage and dark gravy are a treat with the fries and curd. It's extremely flavourful and goes well with the Stout."

Monica points to Damien's book. *Treeline* by Ben Rawlence. "A classic," she says.

"It tells it all ... what was being lost and what it was becoming." He shakes his head and gives her a sad smile of solastalgia. Then he seems to pick himself up. "The book was written over thirty years ago; back then Rawlence imagined that as ecosystems start to falter, nation-states that used to send their military force to maintain the flow of oil would instead dispatch armies to protect the forests that make and send rain." He then laughs mirthlessly at the idea. How ridiculous it is.

Monica nods and rolls her eyes. By the time these

political entities do that it will be too late, she decides; the environment will be too far gone. The time to act has already passed. Ecosystems are already collapsing, particularly in the Arctic.

"If only..." She laughs with sardonic humour. "But skirmishes about resources ... well that's another thing. I'm thinking of how everyone is scrambling for water, like stealing clouds even. Over a hundred years ago, China started seriously modifying weather by creating smart clouds through seeding. They currently make over sixty billion tons of artificial rain a year, pissing off neighbouring countries whose clouds they're stealing. And don't get me started on what DARPA is doing. But speaking of water, I just read the latest statistics on the war in the middle-east between Egypt, Sudan, and Ethiopia."

"Yes, over their dams on the Nile."

"Wars over water have become the norm with climate change."

He sips his cortado and purses his lips in thought, hand brushing the length of his long nose. It's like a mental twitch, Monica decides; both brothers do it, caress their nose and brush their hair with their hand whenever someone slightly unbalances them. As if they are either hiding or pointing out a feature of their face that distinguishes them. She's not sure. At any rate, he's just betrayed that she makes him a little nervous. Good. And, yet, his deep blue eyes fire with intellectual intensity. "I fear you're right, Monica. The Sahara Desert has 'leapt' over the Mediterranean Sea, converting a third of Spain to desert. The ongoing conflict between south and north over water has created a civil war in that country. That is the next step in the escalation. When various parts of a nation fight among themselves and tear each other apart. We don't need wars to create disturbance; we will have civil strife."

"Yes, inner conflict. Like a good novel!"

He almost laughs and nods. "Yes!" His eyes light up for the first time since Isabo left and she decides that it softens his face and makes him terribly attractive. She also notices that, unlike Eric who constantly talks over her, Damien courteously lets her finish her sentence before responding. How refreshing and respectful. Thinking of the two brothers growing up, she wonders how the introvert ever got a word in past the loquacious self-centred extrovert. Despite many similar sibling traits between the twins—like their gate, posture, involuntary hand gestures and speech—they are two very different men. And each makes her feel differently. The more she interacts with Damien, the more she realizes what a prize he is. She admires his reserve, his understated expressions, how he calculates every action, how he speaks with the slight hesitancy of consideration. Eric displays his emotions for all to witness; Damien holds his emotions close, like cherished possessions to be shared only with someone special. When Eric smiles, which is often, he grins with purpose, beaming like the high beams of a car. When Damien smiles, which is almost never, he releases the warm glow of a campfire. Eric gazes with the hunting eyes of a raptor; Damien stares with ingenuous eyes of candor. Both hide their inner core: Eric with bluster and show, a shallow creek whose ripples inveigle like a clever trompe-l'oeil; Damien with the earnest darkness of a deep dystrophic pool, quietly biding his time for the right person to dive in and touch his guarded inner core.

She wants to be that person. But so far he's only let one person enter his dark cloister: Christian Isabo. She's almost certain that Damien is intimate with Christian Isabo, who doesn't hide that he is gay. She saw the brief fire pass between them when Christian introduced her to Damien. How their eyes kissed. She concludes that a sexual relationship with Damien is therefore unlikely for her; but sex isn't everything, she decides. She wants to laugh at her sudden realization. But it makes sense. While Eric has certainly titillated her with wild unbridled sex, Damien promises to arouse her intellect with delicious intrigue. Sex, like chocolate, is gone after a few bites; but stimulation of the mind and the sharing of ideas can be savoured for hours, days or weeks. Even years. And besides, it seems to her that the wanting can often be far more delicious than the having. Didn't Browning once write that a woman's *reach should exceed [her] grasp, or what's a heaven for?* She and Damien are better aligned in their vision of the world than she and Eric. While she may agree with some of Eric's prognoses of the world, his cures for what ails the world don't harmonize with her philosophy. Damien is a deep ecologist like her; that should count for something. Maybe everything.

Damien continues, "I think we will find that in every country there are factions vying for water and willing to use violence and terrorism to get it. It will be a matter of survival."

"Like the president of the United States buying up all the aquifer-rich land he can get his hands on in South America and pretending it's all for military defence."

"Or Robinson doing something very similar right here in Canada. When the Technocrats nationalized water utilities, they created their own huge monopoly of power."

"He who controls the water, controls the world," Monica says, taking a liberty on a quote from Frank Herbert's *Dune*. She winks then adds, "But, *it is said in the desert that possession of water in great amount can inflict a man with fatal carelessness.*"

Damien's sapphire eyes smile with appreciation and his mouth twitches in an almost-smile. "Yes... So, you're a fan of *Dune* and you quote my favourite character, the planetologist, Kynes. *The struggle between life elements is the struggle for the free energy of a system.*"

Monica grins. "*The flesh surrenders itself. Eternity takes back its own. Our bodies stirred these waters briefly, danced with a certain intoxication before the love of life and self, dealt with a few strange ideas, then submitted to the instruments of Time.*"

Damien leans forward, face betraying boyish enjoyment. "*A man's flesh is his own; the water belongs to the tribe.*"

So, this bookworm can be playful, thinks Monica. "*Survival is the ability to swim in strange water.*"

Damien smiles now, a closed smile of genuine relaxed pleasure. It's barely a smile, but the corners of his beautiful mouth have turned up and Monica basks in the abiding warmth growing inside her; she's made him smile and they are resonating in sync. He says, "*The highest function of ecology is understanding consequences.*"

"Indeed!" One of her favourite quotes from *Dune*.

After a silent pause, in which both study the other in appreciative silence, he offers in a quiet voice, "I read your master's thesis on Corporation Farms..."

She's surprised. Eric never once showed an interest in her thesis work.

"It was brilliant and I think you were courageous to choose that topic," he says, eyes sparkling like an ocean.

She feels a blush coming on. God! She never blushes!

"It should have received more traction, but we know why it didn't," he adds.

Embarrassed by her blushing reaction, she quips, "I think if it did, I wouldn't be here, talking to you, but in some stinking Technocratic jail for sedition." She laughs.

So does he. A delicious boy's laugh. And with it, his eyes crease and those stunning blue orbs grow gentle. There. She's made him laugh too! There is a gentle honesty, something close to vulnerability, about him that stirs something in Monica. Something she has never seen in Eric, despite his openness and raw emotional display. She finds herself at ease with Damien. There is no artifice between them, no competition or maneuvering or sexual tension; both are comfortable. This is new and something she quite enjoys. She realizes with stunned joy that she hasn't enjoyed herself more in the company of a man and suddenly recalls wonderful talks with her father, working together in the barn, cleaning stalls, or in the field, milking the cows.

Damien leans forward with a new intensity and she knows he is poised to make his proposition to her. He quickly sits back when the waiter comes with her stout and poutine then leaves. Monica immediately digs in and savours the complex flavours and textures of sausage, fries, curd and gravy.

Damien watches in silence as she takes several bites, groaning out loud with pleasure, then savouring a healthy gulp of stout. Without looking, she feels him watching her eat and enjoys his attention. He finally leans forward again and she meets his intense gaze. "Monica, our mission is to break the Technocratic government from as many angles as possible." No preamble, she decides, and appreciates his direct approach and unflinching candor. "I'm not a proponent of violence, so I'd like to see us use other means to topple the government. I'd prefer to simply help it rot from the inside than attack it outright. But, if we have to use violence, we will." He tips his head to her thoughtfully, assessing her every reaction. "Christian has that in hand, as you no doubt have surmised."

BioGen's Techno-clone technology. "The clones."

"Yes. Those chimeras." His expression sours then becomes thoughtful. "My brother has been dirtying his bioengineering hands with a lot of disreputable and immoral activities in that research and development company of his; all feeding into the Technocratic hidden agenda to use science to control the citizenry and make themselves fat with profit. We want to expose it all to the public. Get them all stirred up, disgruntled with their less than perfect government and far from perfect prime minister. We can do two things at the same time here and this is where you come in. We intend to attack the government's reputation through its ancillary companies: Canadian Enterprises generally and BioGen specifically." He pauses then continues, "Considering your relationship with my brother, we're hoping you can help with the BioGen end of things." She watches his lips firm with effort. "You'd have to break into his best guarded personal security systems and steal confidential files..."

"I've already done that," she answers matter-of-factly.

His eyes crinkle with sudden enlightenment and the inkling of a crooked smile tugs the right corner of his mouth up. He's probably thinking of the various media fiascos he knows she caused, like Robinson's embarrassing mess with the German chancellor and getting Robinson's environment minister sacked. "Of course you have..." He then gathers himself and adds, "You'd be expected to steal highly classified specifications—highly sensitive scientific material to do with some of his, let's say, more nefarious and definitely illegal research, which you will provide to us..."

"I've already stolen much. What do you need?"

He bursts into a wonderful laugh of surprise and sits back in his chair, much more relaxed. Monica smiles seductively. *Gotcha,* she thinks.

"I should have known that you'd be at least two steps ahead of me," he admits. He picks up his *demi tasse* of cortado and takes an appreciative sip, eyes still fixed on her. The light in them is dancing, she decides. Like a deep ocean she wants to dive into. Monica mimics his action and sips her flat white, meeting his beautiful eyes with a steady gaze.

"We're looking for any damning information on their unethical GOF virology, DURCs like virus hacking that could lead to potential maleficent activities such as bioterrorism. Even biological warfare. Like hacked strains of respiratory viruses that are highly transmissible and highly pathogenic. We know, for instance, that BioGen and Canadian Enterprises deal internationally, often with small dictatorships. All this science is political."

Monica has a sudden thought: does Damien know about his brother's secret intention to diminish the human population? He must have some knowledge of it. She's of the impression that those two shared everything; at least, Eric did with Damien.

Damien continues, "We're specifically looking for incriminating information on the origin of the wheat crash in '36 and the secret deals that followed. We know they exist."

"Consider it done."

"You do understand that this will totally compromise Eric's company. We intend to bring him down, along with the Technocrats. His company is everything to him, Monica. You'll be ruining him." He pauses, eyes narrowing slightly to study her carefully. "How do you feel about that?" he asks her and she knows he's really asking 'can you really do that to him if you love him?'

Was she ever in love with Eric?

And in that moment of asking, she realizes that she may have loved him just a little, but now is rather disgusted with him and his selfish antics. In fact, that feeling could easily turn to hatred. How easily she's come to that sentiment! She decides that love and hate are inseparable. They are intertwined like two lovers sharing saliva and sweat, insatiably devouring each other like the Ouroboros. Two incestuous siblings, connected through an umbilical cord of mutual insecurity. When you're in love, you invest far too much in another and lose your soul. She realizes that this release from Eric empowers her with a renewed Amazonian flame. Invigorated, she revels in the power of freedom. Monica finds a genuine smile light her face and responds with self-satisfied confidence, "I feel very good about it, Damien." She likes saying his name. "Very good, indeed."

And now Damien is openly smiling and his eyes grow soft and deep in their gaze. Monica realizes with a flutter of her heart, that his soft gaze is something she has longed for ever since she lost her father. Monica decides that she's grown tired of an effervescent champagne and now prefers the complexity of a vintage red wine. Forget the heady transient delights; she's after darker abiding pleasures.

Everybody wants to rule the world...

SIXTEEN

TORONTO, Corner of Shaw and Yarmouth Streets. July 20, 2046: early morning

Ben Hardy wakes suddenly to the scent of lilac perfume and his wife standing over him by the bed. She's nudged him awake and glares down at him with accusing eyes. He blinks up at her in sleepy confusion. Chloé is already dressed for work in a crisp grey suit and stands silhouetted by the rosy light of a wildfire dawn that streaks in from the east-facing windows. He's surprised she's up so early. Neither of them slept much last night; the smoke from the northern wildfires kept her up all night with wracking coughs. Even the home NIV ventilator didn't do much to help. When she eventually coughed up some blood, Ben suggested they go to the hospital. But Chloé stubbornly refused and just took some pills. Both eventually fell asleep.

Chloé waves a document folder at him. "So *this* is what you were actually doing in Montreal? Gain of function research?"

Ben sits up on the side of the bed and looks up at her, wiping the sleep from his eyes. "What do you mean?" She looks so tall right now. They haven't talked about Montreal days in so long, he thinks. It's painful. He explains in a weary voice, "Most genetic engineering involves gain of function research. It works better that way. Any selection process involving an alteration of genotypes and resulting phenotypes is a type of GOFR. You knew what we were doing, Chloé. You were even part of it for a while. We were looking at virus-host interaction and transmissibility, among other things; ways to increase the wheat crop's resistance to disease—"

"Disease that you created!" she cuts in, voice still raspy from last night's coughing. "I know that was a synthetic virus, Ben. A virus *you* made in *your* lab."

"Yes, yes," he stutters out, fingers nervously clawing through his disheveled hair. "We developed non-natural mutated viral strains that we induced to increase transmissibility for *in vivo* testing—"

"Which you then released!"

"Yes, it got away—"

"No, you *released it*!" she corrects forcefully and goes into a hacking cough. She seizes in halting breaths and continues in a voice still simmering with anger, "Well, BioGen did. BioGen *purposefully* crashed the wheat crops so you could walk in with your new gene-edited resistant wheat crop the next year. How convenient! Remind me how much BioGen made for Canadian Enterprises in revenue from that little piece of convenient luck? Billions, I believe." She shakes her head with growing anger. "Ben! This was no accident. This is criminal!" She throws the folder onto his lap. "You must know how the world suffered from that disaster. So many starved. The conflicts and wars. All so you could roll out your designer wheat and blackmail countries and corporations to buy it! Were the Technocrats in on this? Of course they were; you're part of Canadian Enterprises, after all. And Robinson certainly knew, was 'in the loop,' as they say. Is this about balance of power too? Compromise the dominance of China, the primary wheat producer and consumer?"

Her breaths whistle out of her. Her bronchitis is getting worse, Ben thinks, feeling powerless to help. She suffers terribly with the smoke and the smog-inducing heat. Their house is old with poor insulation and poor air conditioning. Something he hadn't realized when they moved in and did their minimal renos. On top of the smoke, yesterday's heatwave and inversion trapped more city smog than usual, raising the AQI to over 150. That's considered unhealthy for everyone. Suffering from COPD, Chloé is particularly sensitive; anything over 50 AQI is bad for her lungs. She shouldn't have been out yesterday on that field trip to his work place and she shouldn't go out today. Environment Canada predicts that the heatwave and inversion will continue for another five days. But the wildfires are bringing more fine and coarse particulates to the city. Someone warned that the AQI might go up as high as 200 today. Environment Canada issued a warning to people like Chloé to stay home.

Chloé seizes in rasping breaths before adding, "Ben, my only question is, *did you know*?"

"No! Chloé, you have to believe me. I didn't know we were going to release the virus when I developed the resistant strain—"

"Good grief, Ben. You must have suspected. You're not stupid, for God's sake. BioGen's done it before with gene-hacked bananas and potatoes and I don't know what else. You *know* that. It's Vogel's God-damned moniker!" She makes an exasperated sound then says in hoarse breathlessness, "How can someone as smart as you be so ... so..."

"Dumb?"

"Ignorant!" She shakes her head and waggles her finger at him accusingly. "And what about that recent terrorist bombing of Siegel Analytical? BioGen could be next, Ben. That eco-group your sister's husband—Armon—keeps talking about ... the Gaians ... they've made terrible accusations about Robinson's company, Canadian Enterprises, and I'm inclined to agree with them. Especially after *that*." She points to the folder.

Ben looks down at the folder. He opens it and flips through copies of emails to various stakeholders and handwritten memos between Robinson and Vogel about the artificial virus and its release. Stunned, Ben looks up at Chloé. "Where did you get this?" he asks in a hoarse whisper and glances around like a criminal as if they are being surveyed.

She murmurs something he doesn't understand.

He throws the file down on the bed and abruptly stands, seizing her by the shoulders. "No, seriously, Chloé, where did you get that file?"

She shakes him off. "Stop it! You're hurting me!"

"I'm sorry." He lets her go. "But, it's proprietary, Chloé," he continues in a hoarse whisper. "If anyone finds out that you have this, I'll lose my job or worse—"

"*That's* what you're worried about?" her voice rises to a phlegmy shriek, breath rattling out of her.

Ben winces. "You'll wake Janet up..."

"She has to get up for school anyway. But, Ben, this has to stop." She grabs the folder and turns to walk out of the room then stops. "If you must know, I found it in my satchel this morning when I got up. Someone must have put it there for me to find." After a pause, she says, "For me to do something about."

"Wait! What are you going to do, Chloé? Don't do anything stupid." *Like take it to the press.*

"Just watch me."

"You need to stay home. Think of your heart. It's not so good recently." He thinks of her recent hospital stay when the doctors diagnosed her with pulmonary hypertension. The doctor had warned her that congestive heart failure could occur. She doesn't look good; she's pale and he can hear her wheezing laboured breaths. "They forecast dangerous air quality today. There's an advisory."

"Like I said, this has to end, Ben. And it's your turn to take Janet to school today." Then Chloé is out the door.

"Don't forget your mask!" Ben calls after her, then feels lame for stating the obvious. "It's really bad out there today," he adds more to himself as the outside door slams and he thinks that she shouldn't go out at all in her condition, even with a mask. She ended up in the hospital on a ventilator during the last smog-in.

Ben sits back on the bed and grabs his head in his hands. His concern over what Chloé is planning to do is overshadowed by his discovery that there is a mole in BioGen. That's where Chloé was yesterday afternoon, touring his research lab on Devonshire Place with her grade eight science class. He had let his two technicians Preksha and Sang-woo host her class while he was tied up at one of BioGen's commercial labs in Mississauga the whole day. Someone leaked that information to her, guessing that she would take it to the press. Who would do that? Who knew her that well?

TORONTO, Devonshire Place. July 20, 2046: later that morning

Holding hands with his six-year old daughter, Ben walks into one of his several air-purified labs at the small BioGen research facility on Devonshire Place and watches Janet's face light up with fascination. Instead of taking her to school today, he's decided to bring her to work. A little Grade 1 field trip, he decides, thinking to covertly investigate potential moles. Who, besides his two technicians, interacted with Chloé yesterday during her student field trip? Who could have slipped that incendiary information into her satchel?

He doesn't see Preksha and Sang-woo in the outer lab and deduces that they must be in the inner tissue culture lab, working on one of his latest projects. Ben walks his daughter through the outer lab, crowded with shelves and equipment. He points out the laminar flow hoods that line one wall; each hood is equipped with an automated multichannel pipette dispenser and other equipment for gene editing. Several filtered chemical storage units holding various reagents stand beside the hoods. The opposite wall is lined with four incubators, stacked on each other, a glass-door fridge and freezer and a counter with a centrifuge, bead bath, and liquid pumps. He leads Janet past counters in the middle of the room and points out the stereo microscope, the inverted microscope with micromanipulator set, the electroporation unit and transfection unit, automated cell counter and fluorescent cell imager, along with other sundry equipment such as microinjection pipettes with loading tips, petri dishes and other culture dishes, sterile gloves, and various reagents and heating units. Janet looks at it all with wonderment.

They reach a glass wall and door into the inner lab. This is Ben's tissue culture lab, where his technicians are culturing various transgenic calluses and plants.

"That's my little garden," says Ben with a crooked smile as they look in on the growing room, shelves full of culture racks of newly cultured plantlets in plugs, plant masses on agar in test tubes and Erlenmeyer flasks with cell suspensions in liquid on shakers, all under fluorescent lights.

"I like it," says Janet, peering with interest at the various plants growing there.

"The plant tissue culture lab has three separate workspaces for preparing, transferring, and growing various tissue cultures," Ben explains. "That's the growing room, the last stage of culturing. It also leads to a small greenhouse." Then he points to another door at the back of the growing room. "Past that door is the culture room, where my technicians are probably preparing callus cultures. They do that by inoculating explants in agar under fume hoods like the ones we just passed in this lab." Then he grins at her, like he's holding a prize. "Did you know that all plant cells have totipotency?"

"What's that?"

"Well, you've probably heard about stem cells, eh? All plant cells—if suitably stimulated—have all the information necessary for growth and reproduction into a new whole plant. Mature plant cells can also dedifferentiate from a specific type back to meristematic conditions then redifferentiate into something new. Imagine your heart cells able to turn around and make lung tissue!"

Janet stares in total fascination.

"We only need a small bit of a leaf or stem to grow a whole plant. So, in the back room under sterile fume hoods like the ones we just passed, Preksha and Sang-woo are taking explant sources like cut up pieces of a plant's shoot tip or leaf disks and inoculating them in growth media with nutrients and growth hormones under sterile conditions. They're inducing different types of callus cultures—soft, hard, green, white, and brown—depending on the plant and hormone. It takes two to three weeks for the calluses to form. Most of what we do here are callus cultures, protoplast cultures, or cell suspension cultures like those flasks on the orbital shaker.

"The plant calluses Preksha and Sang-woo are growing are masses of unorganized plant parenchyma cells. See those petri dishes and test tubes with what looks like algal masses in agar?" He points to one wall with rows of petri dishes and capped test tubes. "Those are callus and protoplast cultures. The cell suspension cultures are in the flasks on the shaker." He points to the large shaker with flasks attached to it. "We make the calluses usually from somatic tissues after plating onto tissue culture medium. We use auxin and cytokinin to stimulate root and shoot growth. Calluses are great for creating transgenic crops and cell suspension cultures are good for biosynthesizing secondary metabolites—like anti-cancer properties or birth control, for example. We use protoplast cultures—which are basically plant cells stripped of their cell walls—to do gene transfer. Like fusing two different species to create one with the best qualities of both."

While Ben lectures his daughter who pretends to understand him, he searches for his technicians. Neither is in the growing room, so Ben decides to wait for them to emerge from the culture room. He turns to Janet and says with a slanted smile, "So, you already know that what we do here is magic..."

"Mostly gene-editing, right Daddy?" says Janet, eager to make points with her father.

He nods. "That's right, Sweet-pea. Gene-editing is a type of genetic engineering that allows us to insert, delete, modify, or replace DNA in plants, bacteria, and animals. It can change a creature's physical traits, like eye colour, or disease risk. We use a tool called CRISPR, which stands for Clustered Regularly Interspaced Short Palindromic Repeats. It acts like scissors, cutting the DNA at a specific spot on the genome with the help of a special protein, Cas9, and something called guide RNA. We then remove, add, or replace the DNA that was cut. Gene editing includes what we call knockouts—preventing a gene's expression—and knock-ins—a targeted insertion of an exogenous gene at a specific locus."

"Knock outs like in baseball?"

He laughs. "Pretty much. Yes, just like that."

He takes her over to one of the computers and they sit down at it. He opens up several files and shows her several images of various crops and people working in the lab.

"Along with tissue cultures, we do transgenic experiments, that simply means the transfer of genes from one organism into another, which even includes between species to create a transgenic organism. We can engineer plants with a gene that helps them combat a particular pest or be more efficient in photosynthesis. You know what that means?"

"Yes, Daddy! You taught me that!" she says proudly.

"We do a lot of this through gene-editing, which is an effective way to increase tolerance of crops to abiotic stress, things like drought, salinity and flooding," Ben takes on that professorial tone Janet's grown accustomed to as she struggles to understand. "Let's look at rice as an example." He opens a file on the computer that shows an image of a rice crop with a huge table of data. "Rice is most affected by drought and salinity because of where it's traditionally grown. Improving on the seminal work of Zhang from decades ago, BioGen edited rice plants using CRISPR/Cas9 and knockout OsRR22, the gene associated with salt susceptibility in rice, to decrease salt susceptibility. We've also engineered rice to better tolerate drought through gene-editing and cis-genic approaches to reduce stomatal density—" He stops for a moment, realizing that he's using words his little girl doesn't understand. "You know that stomata are openings that let a plant transpire?"

Janet nods eagerly, proud that she knows something of what her father is telling her. "So it can breathe."

He smiles sideways at her. "Yes, but that makes them a major doorway to water loss. So we tell it to make fewer stomata." Then he points to a map of the world on the computer and continues, "Another thing we're doing is editing rice so it can live in cooler climates up north where longer days happen in summer. We use gene drives to change the flowering times of rice plants so they can live in northern latitudes.

"What's a gene drive, Daddy?"

"Gene drive is when mobile pieces of DNA insert themselves into different parts of the genome to help spread a trait through a population. You know what genes and DNA are, right?"

"Of course, Daddy! You taught me!"

Ben smiles. "Good girl. Anyway, engineered gene drives can quickly spread good traits or bad traits—like sterility—through a population. We use CRISPR gene drives to give some allele—a trait carrying part of a gene—an unfair advantage. We use a synthesized DNA sequence—the gene drive—to make sure that the allele with its trait is passed on from the transgenic organism in the lab to offspring. When the transgenic organisms are released and mix with the wild population, the trait spreads through the entire population. It can be a good trait or a bad trait depending on what we want to do: help make a plant salt-resistant or eradicate an invasive species by making it sterile or kill it."

"But, Daddy, the bad trait wouldn't work then, would it? If the offspring become sterile, they'd all die or be sterile before they could affect the rest of the wild population."

Ben lets out a great laugh. "How did you get so smart?" he asks Janet, ruffling her hair. "You're so right, Sweet-pea. Ok, here's how it works: we engineer the trait—say death or infertility—to only occur when two copies are present, what we call homozygous recessive. But, we copy the drive in the germline, so each offspring only has one copy of the altered allele, what we call heterozygous, and is only minimally affected by the genetic alteration. This lets the alteration spread quickly through the population first. Then, once it becomes common, homozygous offspring are produced and the whole population crashes. Clever, huh?"

Janet nods, impressed. Then she looks at him quizzically. "But what happens when something goes wrong? Like that thing back in the '20s when those super pigs got away? Farmers created them by crossing their gene-modified farm pigs with wild hogs. Then they let them go because they couldn't make money on them and the super pigs started eating all our wheat and barley."

Ben blinks in surprise at his six-year old daughter. "Where did you get that from?"

"Mommy told me."

Ben finds his smile tighten into a grimace. He thinks of his argument with Chloé this morning and her terrible accusation. His 'accident' forced them to move from Montreal and ultimately cost Chloé her job at BioGen. And that was a shame; she was a promising microbiologist there, doing interesting work with fungi and lichen. She wasn't fired; she quit, citing ethical reasons. She no longer wanted to be part of a company who played God with life. Perhaps she already suspected their transgressions. She wasn't a fan of Vogel's. She'd told Ben once that she considered Vogel an unethical bully. When they moved to Toronto, she found a job teaching high school science and Ben continued in BioGen's research and development lab as one of their chief scientists. If she was less polite, Chloé would have called Ben's promotion a bribe to keep him quiet.

Ben shakes off the guilt and scrolls down to another onscreen page that shows projects on various plants. "Now, this project is one of my favourites," he says, forcing himself to be enthusiastic. "Plant gene editing for disease resistance, mostly by knocking-out susceptible loci for enhanced resistance. Things like leaf blight, powdery mildew and various viruses."

Ben then catches sight of his two technicians through the large windows of the adjoining tissue culture lab. They've just come through the culture room into the growth room. Both are dressed in scrubs, hair cap and masks to avoid contamination.

"Here, Sweet pea," says Ben, clicking to an educational site with games. "Take a look at these images of plants that have been genetically engineered. See which ones you can identify. There'll be a test when you're done!" He winks. "Just kidding. Find a game you like to play. I'm just going to talk to Preksha and Sang-woo for a minute. They're my plant pathologists."

He leaves his daughter at the computer and enters the growth room. His technicians greet him with smiles and he explains that he's brought in his daughter for a little personal tour. Preksha then proceeds to explain what stage she and Sang-woo are at in their project. Ben listens abstractly, waiting impatiently to open his inquiry: "So, how did it go with my wife's Grade Eight class yesterday? I hope they weren't too rowdy for you."

"No, no!" Preksha eagerly assures him. "Those kids were very curious! And they asked really cool questions, didn't they, Sang-woo?"

Sang-woo nods.

Trying to be casual, Ben asks, "Can you tell me who else the group or my wife talked to or who else was here when they came through the lab?" At their hesitation in thinking, he decides on expediency with a lie. "It's important. We just found out that one of the kids has Covid 29 and I'll need to notify everyone who came into close contact with the school group."

Suddenly serious, Preksha says, "Well, we were obviously here, so you have us covered. Consider us notified. And we were here the whole time they were here of course, so let me think..." She confers with Sang-woo, who shyly mumbles something. "Yeah, so, Randy was here briefly, but he went straight to the greenhouse to check on his plants," says Preksha. "Oh, and Christian, of course, came through. He was great! Because we were mostly in the culture room, he offered to take them through CRISPR and go over the equipment."

"Is that all?"

"Oh, Monica Schlange was with him," Preksha adds. "She asked some pretty good questions too! I think that's it."

"Could someone else have come in when you were in the culture room?"

Sang-woo and Preksha exchange glances. Preksha shakes her head. "I don't think so. It's possible, but no one else was slated in the lab today except us. I suppose you could ask your wife?"

Ben frowns. None of them is the likely suspect for espionage. Isabo practically helped Vogel set up this lab—he was there since the beginning. And Schlange is Vogel's whore. She comes in all the time with him and all she seems interested in is loud sex with Vogel to sickening 1980s music. Maybe he has this all wrong, Ben decides. Maybe someone at the school was the vector and they slipped the files into Chloe's satchel before or after the field trip. That still leaves the leak in question; how the vector would have obtained that information in the first place. But that also opens up the suspect list to anyone at BioGen. It doesn't have to be someone at his lab that day. It just needs to be someone with access to those documents. Over fifty scientists and technicians come through the Devonshire Place research facility. And there are people who come and go from the commercial labs that have meetings with Vogel.

"Ben!" Isabo rushes into the culture lab, breathing hard. "Why didn't you pick up?"

Ben blinks at his colleague and glances at his

phone on the counter beside Janet, who has ignored its buzzing as she played her game on the computer. "I've been giving my daughter a tour and—"

"Your house is on fire!"

"What?"

"And your wife is missing. We tried to reach her. She never arrived at the school."

"What?" He stares at Janet, busy with her game on the computer, and feels his gut plummet with dread.

TORONTO, Shaw Street. July 20, 2046: earlier that morning

Chloé puts on her mask and heads outside her house, immediately feeling the humid heat of the morning. She feels the tightness of her still simmering anger at Ben for being so damn amenable. She wishes he would grow a backbone and say 'no' some time. That prick boss of his runs him dry and doesn't care.

She looks up at the blushing sun in the sky; it resembles a giant orange ball in a permanent sunset, and glows deep yellow-pink in the thick smog and wildfire smoke in the air. She glances back at their stark white brick three-story house. Even it is a compromise they shouldn't have made. The place is nice enough, with lots of character within a nice residential neighbourhood. Sitting on the corner of Shaw and Yarmouth, it was once a café that featured house-made baked goods and a wrap-around sidewalk patio. All that disappeared years ago with the last pandemic. When they moved here from Montreal, Ben found the place boarded up and in poor shape. They gave it a quick fix, but that isn't enough to combat the heavy air pollution they're experiencing in the smog-filled city, particularly now with the heatwaves and northern wildfires. It's leaky. Pollutants seep in easily, making it difficult for her to sleep at night without a ventilator when the AQI is higher than 75, which is often. Why did they have to move here to the city in the first place?

This is not a good place for her, she thinks, reflecting on her severe COPD. She grew up as an asthmatic and both parents ended up with COPD as well. Both Marie and Jean Gaboret had been heavy smokers and Jean worked at GD Electroplating Inc. near Sherbrooke, where Chloé and older sister Lise helped as young girls. Chloé didn't realize at the time that she was breathing in the small cadmium particulates from the thermal processes involved in electroplating. Or that she had the gene for -1 antitrypsin deficiency, giving her a predisposition to COPD. Perhaps Lise didn't get the gene; she hasn't yet developed COPD, despite the fact that she also worked at their father's electroplating plant that belched out cadmium fumes or that she's a heavy smoker. Or is her current lifestyle preventing the onset of COPD? Lise now lives on a farm outside of Toronto, near Port Perry.

Smelling the wildfire smoke through her mask, Chloé heads south on Shaw toward the Ossington Station subway in the rising heat of the morning. It's only 9 am and the temperature is a blistering 34°C; the high-pressure inversion they reported for today will trap more pollutants near the ground. She checks her phone app and flinches at what it reveals: an alarming AQI of over 200 already! No wonder her eyes are watering from the smoke in the air. She's forgotten her goggles again. Everything is bathed in an eerie peach-pink colour—chrome shines like copper, windows glitter with reddish light, and the sun hangs in the sky like a giant orange ball in a permanent sunset. It's quite surreal and unsettling.

Toronto News reported over a thousand individual wildfires in Ontario's northern boreal forest yesterday. Several million hectares of land is burning. Over 5000 people displaced. A single wildfire grew to more than 700,000 hectares, an area larger than the entire Greater Toronto Area. Part of the reason is no rain. They have drought-like conditions. The wood is like tinder, easily sparked by dry lightning. High winds are spreading the fires. Evacuations are occurring everywhere. The poor indigenous people!

The northern boreal forests are not only the home of these people; they occupy one fifth of the globe and contain one third of the Earth's trees, forming the second largest biome, the ocean being the first. If the boreal disappears, the disruption will be catastrophic for both the planet and for humanity. Perhaps it is already happening, she thinks, looking up at the blushing sky. *How will we survive*?

She knows she shouldn't be out in this yellow-pink noxious soup, but Ben just made her so mad, she feels compelled to do this now. The file is like a piece of radioactive metal, burning a hole in her satchel. She must get it to Theo. She intends to drop by his office on Queen Street East in Leslieville before heading to her school in the Beaches for her teaching day. Theo is part of the Fifth Estate; he runs *The Aletheia*, a small independent press both in newsprint form and online. It's not part of the country-wide syndicated media controlled by the Technocrats and for a small press it has good coverage in the Toronto area; so, it will do, thinks Chloé. It'll get the word out. Besides, Theo is a good friend. One she can count on for not cringing at the truth, no matter how politically hot it is. She's decided to go there in person rather than send materials via email or other means. This must reach Theo directly.

Soon after she passes Essex Street, she feels someone following her. She glances back and flinches at the sight: a Techno-clone! Techno-clones are not common in the city; the Technocrats normally deploy them in military issues of national security. Her eyes stray to her satchel and she thinks of the files inside. Are they important to national security? She's downright scared of the clones. They don't seem human anymore, she thinks with another glance at the clone. She takes in his weaponized left arm. His burnished skull of metal and flesh and binocular eyes. Metal tubes snake down his face into the corner of his mouth. He's easily seven feet tall with a long stride and she realizes with a flinch and thundering heart that he's catching up to her.

She thinks to call Ben on her phone then tells herself she's just being unreasonably fearful. She doesn't want to give him the satisfaction of seeing another panic attack of paranoia from her. She's still angry with him. She thinks of calling Amanda, Ben's younger sister on Dovercourt. She wouldn't accuse Chloé of paranoia in the streets. Her husband is thinking of joining the Gaian movement, after all. Chloé knows this even though the Cranes are keeping it a secret from everyone, especially Ben.

She gives up on the phone and tries to centre herself from panicking needlessly. She's about to dart west on Pendrith toward Ossington Station when she sees another Techno-clone, walking toward her. Breaking into a nervous sweat, she abandons her west route and continues down Shaw, picking up her pace. Her thoughts race: what are two Techno-clones doing here in the city? Wishing to avoid them, she jogs across the street, heading east on Barton Avenue to catch the subway at Christie Station instead. Already feeling breathless, she passes several houses to the northern edge of Christie Pits Park and decides to cut through the park's open field to Christie Station. Breaths wheezing out of her, Chloe glances back and spots both Techno-clones walking together. There is no mistake now; they are definitely pursuing her!

Her heart pounds up her throat. They're closing in! She turns to run toward the trees at the south end of the park and spots three more Techno-clones walking towards her. Perspiration beads on her forehead and she stumbles under a wave of nausea. What do they want? She knows what they want and feels the weight of the satchel clutched in her sweaty hands.

Oh, God! There's no one else in the park; the Techno-clones have scared them all away. There's no use calling anyone on her phone now. It's too late. The clones have her surrounded. It will all be over in moments. They close in and she can make out their alien faces of copper-tinged metal and the translucent flesh of amphibians.

Fumbling with the satchel that holds her secret papers, Chloé stumbles and feels her heart race out of control. It thunders inside her like a bird with a broken wing. Her breaths stutter out of her in short spurts. She labours to pull in enough air and realizes that her lips are pursed and she is pulling in shallow breaths. They are not enough. Green spots appear in front of her and she realizes she is about to faint. She fumbles in her satchel for her bronchodilator and pulls down the mask to take in a breath from the inhaler.

With lightning speed, one of the Techno-clones lunges forward and knocks the inhaler from her hand. It flies up and bounces to the ground metres away. She chokes on her first inhale of unfiltered air. It's like breathing in a campfire. Smoke scorches her throat and sticks there like concrete forming, gagging her. Her heart wants to explode.

She's now face to face with them as they crowd in on her, all glistening synth and metal. There's no expression. She makes a foolish attempt to dash past two of them. They close the gap and bounce her back to the centre. Another clone rips her mask off and throws it to the ground.

The clones crowd closer, closing a ring around her. She can't breathe. They silently nudge her with rough metal-synth bodies. Alien faces, half-human and half-machine, fade in and out of focus. She's gasping for air. Her heart hammers like an animal biting her from inside. Her chest writhes and constricts painfully, pressing down on her. She screams inside. *Help! Please!* ... She realizes that she is falling and the clones let her, moving back to give her room. She crashes to the ground, choking on the corrosive smell of campfire smoke. It fills her lungs with burning smoke.

The clones crowd back in, forming an umbrella of dark alien shapes that eclipse the sunset light. Alien heads wink out the light in staccato. They are waiting. She realizes that they are waiting for her to die.

She can't breathe. Can't pull the air inside. Then she feels excruciating pain as her poor palpitating heart rebels and seizes.

Then there is nothing.

—

One of the clones bends down and checks her neck for a pulse. He nods to the others. Another goes through her satchel, removes the file folder, then drops the satchel on the ground beside her. He fetches her mask and puts it back on her face then takes the bronchodilator they'd knocked out of her hand and pockets it.

The five clones then walk in separate directions under the blazing morning sun. They leave the prone body on the scorched field in the rippling heat.

SEVENTEEN

TORONTO, Distillery Lane.
September 9, 2050: late night

Monica rouses herself from the bed, careful not to wake Eric, who snores loudly. Carefully pulling his arm off her, she gets out of bed and tip toes naked out of the bedroom to his office. They've just made love for the fourth time that night and Eric dropped into a heavy sleep moments after. He'd been rough and distracted each time they had sex. Although she likes it rough and wild, he hurt her a few times, as though he didn't care. Monica thinks she knows why.

—

Eric was preoccupied today when they met for lunch and something put him in a surly mood at the end of the day; he was uncommonly laconic at supper. But it seemed that it wasn't to do with her because she managed to distract him in his home office that evening. She'd pushed herself on him, teasing and coaxing, licking and blowing in his ears, despite his gruff rebuffs. He kept citing this new important project but refused to elaborate. Earlier in the BioGen lab, Isabo confided that they'd just landed a huge military contract with the Americans.

Just as she thought her persistence made him angry and he would blow up, he rose with sudden violence, snarling, "*Mein Gott,* woman! *Du bist so eine Schlampe!*" He swept the papers off the desk like a madman and seized her, throwing her butt hard onto the desk. Hands tore her slacks down and he pulled open his pants, releasing his swollen cock. Then he drove into her with wild abandon. He soon ejaculated with a thunderous howl of pleasure before she had the chance to come. No kissing, no caressing. Just the business. When he was done, he pulled out, zipped up and growled at her with a satisfied laugh, "Now, leave me to my work, *Schlampe*! Let me work!"

Making motions to help him pick up his papers, she quickly scanned each as she did. She thought it odd how he even had papers on his desk; he didn't normally keep papers that would incriminate him. Everything was done on computer, using encrypted files. One of the papers grabbed her attention. A printed email from General Seth Willett, Chairman of the Joint Chiefs of Staff to President Tobiasen: it confirmed shipment of a new airborne DNA-based viral agent that makes Caucasians sick, kills people with higher melanin content, and leaves Technoclones unaffected. Side effects of sterility in some heterozygous variants was noted. Stunned, she was suddenly reminded of her earlier suspicion of his selective breeding plans for a Walden Two. This was a recipe for a militarized genocide. "What's this?"

He snatched the paper from her hand and bit out like a Nazi, "It's top secret." Then his surly look suddenly melted and he grinned like a naughty boy. The change was so drastic, it unbalanced her. "I'm going to be the richest man alive," he said with a glib smile. "And our Walden Two is assured, *Schnuki*."

Great Gaia! She forced a smile back, and went to

bed, formulating a plan.

When he finally turned in, no longer angry looking, she embraced him and they made love several times through the night. Then, when he finally fell into a deep snoring sleep in the dark of early morning, she slipped out of bed...

—

As she leans over his desk, clutching the papers he'd earlier strewn in violent passion, she turns quickly to the sound of a man clearing his throat.

Eric stands at the door, still magnificently naked, like her, leaning casually against the door jamb. "Did you find what you were looking for?" he asks in a sarcastic voice.

She overcomes her surprise and straightens, adopting a brazen unapologetic tone, "Yes, I did, thank you. I found it all. All your dirty secrets, Eric."

He crosses the room in two steps and seizes her wrist in a vice grip, forcing her to let go of the papers. They flutter to the floor. His face now seethes with anger. "Did you think I didn't know what goes on in my company? With you especially? That you're a fifth column? Sneaking around my place, taking my private things, leaking the wheat affair to Ben's wife, that ungrateful witch. She was going to leak it to the press." He grips painfully hard, cutting off her circulation. "The only reason you're still in my bed is because it all came to nothing. Robinson's Techno-clones took care of her. They retrieved the materials and got the rest when they set fire to the place. And Isabo! That cunt! I *made* him, plucked him straight out of high school and gave him everything he needed to thrive in my lab. That ungrateful homo slut will get his tonight. I just found out that he's in collusion with my brother. My whiny brother and his precious Gaians! The fucking enemy! He's probably given Damien blueprints to God knows what projects of mine—thinking they're his too. Well, they're not!" He shakes her hard like a rag doll he's about to discard. For a moment, she is frightened. "Are you with my brother too? Are you? Of course you are!" He keeps shaking her. "You're both traitors!" he screams. "I only ask one thing of my people. Loyalty. To *me*! That's all I ask."

"Let go!" she growls out, letting her own fury boil over her fear. "You demand loyalty but you don't give it. You don't deserve my loyalty or my respect!" She shakes him off. "Ben Hardy is your most loyal employee and you kill his wife!"

"For selling me out to the press! If he wasn't so useful to me, I'd have sent him starving in the city for being such a weakling and not controlling his woman."

"He has relatives on a farm near Coppin's Corners, moron! He'll survive when all of us are dead," Monica bites out sardonically. "I should have taken those papers to the press myself—"

"Bitch!" He slaps her hard, knocking her down. Her temple collides painfully against the desk. She sees stars and blacks out for a moment. When she comes to, she is sprawled on the floor and Eric leans over her, anger defused. He looks concerned ... no, more like frightened.

She tries to get up and slumps back to the floor,

dizzy and suddenly weak. Her head throbs with pain.

"Oh God, the blood..." he moans, face white and looking like he's going to be sick. "You're ... bleeding... there's so much blood..."

Monica steels herself. Her hand has landed against his precious copper heron statue. In a singular Amazonian motion, she grabs it, rises and swings the statue hard, connecting with his temple.

Whack! The sound is so satisfying. He drops to the floor, half conscious, and groans in bleary pain.

She drops the statue unceremoniously. It clatters loudly on the hardwood floor.

"Don't get up," she snarls down at him. He's bleeding like a stuck pig. Blood pours out of a nasty gash on his head over his eye. Looking at him, she doesn't feel so bad about her own wound. She picks the papers up off the floor, ignoring him as he curls like a naked baby on the floor, making strange whiny moans.

When she reaches the door, she turns to look at him. His long-limbed body rocks on the floor, no longer majestic like a magnificent hawk. More like a pathetic wounded vulture, she thinks.

Before leaving, she says in a dead calm voice, "Next time I see you, I *will kill you.*"

—

Monica rushes to the bedroom. She hastily dresses into slacks and loose silk shirt, stashes the documents in a satchel that she slings over her shoulder, and is about to leave then stops and opens Eric's locked nightstand drawer with his personal code.

She snatches his loaded Glock, tucks it into her jeans waistband at the small of her back, under her silk shirt, then leaves Eric's flat.

Monica emerges into the lurking smog of the Distillery District and walks the cobbled street, vacant in the deep of the night. The 'gaslight' lamps throw a fitful amber light on the cobbles.

With shaking hands, she pulls on her respirator mask and breaks into a run but immediately feels dizzy and weak. She stops briefly to keep from falling then settles on a brisk walk as she heads to Isabo's place in Corktown by the Don. She's been to his place often, plotting new intrigue and sharing the spoils of their espionage before taking them to Damien. Most of which Eric overheard, she now realizes.

She knows that she's split her head open. A quick appraisal in one of Eric's many mirrors made her woozy at the sight. Blood still issues from her wound and runs down her face. It's already dripped on her silk shirt. She has no time to tend it; Isabo is in danger. He may already be dispatched by Eric's Techno-clones. What good is she against them, even with the Glock? Their armour is impenetrable. Perhaps she can get to Isabo and warn him before they arrive. Expediency is critical.

When Monica reaches his apartment complex on Bayview Avenue, she uses the fob he's given her to let herself in and takes the elevator to the twentieth floor. His place faces Corktown Commons park with a view of the Don River, Toronto's most polluted river. But from the twentieth floor it strangely doesn't look it, she decides with a scathing smirk. It's all about angle of perception and distance, she decides. That's something Eric has always known and exploited. Look at an undulating landscape at noon and you may not be convinced of its rolling hills. The truth skewed is always more attractive than its direct delivery.

When she reaches his apartment, she realizes she's too late. The door is slightly ajar and muffled sounds from within suggest someone else is there besides Isabo. The talk is gruff—the Techno-clone. And whiny—Isabo. At least he is still alive. And Eric seems to have sent only one Techno-clone, thinking that is enough to dispatch Isabo. He's right; except he hasn't counted on Monica being there.

Feeling the thrill of fear, Monica barges in, improvising on the fly. She carelessly throws her satchel that holds Eric's dark secret on a chair and says in a slurring voice, "Chrissy-baby! I wassodrunk, I fellonthepavement—OH!" she cries out at the sight of the seven-foot tall Techno-clone stooped over Isabo. Her eyes involuntarily narrow as she takes in the Techno-clone's impressive form. Its metal skull and armoured body, weaponized left arm that looks like an Uzi glued to his body, face an intriguing mix of synth flesh and technology, binocular eyes, tubes crawling over its lizard face.

Isabo sprawls on the floor, face as bloody as hers but from a smashed nose and mouth. Thankfully, he seems alright otherwise, with no other obvious injuries. The clone was just getting started, she figures.

The clone straightens and its binocular eyes fix on her. She knows it's using facial recognition software to identify her: by now, she's designated a dangerous subversive, thanks to Eric. She thinks the clone ridiculous looking. She'd told Eric to his face once. His precious Techno-clones, Robinson's ferocious guard dogs, look like ugly chimeras created by a loser science fiction writer.

Eyes quickly appraising the room for opportunities, she sways like a drunkard and stumbles forward, saying in a slur, "Watcha lookin' at, ass-clone. Ya never sheen a woman before? Ha! You wouldn't know what to do with one. So, what the fuck are you doing here? Who the hell invited you to our revolution!"

Isabo squeaks out, "Monica! Don't—"

The clone charges her, raising its weapon arm. She swiftly ducks and slides out of its way, dashing straight to Isabo's balcony, which, is, of course, a dead end. She gasps in feigned surprise and looks down. It's a long way down. The clone releases a victorious smile and follows her onto the balcony. She thinks, *gotcha*!

"Don't hurt me, please!" she whines in her best pathetic dumb useless female voice.

The Techno-clone lunges at her and seizes her by the throat, cutting off her air. The clone pushes her whole body backwards, far over the short rail, and she sees the starry sky blinking above.

Hands flail out, fumbling, as she panics, realizing that she's losing consciousness. She has seconds before it's over for her. There! Found it! On the back of the clone's neck.

The clone suddenly jerks as if bitten by something and makes an infrahuman shriek. It lets her go and shakes itself. Monica snakes out from under the clone, who is still bent over the rail. She pulls out her Glock, shoves it into the clone's exposed armpit—its Achilles heel—and fires several times. Then, with Amazonian warrior strength, she heaves the injured clone over the rail. It falls, writhing but not screaming, and crashes twenty floors down on the pavement with a loud bang and clatter. Its metal exoskeleton shatters into pieces and the clone—or what's left of it—remains still.

Monica straightens, panting out sobbing breaths, and manages a predatory smile. Ambitious men are always underestimating her. Even Techno-clones ... *Especially* Techno-clones.

Isabo rushes to the balcony and looks down at the crumpled body of the Techno-clone, lit by outside security lights. A pool of dark blood forms under the smashed metal-synth body. They hear a door slam below, then a window closing, followed by a long dank silence, broken briefly by a dog barking in the distance.

"How did you..." Isabo trails in a whispered voice. "And the armour..."

"You kidding me, Isabo." She shakes her head at him in reproach. "You never watched medieval movies? That's where you stick an armoured knight during hand to hand combat. There or the crotch. As for the 'kill' switch..." She gives him a slanted smile. "Do you think Eric would put these jerks on the assembly line without one?"

"But I helped build them. There's no ..."

"A little addition that only Eric knows about." Which is just like Eric. "And whatever Eric knows, I know." She tips her head with a pursed self-pleased smile.

Isabo releases a sigh of relief and seizes her in a bear hug. "I owe you my life!"

"Yes, you do. Remember that," she quips and pushes him off like he's a slobbering dog. She decides that her dead calm might be shock, but doesn't care. She feels so alive! Tucking the Glock back into her pants under her shirt, she says in a clipped voice, "Listen, Isabo, we need to leave *now*!"

"Yes, yes!" He shakes his head to clear it and gingerly wipes his face where the clone had smashed it. Then he points to her, as if seeing her injury for the first time. "But your head looks bad. It needs stitches or an x-ray, or both ... We need to get you to the hospital."

"Not happening," she says firmly. "Too dangerous. Eric's people are everywhere." She glances at the satchel she'd carelessly thrown on his chair. "Besides, I have something sensitive Damien needs to see *right now*. Eric caught me, which is why I have this." She points to her injured temple. "He wasn't expecting me to leave with it; I think he left it out just to trap me. This is urgent, Isabo. So, let's go. You know where Damien lives," she ends with a humorless smile.

His lips firm and his eyes meet hers in a steady gaze of brief hesitation; then they acquiesce and he nods. "You're right. We better go. But you still need something for that nasty wound or you'll bleed all over my car!"

Isabo grabs a first aid kit and insists she administer herself as he drives them in his Tesla to Rosedale, where Damien lives. He parks on the street a block from Damien's place and they walk to a large old brownstone house then ring the doorbell. They need to ring several times and wait several minutes. It is four in the morning, after all.

The lights finally come on inside and Damien opens the door, wearing a housecoat over pajamas and looking sleepy. His eyes go wide and he quickly ushers them inside without a word. When they are safely inside, he says, face grimacing with concern, "You're both hurt. What happened?"

"A Techno-clone came to my place," Isabo says in a breathless voice and looks like he's about to faint. "But then Monica burst in like fucking Supergirl and took him—"

"It," she corrects.

"She was incredible, Dem! You should have seen her in action! She took down a fucking Techno-clone!"

Monica notices Damien's keen interest. To shut Isabo's embarrassing gushing, Monica cuts in, "I think I finally have the prize we've been looking for." She taps her satchel with a sly smile. "*Everybody wants to rule the world...*"

Damien glances from the satchel to her face and his eyes sparkle like the sea at night under a harvest moon. He looks like a man who's just won the lottery. "We'll take a look right away, but first let's take care of your injuries. I think you're both in shock." He turns to Isabo. "Are you alright to fetch a cognac from the cabinet and bring it here?"

Isabo nods and finds the cognac and some liqueur glasses. He first helps himself straight from the bottle then hands it and a glass to Damien who pours some into a glass for Monica.

"Drink this," he commands.

She gratefully gulps, feeling the liquid burn down her throat like a wildfire. It warms her all over. She finds herself focusing on Damien's bare feet. He has beautiful feet, with long toes just like Eric's...

Damien passes the bottle back to Isabo and urges him to take a seat in the living room. "Christian, I'll help you soon but first I must attend Monica. Her wound is more pressing."

Isabo nods weakly and collapses on one of Damien's fancy arm chairs with the bottle of cognac in his hand. Monica is grateful that Damien attends to her because she suddenly feels giddy and weak.

"You've lost a lot of blood," Damien says calmly. He takes the satchel from her and hands it to Isabo, then takes her arm to firmly support her and walks her into his large downstairs bathroom. There, he instructs her to sit on the toilet. He then pulls out a small pen light and leans down to her height. "Look straight at me. I'm just checking for signs of concussion." He shines the pen light into each eye and nods to himself, satisfied, at the reaction of her pupils. He follows with a series of questions: "Are you seeing double or blurry?" "Nauseous?" "Pain in the neck or severe headache?"

Satisfied with all her negatives, he grabs a kit of bandages and other things. "I'm just going to clean the wound a bit so I can put on some suture bandages to close it and hopefully stop the bleeding. Then we'll sterilize and bandage it, after which you must lie down to recover." He squats down again to her sitting height and starts cleaning and wiping with a cloth. He is very gentle with her, explaining in a quiet voice as he does each thing, slender fingers deftly administering. It's been a long time since someone has looked after her, she thinks, managing to enjoy the moment.

He stops for a moment to study her, and finally asks, "Did my brother…?" He can't bring himself to say more.

"He caught me stealing his files," she says in a weak voice. "We fought. He hit me and I fell and knocked my head."

He nods quietly, brows briefly furrowing, before continuing to clean her wound in silence.

She stares into his sapphire blue eyes, finding them hypnotizing. They are so deep, she falls right into them. Then he is finally done. "There." He looks at her with such kind eyes. It brings tears to hers. She has never felt more vulnerable. "There, there," he says, gently wiping her tears away. "You've been through a lot, my darling friend."

She seizes the words and clutches them to her heart. His scent is wonderful, a combination of musk and lavender and something she can't place. Certainly not like Eric's brash cologne. She is certain that he wears nothing and she is inhaling essence of Damien. Without thinking them there, her lips find his and she is kissing him.

He does not pull away but he does not reciprocate either. When she finally pulls away, he blinks several times and stands up. "Come," he says, as if nothing happened. He pulls her up to her feet. "You must lie down for a while. You need sleep."

The moment has passed and she feels like she's just walked out of a fairy tale.

When they reach the living room, Isabo stands up and helps them to the couch. He helps Damien direct her to lie down and sets a pillow beneath her head. Damien then drapes a blanket over her. "Sleep, darling," he says in that quiet voice that she finds so commanding. Darling! He's called her darling. Within seconds, she is asleep.

—

She wakes to quiet voices murmuring in another room. The morning sun streams in through the sheers of the large south-facing bay window. She pulls off the blanket and sits up, feeling a small headache. But her energy has returned and she feels refreshed.

She scans the spacious high-ceilinged living room as if for the first time. When she first saw it earlier in the dark of night, she was in no state to take it in. There's a large library wall, a stone fireplace, classic wooden furniture, hard wood floors and beautiful Persian area rug. The classic look matches the master of the house, thinks Monica.

She wanders to where she hears the voices of Isabo and Damien talking quietly. Their tone is soft and intimate. They go suddenly quiet. When she reaches the doorway to the large pale yellow antique kitchen, she sees why; they are kissing.

Damien and Isabo sit at the large oak kitchen table, leaning into each other in an embrace. The morning sun streams in from the tall windows and back door, warm light playing on their faces as Damien caresses Isabo's cheek with a hand. A large tabby cat weaves through Damien's legs, then stops to look at Monica with languid curiosity.

The men turn and surprise her by smiling unapologetically.

Isabo's face has cleaned up nicely; there is only a bit of bruising on his chin and a slightly swollen eye. He's dressed in a clean shirt that fits him well, suggesting he keeps spare clothes at Damien's place. She knows they have been sleeping together; the way they sit, shoulders touching with that familiarity of a couple who have recently woken up from slumber.

"Come, Monica!" says Damien heartily. He glances down briefly and introduces his cat to her. "And this is Gretchen, who rules this house." She meows. He grins. Damien is outright cheerful. Is it the cat or Isabo that has that effect on him? Monica decides it's both; Isabo has that effect on anyone, Monica thinks, not moving from the doorway. How wonderful that they have found one another!

Damien stands and approaches her at the door. Then he surprises her with a gentle kiss on the mouth. "Have some breakfast," he says, pointing to the table where three plates are set. She sees a large teapot with honey pot and cream and tea cups set on the table. Damien says, "There's a pot of Earl Grey tea on the table. I'm making eggs and toast."

"*Chouchou* makes a mean omelet!" says Christian, eyes creasing with a huge beaming smile.

Confused by Damien's kiss and Isabo's cheerful

complicity, Monica lets him lead her to the table where she sits with a view outside to the back garden and fir trees. Damien pours them each a tea. As each fixes their tea as they like it, Isabo asks, "How's the head?"

"Better, much better. You're looking better to0," she responds as she pours cream into her tea.

"I had some wonderful TLC," Isabo announces with a giggle and a sly glance at Damien.

Damien ignores him and leans down over the table to study her more closely. "Not too much blood has seeped out. I think the sutures are holding. That's good."

She stares into his timeless blue eyes, looking for an answer, and finding nothing in those depths.

"She'll live, then?" Isabo asks.

"She'll live." Damien nods with a wink. Then he stands up and moves to the large screen on one wall of the kitchen, holding his cup of Earl Grey tea. "Now see here, while you two were sleeping off your terrible adventure with a Techno-clone, I was busy with that little prize you brought me, Monica." He flicks on the monitor. "Here's what's happening now," he says, flipping to the news he recorded earlier this morning.

The CNN anchor Gene Carter is talking: "... Robinson has denied any knowledge of this treasonous and criminal act and has denounced Eric Vogel, firing him from his position as minister of Environment & Technology and demanding his arrest. While a full investigation is forthcoming by an independent tribunal into the matter, it appears that Vogel and a small cadre at BioGen were alone in creating this biological weapon to sell to the Americans. The Canadian federal police have put out an all-points bulletin for Vogel and his two colleagues with Techno-clones dispatched to find them."

Monica stares, hands drifting to her mouth in shock. "Oh, God..." She turns to Damien. "Where is he now? Did they catch him?"

Damien stops the recording and shakes his head. After a sip of his tea he checks his phone for the latest update. "They got the two technicians but haven't found Eric. He wasn't at his place and didn't show up at the lab. My brother's gone into hiding. When he doesn't want to be found, no one can find him. I'm sure he has at least one if not several safe houses in town for moments just like this. I know I would." He glances inquiringly at Monica who shakes her head. She knows nothing of safe houses. Contrary to what she'd said to Isabo earlier, Eric obviously doesn't share *everything* with her. And it's just like him to let his underlings take the fall for him, thinks Monica scathingly. She glances from Damien to Isabo, still seated at the table with her. "What about BioGen? Did they shut it down?"

"No," Isabo says. "BioGen is part of Canadian Enterprises still and will continue as long as Robinson runs CE. He'll likely put someone else in as temporary CEO of BioGen until the board figures out what to do." He turns an inquisitive glance at Damien. "I suppose I could go back to work, then? There's no danger now with Eric on the run, is there?"

"I don't think you should, Christian," Damien says quietly, stroking his long nose with a finger. He puts his cup down and reaches down to pick up Gretchen, who has been rubbing his legs for a while now, then returns to the table, hands caressing his cat. He sits next to his lover, eyes meeting Isabo's look of puzzled inquiry with an unsmiling gaze. "BioGen is still under fire as the lab that produced this awful virus." Damien puts Gretchen down and picks up his cup of tea. "And, I've taken advantage of that." He looks at Isabo with some regret. "I was very busy this morning, *chouchou...*"

Monica stares at Damien. She finds something suddenly quite sinister about Damien's expression, a look of fanatical determination and, for a brief moment, she can't distinguish him from Eric.

Damien lets out a deep sigh. "The information that Monica got from Eric was too incendiary to ignore," he says to Isabo. "You know that, Christian. Remember what you said when I showed you the papers Monica brought? It's our spark. We must take advantage of it to ignite our movement. This is our time. So, I'm afraid that BioGen is no longer a safe place to be, Christian. For you or anyone. It is now a target for a number of violent forces. And remember, it's Robinson who sent the Techno-clone after you. He's secretly in with Eric. They'll throw anyone under the bus if it suits them. And you're a good candidate for that right now."

Monica watches Isabo's look of incredulity. A brief moment of horror washes over him, which he tucks away and replaces with a wave of brooding darkness that he sweeps away with a final look of understanding and acceptance. Monica stares in fascination at Isabo's transformation. She knows that BioGen was everything to him once. But that began to erode and crumble a few years ago when he discovered some of Eric's less than savoury practices: particularly how Eric twisted some of Isabo's projects, like he'd done to that lackey Ben Hardy. That was when Isabo found the brother to replace the brother, Monica thinks, eyes straying back to Damien, who is watching Isabo carefully. Just like she's done, thinks Monica with a faint smile.

"So, here's the deal." Damien appears to steel himself by pulling in a long breath and leads them to his laptop on a credenza by the liquor cabinet. He pulls up some sites on the large monitor on the wall then says to them both, "The news outlets only got part of the story. What they don't know yet—but we do with proof—is that Robinson was in on it from the beginning. What Monica brought with her last night is incredible. We all read it. So heinous." Damien shakes his head and glowers. "To be honest with you two, I find it beyond belief. This is literally a crime against humanity. I'm flabbergasted that my own brother would go this far." He shakes his head again. "I know he was obsessed with reducing the human population. But to do this is..." he stumbles with his words, obviously disturbed. "I don't know how to take it in." After a long moment of tense silence, he recovers and continues, "Anyway, like I said, this is an opportunity for the Gaians to strike at the heart of the Technocrats. So, that's what I'm doing. The truth—all the truth—will out. And the violence will follow." He turns to Monica. "The rest of the story will be leaked to key news outlets. And we've set in motion that huge social media campaign that you helped build. I'd like you to oversee its escalation. I've also green-lit our tactical units and strike teams with pre-selected hits."

"Even Ottawa?"

Damien nods. "Absolutely. Montreal, Vancouver, Calgary and Regina. All the key places. Our people are in place." He checks the time. "And in action already."

Monica envisions Wanda leading her unit.

Monica glances at Isabo, who meets her eyes with agreement. "What else can we do, Damien?"

"You can start by telling Christian all about how you dealt with the Techno-clone. Christian told me that you know about a kill switch? Perhaps Christian can do something about that, eh?" He turns to Isabo with a complex look that includes adoration and admiration. Damien picks up his tea and clears his throat. "There's one more thing. You both must live here! I insist." He looks from one to the other with intense azure eyes. "You are both now treasonous criminals, enemies of the state. Eric will have seen to that. Robinson will have a bounty on both your heads. There is no safe place, except here. In a way, this is timely," Damien admits with a strange almost self-pleased smile. He leans back, stroking his cup of Earl Grey tea, and crosses his long legs. "I was thinking of creating a Triad for when we become the new government, which I think is imminent. That Triad should consist of the three of us right here in this room."

"Agreed," says Isabo, glancing at Monica with a wide grin of acceptance. "What about renaming everything to cleanse the palate, so to speak?"

"Excellent idea. Once we form our new Gaian government, we will have a naming day. We should provide all places with meaning."

"Like using names with ecological significance?"

"Excellent. What should we call our utopia, then?"

"What about Icaria?"

Both men turn haltingly to Monica. Thinking of what Eric said to her long ago, she begins to explain, "It's after Étienne Cabet's socialist utopia that—"

"—Uses small community cooperatives to replace capitalist production," Damien finishes for her. He nods with a smile of approval. "I like it. Eric mentioned it to me a long time ago. I still like it."

"Are you sure you don't mind?" Monica says.

"Not everything Eric came up with was bad," says Damien winking at her. "Now, let's have some breakfast!"

—

It's four in the morning and something has woken her. Shots ricochet and echo in the night. She hears sirens in the distance. More fires are burning out of control. Too excited, Monica can't go back to sleep and sits up in bed.

Yesterday, Damien's living room became Gaia's hub centre and the three of them spent the entire day strategizing and following events, communicating with colleagues, and working on computers over coffees and snacks brought in by Damien's house helper, Dominique. When she first saw her, Monica felt a foolish spike of jealousy and wondered if the pretty young girl was also sharing Damien's bed. She knew better. Or did she?

Monica commands herself to review the events of the past twenty-four hours and her mind reels with the excitement of the day. Like a dam breaking, the latest revelation of Robinson's collusion with Eric through leaked emails exploded from news outlets to social media. All that Canadian restraint fell away as the Gaian revolution made huge strides. The titration they'd created had tipped and they'd finally broken through the inertia barrier.

Gaians tore through the streets inciting mobs. Stories, both true and fake, swept social media and went viral, stirring anger among the citizens. The Gaian seeds that they had sown over the last years and nurtured over the last months now germinated into spontaneous riots in the streets. As a wildfire creates its own incendiary environment, the revolution lit its people with an angry fire that is refusing to be put out. Canadians, normally quiet introverts, are finally releasing their simmering rage at a charlatan government. Beware the anger of a quiet man.

When the three of them last checked, before turning in for bed at 2 am, the entire city had turned into a war zone. Skirmishes were erupting everywhere. Fire bombs already hit several Techno installations, including the giant Porter Medical Labs and other Canadian Enterprises buildings throughout Toronto and its surrounding areas. News of the other cities came pouring in with similar hits. People—mostly Technos—were barricading themselves. Each suburb had its own unrest. News of unrest in the United States resulted in a final storming of the White House by expert insurrectionists using deadly gas. There is speculation that President Tobiasen was also killed in the attack. Robinson, in the meantime, has tucked his tail behind protective security and is now considering invoking the *Emergency Act* and martial law according to reliable insiders. Monica is certain that Eric is right beside Robinson.

Monica and her team incited the fire of revolution in an explosive campaign on social media throughout the provinces. The Technocrats, and Robinson particularly, are being vilified by fifth estate bloggers and independent news media worldwide, even some mainstream media. Robinson's collusion with Eric rapidly made it to mainstream news and from there exploded. Through her many avatars, Monica reminded the public of Robinson's earlier sexual transgressions with Chancellor Magda Zimmermann and that messy business with Spectrum WasteTech in '43. The final nail in Robinson's coffin was his connection with Eric and this heinous virus that promises to devastate the world. Millions of people would fall like flies to DDT. As fast as people would fall to the virus, feckless governments all over the world would fall to the violence of revolution. The dominoes Eric so often waxed on about, would lock in a cascade.

How strange everything has turned out! She thinks of Eric, how he used to love her with such passion. Her thoughts slide to Damien and those kind eyes, that gentle mouth and how he holds himself with the same intensity as Eric but without the arrogance. She brings her fingers to her lips and thinks of his gentle kiss that morning. What did that kiss mean? He'd called her darling the night before...

Suddenly aroused with a burst of wetness, she flings off the covers and gets out of bed, naked. She lets a wild impulse lead her down the hall, bare feet making the old floor creak, and walks toward Damien's bedroom.

With close to hysterical energy, she flings open the door then freezes at the doorway.

The two of them lie in bed, entangled, under the covers. Damien spoons Isabo and has flung his arm over him in a loose embrace. Both are asleep. Gretchen, the cat, lies on the bed's headboard, alert, as if overseeing them like a guardian angel. This is madness! What has she done? Of course Isabo would be in bed with him. She thinks to leave but something keeps her there. She finds herself studying them and thinking how beautiful they look. So blissful in sleep.

She is about to back out, when Isabo opens his eyes and smiles at her, inviting. He raises himself on an elbow and draws her in with his hand. "Come," he whispers. "Take him...Take my *chouchou*..."

Isabo throws off the covers, revealing their naked bodies, one ample and muscular, the other lean and wiry. They are both magnificent, she thinks. Isabo moves Damien's arm off him and makes room for her between them. "Come," he repeats. "We've been waiting for you."

They have? Heart thundering, she climbs on the bed and feels the thrill of forbidden passion coursing through her like an electric current. Damien sighs awake as she comes between him and Isabo.

"Look who's finally joined us in Icaria, *chouchou,*" Isabo says, turning to face them both.

Damien doesn't look surprised and gives them both a lazy smile. His eyes are already dark with desire as he pulls her up against him and reaches past her to pull Isabo in to press against her. Within a moment, she is deliciously entangled between the men of her Triad with nothing but possibilities in front of her.

EIGHTEEN

LONG BRANCH, Lakeshore Road
E. May 23, 2051: morning

Monica looks up from behind a desk to the potential recruit who stands fidgeting in front of her. They are in a large hall of the Small Arms Inspection building, flanked by two guards holding CARifle assault weapons. Part of the guards' faces are hidden under the newest vee-sets with eye-coms neatly attached to their heads; these provide them with recognition software and instant AI intel similar to what the Techo-clones use. More technology the Gaians managed to steal from the Technos, thinks Monica with a sardonic smile. She doesn't care that she's using Techno stuff to fight a war against Technos. The time for righteous integrity will come later, when the war is won.

The hall is well lit through mostly broken industrial paned windows that face the garbage-strewn shore of Lake Ontario. Once used as a multi-purpose hub for arts and culture, the old brick building was abandoned over the years and fell into ruin. A perfect place for secret Gaian recruiting.

The potential recruit is about Monica's age with earnest brown eyes under a mop of chestnut brown curly hair. Despite his obvious fear of her, he shows spunk and confidence by looking directly at her. Good. She prefers someone more mature. Despite youth having exuberance and fast action, it can also be overly rash and temperamental. Most young men can't look her in the face. She knows she's a striking beauty and the target of many covert stares. She has used her physical beauty to manipulate men and women her whole life: those who underestimated her because of it and those who thought to exploit it for their own agenda. In every case, she managed to manipulate their intentions and actions in her own favour. Beauty has many facets. Lately, she wears the fierce warrior-goddess look. The jagged scar on her temple is part of her new archetype; she makes a point of not hiding it, keeping her long hair back to brandish her badass scar. It even carries its own narrative: depending on who the storyteller is, she received it when she single-handedly vanquished a Techno-clone (true, she did) or she received it during a skirmish with Toronto riot police (also true). It's just that she didn't receive the scar from either. But even the carefully hidden truth may yet form part of the narrative: that she fought and overcame the Techno badass of them all, BioGen's bad boy, Eric Vogel. Let the legend grow...

"What's your name?" she asks the recruit.

"Armon Crane, Commander," he says in a steady voice.

She almost smiles at his acknowledgement of her title. She's still getting used to being called Commander. Damien insisted that she embrace a military approach in her guerilla campaigns and summarily gave her the title of Field Commander of the Gaian Army. She'd laughed at him when he first mentioned it. He let her laughter peter out then seriously explained his rationale: "This is a war, Monica; wars need armies and armies need commanders to look up to. Strong and recognizable faces of the revolution. Yours, pardon my saying, is especially attractive in both literal and figurative sense. You and your face will become an important symbol of the Gaian revolution. The Gaians need to be taken seriously and those who join us must feel that we respect them and what they are sacrificing to fight for the cause by putting ourselves out there. We have to take ourselves and each other seriously."

In the end, she didn't mind the title and the recognition. It fed her rather large ego, she admitted. And she found to her surprise that she preferred fighting the war at ground level to her media fight; the visceral appeal of physical combat and commanding night operatives provided a kind of immediate gratification she had never dreamed possible. The only downside was that her many campaigns into the countryside kept her from Damien's and Isabo's bed at nights.

Monica has already recruited dozens of Gaian fighters who report directly or indirectly to her. Wanda Dressler is one of her first recruits, a fellow poli-sci student at U of T. Smart and dedicated. Unflinching and fast. Intuitive yet analytical. One of her best soldiers and a loyal friend. Every member of the Gaians is a fighter, a warrior-soldier. It makes sense, Monica considers. They are at war, albeit a subversive guerilla war.

She opens Crane's dossier and studies it, noting that he is 40 years old, nine years her senior, and grew up on a farm near Guelph, just like her. His parents ended up on a Corporation Farm too. She taps her computer for additional information. Bingo! She stiffens at what she discovers. Crane's wife is the sister of Ben Hardy, one of BioGen's R&D scientists. Monica met him several times when she was whoring with Eric; Hardy is a spineless mealy-mouth flunky who did anything Eric asked him to do. The same flunky scientist responsible for the global wheat crash of '36. Monica turns to Crane from the computer screen and lets a sneer curl her mouth. She raises her arm and flicks her finger twice. Two guards suddenly close in on Crane, aiming CARifles at him.

"How far did you think you'd get as a BioGen spy?"

"I'm not a spy!" he says quickly, eyes flitting like a deer from the guards and their rifles then back to her. "I'm not in league with my brother-in-law."

"He lives with you."

"He's my wife's brother," he defends unflinchingly. She gives him credit for standing his ground. "Their house burned down and his wife died in an accident during the Boreal Scorching smog-in five years ago."

She's well aware of that 'accident.' Techno-clones dispatched Chloé Hardy before she had a chance to go to the press with damning information on BioGen. They set fire to Hardy's house. Monica had been wondering for years how knowledge of Chloé's mission reached Robinson's or Eric's goons. Particularly since Monica was the person who snuck the file to Hardy's wife in the first place. When no one came after Monica, she began to think that the eavesdropper wasn't at BioGen. But Eric knew all along and was biding his time. She now knows that Eric bugged everyone, including Hardy's place. That is so like Eric, Monica decides. Putting surveillance on all his workers. She thinks of all those meetings at Isabo's place where they'd discussed strategies and moves. No wonder Eric was always a step ahead of her.

Crane continues, "Ben's there because it's my wife's house; she took him and his little girl in. They had no where else to go in the city. But I don't agree with what my brother-in-law is doing. He doesn't know I'm here. Even my wife doesn't know!"

She glances at the two guards and flicks her hands for them to stand down. They lower their weapons and move off but stay close.

She places her hands down on his file and narrows her eyes at him, lips curling into a sardonic smile. "Why are you here, then, Armon Crane, sneaking out of your own house like a cowardly burglar?"

He meets her challenging gaze head on. "What BioGen did—what my brother-in-law did and is still doing—is unconscionable. It's criminal. But I am married to his sister. I can't change that. But I can change things this way, by doing the bidding of the Gaians."

A dangerous position he's taken; playing both sides. She leans forward and studies him. "Even if it means blowing up a BioGen facility?"

He blinks at her. He's obviously thinking. When he answers, he meets her challenging eyes with a grave but steady look. "I love my wife. But I'll do whatever the Gaians ask me to do. Like I said, I don't agree with what BioGen is doing for the Technocrats. Robinson is a cheating liar and his government doesn't represent the Canada I hold dear. Suspending elections and forcing Parliament to invoke the *Emergency Act* to instate martial law for so long is against our constitution. Forcing birth control with a lottery is cruel and inhumane. This government is turning into a dictatorship. And the worst of it is they haven't done what they promised with the environment. All they've done is make money on proprietary technology they sell around the world. I believe in deep ecology and support a revolution against the Technocrats and their Techno ways. And I'll stand by it any way the Gaians want me to."

She notices that his eyes haven't shifted. He means it. She can feel the sincerity cascade off him. She leans back in her chair and nods to herself. Here are two brothers who are very different; just like Damien and Eric. What is it with brothers? Of course, Armon Crane is only Ben Hardy's brother-in-law. Still...She shakes her head. Men...

"OK, Crane," she says, giving him a tight smile as gesture. "You'll be with Wanda's unit for a while. In time, if you do well, we'll give you your own unit. Sound good?"

He brightens but still doesn't smile.

Good, she thinks. She doesn't care for shallowness. Now the test: "Your first mission is right now. It's the BioGen commercial facility in Mississauga."

His eyes go wide, but he doesn't react otherwise. "Now?"

"You have someplace to be?"

"No, Commander."

She watches him steel himself for the mission. "Good. *Welcome to your life; there's no turning back.*" She points to a doorway. "Wanda's in there, briefing the others. Go, or you'll miss your chance to be a Gaian."

He nods and leaves.

Monica lets an oily smile slant across her face. She doesn't trust this Armon guy. She's put him with her best soldier. Wanda will keep an eye on him for her. Let him prove his mettle first. It's hard to tell; he might work out to be a real asset, but only if he makes up his mind. If he can't, she might have Wanda kill him. Or kill him herself.

ACUTE

Destruction in creation and creation in destruction are ingrained in the life cycles of everything on the planet and the universe. A forest fire can destroy life but in so doing creates a more vibrant, healthier forest. The vortex, water's natural form of movement, is polar, cycling in a rhythm of contraction and expansion. The opposing forces of polarity generate ongoing cycles of creation and destruction. It is the Ouroboros remembering. Water's restlessness gives living systems the ability to seek complexity and evolve. Water destroys and creates. Water confuses and clarifies. Water dirties and cleans. Water is the driver of creative destruction.

—Damien Vogel, "The Cycle of Creative Destruction," Chapter Two in ENVIRONMENT IN CRISIS, edited by Sophie Rich and Nathan Ehrenbach, Gaia Publications, May 2045

TWENTY

CENTRAL TORONTO ACADEMY, Shaw Street. March 10, 2054: early morning

"Bye, Sweet-pea!" Ben calls after Janet, who ignores him and runs into the school without looking back. He knows that his fourteen-year-old daughter hates it when he calls her Sweet-pea, especially in front of her friends. But he can't help the endearment that he's used since she was born. He knows that she would rather cycle on her own to school, but he's insisted on accompanying her because of the martial law order, the checkpoints, and the curfew.

Drawing in a long inhale of filtered putrid air through his mask, Ben gets on his bike and cycles to work. The smog is already thick this morning, hanging like a yellow cloud of suspended puke as he plows through it. Since the Boreal Scorching in '46, the air has never really cleared up, Ben thinks as he cycles down Harbord Street from Central Toronto Academy. Over three thousand deaths in greater Toronto alone occurred during the heatwave and smog inversion that accompanied the smoke that blew in from the north and settled like a suffocating blanket. It killed his wife. Since then, for the next decade it's been dangerous to be outdoors without protection every summer. That period of mandatory mask-wearing seems to be extending into the fall and starts as early as February, Ben thinks. Air quality is steadily getting worse and Robinson's Technocrats haven't been doing anything about it except declaring martial law to keep the crowds controlled. There's so much wrong with that government, right down to their recent cabinet shuffle. No person of colour remains in cabinet, which is not only unconstitutional, but highly suspicious.

Ben can't help thinking of that awful media disclosure in '50 about that DNA-specific biological weapon that Eric and two BioGen technicians supposedly created. Rumours immediately followed that Robinson not only knew about the weapon but was in collusion with Eric that incited unrest in the streets, and which the Gaians directed into a revolution. Eric was never caught. He just disappeared. Ben finds himself seized by an unreasonable fear: that Eric is still around and the reason he was never found is because he's being protected by the Technocrats who may be thinking of releasing the virus. It would certainly halt the revolution, he considers with a shiver. But it won't stop the boreal scorching and terrible air pollution.

After they lost everything in the fire eight years ago, he and Janet moved into Amanda's house on Dovercourt Road, which has been very convenient for Janet because her school is still nearby. Both his sister and brother-in-law have been so kind, Ben considers as he approaches his first checkpoint on Bathhurst Avenue. He knows that Armon doesn't like him, which makes his kindness even more meaningful. Ben suspects that Armon is a Gaian. But he and Amanda avoid the topic. And Armon remains distant with him. The upside to the arrangement is that the two cousins are together. Despite their ages,

Janet and Leonard are close and good company for each other.

At the checkpoint, two Techno-clones stretch out their weaponized arms to stop him and Ben dismounts as one of them commands for him to surrender his ID. "Where are you going, sir?" The clone asks in a reedy voice. They are always so polite, Ben thinks. Yet, he shivers with unreasonable fear every time he interacts with one.

"To work," Ben says, surrendering his ID to the clone without looking at him directly; he finds them too frightening. He feels the clone's infrahuman eyes gazing at him as it takes his ID in its unweaponized hand. "At the BioGen facility on Devonshire Place."

After a mere glance at his ID—in which Ben knows the clone instantly processes the information in its AI head—the clone gives him back his ID and waves him on. "You may proceed, Dr. Hardy."

Ben gets back on his bike and continues down Harbord, cycling past demolished buildings covered in Gaia posters that feature the warrior face of *that woman,* fierce eyes following him like Big Brother. He reaches the next checkpoint on Spadina where two more Techno-clones ask him for ID. He's used to the clones by now, but still finds himself repulsed and intimidated by them. How could Christian Isabo have designed such a creepy thing? He finds it difficult to think of them as humans. They've been altered so much. Where does one draw the distinction between human and machine? Before Christian suddenly left BioGen, Ben had some interesting discussions with him on the line between human and machine and on the topic of transhumanism, Christian's special interest. The Techno-clones were originally deployed by the Technocrats as federal law agents meant to keep the peace internationally and in military situations in Canada and abroad. But since Robinson declared martial law in '51 and cloistered himself under guard in Ottawa, Toronto has become a war zone and Techno-clones are stationed throughout the city. Movements of citizens are restricted and a curfew with checkpoints has been in effect for over a year.

Amanda is frightened out of her wits, and Ben knows why: Armon is a Gaian. Every day Armon leaves for work but also does Gaian things and Amanda's fear is that one day he won't come home or that a Techno-clone will come for her in his place. She is terrified of them. She's asked Ben time and again to take them all to the country, to his sister-in-law's dairy farm near Port Perry. But Chloé's older sister is the last person to accept the Hardy and Crane families. Ben is sure that everyone on the farm is a Gaian supporter. Amanda forgets what Lise said at Chloé's funeral eight years ago: that Chloé's death wasn't an accident. Not only was Lise convinced that Chloé was murdered; she went on to accuse Ben of having a part in it and of being a Techno-lackey. She didn't come right out and say it, but it was implied, and he feels unreasonable guilt because of it.

They'll just have to ride it out, Ben thinks with a long sigh of resignation as he turns the corner from Hoskins onto Devonshire Place, past a derelict building plastered with more garish black and red Gaian posters that feature a cartoon of that bitch

Schlange. Letters that look like they've been painted there with blood brandish a quote followed by the Gaian motto: *"I'd rather die a free Gaian than live a slave to Technocracy!" Join the Fight For Truth and Justice!* It's a recruiting poster, thinks Ben, shaking his head with a frown. These posters have sprung up everywhere like a fungus; the clones can't rip them all down fast enough.

Ben dismounts when he reaches the grey nondescript building where he works. He still has responsibilities there, Ben decides. He realizes with a pang of regret that his job no longer gives him joy. It has become a chore. Part of it lies with his new boss, Wayne Babich, an administrator with Canadian Enterprises. Babich, who replaced Eric as CEO of BioGen, has an icy temperament and Ben finds him overly fixed on efficiency. He lacks the imagination and maverick drive that Ben found so inspiring in Eric. As Ben locks his bike on a rack outside of BioGen, he sighs under the weight of a longing emptiness. Much of his transgenic crop research has been useful in the Corporation Experimental Farms and agricultural projects overseas. He's done some good things. But he also knows that some of it was subverted and used by the company in ways he had never intended. In GOF research and DURCs aimed at maleficence, just like Chloé had accused. Just like poor Christian and his Techno-clones. Though Christian didn't seem too cut up about it—before he left so suddenly.

Ben bows his head at the bike stand by a spindly gingko tree and studies the brown grass. He misses his wife. Chloé was his rock and his source of balance. She was always so good at pointing the way. He feels lost now. Without purpose. Awful nightmarish doubts have crept in. Was Lise right after all? Did BioGen kill Chloé for what she knew and was about to tell the press? Ben never did find the mole who'd passed the information to her. If Chloé *was* killed by BioGen or Technocrat agents, then who else knew about the leak? His first thought is of Eric's whore. Schlange seemed to be there a lot and without restrictions; she was so curious, always asking questions and being chummy with Christian. Did she give Chloé away? Or was she the leak? He thinks of the Gaian posters everywhere in town with her face plastered on them. Her face stares at him with fierce raptor eyes. A jagged scar trails down her forehead like a warrior's badge. The cartoon emphasizes her cheekbones, firm jaw and sensual mouth painted in garish red. That whore is a good choice for the face of the revolution, he decides; though he wonders at her true allegiance. Her face makes him fearful for another reason: that she left Eric's bed for the 'bed' of the Gaians scares him because she is like a cat, always landing on her feet.

BIOGEN RESEARCH & DEVELOPMENT LAB, Devonshire Place. April 13, 2054: late at night

Armon bursts into Ben's culture lab and Ben jumps in surprise. Armon is dressed in fatigues and his face is smeared in black grease. He stares at Ben in surprise.

"What are you doing here!" Armon shouts angrily.

"Amanda was supposed to keep you home! We need to leave NOW!"

"Why? My work. We're finishing—"

"This place will blow in seconds!"

"But Preksha and Sang-woo are still in the back—"

"No time! I came for *you*! Because of Amanda!" Armon seizes Ben gruffly and pulls him down the corridor into a run. They tear down the exit stairs to the outside doors. "RUN!"

Just as they clear the doors to the outside, a huge explosion throws them violently to the ground. Ears ringing, Ben staggers to his feet and stumbles to Armon, who struggles up and grabs Ben, pulling him away from the building. Armon shouts something to him that Ben can't hear. They move in slow motion, like they are floating. Ben's eyes fix on the building, now blazing with an angry white fire. Another explosion sends them sprawling to the ground again. As they get up, black smoke billows up as a deep infrasound presses on them. It reverberates with Ben's ringing ears. Then he's choking in the smoke and smog. Armon pushes a mask on his face and pulls him into the empty street. No, not empty.

A single figure stands in the yellow smog, watching them from down the street. A woman. Ben recognizes her. Even behind her mask, her figure and face are unmistakable. The woman on the posters. Eric's whore. Just as he recognizes her, she raises a gun and aims at him. He freezes. She shoots twice. Beside him, Armon falls like a stone.

By the time Ben realizes that her target was not him but Armon, she has already disappeared in the smog like a phantom. He knows Armon is dead. Within moments several Techno-clones arrive and Ben hears the approaching sirens of emergency vehicles. He finds his bike and flees before they spot him. Ben is able to use the diversion of the explosion to evade the checkpoints.

Once close to Amanda's home, Ben grows dizzy and shaky. He stops and steadies himself on shaky legs. How is he going to explain Armon's death to her? The man died saving him. Ben gets off his bike, letting it clatter to the ground, and collapses on the pavement, shivering with shock. He slides in and out of consciousness then violently throws off his mask to vomit. It gives him some clarity and he pieces together what happened. This was a Gaian bombing and Armon was involved. But Armon tried to prevent Ben from being there. Armon had told Amanda to keep Ben at home that evening. Ben remembers how she'd insisted he play cards with her and not go to work this night on his project. She didn't know why, so she wasn't that convincing. Then Armon burst into the lab to help Ben escape and got shot for it by that whore. This confuses him. Did she execute Armon for helping Ben or is she still secretly with Eric and executed Armon for bombing BioGen? Someone had to help the terrorists gain access to the building and she was the likely source. It made even more sense if she was the one who put the papers in Chloé's satchel. But why didn't Schlange shoot Ben, too? That doesn't make sense. She should have shot him too, he thinks, letting guilt press him down.

He falls into exhausted weeping as it starts to

rain. First a listless drizzle then rapidly turning into a steady downpour, soaking him in a cold deluge.

He thinks of his two hard working technicians. He'd left them to die in the explosion. They were only there because of him and his project. They still had their future ahead of them; not like him. He's been washed up for a long time now. Since Chloé died. Now Armon is dead. How is he going to tell his sister that her husband is dead because of him?

He weeps hard, sitting in the rain.

TORONTO, Dovercourt Road.
August 15, 2055: mid-morning

"I'm ok, really, Amanda," Ben insists in a gravelly voice to his younger sister. He stands at the door and opens it to leave the house. Ben now drives Amanda's car to the new BioGen lab that sprung up since the research lab on Devonshire Place blew up. BioGen set up a makeshift lab in Etobicoke, borrowing from two other intact labs in Mississauga and Guelph. Each time he goes to work, he knows Amanda fears for his life. "I've been off work for over a week now. The work is piling up." He feels antsy; when he's not at work, he feels like people are scheming behind his back. They never did sort out the information leak at the Devonshire Place BioGen facility. The mole could have been Schlange, though she'd been absent since Eric left the company. It's entirely possible that there are more moles throughout the remaining facilities. At least when he's there, he can monitor the nuances of the revolution and internal BioGen politics.

"You still don't look that great," Amanda says, looking him over with a frown. "I'm keeping the kids home for another few days to make sure. You should do the same."

The entire family, including the kids, succumbed quite suddenly to what seemed a new kind of respiratory 'flu' virus a week and a half ago. Coughing and hacking and feeling weak and listless, they all spent most of the week in bed. Amanda, who alone experienced a much milder case, was taking care of everyone, doing the shopping, making meals and tending to all her bedridden wards. She was a real trouper, thinks Ben, who recognizes that she is obviously still in mourning. It is a little over a year ago that Armon died in the BioGen explosion—at least that's what Ben told his sister: that Armon died trying to save others, which was true in a way. Ben doesn't feel like a burden; he figures he and Janet are helping her cope. Amanda is a nurse by profession, though she gave it up last year to look after her family. But once a nurse always a nurse. Looking after them is good for her, he tells himself. And Janet and Leonard are good company for each other.

Amanda followed the spread of the epidemic on the news and kept Ben apprised: the bug first hit the eastern provinces with Toronto hit the worst. It was likely ground zero. Patient zero, who was likely infected here, then spread the disease when they traveled out of the city. CDC is suggesting contamination from some zoonotic source, like a sick bird; others speculate an accidental release of a GOF research virus from some lab. Within a day, the entire city was sick—except for the Techno-clones, who kept guard throughout the city. Its incredibly rapid spread meant that the virus had to be air-borne. Days after, the bug had spread through all of North-America and Europe. By the time it hit Asia, Africa and South America a week later, it was killing people. It seemed that even as the people who first got sick were getting better, other people—who weren't sick to begin with—were suddenly dying. It soon became clear that those dying were almost exclusively non-Caucasians. Virtually all Caucasians recovered but some had side effects such as infertility or sterility—discovered through the onslaught of spontaneous abortions and miscarriages. They're calling it the White Plague, because those with non-white pigment are most affected, leaving whites in supremacy. The term was originally coined by some conspiracy theorist as a sarcastic pejorative, suggesting that the virus was manufactured and purposefully leaked by Technocrats with a white supremacist agenda. Yet others, true racists, embrace the term as being delivered by God to purge humanity of less pure elements.

Janet walks into the living room with Leonard, both coughing. She turns to her father standing at the open door and quips that this White Plague is acting like his gene-hacked plants. She adds in a hoarse gravelly voice, "It reminds me of those bad traits used to eradicate an invasive species by making it sterile, or die, depending on its genetic makeup."

Ben's heart suddenly races.

"You remember, Dad?" Janet continues. "You explained that to spread a bad thing, it had to be active only in its homozygous recessive state, cloaked first in a heterozygous state to allow it to spread before it took effect in its target. In this example, to kill all non-whites. Crazy, huh?" She laughs, obviously not taking what she said seriously.

"I remember," Ben says in a voice close to a whisper. He doesn't laugh or smile. Everything has just clicked into place. The precise nature of the virus, its vectors, its spread and its ultimate targets. For once, are the conspiracy theorists right? His gut grows heavy with the sudden thought: what if this virus was indeed manufactured? What if it was specifically made to act differently according to a person's melanin content? Quickly on Caucasians but only to make them sick, and more slowly but lethally on non-Caucasians? The Caucasians, who only got sick from it would spread the disease to highly melanised people, who later died from it. Just like Janet said.

He thinks of the media release back in '50 about an airborne racially targeted DNA-virus developed by Eric Vogel that was intended for shipment to the United States military. It never happened. The whole operation was shut down and the responsible BioGen technicians arrested. But they never found Eric. Could this be that virus? Did Eric finally release it? Where is that son of a bitch? Sitting in a Technocrat safe house?

Ben stands at the door, frozen in terrified thought. He swallows down the gorge rising in his throat and stares at Amanda for several moments. Then he shuts the door.

"We need to leave the city," he breathes out to her in a voice choking with fear.

TWENTY-ONE

GABORET-BOISSONNE FARM, Goodwood Road. September 30, 2055: late afternoon

The Gaboret-Boissonne farm is a small piece of land 70 kilometers northeast of the city. His mother had told Leonard that the farm was reduced some time ago to its paltry two-acre lot from its original hundred-some acres as a horse breeding operation producing world class jumpers.

As the car turns into the long gravel driveway with overhanging poplars, Leonard gets his first glimpse of the large three-story house, guarded by several gnarly oak trees and a large orchard of apple and pear trees behind it. On one side, the orchard is flanked by a chain link fence, and on the other by a partially complete new more secure wire fence—obviously a work in progress. Both sides of the property are given over to scrub forest, mostly Scots pine and cedar with maple, birch and cottonwood. A large barn that looks like it was once painted green sits behind the house and beside the barn is what looks like a garden, completely enclosed in its own intriguingly high well-maintained wire fence.

Leonard's mother had earlier shown him a picture of the house to prepare him for their new home, shaped like a squared-S, with gabled roof and lintel on the emergent side, and the tower, hugged by a rounded veranda, making up the 'back of the S. Sticking out behind the tower was another portion of the house. The old mansion was built over a century ago; it represented classical High Victorian architecture. His mother had pointed to the classical gables and the Doric pillars of the porch that displayed the epitome of picturesque eclecticism. Spotted by dappled sunlight that streamed in through the large oaks, the house looked strangely bright and cheerful. Bright red creepers adorned the livid stone-brick façade, the contrast almost garish.

But that image was taken in the morning. It is not how he sees the house now, as the shadows of evening move in with overtones of gloom and the creepers look dark like clotting blood. The walls are a dull shade of nondescript colour and the little sparkles of reflected sunlight in the windows are winking out one by one.

As the car drives up the long gravel driveway, his cousin Janet, seated beside him in the back seat, grumbles that the place reminds her of the haunted Manderley in *Rebecca* by Daphne du Maurier. He has no idea what that means, but he decides that he doesn't want to read that book now. As the car approaches the front of the house, Janet points out the barn and the fenced-in orchard and garden that he's already noticed. The sturdy fence is obviously built and maintained to withstand many winters and to discourage trespassers, made of sturdy maple posts and wire that is likely electrified. He notices Janet's sudden pique of interest and feels relief that it draws her out of her dark mood, which has been a pain the whole drive here.

Leonard's Uncle Ben and his mom, seated in the

front, speak in hushed voices. "It looks so run down," Ben whispers to Leonard's mom. "And the forest looks..."

"Sick?" Mom says.

Ben forces on a cheerfulness Leonard knows isn't there. "It's fall, Amanda," he replies more upbeat. "Wait until the spring. You're so accustomed to the city, you've forgotten the four seasons."

But Leonard notices the spots of fungus infection on the leaves of the sugar maples that are turning brown, not orange. Many of the pine needles are brown or yellow, like they're giving up. The increased heat is affecting them, he decides. There is more brown in the deciduous trees than the vibrant reds, yellows and oranges that he expected. He'd read somewhere that if a birch tree's leaves in autumn are green and brown, instead of yellow and red, the winter will not be cold and dry but wet and mild. Yet another changing climate phenomenon. Nothing looks vibrant and Janet's surly mood isn't helping.

His mother opens her mouth to retaliate his uncle's earlier comment but she stops when Ben's brows rise in warning. She closes her mouth and lapses into thoughtful silence, cuddling five-year old Bobby, who's fallen asleep beside her.

During their drive here from the city, Janet had moped quietly. When she wasn't quiet, she was tormenting Leonard with kicks to give her more room or lashed out at him with cruel comments on his looks or height or clothes. She can be real mean sometimes, he considers. He ended up letting her stretch out her long legs into his side, squeezed as close to the window and staring out at the countryside. He'd hoped to see a more vibrant wilderness; everything in the city with its intense smog looked sick and dying—which he supposes it is. But he was disheartened to find that the forest in the countryside didn't look much better. He wanted to cry, but he held it in so Janet wouldn't see; he'd never live that one down. He'd read an old 2022 book his mother gave him about the moving treeline with climate change. The predictions it made have already been surpassed. The book predicted that the taiga treeline moving north would obliterate the tundra; what's really happening is that the treeline is disappearing as the trees burn up. The boreal fires are hotter and longer, and the ground is drier. The tree roots can't suck up enough moisture, so the trees can't breathe and can't defend themselves from disease. They stop growing and produce less oxygen for humans to breathe. They become tinder, bursting into raging fires and the black smoke chokes the air so nothing else can breathe—

The car stops.

The door to the house opens and two people step out onto the porch. They don't wear masks. One is a young dark-haired woman with a short bob of dark hair and a pretty face with a ruddy complexion; tight jeans define her slim figure and she wears a man's faded blue shirt with the arms rolled up. The other is a tall well-muscled man with long tangled honey-blond hair He's dressed in faded jeans and red checkered shirt. Both approach the car, she with springy steps and he loping slowly behind.

"That's Nicole!" Ben brightens notably. His eyes then narrow with something akin to suspicion. "Not sure about the fellow. I don't remember him from when I was here last." He frowns slightly. "Then again, that was over twenty years ago, before Cloé and I moved to Toronto..."

Ignoring the approaching reception, Janet leaps out of the car and runs toward the fenced-off area. Leonard feels compelled to follow, but lingers dutifully to participate in their reception.

Nicole flings her arms around Ben. "You look wonderful!" she says in a girlish voice. Then she turns to Leonard's mom who's extricated herself from Bobby, now comfortably sleeping on the passenger seat. "I'm so sorry about Armon, Amanda." Nicole hugs Leonard's mom. Then she turns to Leonard. "And you must be Leonard. You're growing up so fast!"

Leonard nods and smiles awkwardly. Thankfully, she doesn't grab him and squeeze him like a child.

Nicole turns to glance at Janet's disappearing figure then turns to Uncle Ben. "Janet? She's fifteen now? My God, she's grown into a young woman!"

"But she stayed girl enough to be rude, I'm afraid," Ben adds with an apologetic look.

"That's all right. She's excited about the place. That's more important." Then she turns to introduce the tall man beside her. "This is Viggo Nilsen," says Nicole. "He used to run a farm in Sweden then farmed in northern Manitoba with his brother for a while until the fires got so bad he had to leave. He's helping us with a bunch of things on the farm. He's one of Sylvia and Rishi's friends from the old days."

"A pleasure," Viggo says in a baritone voice and steps forward to shake hands with Ben and Leonard's mom. Then his brilliant blue eyes land on Leonard. He surprises Leonard by looking him straight in the eyes with a penetrating stare and offering his hand to shake. Leonard accepts Viggo's large calloused hand, both impressed and embarrassed by the attention; usually grownups ignore him. Once Viggo returns his attention on the other adults, Leonard covertly studies him more carefully and finds the man a puzzle: he looks both a labourer and an intellectual. He's dressed like a farmer with a rugged stubble-covered face, tanned and weathered from the outdoors; but his intelligent eyes and firmly held mouth betray the reserve of a man who studies and analyzes things. Like himself, Leonard decides, at once liking Viggo.

"The rest are inside," Nicole says and turns to the house. "Shall we? We'll get your stuff after and let Bobby have his nap. He's safe there."

As the adults disappear into the house, Leonard catches up to Janet who has already stationed herself by one of the maple posts of the fenced-off garden. She looks disappointed. She's discovered that it is just an ordinary garden with a chicken coup inside.

"Why is it all fenced in like that then?" Leonard asks. "It's got extra fencing from the rest." His eyes light up with a sudden thought. "Maybe they're growing illegal plants. You know, like opium and stuff."

"Don't be an idiot!" Janet remarks severely. "You slug! They're just ordinary winter vegetables."

She's right. Leonard recognizes lettuce, cabbage, carrots and potatoes. Nothing exotic.

A sudden rustle from behind makes them turn just in time to catch sight of a large tabby cat as it disappears into the bushes. Returned to her earlier morbid mood, Janet wanders the property aimlessly, heading toward the barn and kicking up leaves. She suddenly stops, alerting Leonard to another rustle in the bushes. It is not the cat.

"Don't move!" she hisses in a whisper to him, hoping to take it—whatever it is—off guard. After a long moment of frozen anticipation, she springs forward and tackles the bushes blind.

It grunts. Then a voice shrieks, "Let me go, bitch! Get off me!"

Leonard dashes over as a teenage boy about Janet's age pushes her off him and scrambles to his feet. He glares at them out of a darkly tanned face. Disheveled honey-blond hair that looks like a neglected mop hangs over brilliant blue eyes and tangles down over his shoulders. He turns on Janet. "What d'ya mean by tackling me like that!"

"You were spying on us!" she retorts, getting to her feet.

He brushes the leaves and debris off himself with a haughty air. "So what!" he says. "I live here! You're trespassing!"

"We are not!" Leonard shouts and inflates his chest, trying to look bigger.

"Shut up, you little snot!"

"Don't you talk to him like that!" Janet threatens fiercely. "Or I'll beat you up. Fucking asshole..."

The boy laughs in mockery. "Stupid bitch—"

She swings a left hook and catches him in the face.

Both go down into a rolling fight. Leonard stands by, watching with awe. His cousin is so impressive: a girl—a young woman—who fights like a dog and swears like a sailor.

At some point, the boy scrambles up and flees to the house. Leonard notices blood on the boy's face.

As Janet gets up, brushing herself off, Leonard warns hysterically, "He's going to tell his mom and we'll be sent away!"

"Oh, shut up, turd!" Janet says sharply. "You're such a sissy, Leonard. Grow up! No one's sending anyone away." But she looks far from confident.

—

"We're so glad you could come," Lise steps forward as Ben and Amanda enter the foyer of the house. Some things never change Ben thinks, meeting her critical gaze. She is the undeniable ruler of this household with a regal, authoritative presence that pervades a room as soon as she enters it. Words are often not necessary; her expression is enough to manifest her needs. Ben remembers first meeting her and being frightened of her.

Lise embraces Ben and Amanda. "It's been far too long," she says. "It's so good that you made it out of there; I can't imagine how bad it is in the city with the virus and air pollution." Despite her friendly and caring exterior, Lise maintains a frosty cool that never vanishes. Not even when she smiles. Lise resembles her younger sister, but Ben finds everything about her more marked and austere: masculine lips, drawn-back hair, steeply arched brows, dark critical eyes, and a roman nose framed by a thin long face.

Ben, who hasn't seen his sister-in-law since the funeral of his wife a decade ago, feels the past creep back into his life. There are things he would have liked to forget. Disengaging from Lise, Ben pushes a smile at Aloïs, standing in quiet reserve beside Lise and drawing several inhales from his pipe. Ben leans forward, forcing himself to unflinchingly look at those judging eyes, and shakes his hand firmly. "It's good to be here," he says, glancing between his two hosts and realizing with awkward humility that he and his sister and their kids are here at the graces of these two and he owes them a debt of gratitude. The last time they saw each other there was still tension from the things that had happened.

Sylvia and Rishi enter the foyer from the living room and greet Ben and his sister with strong handshakes. Dressed in practical farmer's jeans and cotton shirt, Rishi is tall and wiry. He wears his long graying hair in a ponytail and has left his almost gaunt face in a scruffy beard. Rishi has managed to not get killed by the airborne virus by remaining isolated and he obviously feels secure in the knowledge that Ben's group are no longer infectious. No one wears a mask.

Rishi and Sylvia look like hippies from the past and have been on Lise's farm for so long it seems like they too are family. They've been together as common law for over two decades and judging from their appearance they haven't changed from their bohemian nature since Ben last saw them. Their son must be about Janet's age, Ben considers.

"Welcome back, Ben," Rishi says, offering his

hand to shake Ben's. Ben takes it with an appreciative smile. Rishi says no more, though, and Ben feels pressed down by the thickness of the silence.

Sylvia moves in, her long tie-dyed dress flowing with the movements of her slim figure. She gives him a weak hug and he feels her bony arms. Then she hugs Amanda. "How's Leonard?" she asks in a quiet voice meant only for Amanda. "How's he bearing up without his father?"

Amanda pushes a smile and glances nervously at Ben. "He's good. He loves his uncle and his cousin. They're great company. Thanks for asking."

"Let's all sit," Lise says, urging everyone to sit in the living room. "I've got some tea brewing on the stove."

Everyone moves to the spacious living room and takes a seat on one of the several plaid armchairs. Bathed in bright light from two large bay windows, the room looks like a retro-modern collection from a 1960's rummage sale: a worn paisley couch and puff style ottoman, studio armchairs with fake wooden arms, kidney-shaped walnut coffee tables, mismatched area rugs and an eclectic mix of lamps, including a large Tiffany lamp and even several lava lamps on the fireplace mantel: together with some old landscapes on the walls, the design has a kind of granny chic feel. The large fireplace is more than decoration, thinks Ben; it looks well used.

Still feeling awkward, Ben says, with a glance at Nicole, "Well, you know what's been happening in the city. So, what's been going on here recently?"

"Plenty!" "Not much," Sylvia and Nicole say at the same time.

"What Sylvia means is that a lot of silly things have occurred," Nicole says quickly with a warning glance at Sylvia. Ben detects an uneasiness in the room.

Failing to grasp Nicole's hint, Sylvia blurts out in close to a retort, "Well, if you call being attacked twice in the last three months by stragglers and Rishi nearly killed by one of them *silly*!"

Nicole groans loudly and glares at Sylvia. The others look from one to the other in discomfort.

Sylvia sweeps her gaze over them all, eyes challenging. "Well, what's wrong with telling them the truth?"

"Because ... well, look at Amanda's face," says Nicole.

Amanda has turned pale and looks like she might faint.

Lise, who stood up to go get some tea, says to Ben, "I'm sorry you have to find out all the gruesome facts the first five minutes of your stay here, but the truth must be told sometime." She waves a hand at Nicole, looking expectantly at her and adds, "They might as well know the whole."

Nicole takes Lise's cue with a big sigh. "OK, well, some of us—I won't say who—didn't want you to come for a number of reasons. But the vote was in favour, so here you are. To explain, since the '30s—well since the wheat crop crashed in '36—lots of farms have been experiencing catastrophic crop failures and went bankrupt. Supplies became hard to get."

Ben feels his chest constrict with the truth. Everyone in the room knows that he was responsible for the wheat crop crash—thanks to his transgenic fiasco. BioGen already knew about the general crop failures for years. It was, in fact, this very phenomenon that Nicole was referring to that BioGen was attempting to address. Wheat was already in trouble when Ben crashed it. And it wasn't just wheat that was in trouble.

Nicole goes on, "You may have heard it in the news. Then again, you may not have; I always forget who runs the media," she says naively, as if she's forgotten where Ben worked. "Anyway, only those who could afford the synthetic fertilizers and huge costs for proprietary seeds could go on and make a profit. To be honest, the only people who could do that were the Corporation Farms. They didn't have to pay the ridiculous astronomical prices for seeds every year or expensive fertilizers and pesticides needed for these climate-resistant crops. But you'd know that already..."

...Because you developed those seeds and pesticides in a proprietary model to milk every miserable farmer dry, he adds in his head for her. He suddenly concludes that coming here was a bad idea...But where can they go? Going back to the city would be fatal.

"Lots of folks went out of business," Nicole continues. "Then the supply chain started choking up. Partly because of the DNA-virus and partly because of the warring factions and road blocks. People couldn't get supplies even if they could afford them. Some things just dried up completely—and that was well before the virus hit. People stopped trading and started hoarding. In the last several years, because of all the strikes and unrest in the urban centres, lots of misinformed folk from the cities flooded into the countryside."

She seems to include Ben and Amanda in that

assessment, which is unfair. It seems that these folks have no idea what's happening in the city. How the Gaian terrorists are rounding up Technos and stringing them up in the streets. The bombings of Techno facilities. The mob riots between factions and the police barricades and roundups. People disappearing or dead bodies found in alleys. They aren't just rumours. It isn't safe there for anyone, whether Gaian, Techno, or neither. If these folks are getting their information from the news media, they aren't getting half of what's really going on. They may have had good coverage on the virus raging there, but there's so much more going on. They have no idea how perilous it's been for Ben and his family in the city. Most people still blame BioGen, not Eric, for the virus. Most BioGen facilities have already been bombed and gutted and a Gaian noose is waiting for him.

"...Some people went back—those that could," Nicole goes on. They must have been more than desperate or delusional, thinks Ben, for them to return to the city where virus and violence still rage. "Of the rest, some lucky people got jobs in the Corporation Farms. But the rest had nowhere to go; they starved and became desperate. First, they started raiding the Corporation Farms and stole food. But the Corporation Farms just built bigger and better fences and set up guards who shot anyone who got too close. Like the bloody Berlin Wall. So, they started looking elsewhere—here for one. Aloïs calls them stragglers. It fits. They're straggly, starving desperate people who belong to no particular group. Anyway, they've taken to forming packs because it's easier to raid a farm that way. They've hit so many of us now. Even when we aren't hit, we suffer; along with the attack on Port Perry, stragglers recently raided and burned down Willowtree Farm, which used to trade our labour—farm labour by Viggo and Rishi, for instance—for meat and other farm staples. That's all gone. Which is bad because we lost our cows and horses long ago." She glances at Rishi. "And Rishi here had a close call this summer when they attacked our farm and one of them stabbed him in the shoulder. The straggler was aiming for his heart and missed. They got most of our animals, even Wizard, our old guard dog. We still have our chickens and a few goats. But no cows to milk and no horses to help with plowing. Miranda—our old tabby—is still with us, of course, but that's because she's half wild already. The stragglers have been harassing us consistently the last few months. There just seem to be more of them. Twice they were partly successful. You must understand that it is our lives they are robbing from us. Every time they get a chicken, it's fewer eggs for our families. Every time they rob our orchards or gardens, or take our animals, there are fewer things for us to eat and live by. Without these things, we'd have to become stragglers too."

"How do we fit in?" Ben asks

"You make four more mouths to feed," says Aloïs bluntly in his usual monotone. He obviously considers Bobby negligible or has mathematically summed up the children based on biomass.

Feeling strangely unwanted, Ben offers, "I have close to two thousand dollars. It could come in handy when we need it."

"Until the economy completely crashes," quips Aloïs. "And it will soon crash, when the Gaians succeed in taking down the corrupt government. The economy has already taken a dive. Better to have brought supplies."

"There's our car..."

"Useless, except for the engine, maybe..." Then almost sarcastically, "Or for you to escape..."

More desperately, "I'm considered a pretty good mechanic—"

"A lot of good that will do us unless you're good with power generators and water purifiers. Besides, we have Viggo, here, who knows everything about machines."

"Dammit! We're alive and we deserve a chance too! Our children deserve a glimpse of the future. We owe it to them. You owe it to us!"

"We don't owe you anything!" says Aloïs sharply, finally betraying some emotion.

The silence that follows presses down on Ben like a giant hand of reproach. It all comes back to haunt him: his transgenic horror unleashed on the hungry world; the suspicions of his role in BioGen's supposed collusion in the international power struggle for the control of food security; even the suspicion of his complicity in Chloé's death. That one hurts the most. Immediately after Chloé died, Lise made the bold and insistent claim that her younger sister's untimely death in Christie Pits Park was no accident. The police had concluded that her mask was probably faulty and she'd forgotten to bring her bronchodilator and panicked then died of a heart attack when confronted with the severely high smoke in the air. This was all too common among people suffering with COPD. But Lise insisted that Chloé would *never* forget her inhaler. Lise suggested that someone had killed her younger sister to shut her up, despite no sign of a struggle. Though Lise never said why, it was clear to Ben that she knew something of Chloé's discovery about BioGen's criminal activities. Ben's face puckers with the memory of his argument with Chloé just before the tragic event. They'd argued about what she knew and her intention to divulge all to the press. Had Chloé told her sister before coincidentally dying right after their argument? What if Lise is right? When he was given Chloé's personal belongings, he'd checked her satchel for the incriminating file she'd taken with her that morning. Her phone and wallet were there; but no file. When he checked her phone archive for texts and calls, there'd been nothing to her sister.

"Hold on, Ben," says Nicole with a quick glance at Aloïs, now returned to sucking on his pipe with indifference. "Please don't take this wrong. You're welcome to stay. We understand your situation and you have a family. We voted positive and that stands." She glances around the room at everyone. "Only we want you to know that this place isn't a retreat. It's just another situation of the same overall problem. We need to ration and work within strict restrictions and we need to protect what we have. It won't be easy for anyone, even the children."

Amanda's eyes glisten with tears and her face now puckers with distress. It is clear to one and all that this is not what she expected.

Nicole sighs ruefully with a long glance at Amanda. "Listen, it's not as bad as it looks. This is supposed to be a joyful reunion. We should take a lesson from the children who—"

Simon bursts through the front door into the living room and runs to Sylvia. He's in tears. Blood flows from his nose and cracked lip. He wails loudly like a child about the mean children who've come and trespassed on their place.

Sylvia tries to calm the boy down. "Stop crying, Simon. Who hit you?" Her voice has become vengeful.

"That girl! The girl who came with *them*!" He points an accusing finger at Ben and Amanda.

Sylvia looks from them back to Simon and her anger shifts to the boy. "Why did she hit you?" Then more forcefully, "Simon, what did you do to provoke her?"

"Nothing!"

Ben offers, "He may be right. Janet's been in a bad mood. She didn't want to leave her friends in Toronto and..."

"I still want to know why she hit you, Simon," Sylvia persists then turns to Ben. "Because I know him. Boys his age are so impolite." Then back to Simon, "If you don't tell Sylvia now, Sylvia will smack your bottom till it's blue!"

Rishi pulls Simon away. "That's no way to handle it. You can't spank him; he's almost a man—"

"—He's still a child."

Just as the parents begin to argue, Janet and Leonard run into the house. Leonard runs to his mother, who embraces him as if to guard him. Janet runs straight to her father and says quietly but forcefully, "I want to go home! Please, Daddy!"

Ben glances at everyone then looks down at his disheveled daughter. "Listen, Janet, I want you and Simon to make friends. I don't care what happened. We're guests here. Now, go say hello." He urges her forward.

She recoils. "But he called Leonard a snot!"

"Go!"

The two combatants eye each other coldly and exchange a frosty hello from their respective corners of the room.

As if a spring is let loose, the adults burst into laughter and relax.

"Now, I'll go get that tea," says Lise.

TWENTY-TWO

GABORET-BOISSONNE FARM, Goodwood Road. October 10, 2055: mid-afternoon

The day is blistering hot as Janet and Leonard investigate the main road they had initially taken to get here: Goodwood Road. Lise has lightened their chores today because of the heat and they are now free until supper. Despite the yellow haze that covers the sun like a spider web, it seers down like a heat lamp. As they walk up the path toward the gate that leads to the road, Simon, who is casually leaning against a large oak tree and chewing on a long grass stem, watches them in his characteristically detached manner. He too craves distraction and to no surprise to Leonard, springs onto the cobbled path in front of them and succeeds in making the path too narrow to walk abreast as Janet and he are doing.

Leonard opts to fall back and walk behind her instead of losing his dignity by walking through the tall grass to get around Simon. That is his mistake. Janet passes Simon by, ignoring him without onslaught. But as soon as she passes him by, Simon jumps to the centre of the path, legs straddled and arms stretched to block Leonard's way.

Leonard halts.

Simon feigns several times to let him pass only to block it just as he is about to take it. Simon goads, "Go this way! No, this way, stupid!"

Too proud to summon Janet's aid, Leonard remains

silent and watches his abstracted cousin continue on, unaware of his dilemma. There is no way he can fight Simon, who is much taller and bulkier than he is.

Just as he feels vanquished and Simon emits a loud peel of triumphant laughter, Janet turns. "Hey, Scumhead! Leave my cousin alone!"

Simon laughs again. "Go on, snot! Your *mommy* wants you."

Abandoning his pride, Leonard runs to catch up with Janet and glances fearfully back at his tormentor.

Eventually, Simon joins them, ignoring Leonard.

"What are you doing, Sewermouth?" he asks Janet, and climbs the fence to sit beside her. Leonard notices that he leans his shoulder up against hers in an overly familiar way. And she doesn't seem to mind.

"What's it look like?" she quips. "I'm watching the road for cars."

"That's dumb!" he says. "There aren't any and you know it. There haven't been any cars for months—"

"Except ours."

"Except your dumpy car."

They all grow silent and Simon falls in with their silent contemplation. But he quickly tires of sitting under the scorching sun of midday, doing nothing, and breaks the silence. "What's it like in the city?"

Janet turns and looks at him strangely. "I was just thinking of the city."

"I haven't been there since I was a kid!" Simon confides, obviously thinking himself no longer a child.

"Really?"

Leonard recognizes that look of sinister inspiration

in Janet's hazel eyes and prepares for fascinating tales, fantastical science fiction, and outrageous lies about the giant megalopolis of Toronto. He is not disappointed.

"Did you know that Robinson eats raw meat?" she taunts at one point. Then there are the intoxicated crowds that gather nightly and seek any desperate fool in the streets to publicly hang for their own sadistic satisfaction. Unfortunately not far from the truth, thinks Leonard.

Simon is hypnotized, aghast with lurid fascination. Even Leonard, who knows better, finds her tales incredibly engrossing. Partly because most are inspired by a spark of truth, just embellished with her lurid imagination.

"Simon!" Nicole's voice rudely interrupts from the house. "Your mother wants you in the kitchen!"

"Can't it wait?" he whines. "Janet's telling me about the public hangings in the city!"

"Is she?" Nicole says. "Your mother's waiting for you to help in the kitchen. She said you're meant to help her do the pickling. Janet's stories can wait... NOW, Simon!"

As Simon runs into the house, Nicole passes him and reaches the fence where Janet and Leonard sit. She looks at Janet gravely. "Why do you tell him those gruesome lies?"

Janet puts on her best innocent face. "What gruesome lies?"

"You know what I mean," says Nicole seriously. "When you left the city none of that was going on—public hangings and mass bombings—though one can't be sure in the future. The point is that someday we may all want to return to the city. We may have to. And you're giving Simon a terribly wrong and horrible impression of it." She smiles a little. "Try the truth. He'll still listen. You're a smart girl. You don't need to create fabrications to impress people. Be yourself, honey."

Leonard doesn't understand. For him, Janet is being herself already.

After Nicole leaves, Janet gives him that look. It means 'really?' They both know that despite Janet's embellishments on the violence, Nicole's version of what is going on in the cities is naïve and wrong. Public hangings and mass bombings are definitely happening there. It makes Leonard wonder about the adults' perception of reality.

GABORET-BOISSONNE FARM, Goodwood Road. November 2, 2055: early afternoon

Every morning in the winter, Janet and Leonard do chores in the barn, turning the hay and playing with Miranda's new kittens, tending the chicken coup, and feeding the chickens and the goats. As a reward to themselves, they play a game to amuse ourselves, skulking around the big house playing spy. They create a fantasy based loosely on how they feel about the adults they've been thrust amidst. Naturally, the place becomes a maximum security prison and Aloïs becomes the villainous warden and Lise his trusted sergeant. All the other adults are prison guards to be avoided at all costs—even Nicole, who Janet likes now because she started teaching Janet archery, which is great fun. Their mission is to rescue Miranda from the prison and transport the cat to the safety of outside, which is where she wants to go anyway.

They keep their game a secret even from Simon. Leonard knows that Janet's true reason for secrecy is primarily her own awareness of the silliness of the game and her knowledge that were Simon to discover it, she'd never hear the end of it. The justification she's given Leonard is that Simon is sure to tell his mother who would put an end to the game. Which is true, Leonard decides.

One hot afternoon in November, after their chores, the two prowl the upstairs bedrooms, looking for the cat, who they usually find lounging like the Queen of Sheba on someone's bed. They find her lying asleep on the bed in the spare bedroom and are about to grab her, when they are suddenly alerted by the sound of two people walking up the stairs. The cousins scramble into the large stand up closet and close the door as two people walk in. Leonard smells moth balls and dust as he crouches down to face Janet, who he can make out rather well from the sliver of light through the crack in the door.

It turns out to be Lise and Aloïs. They argue about the crops in the garden. "If the Technocratic Agriculture Police ever come to inspect us, like they keep promising, we'll be screwed, Aloïs," Lise says in a frosty voice. "We have to get more creative about storing our seeds."

Aloïs replies in a clipped voice, "They'll never come to this backwater farm. This place is no man's land, Lise. You saw what happened to Goodwood last month; totally razed and looted. And no one came to help. Just like Port Perry. This whole region is a wasteland and no one wants it or cares. It's all a scrap yard. Now with the revolution getting more violent, TAP has better things to do these days, I think."

"Doesn't that scare you, though?" Lise says then suddenly shouts, "Shoo, Miranda!"

The children hear the cat meow her objection as she is no doubt pushed off the bed.

"Now, where did I put it," says Lise. "My sewing kit..." Leonard hears her opening a dresser drawer. She adds to Aloïs, "Mark my words, Aloïs; when we lower our guard, that's when things happen."

Leonard involuntarily wriggles his body, fearing Lise might open the closet in search of her sewing kit. Janet makes a nasty face at him and gives him a phantom smack to keep still. "Ah, there it is!" Lise says more cheerfully to his relief. Soon enough they leave and go down the stairs, still talking about seeds and the farm police. The children sigh with relief and Leonard releases a fart he's been keeping in.

Janet bursts out laughing and Leonard giggles. Then Janet quickly shushes him. Two pairs of feet shuffle quickly into the room and the door closes accompanied by a woman's giggle. Janet puts her finger to her lips, signalling for Leonard to remain still and quiet. They look at each other, wondering who it is.

"Darling, no one ever goes there," Sylvia says in a strange voice that drowns with emotion. "We could sneak there right now. Please, darling, no one will see us!"

But it's not Rishi, her partner, who answers; it's Viggo, their friend. "Älskling, Älskling...It's too far away! I need you *now*! Right here!" baritone voice pleading. "See what you've done?" he says in a husky voice followed by a groan.

Sylvia responds in a sighing voice, "Oh, Viggo!"

"Do you feel me? *That's* for you!" A shuffling sound follows and Sylvia utters a squeak. Are they struggling?

The cousins stare at one another in the cramped shadows. Janet's eyes go wide.

"Oh, my darling!" Sylvia moans out with a long sigh. Then urgently, "Not here! Oh, Viggo, my love, someone will—"

"No one's in the house!" He says with gruff urgency. That's not true, thinks Leonard. Lise and Aloïs are downstairs. Then Viggo adds in a playful voice, "*Komma,* Älskling *...jag måste ha dig nu...*"

The sound of loud kissing filters into the childrens' cramped enclosure and Janet mouths at Leonard: *they're kissing*!

Leonard mugs back at her to show his astonishment and repugnance. He is surprised to find that he is disappointed with Viggo. The man had become something of a hero to him. An icon: a man who worked the land with his hands but used his brains to solve problems. Leonard suddenly feels vulnerable. If Viggo and Sylvia discover them eavesdropping on them, Leonard will be so ashamed.

The sounds that follow are confusing. Shuffle of feet and the rustle of clothes and things falling on the floor then the squeak of the bed, playful giggling, then more kissing sounds. The bed keeps moving and squeaking. Now heavy breathing, panting, and moaning sounds from both Sylvia and Viggo filter through the closet door. It goes on and gets more loud and frantic.

Leonard clamps his hands over his ears. Are they doing what he thinks they are doing?

Janet flings her hands to her reddening cheeks and her eyes go wide. She mouths at him: *they're FUCKING*!

Leonard shuts his eyes tight, which he knows is silly because he can't see past the closet doors anyway.

This torture seems to go on forever. Then Sylvia wales out several times like she's in awful pain or something—except she cries out Viggo's name adoringly—and Viggo follows with a growling shout of release like he's having a successful bowl movement after being terribly constipated. Within moments Viggo unleashes a hearty laugh and Sylvia giggles some more.

"My Älskling," Viggo breathes out adoringly. And then they are kissing loudly again.

Janet shakes her head in amazement at Leonard. She mouths: *oh, my God*!

The two adults are quiet for a long time and the children look at each other in puzzlement and frustration. Surely they haven't fallen asleep! Leonard starts to feel cramped. He feels pins and needles as his legs fall asleep. He tries to move them. Janet grimaces at him and shakes her head at him vigorously to indicate for him to remain still. The last thing they want is for the adults to hear them. Leonard is just so glad he farted before they came and now fights a fit of the giggles.

Finally, Sylvia murmurs, "Oh, Viggo, my sweet darling ... Every time is like the first time ... Why did you ever leave me?"

Viggo says in a deep languid voice, "You know why..."

Leonard can tell that they are kissing again and rolls his eyes at Janet who responds with a shrug. Sylvia sighs out, "Oh, Viggo, your body ... it's so gorgeous."

He chuckles. "So is yours, Älskling." More kisses.

"But I don't have all your scars ... They're like badges of honour. What stories they could all tell of your life up north and in Sweden..." The children hear him sigh with pleasure; no doubt she is stroking all his scars and kissing them better. After more kissing sounds, she asks, "What about this one on your butt?"

He laughs quietly. "That was when the threshing machine broke and I landed on one of the blades."

Ouch! Janet mouths to Leonard.

"Ouch!" Sylvia says in sympathy and kisses him loudly. On the butt, obviously.

"And this one on your back?"

Janet now rolls her eyes in exasperation. How many scars does he have?

"The fire of '39. One of many no one in the city even remembers because they never heard about it." After another silence, he continues in a contemplative voice, "This is such a big country ... Most of these devastating fires don't even make the news. Unless it's the Boreal Scorching of '46 because it affected the city with so much smoke."

Leonard hears his stomach growl and grimaces at the sound, hoping the adults don't hear. They haven't had their lunch yet. Realizing that he's hungry, Leonard hopes Viggo doesn't have a hundred scars for Sylvia to kiss each one adoringly.

"What was it like, having to battle the fires every summer?"

"Try all year, Älskling. With climate change and no rain or snow, there is no fire season. All year is fire season. You asked what it's like? ... It's like the apocalypse. It starts with the air and the sky. Each day it would get more hazy and the sunsets were bright orange. Some would see that as beautiful, but we watched it with dread. Then, depending on the wind, we would smell the smoke, thick like a campfire and we could see columns of ash, yellow and dirty, billowing over the forested hills. The smoke is so dense everything goes dark and you can't see more than a few metres ahead of you and it stings your eyes and hurts to breathe. When it rages close, the flames move faster than you can run, leaping across roads and rivers. You don't have a chance. Did you know that it can burn so hot that the air in front can be 800° Centigrade? It instantly dries the trees ahead and they burn so fast they crack and explode. A wildfire creates its own weather and wind, building its own world for more of itself. And then after, it's all black or grey and smoking and full of flying ash. And so quiet. One time, I found an old trapper's cabin after a fire. There was a box of tools melted to the rocks. The old trapper was gone and we hoped that he made it out alive."

After another silence, "You never told me what made you finally come back. After all those years you were up there, fighting the fires ... What made you leave and finally come back to me seventeen years ago?"

She's asking him all the hard questions, Leonard decides.

Janet grabs his hand and squeezes it. She looks at him strangely, eyes big, like she's just figured out something important.

"You know I never really left you, Älskling. Even when Rishi came along, I stayed for a while. But I couldn't stay. You're always in my heart. When my brother... when Björn died in the wildfire that took our cabin that spring, I just couldn't rebuild anymore. I couldn't—"

They all hear it at the same time and freeze. A loud slam of the front door downstairs. Someone has just come into the house. Then a man calls out: "Syl! Are you here?"

It's Rishi!

Leonard involuntarily stiffens. He hears Viggo and Sylvia scramble. Probably putting on their clothes.

"Window!" Sylvia whispers urgently. "I'll go downstairs to meet him."

Leonard hears them kissing again, followed by some mischievous giggling. Then the window creaks open reluctantly and there's more shuffling as, no doubt, Viggo crawls out the window.

The bedroom door opens and Sylvia calls down the stairs, "I'm here, love!"

The cousins hear Rishi walk up the stairs and Sylvia walk down. "I was taking a quick nap in the spare bedroom," they hear her say to Rishi as they go down the stairs together.

"That was some quick nap!" Janet whispers to Leonard. Rishi responds to Sylvia with something they can't make out as the couple wander off to another part of the house. The children then hear the other adults conversing in muffled voices. Janet looks at Leonard with new intensity. "Let's get out of here!"

She gingerly opens the closet door and the two creep out with a quick glance at the open window where Viggo had crawled out. Leonard follows Janet as she tiptoes to the window. They catch sight of Viggo as he disappears into the scrub forest. He's crawled down the downspout with the agility of a young Romeo and the ease of someone who practiced it many times.

Janet turns to Leonard with a victorious grin on her face.

Leonard doesn't realize that his mouth is agape until she tells him to close it. "What are we going to do?" he asks her.

"Nothing," she says seriously, still looking out the window. "Absolutely nothing." Then she turns to him with a roguish grin. "I always did wonder why Simon had such a wonderful head of blond hair with Rishi as his father. Sylvia is a blond but a strawberry blond. Simon is more of a honey-blond—*just like Viggo...*" She hikes her brows at Leonard with an air of triumph. "And those blue eyes of Simon's when both parents have brown eyes. Now, that could simply be that the parents are both heterozygous and carry the recessive blue gene. But look at Viggo...He came down to the farm seventeen years ago. Simon is sixteen. You do the math, Leonard. A year after he gets here..."

"Simon is born!" His mouth gapes open again. "Do you think Rishi knows?"

Janet throws her head back and makes an exasperated sound. "Leonard! You slug! With them skulking around like that and Viggo escaping out the window? What do you think?"

TWENTY-THREE

GABORET-BOISSONNE FARM, Goodwood Road. May 13, 2056: morning

By mid-morning the smell of Toronto is almost gone and the sun feels like a heat lamp on Leonard's face as he steps outside the farmhouse. The air ripples under an azure blue sky and the fields buzz with crickets and bugs and the occasional loud drone of a bumblebee. It feels like summer. The winter was long and cold; the adults had imposed severe rations, but the children didn't care so much. Janet and Leonard had enjoyed their first country-winter, making snowmen and forts and sliding down the little hillside in makeshift sleds. By late March, most of the snow disappeared. Leonard watched the buds appear and transform into diaphanous leaves, colouring the forest in a hazy froth of light green. Like a brush dabbing the forest floor in a glorious watercolour. Using a nature guidebook that Lise gave him, Leonard eagerly identified oxalis, trout lily, trillium and ferns that covered the ground.

The crops were seeded in early April. Those that could withstand the still frosty mornings such as spinach, onions, and dandelions were seeded outside. Others were set to germinate in the extended greenhouse that they had all helped build last winter. Rows of little clay pots with tomatoes, radishes and lettuce resembled a miniature green and red army of soldiers. Janet's father, Ben, turned out to be a skillful carpenter and, with his family's contribution in building the greenhouse, came their final acceptance by the others on the farm. The Cranes and the Hardys all feel better for it. Except Janet, thinks Leonard. For her it's complicated; things are always complicated for his impetuous cousin. For instance, is she friends with Simon or enemies? One moment they're laughing together about something and all chummy and clingy even, excluding him altogether; another moment they're at each other's throats screaming bad words. One time he caught them actually kissing! It's as if she's obsessed with him and Leonard is forgotten. Are they like boyfriend and girlfriend or something? If they are, they sure are fighting a lot. Like Janet's parents used to.

Grabbing Bobby by the hand, Leonard scrambles after them as they head for the forest, not waiting for him and Bobby. Janet and Simon are both tall and long of stride. They wear functional bows and arrows slung over their warrior-like shoulders like soldiers heading to battle. As usual, Bobby and Leonard trot behind like their pet dogs. The four of them are setting out for a picnic, equipped with arms (an imperative requirement on an outing).

Up to last month, their parents had restricted them to the confines of the small farm's enclosure for fear of stragglers. But the farm's last skirmish with a small band in January that Viggo and Rishi had easily chased away suggested that they might be relics of a breed that the harsh winter had destroyed. The adults seemed to agree that the emigration from the cities—the heart of the revolution—had petered out; those who were already in the country must have found a place to stay or they had wasted away in the bitter cold of the winter, the adults reasoned. So, even though the children had already secretly gone far beyond the dilapidated fence many times before, they could do so now with the sanction of their guardians. And even though Leonard is glad of their sanction, he worries about their reasons. To start with, the winters have not been that cold.

Are the cities all dead or have they been resurrected with new rulers? The virus killed so many people already. Of those left, are they Gaians or Technos? When Leonard's family left the city, it seemed like the Gaians were winning but it was a real war zone. Who's to say? The adults don't discuss this, which puzzles him. Isn't it important to them? Now, with the stragglers supposedly gone, the adults seem less concerned with what goes on in the cities and more about their failing crops. He's just a child, but he finds their lack of concern dangerous...

—

It's almost noon as they walk along an old worn path that winds its way through the mixed coniferous-deciduous forest. The path was created over a hundred years ago by their ancestors who used it as a short cut from estate to estate. The twin estate to the farm has long since burned down and the path is seldom used. It leads the children to a clearing, alive with the buzzing of insects. Their eyes squint momentarily and adjust from the filtered light of the forest to the brilliance of direct sunlight.

Leonard stands for a moment and draws in a breath, appreciating the change in the smell and consistency of the air from the sharp pine pungency to the sweet fragrance of cherry and apple blossoms. The sounds, too, have changed subtly from the yodels, fluting and whistling of veerys, thrushes and warblers to the arrogant and abrupt throaty screech of the red-winged blackbird and the repetitious chipping or twitters of the sparrows and chickadees.

Simon and Janet are arguing as usual by the time they reach the forest on the other side.

"Lise shouldn't call Dad Frankenstein," Janet grumbles. "He isn't a monster."

"It's 'cause he *made* monsters, stupid," Simon snorts. "Frankenstein's the name of the mad scientist, not the clone monsters he made."

"He's not a mad scientist either," she defends. "And they're not monsters!"

"The Gaians say they are," Simon says, picking his teeth casually. "BioGen is just part of Canadian Enterprises, which everyone knows is owned by that asshole Robinson and his Technocreeps. Those Corporation Farms are just feeding the bio-techno machine, making synthetic crap and forcing farmers to buy new seeds every year because they're protected like intellectual property. The farmers can't even use the seeds from the previous year's crop! My mom says that BioGen's technology is irresponsible—patenting synthetic seeds and making Nature redundant. She says people like your dad are wrecking our ecosystems. They're destroying our diversity, and evolution and stuff."

Leonard doesn't think Simon knows what those words mean.

Janet makes a sound of disgust. "What does Sylvia know; she's a misguided hippy environmentalist," she parrots what Leonard heard her father once say. "Besides, Dad just made a little mistake once. Some DNA escaped and went rogue on them. Part of the risk we have to take in GE crops."

"Yeah, like widespread famine," Simon mutters, shaking his head at her. "And what about that DNA virus?"

"My father had nothing to do with that!" Then she adds with a frown, "Lise sounds like a Gaian . . ."

"So? Being a Gaian isn't so bad." Simon shrugs and absently rakes back his mat of hair with both hands. "She doesn't like what your dad was doing there. Lots of people think it's wrong. Mom too."

"She's just scared they'll find us," Janet grumbles then murmurs more to herself than to Simon, "Your mom's scared of everything. And besides, the revolution might fix things."

"My father says that nothing's going to happen until a natural disaster like climate change—"

"Which is already here, goof!"

"And he says that after the natural disaster, the people who are left will start all over again."

"What does your father know!" Janet says scornfully. "He can't even see in front of his nose—just ask Sylvia!"

"What are you talking about?"

"Janet," Leonard pleads, voice lapsing into reproach. "You're not supposed to tell anyone, remember?"

She turns on him. "And I wasn't going to, turd! You big blabbermouth!"

"What aren't you supposed to tell me?" Seeing her adamant silence, he turns on Leonard. "Tell me! Tell me or I'll punch your head in, you little snot!"

"I told you not to call my cousin a snot!"

"Ya? Well, then don't call my father dumb!"

Janet lets loose a scathing laugh. "I didn't, but you just did!"

He seizes her wrist. "You take that back!"

She gasps at his clutch then shocks Leonard by dropping her gaze and apologizing to Simon. "I'm sorry. I don't think your dad is dumb." He gives in and lets her maneuver out of his grasp, panting with excitement. As soon as she is free, she bursts into a guffaw and leaps out of range.

Simon decides not to pursue her. Perhaps he's too hot, Leonard thinks, and feels relief.

As they step out of the cool dappled forest into the warm sunshine of a lilac-sumac savanna, Simon announces that they should eat some lunch. Leonard is happy to comply; so is Bobby, judging by his face lighting up with a smile.

"It's only ten-thirty," Janet objects.

"Well, I'm hungry. So, it's time to eat."

"You can't tell *me* when to eat," Janet says tartly. "Pig!"

"That's because you only brought along some crackers while I made three sandwiches—all for me! You're never prepared," he says smugly. "And now you're jealous!"

"I'm not jealous," Janet says haughtily. "I'm just

not hungry."

"You are."

"Am not!" Her face goes pink.

"Are too, dork!" He laughs then promptly sits down on a patch of matted long grass amid the lilacs and swings out his backpack. Without waiting for the three others to agree or even join him, Simon fishes out a peanut butter and raspberry jam sandwich and bolts it down with gluttonous pleasure as Leonard stands nearby, longing in silence. Simon isn't a particularly tidy eater and leaves a smear of red jam on his chin. Leonard notices that his cheeks are flushed already from the heat and sweat glistens on his nose and forehead.

Janet stomps around then finally drops down to sit in the grass and throws her arms against her upraised knees, glowering at Simon. Even if she *is* hungry she isn't going to admit to it now. Leonard is ready to confess his hunger in hopes of receiving a morsel, but Janet glares at him as if she's read his mind. His shoulders droop in defeat. Bobby whimpers. They all ignore him.

Once Simon finishes his first course of lunch, they plunge back into the forest out of the burning sun and into a white pine stand with oak trees, yellow birch and tall aspens. The deer flies buzz furiously around their heads amid wild arm waving and frustrated outcries. Simon leads them up a hill toward a large hemlock grove. He scrambles a steep incline to a narrow long ledge that may have once been a path. The forest floor is carpeted with dead needles and tiny fallen cones and dotted with young maple saplings. Like a man who has found gold, Simon bends down and gathers a handful of cones then darts behind a tree. Janet, who has waited for Bobby and Leonard to catch up before she scrambles up, shrieks at the deluge of cones Simon flings at her face. He sniggers as she practically falls backwards on top of her cousins then swears furiously at Simon, her face red with embarrassment.

"Come on!" Simon says enthusiastically. "Let's play war!"

Eager to play, Janet runs for cover and gathers her own arsenal of weapons.

"You can't use your hands!" Simon warns just as Janet is about to throw some cones at him. "You have to make a slingshot using a tree like this." He squats over a young sapling and bends its branches into a mutilated mess, fits a cone into his makeshift catapult, pulls the sapling back then lets it spring naturally towards Janet. The cone flies past her head, barely missing her. Both participants shriek with pleasure.

As Janet and Simon collect their cones, Bobby and Leonard, left out of the game as usual, sit back like a dutiful and appreciative audience to watch their creative entertainment. The warriors shoot in earnest, sometimes hitting their opponent with a victorious cry, other times—most of the time—missing widely. In the process the poor saplings they use are swiftly demolished and they must forage for a new catapult.

Bobby tugs Leonard's sleeve and points far into the forest. Leonard gruffly tells him to let go. Bobby insistently pulls and points again. This time Leonard looks and listens. He thinks he hears something and sees some movement in the forest. Beast or person? Or just a bird? Maybe a squirrel. Still...

"Janet!" He touches her arm and whispers loudly, ready to tell her about the possibility that someone else is there in the forest with them.

"*Not now,* Leonard!" she commands, shaking him off and dashing to a new catapult.

During a forage she trips on an exposed root and falls headlong to the ground with a hollow thud. When she doesn't get up right away, Simon jeers, "Hey, clone monster! Get up!"

She jerks to her feet, wiping her head, and pushes back her thick mane of straw coloured hair to tuck it behind her ears. Leonard notices a cut on her dirt-smeared forehead. "Don't call me that, you moron!" she spits out, temper flaring and not noticing the blood trickling down her forehead.

"*You're* the moron! You never do anything on your own," Simon bites out. "That's 'cause your dad made you out of spare parts back at the lab!" That line is usually reserved for Leonard and he is used to it. But Janet can't bear the insult.

"You shut up!" she screams. "I'm tired of your snotty remarks about my dad. You can keep them to yourself"

"Until he gets us all killed when the Technos come looking to take 'Doctor Frankenstein' back to his lab!" Simon mocks.

Janet rushes him, hands lashing out like raptor's talons. He jerks out of her clawing hands and tackles her. They roll among the dead leaves, hands swiping and legs kicking. Leonard can't tell who is winning but both are crying. Bobby fretfully grabs Leonard's arm and whimpers like a dog.

"Stop it! Stop it!" Leonard pleads and tries to pry them apart. He finally succeeds but only after receiving a kick in the stomach.

Simon stands up first, nose bleeding and an eye already swollen. "You bitch!" he screams down at her as she pushes herself off the ground and wipes her dirty tear-stained face. "You crazy bitch! You don't care about the others. You're just like your dad: he should have thought about us before he went and made all those monsters! Before he brought you here!"

"Go to hell!" she shrieks. "You haven't a clue what he was doing. He was feeding the hungry of the world!"

"Yeah? Meantime our toxins and viruses are killing everyone we're feeding!"

Janet stomps her foot. "You're so narrow-minded, just like a Gaian. Just like Sylvia!"

"My mom isn't a Gaian!" he screams back, as though it is an expletive.

"Well, a stupid slut, then! She's been screwing Viggo since he got her pregnant with *you*!" It came out like a rushing torrent, beyond her control. Leonard realizes that her outburst shocks her as much as it shocks Simon, who stares with his mouth hanging open.

In the frozen silence, Janet swiftly retrieves her bow, scattered arrows and quiver and gruffly commands, "Come on, Leonard. You too, Bobby." She takes Bobby's hand with a last glare at Simon who stands in confused silence, brushing off the mess from his shirt and pants. "We're going home." Without waiting for Leonard to decide, she leads them at a brisk pace, crashing through the woods, back to the farm.

"Do that!" Simon yells after them. "Go home! All the way to stinking Toronto!" He sits down on a rock to sulk and, no doubt, mull over Janet's bombshell. Leonard turns his head for a last glimpse of Simon as Janet tugs Bobby hard down the hill.

"Shouldn't we wait for him?" Leonard asks innocently when he loses sight of Simon.

"He can find his own way home," she mutters, tugging Bobby, who can barely keep up. "He led us here, didn't he?"

Leonard staggers over the rough terrain to keep up, secretly praying that Janet knows the way. It isn't Simon he is worried about. The sun disappears behind carbon-coloured clouds. The clouds scud overhead like prey, chased by a biting wind. It howls and sends the Trembling Aspens thrashing above the cousins. Their lanky poles clank like bones to the moaning wind as the leaves hiss an angry chorus.

Thinking of the sounds Bobby and he heard in the forest earlier, Leonard asks, "What if we meet a bear?" and starts to feel unsafe.

"There aren't any bears in the forest, Leonard," Janet says shaking her head sarcastically at him. "Besides, I have my bow and arrows." She taps her quiver and bow smugly. She's right, he decides, pacified by her confidence. She's good with that thing and he is a little surprised that she doesn't remind him of the four rabbits and two coyotes she killed the other day while all Simon had managed to do was wound a rabbit with his. Janet has become a skilled huntress, providing food for the families. Viggo taught her how to skin, gut, clean then joint a rabbit for cooking. Leonard tried to watch but got too squeamish when she cut it open and pulled out its guts.

Now under the dark shadow of gloomy rain clouds, the forest canopy flails in the wind, sounding like the rush of an angry river. Bobby starts to whine and refuses to take another step. As he pushes his little brother on, Leonard complains over the wind: "I told you we shouldn't have brought Bobby along."

Janet glances back with a withering look. "We went a little too far, that's all. Otherwise, it would have been alright—Bobby! If you don't start walking a little faster, we'll leave you behind!"

Real fear tightens his little brother's face as he picks up his pace. Leonard decides that Janet is a mean ogre and, thinking of her awful disclosure to Simon, he can't help a barb: "That's not what Mommy thinks. She says we're not old enough to take care of Bobby by ourselves. You and me and Simon going into the woods for the day is one thing, but taking Bobby ... she'll kill us!"

"For pity's sake, Leonard! I'm not as dumb as Amanda thinks." Janet fumes then mumbles irritably, "She always under-estimates me..."

They break through the perimeter of the dense forest to the farm as rain pelts them like missals. It instantly drenches them. As if the stinging rain warned her, Janet grips Leonard's arm to stay him and he sees her eyes harden as she throws swift glances to the open garden gate and the greenhouse whose door is ajar.

Leonard squeaks in surprise as she clamps a hand over his mouth. "Shh! Hold still!" She points to Bobby. "Keep him quiet!" She glares at him under streams of wet hair. Then she lets go and Leonard hugs Bobby to him. Both can't stop trembling. Bobby looks up at his older brother with puzzled distress. Janet snatches her bow and loads it with an arrow. As if in response to her move, the front door of the farmhouse creaks open and a large unshaven man with unwashed hair and eyes glinting of malice lumbers out. Leonard notices a dirty white band on the arm of his worn checkered jacket. A large automatic weapon hangs carelessly over one shoulder. He carries a loaded sack in one dirty hand and a large blood-covered knife in the other.

The man spots the children and Leonard hitches his breath, stiff with terror, not daring to blink the rain off his eyelashes. His arms crush Bobby to him. The man grins, baring yellow teeth, and stomps toward them. Leonard pushes Bobby behind Janet and he clutches her leg.

Janet raises her bow. The brute laughs at her and keeps coming. She draws the bow back and lets the arrow fly. It sinks into his chest and he inhales sharply, eyes bulging in disbelief. Then he charges them. Leonard cringes and feels a warmth between his legs. He's wet himself. Janet stands like a statue, her arm a blur of reloading, and strikes the brute with two or more arrows before he finally staggers, metres from them, and falls with a great thudding splat, face down in the mud.

Janet stands like an amazon and points to the

grimy white armband on his right arm. "That must mean something," she says in an earie voice of quiet control.

Gruff laughter from the barn warns the children that there are more men. Janet seizes Leonard's arm and nods hard at Bobby, instructing Leonard to grab him. They dive for cover in a small thicket by the cherry tree just as Simon breaks through the forest into the clearing. Leonard shivers, cowering in their wet hiding place, and clutches Bobby, hand clamped over his mouth to keep him quiet, as several large men march past them toward the dead man. Toward Simon. The leader stands easily a head taller than the others—at close to seven feet tall. With vulture eyes and hawk-like nose. Copious raven hair is pulled back from his forehead, forming a crest. A terrible ragged scar on his temple pulls slightly at his eye, making him look like a pirate. The strong profile reminds Leonard of a vicious bird of prey. Rain drips from his beaked nose. Even in the rain, he looks magnificently terrifying.

Simon stands not far from their dead colleague, dripping hair hanging in his eyes and bow in his hand. He stands in frozen terror, instantly realizing his predicament. The stragglers make the logical conclusion.

Simon's eyes fleetingly stray, searching hard, beyond the thugs to the sumac-buckthorn thicket where the cousins huddle. Does he see them there? Before Leonard can see more, Janet shoves him and Bobby down into the wet dirt. What he doesn't see he can only imagine as his heart slams up his throat:

blue eyes and hazel eyes locking, their anguished message of agreement. The rest he hears through the hissing rain: a slashing sound, a clipped gasp and a thud. Bobby tries to wriggle free as both boys choke in the dead leaves, inhaling acrid humus. Leonard holds Bobby fast and dares not struggle against Janet's firm hold. Hot tears sting his eyes. Janet's firm hand, now shaking, keeps him down for an eternity of smelling dirt and rotting vegetation. Of feeling the wet prickle of soil and dead leaves against his face. Of listening to men's grunts and malevolent laughter and shuffling steps that slowly wither to a constant sizzle of rain.

When Janet finally releases them, Bobby and Leonard spring up out of their living tomb of soil and rot. Leonard blinks back tears and tries not to look at the pale shape lying on the ground that was once Simon. But he stares even as gorge rises up his throat. He stares at the head that looks almost severed from the rest of the limp body. It has been almost slashed right off. Vacant startling blue eyes stare out of a frightened face. Leonard stares at the dark river of blood that covers the wet ground and somehow leaves the lifeless body untainted.

He knows perfectly well what just happened: Simon took the hit for them and Janet let him. The first and last decision they made together was one made in terrible complicity.

Before Bobby and Leonard struggle out of the thicket, Janet is already sprinting past the two corpses to the house and up the entrance stairs. She disappears through the open entranceway.

Suddenly terrified to be alone, Leonard seizes Bobby's hand and chases after her in the rain.

She emerges and meets him at the door, barring the way. Her face is sheet-white but a fierceness in her dark eyes freezes him in place. She looks suddenly all grown up.

"We need to leave ... NOW!" she barks at Leonard.

"But, Mom and Uncle Ben ... and—"

"All dead!" she says in a strangled voice devoid of emotion. She gruffly pushes both boys down the entrance stairs, not giving Leonard time to register that his mother was brutally killed along with all the other adults.

As they pass the barn, he hesitates, blinking away the rain. "But who will feed Miranda's new kittens?"

"They'll feed themselves, Leonard. They're wild cats." Then with another shove, "Now get moving!"

Just as Leonard decides that Janet is mean and he hates her, they see it and stop dead: Rishi hangs upside down from a large branch of the oak tree by the road. Hands dangle limp over his head, covered in blood. His body swings aimlessly this way then that way. Janet grabs Bobby and shields him from the site as Leonard shivers with the thought of their entrance. Had they fooled Rishi by coming in boldly by the front gate? They didn't look the stereotypic straggler; as Janet pointed out, they were well-fed and dressed, though disheveled. Had Rishi greeted them in his friendly way? Had their raptor-like leader offered some friendly greeting then slit Rishi's throat like he had Simon's? The knife is swift and quiet, the purveyor of surprise.

"Let's go!" Janet pushes Leonard forcefully past the tree and down the main path to the road. She pushes him so hard, he does a stagger-dance and almost trips into a fall. He wants to yell at her to stop pushing him around, but he's too frightened of her.

TWENTY-FOUR

GOODWOOD ROAD,
May 15, 2056: late afternoon

Dark clouds rumble and press down as a brisk wind whips across their faces. Within moments the sky opens, releasing a steady drizzle that swiftly becomes a heavy downpour. It's a cold rain. The wind beats against their faces, driving the pelting rain against them like a deluge of miniature missals. Janet drives them on, walking ahead and leading the boys like she's a sergeant in the army and they are her little soldiers. It has been unnaturally cold and raining on and off the whole time they have been walking these three days.

The road is narrow, made for one vehicle, and rutted quite deeply in some places. It beats some of the rough trails they've been on though, thinks Leonard. Janet insisted they stay away from any main roads like Goodwood Road. They've been using old equestrian trails and deer trails and small local ATV lanes as they make their way east. It will take longer for them to get to some safe place, but they will also be less likely to be found by stragglers.

The wind lashes his sodden hair across his face, forcing Leonard to keep pulling strands out of his eyes. It's a melancholy wind that howls like a lost soul, searching for its mother. It moans through the trees, creating a chorus unique to each forest. The hemlock, beech and maples sizzle and groan. The poplars and locust trees creak and clank as their lanky tops sway in the lonely wind. The swamp cedars hiss and trickle like a running brook and occasionally utter a squeak like an old door opening for a stranger. The tall pines groan and boom like cracking ice as the wind scrapes across their stiff trunks. As Leonard passes one of these magnificent trees, his hand runs across its trunk and he feels the gnarled rust-coloured plates of corky bark.

They walk in single file, usually along the middle ridge of the rutted dirt road. Where the trees are close to the road and hang over it in an arch fashion, their branches droop low, heavy with rain. Some are low enough to brush against their heads. At times they must thrash their way through a crowd of soaked honeysuckle and buckthorn that has overgrown the disused road or trail.

Bobby starts whining again, complaining that he's hungry and wants his mommy. Leonard sighs. How can he tell his little brother that their mother is dead, likely with her throat slit like Simon, along with Janet's father and the others, even cynical Lise. Leonard is suddenly reminded of what Lise said when Janet and he were hiding in the closet: *mark my words, Aloïs; when we lower our guard* that's *when things happen* ... They had all lowered their guard...

Leonard shushes Bobby, afraid that Janet will turn and bark at them with repressed rage. She's become a different person, driven, hard, and cruel. Someone he's afraid of. But someone he will follow anywhere.

He can't shake off the lurid image of Simon lying on the ground, head practically severed from his body. Blood everywhere. Telling Simon that his mom was screwing Viggo was the last thing she'd said to him before he died so cruelly. How must she feel? Leonard would be overwhelmed with guilt. Especially since she shot that straggler. Did she really have to? Because that was what incited them to kill Simon—to avenge what Janet did. Would the brute have chased them if they'd simply run away? And could she not have created some diversion when Simon appeared so he might have escaped? Forcing the cousins to remain silent as the straggler slit Simon's throat must eat into her. Leonard struggles to imagine what his cousin saw in the house; she even doubled back to grab supplies and backpacks for each of them before they started their trek. She'd pushed the boys into some bushes and told them to stay in hiding while she ran back and fetched some things, like an old compass Nicole had given her that she now consults to steer them to safety, and an old map she keeps in a waterproof baggy.

They have been walking for three days and haven't seen anyone. That's a good thing, Leonard supposes. But he keeps wondering if they're lost and wandering blind in the forest and Janet just doesn't admit it. Leonard knows she's proud like that. He's seen her and Simon go after each other because of it.

One night they found a small cabin on an abandoned trail in the pine forest and took shelter there amid some small rodents. But otherwise they slept on the wet forest floor. They foraged for wild berries and ate from what Janet had hastily packed in their backpacks: mostly junk food, which was easy to pack. Now there's nothing left and they are tired, wet and hungry. Leonard doesn't ask Janet why she doesn't hunt for a rabbit or squirrel because he knows why. He watched her try once; she'd sighted a rabbit and notched the arrow in her bow; but she couldn't release the arrow. He saw her arms shake with the effort and give up. He thinks she cried after. She didn't try again. He won't press her to hunt for them; the last time she used that bow and arrow, she killed a man. He wonders why she still carries it.

Finally realizing the significance of the direction they are going, Leonard shouts over the rain to her back, "Why are we heading east? Isn't the city west of us? We can't go all the way to the city. It's too far! We'll starve!"

She keeps walking and mumbles to the rain, without turning her head to face him, "You just figured that out now? Turdy slug...Some boy scout..." Then in a louder voice so he can hear, "We're not going to the city."

"Then where *are* we going? What about Goodwood? Can't we go there for help? There were lots of houses there and a main street with shops..."

She stops and turns, letting the boys catch up to her. She aims a scathing look at Leonard. "Seriously, Leonard? Don't you remember Aloïs telling Lise? Goodwood got torched. Right after Port Perry. Whether it was Techno-vigilantes or Gaians or just angry arsonists, there's nothing there now. So, we're going to the nearest Corporation Farm. I'm pretty sure that they are still there. They're northeast of here. They'll help us. Now, let's go!" She pushes

Leonard gruffly ahead of her and pulls Bobby into her arms, carelessly splashing through the potholes in the road.

—

The rain refuses to stop. They seek refuge in the dark forest; they eat there and try to sleep on the wet moss and slimy leaf litter as night falls. The rain continues in a steady fall, sizzling and plopping through the vegetation. The attempt proves futile and Janet resolves to continue through the night. Taking the weary Bobby in her arms, she leads them on, marching awkwardly in the dark and stumbling through the dips in the road.

When the rain finally stops as the morning sun rises over the horizon, Janet announces that they are stopping to rest. She finds a small clearing in the cedar-pine mixed forest on the edge of a swamp among the red osier dogwoods, swamp milkweed and marsh grasses. She settles against a hollow of a large willow tree with Bobby nestled on top of her. Leonard finds a spot across from them on a mossy log where he inhales the acrid-sweet smell of dirt and rotting wood. Everything is still wet; but that doesn't matter; so are they. Bobby curls up in Janet's arms and falls asleep almost instantly. Janet closes her eyes and, though Leonard doesn't think she sleeps, she leans back to rest.

He steals a long glance at her. Her straw-coloured hair tangles dark across her brow and curls over her shoulders like string. She looks oddly at peace, though he is sure her sanguine expression veils a tumult inside. He can't imagine it and wants to cry for her. Instead, he thinks of his mother and yearns for her comforting hug. What *did* Janet see in the house? How did Leonard's mother die? He so wants to know, yet he dreads to know.

A heavy mist covers the forest floor like a spider web that coats the young alders and birches. It makes the trees look like ghosts. Through its haze the rising sun appears like a fuzzy ball. A fine halo surrounds it and sends refracting rays in every direction. Its light streams through the trees, casting long shadows and streaking the air with silky lemon threads. They touch Janet's face, giving her an inhuman quality.

Out of the quiet emerges an odd sound like the distant thrum of a pneumatic drill. The drill evolves into oscillating waves of aggressive percussion, interspersed by distinctive croaks. Frogs! Hundreds of them among the reeds in the shallows of the swamp. Leonard wants to laugh and smile to himself, despite his miserable state. Their chorus, insistent and rhythmic, celebrates the morning with hope for another day. For them it's just another day.

The outlines of the pine and cedar trees gradually grow more solid as the haze lifts. Torched by the morning sun, the scaly upper trunks of the tall Scots pine glow like copper candles, even as their lower grey trunks remain in shadow. Leonard remembers his mother telling him about this tree. It's an interloper. She told him that the Scots pine was introduced to North America a hundred and fifty years ago to stabilize deforested agricultural lands, because of its hardy nature and ability to thrive in the poor soils of disturbed habitats. Like all invasive species, the Scots pine was invited in; but when it got too successful, it was vilified for the very reason it was brought in. He doesn't know why, but he feels sorry for it.

An occasional gust shakes the leaves with a stern whisper and they weep rain. Drops spatter them. Bobby whimpers in his sleep. A large maroon butterfly with ragged pale-yellow edges and bright blue spots flits around Leonard and lands briefly on his knee. He holds still and stares as it flaps its wings. Janet would say that it's a sign but he doesn't believe in any of that shite. Instead, he identifies it. It's a Mourning Cloak, probably looking for a maple tree to feed on its sap.

Janet flinches; she's fallen asleep and is dreaming, probably having a nightmare. Leonard can't imagine what and doesn't want to. To see her own parent brutally killed. How had they killed her father? Leonard's mother? Did Janet find Viggo and Sylvia naked together in secret lust while Rishi was already swinging from the oak tree? How long will it take for his body to rot off the rope? The flies must have already found him, buzzing around his head, laying their eggs—Oh, god! Let it all stop!

He cries out and jumps, realizing that he'd fallen asleep. As he blinks his eyes open, he catches Janet watching him with owl eyes. She offers a sad smile of reassurance and her eyes grow gentle like a bed of soft moss. Then, like a light winking out, the kindness vanishes. She sighs then says in a hollow voice that simmers with deep rage, "They were fools."

"Who?" Leonard asks in a trembling voice.

"Dad. Nicole. Your mom. All of them. Lise, especially."

It's as though she knew exactly what he was thinking. "What d'you mean?" he asks timidly. He knows that he will never ask her about what she saw in the house. The horrible death inside. That memory of her as she emerged from the house, standing tall like a pale goddess, will endure as if branded into his retinas. When she fixed her gaze on him with such intimidating fierceness, he knew that the old Janet was gone and he was looking at a new being.

"They forgot that a revolution is like a viral pandemic," she says, lips curling with brooding memories. "Isolation gave them a false sense of security; they thought that as long as they stayed as they were, the disease would just waste itself away and they could continue, like before. But just like a viral pandemic, revolutions morph and adapt. Lack of communication with the cities killed our parents, Leonard. They thought that no news meant they were safe. It meant the opposite. When Dad's radio died and Aloïs's computer stopped getting the internet, the news stopped. It was quiet after Goodwood went down. That should have been the warning. But the grownups didn't care or think it through. They thought that if the cities were destroyed in revolution, counter-revolution, retaliation and counter-retaliation, that was ok so long as our little hideaway—only seventy kilometers from the city—was untouched by the war there. But they should have cared, they should have been suspicious. Because it was all untrue."

Leonard remembers thinking that very same

thing the day of the tragedy. He remembers Lise's words of portent: *mark my words, Aloïs; when we lower our guard* that's *when things happen.* They even gutted his mom's car for parts to use in the tractor and field generator. They'd turned their escape car into a piece of junky scrap metal.

"Those stragglers didn't die off, Leonard," Janet goes on, wild eyes dark with intense energy. "Those quiet months of no stragglers—that was them being recruited as the fight in the cities moved to the country. They were being recruited by Gaians or Technos. Those men used to be stragglers but they're now techno-vigilantes—did you notice the white arm bands?"

Leonard nods. He had noticed.

"Gaians use green and Technos use white; I remember that from the city. These men were well-fed and well-armed. Those CARifles cost a lot. They were organized and had a plan and a strategy. They managed to kill everyone without raising a warning."

Leonard had thought of that too. The raid was no ordinary raid; these men had been taught strategy. They were part of an organized effort.

She reaches across with violent speed and grabs Leonard by the arm, making him flinch. She lets go and says in a dark voice he no longer recognizes as hers, "Their leader was no ordinary straggler, Leonard. He was a Techno and now he's a Techno-vigilante. I think I recognize him, Leonard. He was my dad's boss." She stares at him darkly and those nightshade eyes slice into him with some terrible truth. "This was a targeted kill. They were after my dad and anyone who was with him. They killed him for running away, for knowing too much, for giving away secrets ... heaven knows..."

Leonard stares at her in horror. The thought that everyone had died because of his uncle is too much to bear. He refuses to believe it. But he didn't see what Janet saw in the house. And he doesn't ever want to know. His mind strays to Simon's uncanny prescience when he suggested that they would come for Janet's father one day.

"The revolution isn't over, Leonard; it just entered a new stage of guerilla warfare."

Leonard blinks at her and wants to look away from her penetrating stare. She sounds like Lise, only far more frightening.

"We have to find that Corporation Farm before we starve or get caught by techno-vigilantes or Gaians. As far as I'm concerned, neither is good for us."

She wakes Bobby and gets up. That's the signal to start moving again. She leaves Leonard to tend to Bobby even as he whines in objection. Janet doesn't wait. She pulls on her backpack, snatches her bow, shrugs on her quiver, and is marching ten paces on the road ahead of them by the time the boys scramble out of their temporary shelter among the wet rotting leaves.

That's how they typically go too. Janet ahead by ten paces, scouting for any danger and Bobby and Leonard trudging behind in brooding silence.

TWENTY-FIVE

CORPORATION FARM, Northeast of Toronto. May 16, 2056: late morning

The heat of the day beats down as the cousins reach the top of a hill. Janet suddenly stops. Having taken to walking with his eyes on the ground, Leonard collides into her and Bobby into him. They've been trudging along this overgrown rutted road for hours since they rose in a misty dawn. With eyes cast down in a kind of daze, mind hypnotized by the sound of their boots crunching on the gravel-dirt path, Leonard had entered a doleful haze, letting Janet lead the boys without having to think.

Below, stretching for kilometers to the horizon, bathed in the sunlight of a cloudless day, lies an undulating expanse of farmland. Leonard's eyes track the rows of cultivated crops, some kind of grass or corn, that stretches out to a line of trees in the distance. Some of the large farm is untilled, with plots of natural grasses and herbaceous vegetation. Another section is bare earth. Leonard makes out workers and machines doing something in the distance.

He follows Janet's gaze to the old paved road, which they have been avoiding, that snakes beside the farm below them. A tall sturdy chain link fence with barbwire encloses the farm and stretches to the disappearing horizon on all sides. He bets it's electrified. Not too far down the slope and to the left of the main road within the enclosure are several large grey buildings, the largest one shaped in the form of a cross with its short end facing the road. A dirt path leads from the building to a gate to the main road.

To the west of the building, a turbid stream winds a languid path that snakes across the natural part of the farm, its banks crowded with dark brambles and young alder and willow. Behind it in the distance, Leonard makes out a red blot in the brown-green, rippling in the heat; some sort of machine that creeps slowly across his path of vision. He then spots several machines on the already tilled ground closer to the gate. Janet spots them at the same time.

"There!" Janet shouts and glances from Leonard to Bobby, who looks at her wide-eyed. "See? It's a Corporation Farm. I told you!"

Both boys stare at her, not knowing how to react. For a brief moment she has reverted to the cousin Leonard played spy with, eyes beaming and face radiating optimism.

Impatient with the boys less than enthusiastic response, Janet promptly hoists Bobby up in her arms with a grunt. "Come on, you slugs! This is our salvation!" Not waiting for Leonard, she struggles down the hill with Bobby toward the road they'd so carefully avoided their entire journey and makes her way unabashedly to the front gate of the Corporation Farm.

It's locked shut. Janet rattles it impatiently.

"Janet! We should go!" Leonard whispers, throwing fearful glances around them and feeling terribly vulnerable. His body starts to shiver uncontrollably.

A man emerges from the small gatepost, He holds a rifle under his arm and stomps toward the gate, looking fierce and angry as though the children have interrupted his nap—which perhaps they have, thinks Leonard. The arm pits of his sage green shirt are dark with sweat.

Bobby wails and squirms in Janet's arms. She drops him down and he scrambles behind her. Leonard fights the urge to do the same. The guard shouts belligerently for them to leave.

"Where's your foreman?" Janet demands in a steady voice. Sweat beads on her forehead. She looks a frightful sight, thinks Leonard, feeling suddenly self-conscious of their appearance. They look like stragglers.

"Get on! Go!" The guard waves his arm like we are stray animals to be shooed away. "He has no time for three starving urchins!"

"Is that him?" Janet points to a large man standing in the closest field who appears to be surveying several workers.

"No. That's Lambert, the assistant foreman. The foreman is on the other side." The guard points to an ATV in the next field over, close to one of the buildings. "That's him. Lucien Gadbois." Then he turns back to the children with a brusque sweep of his hand. "Now, go before I shoot one of you for target practice!"

Janet doesn't move. "Tell Mister Gadbois that the daughter of Ben Hardy is here to see him. He will know me!" she announces in a haughty voice.

Leonard stares at his cousin. She looks convincing but he knows better. He supposes it is remotely possible that the foreman might actually know of Ben

Hardy. Janet's father was, after all, one of BioGen's chief scientists in transgenic crops research. It makes sense that this farm is using some of his genetic creations. It doesn't mean they know the designer.

The guard seems to think it over, though. At least he isn't turning them away or shooting at them. Is she somehow convincing him despite her disheveled appearance?

"Stay!" he finally says. "I'll be back. If you're lying, I'll be using you for target practice; if not, you have nothing to worry about." Then he trudges over the muddy furrows of the newly tilled field toward the ATV where Gadbois sits like a king on a thrown.

As Janet watches him carefully, Leonard finds himself saying, "Why did you lie to him? They won't know you! He'll come back and shoot us!"

"Shut up!" she snaps back, eyes locked on the guard and the foreman on the ATV. "They won't shoot us. That's a waste of ammo. They'll just throw stones at us and chase us away like dogs."

It isn't long before the guard returns to the gate. He isn't smiling. Not a good sign.

The guard breaks out into a wry grin. "The foreman says you're a foolish girl to set such store in a name of no importance—"

Janet cuts in, "My father designed the crops you're seeding right now! If your foreman doesn't know him, he *should* and that makes *him* the fool!"

The guard laughs sharply. "I'd shoot you for that insulant tongue but it seems Mister Gadbois wants to take a closer look at you." He slings his rifle over his shoulder and opens the gate. "Come on." He points the children across the muddy field toward the parked ATV. “That’s him.”

On closer inspection, Leonard realizes that Gadbois is a fearfully large brutish man. Seated on top of the ATV like a sloven king, he oversees several huge vehicles that worm their way across the vast field, tilling and seeding. He looks far from friendly.

Janet glances back at Leonard and Bobby with an encouraging smile of victory. Step one accomplished; they’re in. Now they just have to convince the brute to let them stay.

—

Bobby and Leonard cower behind Janet as she strides with long steps toward the foreman seated atop the ATV. He slouches, legs spread apart, sun burnt belly distended under a shirt stained with grease, old food and sweat. Leonard fixes on the metal contraption strapped to his head. It hides part of his face—one of those vee-sets that Leonard heard about that connect you to AI. Vee-sets were just starting to get popular in the cities when the revolution hit. He really wanted one but his mom wouldn’t hear of it. His dad was a Gaian, after all. Leonard remembers thinking it ironic when he heard that Gaians started using Techno technology to fight the Technos and their ‘evil’ technology.

The foreman spots the children and Leonard fights from stopping his stride. The brute aims indolent eyes that flicker like a scorching flame in their direction. “What have we here?” he bellows as the children approach. “Urchins for dinner?”

Leonard shrinks back. Greasy black hair coils like knotted rope to the forman's shoulders and his umber eyes survey the children with detached curiosity. He looks like the Techno Janet just killed and in sudden panic Leonard wonders if he knows. She raises her chest, which showcases her womanly bosom, and tilts her head back proudly, exposing her neck. Her face is smeared with dirt and her hair is matted and tangled with leaves from spending the night in the forest. Backlit, her chaotic hair seems to give off its own light as though it's been dipped in heaven. How she's grown so tall!

"I'm Janet Hardy. My father designed your crops," she says. She's playing a dangerous card, Leonard concludes, thinking who killed their parents. Techno-vigilantes.

"Oh, yes, the infamous BioGen geneticist." His voice reeks of sarcasm. "But you look like a refugee from Hell, not some daughter of a Techno genius."

She says in a clear voice, "We've been walking for days. Techno vigilantes raided our farm near Coppin's Corners and killed our parents."

The foreman snorts. "Then you must be little green Gaians to barbecue on a skewer—"

"We're just *children*," she counters. Leonard has stopped thinking of her as a child since she ... he can't even form the words. But because of it, as far as he's concerned, she's all grown up now, pleading their case: "We don't belong to any side," she goes on. "We're kids. You can see that plainly enough. Please, you must help us, give us shelter. We have nowhere else to go. We work hard and we don't eat much."

Gadbois snorts out a coarse laugh. "Who said anything about keeping you? You're too much trouble: a baby and two insolent—"

"He's not a baby!" Janet defends Bobby, cowering behind her, hands clutching her leg. "He's just frightened. We can all work—we were all farmers. If you turn us away you'll be sentencing us to sure death. We'll starve!"

He gives her a wincing smile then points and barks out, "But you have a bow and arrows; you can hunt—"

"It's just for show." She throws the quiver and bow to the ground with disgust. "I don't know how to use it," she says to the ground. A lie, of course. When she returns her gaze to the foreman it is with plaintive eider eyes that shimmer anguish and darken with pain. "But those bands roaming the countryside—the Technos and Gaians—don't care who they kill. And when they find us, they *will* kill us."

Leonard thinks of Simon.

Janet's hands reach out in supplication. "Please, sir! Please help us. We'll make it worth your while..."

The foreman's expression softens and his gaze sweeps her body. Leonard doesn't like how he looks at her, like a beast with eyes that devour. It terrifies him. But she's charmed the beast with her ingenuous eyes, pretty face, and womanly allure and he takes them into his lair.

TWENTY-SIX

CORPORATION FARM, Northeast of Toronto. July 5, 2056: mid-afternoon

Leonard gazes at the flat horizon that trembles in the blistering heat. The sun beats down on him and the dry field. The workmen and women have left the shiny beetles slumbering in a neat row as they retire inside. Janet and he weed the hardpan and little brother Bobby sweeps the kitchen floor, while the workmen drink in the cool interior of the Corporation Farm workhouse and complain loudly about the poor conditions. Leonard can hear them from here. Too little food, too much work, they shout. They argue about the revolution. The breeze flings their words in his direction. "You're a God-damned Gaian, Birch. What the hell are you doing in here? Gaians are destroying our society—"

'They're saving the fucking planet, ass hole!"

"Oh, yeah? Not until they fuck all of us first with their green shit!"

"Look around you, Lambert. We're already fucked. Technos are pissing away this planet. Why do you think our boujee Techno bosses take their guns to bed with them? Come to think of it, you're a fucking Techno, Lambert. You take your gun with you to bed, huh? You scared of us lowly workers? You scared of the revolution? Maybe you should be!"

"And maybe you should be out there with your fucking revolution, Birch! Go die for the trees!"

Chairs scrape. Leonard braces himself for the inevitable brawl. He's heard those two argue before. They are actually friends, but when they are drunk they turn on each other like rabid animals. Raised voices from the others join in and take sides. Soon they will spill out of the barracks, fists flying.

Shielding his eyes from the sun, Leonard watches his cousin dance lightly over the clods of dirt to the cistern outside the kitchen for a drink of water. The flush of heat glows on her face. Ignoring the commotion inside, she waves to him and her smile draws one out from him. At some point, he's not sure when, she has become his hero. His compass and his strength. They've been here two months and been set to work like adults. Janet has kept Bobby and he going with her spirited optimism and playful sense of humor, telling stories, singing to the boys, and sharing terrible jokes. If something ever happened to her, Leonard thinks he would die on the spot.

It is her sixteenth birthday today. No one will know and Leonard wipes the surging pleasure from his mind. There will be no birthday cake. No presents. At least they are alive and safe. That is her present. The revolution, which sweeps the country like a violent storm, carves cities into rubble. It casts families across the landscape like pebbles in a rough sea. It left their entire family dead in its wake, made his cousin a killer and all three orphaned itinerants, fleeing with the hope of shelter. But Janet led them here to a safe harbor. It's hard work but they are alive and safe...for now.

A gust of wind blows up from behind, dulling the

voices inside. Leonard smells rain. The distant roll of thunder murmurs of a coming storm.

Janet raises a cup of water from the cistern to her mouth, then lets it drop and runs into the kitchen. Leonard is annoyed that she has abandoned him to tend the field alone. The workhouse has grown quiet. Perhaps the workers have all fallen into a drunken stupor. The gusts rise to an open-mouthed roar and sting his eyes with dust. Coal-black clouds chase each other like predators. After a while he walks slowly to the kitchen, shielding his eyes from the flying grit.

Hearing malicious laughter inside, he hesitates at the open door then forces himself to creep forward. He peers around the threshold then freezes, stiff with fear. His brother huddles, naked, on the floor. His dark clothes lie strewn like dried blood at a slaughter. Lambert stands over him like a vulture. His cousin writhes against the strong hold of several men. Her face is pale with alarm and her eyes dark with terror. The men laugh and rip off her clothes. The large man called Birch lurches toward her. He's naked from the waist down and growls in a drunken slur, "Here's the witch who convinced our piss-pot Techno foreman to give away our food! Well, here's some dessert for you!" He drives into her, rough and insistent, his grunts to her cries a discordant duet of lust and pain.

Lambert points to Leonard. "Look! The other kid!" They all turn. For a moment—an eternity—Leonard's eyes lock with hers. They plead for his help.

He bolts.

Her screams chase him stumbling across the

uneven soil. He hears coarse laughter and refuses to glance back. He trips on a rut and his face hits the ground. He scrambles up, tastes dirt in his mouth, and fights into a gallop. Gulping in air. Ears ringing. Eyes blurred with tears. Nose bleeding.

Run. Stinking son of a bitch. Run. Run.

He's left her there, screaming. And, because he didn't stay to hear the screams end, he knows they never will in his mind.

He hides, shivering in the willows by the stream, as the earth grows black and rain pelts him. The onslaught is over in minutes. It leaves him limp like rotting vegetation. He watches the shafts of sunlight pierce the dark mantel and touch the landscape with an unearthly glow and inhales the skunky smell of marsh plants. As the shadows of the afternoon enfold him in their skeletal embrace, he forces himself to go back to help those he's abandoned. He stumbles out of his garden of moss and grass and scuttles over the vast field, sliding into hardpan pools. The wet clay clings to his boots and weighs him down as if to challenge his resolve. He hesitates as he nears the building, straining to listen for any sounds. It's quiet.

Terrified, he creeps into the kitchen, eyes darting, and he finds her curled like a wounded deer on the floor where they've left her. Blood smears the floor and her exposed legs. Bobby lies pressed against her, asleep, and she strokes his whimpering face. She looks up at him with sunken epidote eyes. Her gaze is not incriminating, but not inviting either. He wants to embrace her, let her cry in his arms. Instead he turns his head away and stands fixed like a stone, cold and heavy.

She struggles to raise herself off the floor without his help, then scoops Bobby, quivering, in her arms. She silently pulls on the rest of her tattered clothes and limps back to the sleeping barracks. She doesn't look back to see if he is following.

—

The days bleed into months and both Bobby and Janet appear unharmed. She looks like she always did, face quietly sanguine and eyes glowing like a warm campfire. But Leonard senses a distance from her and from Bobby too. He clings to her like a rescued pet and never looks at Leonard, who now avoids them both. When she and Leonard work the fields, they remain silent and lose themselves in the hard work. When their eyes meet, he imagines reproach in hers but knows their gaze only reflects his own emptiness.

He knows they're still molesting her and probably his little brother too. He figures it is mostly Birch and Lambert, but others might also be involved. He sees the two men scheming in the mess hall and throwing churlish glances at them as they eat. Janet shares nothing with him and Bobby has grown silent. When he does talk it is only to Janet in quiet whispers, so even Leonard can't hear what they say. How he longs for one of her terrible jokes!

He's terrified to do anything, to get noticed. He wants to disappear. For now, the men leave him alone, even when he is ordered to clean the latrines, which is where he thinks the molesting occurs.

When he is not working, he crawls and hides under the porch floorboards where the dirt smells acrid and he spies on the workers from inside his dark enclave. He feels cursed in his fortune. Is he successfully evading them or do the bastards leave him alone because they sense his worthlessness? He crouches there and recites poetry like she used to at bedtime to the boys.

To see a world in a grain of sand, and Heaven in a wild flower.
Hold infinity in the palm of your hand and eternity in an hour.
He who binds himself to a joy does the winged life destroy;
He who kisses the joy as it flies lives in eternity's sunrise.

She no longer recites poetry at bedtime. She stopped singing. After kissing Bobby on the forehead and wishing Leonard a good night, she slips quietly into her bed. Within minutes, Bobby crawls into her bed, looking for comfort, and she doesn't send him away. Instead, she pulls him to her where he falls fast asleep. Leonard lies stiff under the moldy covers and listens to her hitched breathing in the bed beside him. He knows she's crying herself to sleep. He doesn't sleep. He's afraid of his dreams. Instead he imagines what it might have been like if they'd managed to reach the city.

TWENTY-SEVEN

SCARBOROUGH, Steeles Avenue.
August 10, 2056: mid-afternoon

The ruins of the city ripple in the heat like a bad movie. The sour-sweet stench of industrial pollution and wildfire smoke hangs in the air like a thick choking blanket. The sun is a dirty stringy ball in the yellow smog. Murat rakes his fingers through sweat-covered hair then replaces his metalloid vee-set and mask gear and paces the exposed second floor of the dilapidated building. His squinty gaze pans the city, which now belongs to the Gaians. Haze the color of rust lingers over phantom pools on the horizon.

"It's hot as hell," he complains, shrugging his Computerized Automatic Rifle over his shoulder. His camouflage fatigues cling to his body like something he needs to shed. "I'm dying in this stinking heat." Flies buzz noisily around his head and he flaps his gangly arm madly in the air. "Damn varmints."

Slouched against some rubble, Rick ignores him and runs diagnostics on the CARifle stretched out on his lap, verifying the output data on his eye-com. Rick's sullen face is barely visible under the vee-set strapped to his head and air mask over his nose and mouth. Murat pulls down his vee-set and mask then brings out a stick of gum, unravels the wrapper and pushes the wad into his mouth, revealing dirty teeth. Smacking his lips, he savors the mint flavor and tosses the wrapper before putting his mask back on.

"Ass hole!" Rick snaps. "Pick that up."

Murat snatches the wrapper. The rifle slips off his shoulder and clatters to the ground. Forcing on a nervous grin he scrambles to pick up the weapon then steps on the vee-set he's yanked off earlier.

"We're Gaians." Rick's finger stabs the green band on his arm. "Protectors of the Earth, ass hole." He turns back to his CARifle and mutters, "Just like a filthy Techno. . . no idea why you're doing anything."

Murat replaces the vee-set and mask on his face and slings the CARifle over his shoulder. He sags under its weight and lets his gaze stray to where the roof has been blasted away. The air smells of smoke and burning metal. He blinks away the sweat that runs into his eyes and squints at the sun, suspended in a yellow cloud of grime. "Those lousy Technos caused this heat wave. We're turning into a desert!"

Rick ignores him and keeps tinkering with his weapon.

"Hell, if it weren't for this revolution," Murat continues, "the planet would be toast already..." he trails, lost for a moment in a terrifying place. More flies buzz furiously around his head. "Get off!" he shouts and shakes his head violently. He frowns and mutters, "We better see some action soon." Murat pokes the rubble with his rifle. "When I took this post I was glad I'd be toasting any coward Technos trying to escape the city." He raises his rifle, aimed at an imaginary target and makes clicking sounds with his tongue. "When I asked the Gaian committee for this post—"

"Ass hole!" Rick spits out. "You didn't ask for it; they assigned you, Baykal."

Murat half-grins under the mask and shrugs.

Rick pulls his mask down for a moment and spits on the ground. "I know your story, turd. You hid in some hole during the whole clone siege. Waiting to find out who won so you could take their side."

Murat inhales the gum and coughs.

Rick sneers. "I figure Commander Schlange put you with me so I'd keep an eye on you. Make sure you don't run away like them other Technos." He rubs the greying stubble on his creased face and his eyes narrow to slits. "Hell, you were probably a Techno before we found you. Come to mind, you look like one of them..."

Murat's heart pounds. He follows Rick's gaze to his smooth hands then glances toward the outskirts of town and feels his throat swell. He thinks of the Canadian Enterprises shop he worked in until that man with the horse-face came and asked him all those questions about his sister, insinuating that she was leading a Gaian underground: which she was. Shivering inside, Murat says in a hollow voice, "Techno-clones murdered my sister. I could kill—"

"You could never kill anyone, ass hole. And how is it that *you* got away, huh?" Rick raises his brows.

Murat strokes his rifle with short nervous motions, face burning. Rick makes a scoffing sound and returns to his diagnostics. Murat swallows, wondering if he is going to vomit. He forces down the intrusive nightmare: his sister being bludgeoned to death in her city-center apartment the night the horse-faced man had questioned him. Murat had been too frightened to even warn her. Instead he sat in the silence of his apartment, hands poised over the vee-com, and watched the lights of the city strobe like an old movie reel across his wall. Early the next morning, a friend of Shule had vee'd Murat with the news of her death and he fled to the streets, afraid to return to the shop or to his apartment. He hid in Metro Park and watched Techno-clones, half-human and half-machine, raid house after house, ruthlessly deploying their machine-gun arms and killing everyone. Then one night the Gaians bombed the Metro Tower Complex, knocking the lights out of the city—and him. Some Gaian found him passed out among some rubble and now he's with Rick. Murat blurts, "Didn't you lose family?"

"My family are the Gaians. So are yours, ass hole. Remember that." Rick checks his vee-set and pushes himself off the ground. "Let's grab a bite. No one's coming now in the middle of the day."

Murat nods, trying to smile. The thought of food revolts him. As he turns, Murat spots a man, woman and child—all wearing masks—on the street below. They furtively make their way toward the building they stand on. "Hey! Look!" Murat points, gulping in air and chest heaving.

"Where the hell did they find time to have a kid in all this," Rick snarls. "We should shoot them all."

"Yeah! We should!" Murat cries in a shrill voice between racing shallow breaths. "All that technology and then those awful clones."

"You talk too much, Baykal," Rick says. He checks the setting on his rifle. "Let's go."

They scramble down from their perch and drop in

front of the three travelers. The woman shrieks and gathers up the whimpering three-year old who buries his face in her chest. She is young, about Murat's age, and might be pretty, except her dirty hair hangs in a tangled mat over a face gaunt from lack of food. Avoiding those saucer eyes that stare at him from cavernous pits, his gaze slides to the scrawny man. The man casts his eyes down and shoves his hands in his pockets.

"Where d'you think you're going?" Rick challenges, pointing his rifle at them. "You know there's a curfew. No one's allowed in or out of the city."

"But we're not Technos," the man stammers. His eyes dart from the green band on Murat's arm to Rick's rifle.

"You're either with the Gaians saving the planet or with the Technos who're destroying it," Rick says. "There's no in-between, ass hole."

Sensing her husband's hesitation, the woman straightens up. "Our child's so young," she says in a quivering voice. Her gaze darts between Rick and Murat. "He's starving here, in the city. He knows nothing of revolution or war. We have friends in the country who can feed him. Surely you can take pity on him and let us go. We can't be of use to you burdened with him—"

The gunshot rips through the air. Murat flinches.

The impact tears the boy from the woman's arms and splatters her face with blood. Murat's gaze lurches from Rick's CARifle to the child sailing to the pavement as the mother reels backwards. She scrambles to the dead boy—what's left of him—and falls to her knees.

"Liam!" she wails, scooping up the limp destroyed body and clutching it to her breast, rocking. "My baby!"

"Oh, God! Oh, God!" The man dances nervously around his sobbing wife.

"Shut up!" Murat shrieks, shivering adrenaline. He forces down the vile fluid that wants to come up. "Shut the fuck up!" He stabs the air repeatedly with his rifle.

"No more burden," says Rick with icy calmness. "Now, go back and do your duty for the planet or I'll have to shoot you as well."

The man seizes his wife but she refuses to get up. Her chest glistens with blood as she clutches the dead child and rocks in a kind of stupor, moaning. The father yanks her to her feet with violent force. "Sylvia! Come on!" After a terrified glance at Rick, the man pulls her like a puppet down the street.

Releasing a frantic energy, Murat sends a stutter of shots around them. "Faster, Technos! Faster!" His gaze darts fearfully to his brooding colleague. Then he laughs hysterically when one of his shots catches the man in the shoulder. The man twitches, stumbles briefly then drives on. "Th-that'll teach 'em," Murat stammers, watching their figures ripple in the distance. He avoids a glance down at the dead boy surrounded by a dark pool of blood. It already shimmers with flies. His ears ring in the crushing silence. Until the flies swarm around his head again, buzzing like a bad channel-connection.

—

"Get over here, ass hole!" Rick hisses from behind a pile of mortar and brick. Murat scrambles over to Rick, hunching up his shoulder to keep his rifle from falling off. He dives next to Rick and peers over the top of the pile. What he sees makes him shiver. Seven large figures march toward them in V-formation, brash steps clanking in unison, burnished skulls glaring in the heat. Murat fixes his stare on the leader, whose binocular eyes protrude over pale cheeks. A metal snake slithers across his left cheek, molded to his translucent skin, and slides into the corner of his mouth. Murat's eyes dart to the clone's left arm. All metal and technology, it glints menacingly. He's half-human, half-metal. A Techno-clone.

"Shit," Rick whispers in a hoarse voice that betrays fear. "I thought we got them all." He unclips the lock trigger to his CARifle with shaking hands and adjusts the eye-com of his vee-set. Murat sees fierce determination supplant the fear in the old man's eyes. "They're not taking me before I get a few ass holes first." His eyes narrow as he aims.

Murat's heart pounds and he shrinks down, trying to make himself as small as possible. Rick's rifle squeals. The leader jerks back and falls. The other Technos scatter. Rick springs up. "Baykal! Cover me!" he shouts. Shots scream out of his rifle as he darts after the fleeing cyborgs. "Bastards! You're killing my planet!"

Murat watches two more Technos fall before a clone's shot catches Rick. He twitches, spins and falls. The vee-set flies off his head and his CARifle clatters meters in front of him. A cloud of dust rises around his twisted body as Rick gropes for the rifle. "Cover me, ass hole!" he snarls through his mask. Murat trembles, stiff with fear.

The four remaining clones cock their weapons and walk toward Rick's squirming body.

"Baykal! You ass hole!" Rick wheezes. A clone steps on his outstretched arm. Rick's head jerks up. The Techno kicks off his air mask. Then he aims and shoots. Rick's head—what is left of it—falls back. The clone steps over Rick's body and looks straight at Murat. Alarm pounds in his head as Murat shrinks down and presses his shivering body against the bricks until it hurts.

He hears steps crunching toward him on the rubble. Fear shakes him like a vile wind. He wets his pants. He squeezes his eyes shut and hears shots scream like a tortured woman over his head. The bricks crack and ping, spitting grit into his face. Something large thuds beside him. His ears ring in the silence that follows. One eye squints open and he sees the Techno-clone lying next to him, weapon-arm splayed out and motionless.

Something springs onto the rubble pile above him and Murat gasps at the slim warrior with a cyborg face. The warrior pulls off the vee-set, and a thick mane of dark brown hair tumbles down around the face of an angel. She leans forward to touch his shoulders gently. "It's okay, soldier," she assures him in a liquid-honey voice. "I'm a Gaian. You're safe. I got them all." He sees the green Gaian arm band on her left arm for the first time. "I'm sorry I arrived too late to help your partner." She bends on one knee to check him for injuries. "I'm Wanda. You don't look hurt. We'll have you back on duty in no time."

His throat closes and everything shuts off.

SCARBOROUGH, Guildwood Pkwy.
August 18, 2056: late-afternoon

Murat and Wanda pick their way carefully down the ruins of Poplar Street in the rippling heat. The bombed suburban area is littered with chunks of brick and mortar, glass fragments and garbage. Shrugging to keep his CARifle slung over his shoulder, Murat adjusts his air mask and vee-set goggles. He glances anxiously behind him through the thick smog. The inversion has trapped the heat and the particulates, creating a puke yellow cloud hard to see through.

The cloying stink of diesel fuel and decaying food amid a general skunky smell of gritty air makes him feel sick. The air masks only do so much, he decides and adjusts the vee-set on his head to better see through the thick smog. Flies buzz around his head, making him twitch.

Wanda rolls her eyes. "You're not getting squirmy on me again, are you?"

He forces a smile at her under his mask and hangs his head. Wanda insisted that he join her patrol. He wonders if it is to protect him or to set him straight. He envies her drive and courage. He steals a glance along her lithe form, somehow still attractive in camouflaged fatigues, and bright green arm-band tied to her left arm. He guesses she is about his age, twenty-five, but she seems much older, more sure of herself. He focuses on her full lips, held firmly in reproach. The vee-set hides part of her face, including one eye behind the AI eye-com and goggles. Beauty and machine-beast. She doesn't seem to have a problem embracing the Techno's tools to fight a war against the Technocrat armies.

"We're just going to blow away a new hideout where some Technos are building vee-coms," Wanda says. That simple. "They're holed up in the suburban desert, out of prying eyes ... they think..." She winks at him.

Murat frowns. "Something about this makes me feel creepy," he admits. "What if the tip we got is wrong? What if it isn't a hideout and this is an ambush?"

"They aren't that organized. It's not like there's any government left. Robinson's in prison, awaiting execution. The rest of the Technocrats are dead. Their armies are mostly deserting and joining the revolution. Why do you even think like that?"

"But they say the Technos are building a new army too. Some say they've created a new set of clones even better than the last ones."

Wanda rolls her eyes. "They say, they say! Who the hell is *they*? Those clones I saved you from are original models, Murat. There's no new army and there are no new clones. Thanks to the Isabo Key, we disarmed most of them in one full swoop. That man is a genius!" she ends with a wistful smile.

She's referring to the knowledge that Commander Schlange provided about a Techno-clone kill switch from which Dr. Isabo was able to devise a device to trigger it remotely. It was basically the end of the Techno-clones. But some have remained; perhaps another model, which has Murat worried. He grumbles, "But not all of them..."

"You've got a bad attitude. We destroyed all their labs and shops. There isn't a single Canadian Enterprises or affiliate building left standing. They can't make more clones," she said. "There's just a few of the odd Techno-clones left, like the ones you had a run in with last week."

He shrugs and tries to hide the worry on his face.

Her expression softens. "Oh, Murat." She sighs, reminding him of his older sister. She didn't see it coming until it was too late either. They're sitting ducks. He glances at the green band brandished on his left arm. Techno vigilantes lurk behind every corner, just waiting for him. He's advertising himself with the stupid thing: *here I am. Come and get me*! As for the vee-sets and eye-coms and fancy CARifles — Hell, it's all Techno-equipment. Some of it he even helped put together at Canadian Enterprises. What a joke!

"Wanda, how do you know you're on the right side?"

She halts and turns, now looking really ticked off. "Listen, Murat." She plants her long legs apart and gazes at him sternly. "I'm on whatever side *she* is on because she is the goddess of the planet!" She points to a worn poster on the one good side of a demolished building. It's ten metres high and painted with the fierce face of Monica Schlange.

Wanda laughs at Murat's confused reaction. "When she recruited me, I thanked her and told her she should rename herself Gaia, guardian of the environment. She just laughed; she's so humble even though she killed more Technos than anyone I know for the well-being of the planet. Without the planet, we are nothing, Murat. Without its guardians, like Commander Schlange, we are dead." She shakes her head at him and narrows her eyes. They bore into him and he fights from shrinking back. "You can't spend your days being afraid of death, wondering who's going to win. You can't choose how you die, but you can choose how you live, Murat. That's what you take with you."

She sounds just like his sister. Shule always knew what she wanted. She'd been so sure about her choice against the Technos. He remembers her railing at him about his own indecision. "Murat, make up your mind," Shule said in her soft voice, "then live by it." Or die by it, Sis. He squints and shrugs with another glance at the huge poster. Commander Schlange's eyes seem to bore into him with purpose. He'd heard some incredible rumors about her and that scar that slashes across her forehead: the story is that she'd received it when she'd single-handedly fought off a Techno-clone: it was the very first incident of a human defeating a clone and essentially in some ways started of the revolution. Maybe if he had been recruited by Commander Schlange, she might have fired him up like she had Wanda; but she didn't recruit him and he still feels conflicted.

Sighting the house on Guildford Parkway on the bluff, Wanda checks her paper with the address and nods to herself. She begins to walk briskly. "Come on," she says, pointing to a large house behind several tall dead-looking spruce trees. "Let's get in there and blow away that filthy Techno hole for Gaia."

Murat scrambles after her, not wanting to be left behind.

Wanda slides to a window of the veranda with fluid elegance and lobs a gas bomb. It smashes the glass and explodes inside. A noxious blue gas billows out of the window. Wanda and Murat unsling their rifles, race to the door and wait. Murat's heart pounds. He breaks into a sweat. This is the part he hates.

The door flies open and a family emerges, coughing and groping with tearful eyes. First a man, then a woman, herding out two young children. Aside from her eyes widening with surprise Wanda doesn't hesitate: she opens fire, catching them all before they have a chance to scream or bolt for safety or use the weapons clutched in their hands — even the kids. Careful not to look anyone in the eyes, Murat winces as he fires. His CARifle punches gaping holes into what he knows is already a dead man.

Wanda sprints past the bodies and disappears inside for a few terrifying moments. She emerges in a rush and points forward for him to follow. Murat springs after her as she pounds down the stairs without a second look at the sprawled mass of bodies and throws herself behind a pile of rubble. The building explodes and grit and dust fly out like a spouting volcano. Wanda gets up and wipes her hands on her fatigues. They can barely see anything through the thick dust billowing up from the wreckage. Her face glowers. "Those bastards are using kids now. They make me sick."

Still, she didn't hesitate to shoot them, Murat thinks.

"Kids with guns," she says, disgusted. "God, what'll they do next?" She turns and strides down Guildwood Parkway, Murat scrambling behind her.

Murat stops shaking once they pass the abandoned high school and head toward Guild Park where the sweet pungent smell of rotting food and burning metal is welcome. She's taken him back to firm Gaian territory. Wanda turns to him, eyes wrinkling in a smile. "Do you think the Gaians will hold elections next year?" She obviously intends to set him at ease.

Murat begins to relax. "I don't know—"

A sharp tug on his left arm jerks him off his feet. A gun shot rings. His arm explodes with pain. Tears spring to his eyes and he feels sick as he falls.

Wanda crouches instantly and swings her rifle in the direction of the sound of the blast. Murat sees her take a sighting on a nearby building through her eye-com, aim and shoot twice. A figure topples. It sails down the three-story building and thuds meters away. Murat sees his white arm band: a Techno sniper.

Wanda scrambles to Murat and bends over him. Her face softens with concern. He follows her gaze to where his arm is bleeding profusely. It is torn apart at the elbow and the lower arm lies in an unnatural position. His head rings with panic as a wave of nausea overwhelms him. "It hurts, Wanda," he croaks out.

"I know," she says, touching him gently. Urgent

again, "Stay still. I'll put pressure on the wound with. . ." she looks around frantically, "this," and unties her green arm band. He grimaces with pain while she ties it on his gaping wound as tightly as possible. It isn't enough. The blood continues to seep out. Wanda dashes to the destroyed figure of the Techno sniper, removes his white arm band and returns to Murat. Blood has soaked both green arm bands, turning them black. She ties the white arm band as tightly as possible, well above the wound. It seems to work as a tourniquet.

"Come on," she commands. "I'll get you some help. You'll have to walk, Murat." She hoists him up using his good arm. He stumbles to his feet and passes out briefly. When he comes to, she is dragging him through a short cut to the main part of the park. He forces his wobbly legs to keep up with her pace. "Good." She nods, panting as she bears most of his weight. "Not much farther and we'll get you some help. There's a rally at Hanging Circle; we'll find some help for you. You can do it, Murat."

He focuses on her one eye that he sees, bright with determination, and knows that he will follow her anywhere.

They emerge into Hanging Circle. An angry Gaian mob throngs around a makeshift scaffold. They shout as the body of a Techno partisan swings slowly on the rope. A girl at the edge of the crowd calls above the general raucous. "Look!" she points to Wanda and Murat. "More Technos!"

Murat glances from the girl to the white Techno band on his arm. His stomach lurches.

The crowd rushes them like a violent storm. Wanda drops Murat and he collapses to the ground. He expects her to pelt out of there to safety but she stays with him and swings her rifle up. "We're not Technos!" she screams. "We're—"

The angry mob is upon them. Someone hits her. The rifle falls and she totters. The crowd holds her up. They tear off her vee-set and goggles and smash her face. She goes limp but they keep beating her. His body clenches like an insect pinned against a wall, watching them beat Wanda in staccato.

A dark silhouette obliterates the glaring sun overhead. A shovel, brandished high, swings down as if in slow motion. When it strikes his face, it only stings for a moment.

TWENTY-EIGHT

CORPORATION FARM, Northeast of Toronto. April 12, 2057: late afternoon

The rain pelts their backs as Janet and Leonard weed the young corn field. They are the only ones out in the heavy rain; the workers have retreated inside in a long 'coffee break,' waiting for the rain to stop, which judging from the clouds won't be soon. It's close to a year since the children came here, looking for shelter. This turned out to be something other than a shelter, particularly for poor Bobby and Janet, but it does feed them and they have a roof over their heads when they bed down.

Janet stands up suddenly and tells Leonard to stop weeding. "Do you hear it?" she asks him as he straightens. The rain spatters their faces as they listen. Leonard tries to hear something, not sure what he is listening for, except that Janet seems excited by it. More excited than he has seen her in a long time.

Then he hears it: the steady marching of feet. It comes in waves with each gust of wind.

Janet turns to him, almost giddy with excitement. "Do you think?"

He wonders what she means. Could it be the Gaian army that they've heard rumors about? Could it be them descending on the farm? His cynical mind then wonders why that is a good thing. Technos, Gaians, they're all the same to him when it comes to being treated like a human being. Although, he has to give the Gaians the benefit of the doubt. His conclusion is only based on how the Technos and Techno-vigilantes treated them. Maybe the Gaians are of a more noble breed. His father was one, after all. He seemed to think they were worth fighting for, dying for. Then again that brute Birch who keeps molesting Janet is a Gaian supporter...

Janet seems to think this Gaian army is a good thing, because she's dropped her guard to let hope in.

"Let's go see what's happening!" she says, face lighting up like Leonard hasn't seen in a long time.

"We shouldn't," he objects meekly, still reluctant and suspicious. The last time they lowered their guard, their family was brutally killed.

"Come on!" She runs to the gate without waiting for him and doesn't look back. He drops his shovel and runs after her, more out of habit than anything else. When he catches up to his impetuous cousin, she's already leaning against the high fence, face pressed against the wire crossings, looking eagerly down the road. Listening. He is still panting from his run, but he can hear it too. "Look!" She points. At the same time, he spots it too: a convoy of men and woman on foot, walking abreast and trailing up the road. A few are on horseback. Janet seems to ignore that they look ragged, soaked through and tired. Only the ones on horseback are in raingear. The commanders, he guesses. Among the marching men and women, he recognizes some old government uniforms with lapels torn off and green Gaian armbands wrapped over their army stripes; recent converts to the rebel army. They march down the farm lane from the main road in silent determination. No smiles. No victorious singing like he'd imagined from their saviors.

Undaunted by their shabby appearance, Janet turns to him with excitement. "I told you they'd come to liberate the farms! They've even recruited the government army!"

She runs to the gate and Leonard panics at what he thinks she is going to do. "Wait, Janet!"

She ignores him and opens the gate.

They stand at the open gate, expecting the troop to stop and greet them; one way or another.

When the first men reach the two cousins, frozen smiles etched on their faces, one of them pushes the children violently aside into the mud and laughs. "Craven bourgeois! They have only children to defend their fort!"

The two struggle to their feet as the Gaian soldiers trudge by. They have to scramble out of their way or get trampled. As they do, something rears behind them with a straining sound of objection. A horse and rider! They've frightened a horse. It rears up and throws the rider. The rider falls with a hard splat that makes Leonard wince. He shivers as the rider gets up and stomps toward them like a predator. Janet stands her ground and grabs Leonard's arm tightly to keep him from cringing back.

The rider is a women. No, an ice queen. She's imposingly tall with an athletic build and an austerely beautiful face framed by long dark hair, held back in a ponytail. Leonard guesses her age to be in her thirties or so, younger than his dad if he was alive anyway. A badass scar slashes across her forehead, confirming her as dangerous. She must be some kind of commander, given that she's on horseback and dressed in raingear. As the troop continue through the gate, marching past them, the ice queen looks the children over with a frown and narrowing coffee-coloured eyes. Rain spatters her face and Leonard finds himself focusing on the scar on her temple, how the raindrops are caught by it and run down along it then stream down the side of her face to her chin. He starts to shiver uncontrollably. But as suddenly as she turned to them, she turns away—releasing him from his torpor—as if she's no longer interested in them. Like a lithe ballet dancer, she bends down to fetch her rifle without stopping and walks with springing steps to her horse.

Janet calls out, "We opened the gate!"

The woman stops and Leonard wants to kick Janet. The ice queen turns to look at them again and now studies them with renewed interest. She approaches. Leonard's shivering returns. "What are you doing here?" she says in a clear alto voice. "The Corporation Farms don't allow children."

"We're not children," Janet says too quickly then adds, "Not anymore."

Leonard wants to cringe at her rebuttal, thinking it will anger the woman. But the ice queen studies Janet with curiosity instead and her lips curl with a sardonic smile. "You might be right about that," she says thoughtfully. "How did you get here?"

"Techno-vigilantes killed our parents and friends on the farm. We walked here from Coppin's Corners,"

Janet says evenly. "We convinced the foreman to let us work here for safe lodging. But they have been cruel to us."

"No doubt," the ice queen says, umber eyes narrowing at Janet. "What are your names?"

"I'm Janet and this is Leonard."

The ice queen suddenly looks hard at Janet. Almost as if she suddenly recognizes her and something has clicked into place for her. Then she aims knife sharp eyes at Leonard and he melts in fright.

"The Techno-vigilantes ... Were they led by a very tall man with a hawk-like nose?"

"Y-yes," he stutters out. "How?..." he lets the question trail.

"Let's just say his reputation precedes him," the ice queen says with sardonic humor and adds, "I'm Commander Schlange of the Gaian army."

Janet blinks suddenly and stares. "*Monica* Schlange?" Even as she blurts that out, Leonard senses Janet stiffen with regret and fear. But she commands herself not to show it. Something has triggered her fear and he recognizes that look of regret, like she realizes that she revealed too much. Like the time she impetuously blurted out to Simon about his mother's sexual trysts.

The ice queen smiles with sardonic humor at some inner understanding. "So, you are the daughter of Ben Hardy, the unfortunate scientist at BioGen."

Leonard sees Janet involuntarily swallow. This is the connection she regrets the ice queen making.

Then the ice queen turns to Leonard again with that potent stare, gripping him like prey with lethal eyes the colour of mineral pitch. "That makes you Leonard Crane, son of Armon Crane, the Gaian traitor."

Leonard cringes at her undue attention on him. He's unable to move, terrified of what she said about his father. Why did she call him a traitor? She releases him and lifts her gaze to the darkening sky then lets out a wicked laugh of ironic amusement. Then she adds cryptically to herself, "Eric, you bastard, you keep following me, even to the ends of nowhere...*Everybody wants to rule the world...*" She turns back to the two cousins and abruptly commands, "Take my horse to the stables." Slinging her rifle over her shoulder, she leaves thm at the gate and joins the train of men and women marching on foot into the farm.

By now there is a commotion by the main building. Corporation Farm workers and Gaian soldiers mix in a loose crowd, shoving, arguing and shouting but also talking and laughing like old friends. As Janet and Leonard lead Schlange's horse to the barn, they catch some of it as allegiances are quickly formed. It seems that there are more Gaian supporters than previously known at the Corporation Farm. That makes sense to Leonard; if he was one of the workers, he wouldn't make his Gaian support known to this bunch, run by Technos. Birch is a rare bird in openly showing his Gaian support; but he has a small cadre to protect and fight for him during those nasty brawls, and Lambert, his superior, is an odd ally given he and Birch share a taste in molesting children.

Within moments, Brutus—as Janet dubbed Foreman Gadboiss, crambles ungracefully to the top of an ATV tractor. Panting with his effort, he shouts to his men, already mixing with the soldiers in the rain. "These Gaians offer you freedom but they come armed with our own Techno weapons to enforce it! Weapons they stole from us! They deceive you! They offer better conditions for you but they don't say how that can be achieved. The work still needs doing. They offer empty promises that—"

A loud bang rings out and Brutus topples from the tractor into the crowd.

Schlange leaps up like a cat to take his place. She waves her CARifle in the air and shouts in a clear commanding voice, "I'm Commander Schlange of the Gaian Army! Consider yourselves liberated!"

Many in the crowd cheer.

"We're not using these rifles on honest workers; only on capitalist chauvinist pigs like that one! You too can wield a weapon like this if you prove worthy. We don't offer you better conditions. We're too honest for that. Indeed, we see much work ahead of us. But you will know that you are free. You work now for yourselves—not for some rich capitalist Techno pig." She raises her rifle in a flourish. "Robinson is dead!"

More in the crowd cheer.

Leonard notices that all the workers and soldiers are cheering together. Janet and Leonard trade a knowing look. It's obvious that Robinson had no friends on either side of the revolution.

Schlange adds, "Robinson was executed by a Gaian tribunal earlier this morning. The Technocratic dictatorship is officially dead. You are now free!"

The cheering grows wild and Leonard realizes

that Brutus is being beaten and stomped to death by the crowd.

"Come on," Janet urges, pulling at the horse. "We need to find Bobby and get out of here!"

"But, why?" He's confused. "Isn't this what we were hoping for? To be freed from those cruel Technos?..." *...The same ones who've been raping you?* He adds to himself. Then again, he considers that the brute who's been assaulting her is a Gaian supporter. The whole thing is all too complicated, he decides.

"It's because she knows who we are!" Janet bites out. Once they are in the stable and have tethered the horse, she explains, "When those Techno-vigilantes came to the farm...they..." she hesitates and Leonard realizes with a feeling close to panic, that she is steeling herself to tell him what happened in the house. He doesn't want to hear it. He *never* wants to hear it. "What I saw in the house—"

He clamps his hands over his ears and clenches his eyes shut.

She grabs his arms and wrenches them violently down then snaps at him, "Listen! You have to hear this!" She launches with new resolve, "When they came into the house, they killed Father last. They forced him to watch them violate his sister—your mother—and Nicole, and torture the others. Then they killed him last."

"H-h-how d-did you...?" How did she figure that out? He starts to shake.

"God, Leonard! You really want to know the details? Mostly, it's motive. They wanted him to watch."

He stares, horrified, at her. She stares back at him with intense eyes the frightening colour of a stormy sea swell. He has to look away. He's so frightened. Of that ice queen. Of the mob stomping Brutus to death. But mostly of Janet, now staring at him with beryl eyes that cut into him with a truth he's not ready for.

She releases a huge sigh. "Remember I told you that I thought I knew the man who killed Simon? Well, I'm sure of it now—thanks to what that Gaian commander said. The vigilante leader was my father's boss at BioGen. Eric Vogel. I remember seeing him when I visited Dad's lab several times before it burned down. Some say Vogel was responsible for releasing that awful virus that killed half the world. I think they're right. When Dad's lab blew up, something happened. Your dad was killed but my dad wasn't. Vogel disappeared a while before but some people think he was secretly with the Technocrats the whole time until he turned into a Techno-vigilante and came to our farm and killed everyone. This was some kind of revenge for something Dad did or didn't do. Or just for knowing too much and abandoning Vogel's company. Remember, how we left the city in a hurry?"

Leonard nods vigorously, still shaking.

"Either way, it was some kind of pay back. Maybe because your dad was a Gaian and Vogel might have thought my dad was a traitor. Or 'cause my dad survived that explosion which was meant to kill him." She throws up her hands. "I don't know!"

"OK, b-b-but..." he stutters out, boggled by her revelation but somehow managing to need context for their current situation. "What does that have to do with the ice queen knowing who we are?"

"The *who*?"

"Commander Schlange."

"Because the ice queen was Vogel's lover."

There's a long moment of silence as it all comes together.

"Shit..." he breathes out. Then he wonders how a Gaian can be a lover of a Techno.

"Yeah, exactly ..." she says, as if agreeing to his thoughts. "Didn't you hear her use his name just now? And she described him perfectly, Leonard!"

He nods. He had wondered who this Eric was that she'd referred to in her earlier comment to herself. She called him a bastard. Maybe they aren't lovers anymore, but they're still connected; like Viggo and Sylvia were when he went up north for so long before they got together again and made Simon...

"Come on." Janet pushes him on. "We need to get Bobby and hightail it out of here while we can. We can use that mob out there as a diversion and hope like hell that she's too busy with all that to notice that we're gone."

Leonard nods, refusing to worry about where they will go.

They race to the cookhouse where they find Bobby washing the floor. When Bobby sees them, he rushes to Janet and hugs her, burying his face in her clothes. He murmurs into her chest, "Who are those mean people?"

"Just mean people, Bobby," she responds, stroking his head. "But we're leaving. Only, be quiet so nobody notices us, ok?"

Bobby nods. "Are we going home?"

Janet glances at Leonard, pond-green eyes betraying anguish. "Something like that," she says to him, forcing a smile. "Now, be quiet!"

The crowd is still sufficiently distracted for the children to reach the stables unnoticed. Looking on from the stable window, Leonard watches the workers bully their former employers.

Janet takes the reins of the Commander's horse and leads it to the stable entrance. She turns to Leonard. "Take Bobby's hand and follow me closely. When I jump up, you hand Bobby to me and climb on behind me. Then hold on tight because I'll try to get us into a gallop."

The rain stops as they make it to the gate, which is unguarded for now. Janet mounts the horse and Leonard hands Bobby over then clamors on. As he does, he noticees the commander looking their way. "She sees us!"

Janet kicks the horse into a cantor and Leonard hangs on to her with difficulty.

Within a few moments, the commander is riding next to them on another horse. "Stop the horse!" she commands.

"I can't!" Janet shrieks. Leonard realizes that she means it and she's not in control of the horse. Janet has lost the reins and is clutching the horse's mane. He is hanging onto her and Bobby tucks into Janet for dear life.

The commander comes beside them and leans over to grab the rein that Janet dropped and slows both horses to a stop.

Despite their failed plan, Leonard feels great relief.

The commander pulls their horse around and leads them back to the stables. When they reach the stables, she says in a tone of rough reprove, "Don't think that you're worth running after. The horse is too valuable to lose to a couple of horse thieves—"

"We didn't steal it!" Leonard stutters out then amends, "that is we..."

Janet finishes for him. "We were only borrowing it—to get to the city."

"*The city*!" The commander looks suddenly amused and lets out a sardonic laugh. "What would three urchin brats do in the city?"

"We have friends," Janet lies hastily. "Please let us go. We'll send the horse back. You can depend on us."

"Friends!" the ice queen bites out and follows with a sharp laugh. She spits out, "Your friends are dead." She shakes her head at Janet. "You're a very foolish and impudent child."

Leonard's heard people call her that before.

After they dismount and walk the horses into the stables, the ice queen stops and says with resolve, "You're better off here, under my protection. You'll have food, shelter and work to keep you busy and out of mischief. *Welcome to your world...*" With that strange last remark, she hands the reins of both horses to Janet, trusting that she will tend to both horses and not try to run away again. When the commander reaches the stable doors, she turns and adds ominously, "Don't try to escape again. I'm stationing a guard at the gate with explicit instructions to shoot any deserters—no exceptions. Children included."

Then, with a few long strides, she's out of the stable and out of sight, steps squishing on the sodden ground.

Janet looks at Leonard with dull eyes. He can tell that the fight has been kicked out of her and she's resigned to their lot, whatever this new regime brings. When she's not hopeful, he's not hopeful. He already feels his energy drain away.

"I thought we were going home," Bobby pipes up, reminding them of his presence.

For some reason Janet finds it all suddenly amusing and bursts into laughter. It's probably just the laughter of exhaustion, Leonard decides. But he can't help joining her infectious laugh. He's missed her laughter. And it sure beats crying.

"This is home for now, Bobby..." she finally says ruefully and reaches out to pull Bobby into a hug. Leonard stands there in wooden silence, wishing she would do the same to him.

—

That evening, Monica enters the mess hall and takes her place at the head table. Refreshed from a long hot shower and dressed in dry Gaian army fatigues, she faces many rows of workers, seated at long tables and ready to eat the steaming food set before them. Her second in command, one of her Black Guard, announces in a loud clear voice of authority, "All rise! Commander Schlange of the Gaian Army!"

A thunderous scraping of chairs accompanies the workers all rising to their feet and looking at her with various looks of expectation. She surveys them quietly, eyes slowly sweeping the room. Some look grave. Others sublime. Yet others nervous. And then others—perhaps most of them—veil their emotions beneath blank looks. All wonder what this day brings.

After her brief appraisal of the workers, Monica says with quiet authority, "From this day onward this farm will no long be called the Corporation Farm. It is Commune Farm-5, the fifth farm that we have liberated so far. Our war with the non-partisan traitors is not over, so I depend on your loyalty and diligent service to help us finish it. There is no room for chaos and anarchy. Therefore, until the crisis has passed and the subversive forces have been completely crushed, you will submit to provisional rule. As your appointed leader, through the provisional Gaian government in Ottawa, I will exercise my right to engage in whatever measures will be necessary to keep this farm in operation. If I or my subordinate commanders see any sign of dissent, we will show no mercy in dealing with them. You will obey everything my Black Guard tell you—they are my immediate subordinates." She glances briefly along the perimeter and the corners of the large mess hall, where her Black Guard, dressed in all-black and armed with CARifles, are stationed. "Failure to comply will end in punishment, which may constitute expulsion from the work camp, or worse. The state will tolerate only honest workers. Laziness is the mark of the petty bourgeois capitalist. So, see that you work hard for yourselves and the planet!" She grabs her cup of wine and raises it. "To Gaia!"

"To Gaia!" shouts the room.

Monica sits down, followed by the workers and another thunderous scrape of chairs. She spots the three children, seated near the back, and realizes with a smile to herself that she's been searching the room for them.

The older boy lifts his doe eyes to meet her gaze with an earnest look that mixes suspicion with hope. But, the girl, Janet Hardy, avoids her omnioptic gaze; she makes a point of looking at the food she picks at. Monica continues to study the girl, finding herself fascinated. Something restless flickers behind the girl's eyes. An anguish she curbs beneath a fierce determination. Monica suspects the girl was mistreated, but not broken by it. She showed courage and resolve today. Janet Hardy is no mealy-mouthed lackey like her father was. She carries warrior blood inside her; perhaps it comes from her mother, Monica decides. The girl and her two cousins were dealt a miserable hand, fraught with terrible irony, and Monica acknowledges having played a part in that terrible irony. First by involving Hardy's wife in her espionage, then by indirectly pointing Eric to Hardy's family farmstead near Coppin's Corners, and then by not killing Hardy in the BioGen explosion. If she'd killed Hardy that night, his entire family would likely have lived.

She remembers that smoggy night on the street as the burning building gave off acrid fumes of sulfur and burning plastic. Despite Hardy's repugnant servile nature, Monica could not bring herself to shoot him. He'd suddenly reminded her of the cows she looked after with her father. Vulnerable, ingenuous, and protective of their young. She let him go back to his family. Then Eric tracked him and dispatched them all like a cruel predator. Monica knows it was Hardy that Eric wanted to extinguish—just for getting away. That's Eric's style. Eric and his miserable straggler vigilantes destroyed that little farmstead out of wicked *schadenfreude*. Monica sighs at the ego-driven tragedy and mourns the price children often pay for adult follies.

A corporation farm like this one had destroyed Monica's own family when she was thirteen. It killed her father. It turned her mother into a whoring drunk. It ripped Monica's innocence out of her and bled out her naïve faith in humanity, drop by drop.

Janet's feral eyes finally meet hers and Monica experiences a flash of delight as she locks stares with the girl. They are the fierce eyes of a wounded animal, Monica considers. Their colour shifting with the light from siskin to the deepest green with flecks the colour of fertile soil. Moved by inexplicable compassion, Monica resolves to ensure the children's safety. Moments later she recognizes that it isn't the girl's humanity that arouses her compassion; it is her animal honesty.

TWENTY-NINE

COMMUNE FARM 5, Northeast of Toronto. April 21, 2057: early evening

It's just after supper and Janet and Leonard work in sullen silence in the co-ed washroom. Bobby is sick in the infirmary, so one of the Black Guards has ordered Leonard to take his place. Janet kneels on the floor, scrubbing, and he cleans the toilets. They both think the Black Guard cruel to order them to work now; they've both been working the fields and the barns all day and the evenings are meant for rest. But this is just normal; the work schedule is the same as before. Unfair. The only thing different is that he, instead of Bobby, cleans the latrine; usually Leonard is ordered to the kitchen to wash dishes.

In fact, little has changed for the children since the liberation. Aside from a change in regime, their chores and their treatment hasn't changed. The workers do what they did before. Even the bosses have mostly remained the same—regardless of allegiance to Gaian or Techno—all left to prove themselves under the new regime and the stern oversight of the Black Guard. And with their presence, Leonard notices a lingering veil of muted restraint in the men. As if Commander Schlange's judging eyes inhabit the very corridors as the men go about their work. As if they are all in fact being surveyed; which, Leonard considers, is likely. The Black Guard are just another version of a Techno-clone, he decides; they too see everything and dispense order with ruthless precision.

This is the new regime. Leonard overheard the chatter in the mess hall and elsewhere; the new Gaian government in Ottawa has established a Triad of provisional rule, made up of three Triad Commanders: Damien Vogel, Christian Isabo, and Monica Schlange, their commander at the farm. The workers have been trading rumours that the government intends to create a committee of deep ecologists, called the Circle, who will, in turn, oversee the mayors of cities. Leonard overheard Birch call the cities Icarias. He thinks of the myth of Icarus and wonders at the choice. Are they dooming them all to the fire of redemption?

So, Janet and he clean in silence and dream of better times. His are of home with his parents and little brother before his dad was killed in the revolution. He wonders what Janet dreams about. She also hasn't changed much since the liberation. With the exception of the day the Gaians came to the farm, when Janet displayed a reckless optimism, she has reverted to her guarded reticence and silence—which includes not talking to him. He tells himself that he deserves it and accepts it.

The door suddenly bangs open and two men barge inside, laughing, arguing and swearing. Leonard's heart plummets. It's Birch and Lambert, and they are already drunk. The door slams behind them and the penny drops for Leonard: this is why Bobby is 'sick'; it's that time in the month. Now it's finally Leonard's turn to get raped, and he finds himself resigning to it. After so many months of waiting and dreading this torture. He deserves this too. Lambert lurches to the toilet he's cleaning and pulls out his dick to take a leak. He turns to Leonard with a dirty laugh, spilling urine carelessly on the boy. Leonard swallows down his gorge, preparing for violence. When he's done pissing, Lambert points his dick suggestively at Leonard. He cringes back, trying to be brave. Lambert drawls to Birch, "I think this little slutboy would love to suck my cock, eh?" He follows with a churlish laugh.

"Go at it, Lambert!" Birch growls at him and seizes Janet's arm. "I've got Missy here!" He pulls her gruffly off the floor. She inhales sharply and cries out.

"Hey," says Lambert, suddenly sobering up. "Remember the order, Birch. Commander Schlange's explicit orders are *not to touch the kids*—"

"Those orders are for Technos, ass hole!" Birch grabs at Janet's clothes, already pulling them off. Janet struggles to get free and he strikes her in the face. Both Janet and Leonard cry out. Birch laughs, dirty teeth snarling. Leonard's heart pounds like it wants to escape his body as he decides he won't just stand and watch the brute rape his cousin. *This time,* he'll do something. He prepares his body to pounce on the brute who crows, "I'm a Gaian. I do as I please—"

The door bangs open.

"No. You don't." The ice queen stands at the door, looking taller than Leonard remembers her. Eyes flashing with sparks of lightning. She's imposing, dressed in black leather jacket, jeans and black boots. She looks like she's just come in from a ride, bringing in with her the fresh scent of wild grass. The scar on her right temple, lighter than the rest of her forehead, is a fierce beacon. Leonard focuses on the sidearm in her hand. She raises it and shoots Birch in the head.

Birch lets Janet go and she stumbles back as he falls with a loud thud on the floor. Dark blood pools around his head on the floor Janet just cleaned.

The ice queen's almost black eyes flick to Lambert and she tips her head slightly toward the door. It's signal enough for him to skedaddle. Lambert scrambles past Schlange and out of the washroom like a scared rabbit. Leonard hears him pelting down the hall.

The ice queen glances between Janet and Leonard with probing eyes. Does he imagine it? A brief instant as those umber eyes grow gentle and deep with a flicker of compassion? Then it's gone, if it was ever there.

"*Welcome to your life...*" she says casually. "*Everybody wants to rule the world.*" Then more gruffly, "Clean this up," and leaves them.

Still panting from her struggle, Janet studies the dead body of her rapist then turns to Leonard. God knows how many times he had raped her in the last eight months. But not today. Not today! A strange little smile tugs her lips up on one side and her eyes shine with hope. "I guess things really are changing here."

She takes two long steps and seizes Leonard in a strong embrace. As he sinks into her arms for the first time in eight long months, she gives in to the tears she never shed in front of him since that initial molestation. Convulsive tears well up from deep inside, where she'd buried her pain. But these are tears not of anguish at the cruel hands of the dead brute on the floor—they are tears of relief that it is all over. For her and for little Bobby. The two cousins both heard what Lambert acknowledged and what the ice queen ensured (thanks to her impeccable surveillance system): that no one is to touch the children. Leonard is incredibly grateful. Then, why is it that the only thing he can think of is how the ice queen stole his last chance to redeem himself? She blasted in like Wonder Woman before he could pounce on Janet's assailant and prove himself. He knows that he could not have accomplished what the ice queen did, but he still feels cheated.

THIRTY

COMMUNE FARM 5, Northeast of Toronto.
September 9, 2057: mid-morning

"You forced him to beg for mercy, then you shot him in the head! In front of the whole *verdammt* world! *Guter Gott*!" Damien shouts across the computer screen that faces Monica. Even Damien's cat, Gretchen, mimics his disquiet by standing stiffly on his lap, refusing to lie down.

Monica slouches at her desk in a show of insouciance. She has taken to skipping regulation dress protocol by wearing her riding clothes—jeans, crisp white shirt and black leather jacket and boots—feeling invincible and beyond reproach. She lifts her head, chin pointing at Damien in a pouting scowl. "Fairweather needed to die. The sacrifice was necessary. And we needed to make a show of it for the public. Show him up for a coward and a Techno lackey. Shut this unfounded optimism down."

"We're killing ecologists now?"

She leans forward, face close to the screen with a fierce glower. "You know why, Damien. His brand of ecology is dangerous to what we need to do—prepare everyone for life inside, safe from the harsh climate and these raging toxic storms. It's only getting worse and you know it. I know you saw the latest vids from out west. The choking smogs in Vancouver that killed thousands ... We need everyone onboard Project Icaria. All that work to seal buildings and create new self-enclosed systems needs everyone's full support. There's no room for thoughts about a global cybernetic control system that promises something the environment won't be delivering for a long time. You heard the argument Techno-followers are making on social media. They're using Fairweather's damned stable chaos theory to predict that the Earth will just adapt and recover and we can go on doing what we've been doing for centuries—without sacrifice. Just like the Gaia Hypothesis before that. That is so wrong!"

"But calling him a dystopian? What the hell is that? Are we making up words now?"

"It's the opposite of utopia—"

"I know what dystopia means! *Verdammt,* Monica! The Earth *will* recover..."

Yes, but not necessarily the way humanity would like, thinks Monica. *And not with us there...*

To her silence, he adds, "This will all turn around and be safe for us... we *will* go back outside..."

Should we? thinks Monica. "Not likely for centuries, Damien. You know what our own scientists say."

"More like decades, Monica. Didn't you see Tsutsumi's report?"

"And didn't you see Yevstappi's report? Her projections were even based on an optimum scenario of not only achieving zero GHG emissions within five years but also significant decarbonisation through key mitigation measures such as clean energy and enhancing carbon capture. Before the norming is the storming and nature is set to storm for a while."

"Well, it's all up for debate," he concedes, waving a hand with frustration. "We just don't know enough about all the variables and how they are working and changing with climate. Plus there are ways we can use technology to enhance our abilities to be outside—"

"That sounds an awful lot like Techno talk, Damien," she cuts in, voice sharp with warning. "Tread carefully... Do you remember the eight Principles of Deep Ecology? Sessions and Naess were prescient when they gave us the Fifth and Sixth Principles that need addressing: this excessive human interference, primarily with technological, economic and ideological structures."

He firms his lips at her accusation and nervously brushes the length of his long nose. "I just can't abandon outside..."

She almost smiles at his nervous reaction and knows she has him on the defensive. For some reason, he no longer sees the bigger Deep Ecology picture, particularly given Eric's virus attack and the unforeseen compounding effects of climate change and industrial pollution. It's time to segregate the blight of humanity from the healing planet.

"What's your point, Damien?" she snarls out.

"I'm saying that we must not abandon hope of going outside."

"Of course not, but we must maintain public support for Project Icaria. Keep the public on our side and productive. We don't want to spread false hope; that's what this execution is all about. Stopping the spread of false hope. The public must believe that the best choice *right now* is to seal the inside and stay inside because the environment may never be right for us outside...Because we don't know when it will be." More like the other way around, she thinks scathingly. She knows humanity will never be right for the environment. Seeing the crack in Damien's defenses, she adds with a pursed-lip smile, "So, we make an example of this idiotic use of this theory that undermines the utopia we are building. We do this to keep the people happy and on track, willing to build a world inside. To keep us safe from a harsh and angry environment that's only getting angrier..." *And keep the environment safe from us.*

Damien sighs and looks away from the screen at something in the room. Is Isabo standing there, advising him? Monica hasn't seen either of them in close to a year. She's been out in the field securing territory and running the experimental farms, while they've been cavorting in Damien's warm bed the whole time. They probably don't miss her and those wonderful threesomes. Damien nods, as if to himself; but she knows that Isabo has given him a signal to agree. God! He's already getting old and tottery, relying on Isabo to make the hard decisions. Isabo, who knows nothing of strategy!

"Alright," Damien says with a forced smile of truce. "I see your point, Monica. You're right. Carry on, then." He switches off abruptly. He's not happy. He doesn't need to be, she decides, and leans back in her chair with a long sigh of satisfaction.

She reaches down to the locked drawer of her desk, unlocks it and pulls out a small worn dog-eared paperback. She draws her fingers across the creases of the book then opens to the title page and reads

Eric's messy scrawl: *To my beloved Monica. Here's to a brave new world! love, Eric.*

Perhaps in the end, Eric is right about everything, she considers and slips *Walden Two* back into the drawer with a sardonic smile. Eric is right about it all; except for one thing. In his own hubris, the bastard never abandoned faith in his human self; his way was a cheat—create malleable drones through behaviour engineering. Feeble-minded drones he despised, which would make it easier for him to dispassionately manipulate them, subjugate them, execute them. Monica has a more appropriate and efficient way. "Let them grow up with a lie. They don't deserve the truth," she murmurs to herself. She'll save the world by keeping humanity from it.

Slamming the computer shut, she gets up and leaves her office.

—

After a moment of silence, Leonard slips out from his hiding place behind the large credenza and large planter. As instructed by the Black Guard, he had been cleaning Schlange's office in her absence. But when she suddenly entered the outer room, and knowing she hated anyone being in her office, he slipped quietly into his hiding place. He had gotten good at hiding and staying quiet. What he heard has his heart racing. What does she mean by 'building a world inside'? Her last comment to herself tells all. Leonard wants to share what he learned with Janet, but she doesn't listen to him. They don't talk.

THIRTY-ONE

ABANDONED CABIN, Kawartha Lakes Region. December 25, 2057: sunset

A light snow is falling in the clearing of the swamp forest as Monica steps lightly toward the front door of the log cabin. Her boots seem to crunch the snow far too loudly in the silent forest for her liking. It's that time of the day when nature stills as it approaches the verge and a hush falls on everything as if waiting. She glances briefly up to where the cedar tips now glow as if dipped in the darkening pink and orange sky of sunset. The odd pine trunk lights up orange like a candle on fire. Even the snow, where touched by the setting sun, blushes with a pink glow.

Monica carefully opens the unlocked door of the small log cabin and quietly enters. Predatory eyes quickly sweep the room, taking in the fireplace where a small fire crackles, an old cloth sofa, chairs and small wooden table over a worn red and grey patterned rug. A mug of coffee sits on the table beside an open pocket book, spine up. It's *Treeline* by Ben Rawlence. She thinks it odd that this is the very same book that Damien Vogel was reading when she first met him at that pub in what was still Toronto, so long ago. The owner of the coffee and the book isn't here. She feels the cup; it's still warm. She steps furtively to the kitchen in the back. The back door is ajar and she sees fresh tracks in the snow leading away. *Gotcha*!

Ditching caution for speed, she dashes outside

and spots a dark figure struggling through knee-deep snow. He's making for the dark line of trees. In the short time she's been in the cabin, the sun has completely set, dipping the trees into inky darkness and leaving an intense orange glow in the sky overhead. Within seconds, she catches up to him and recognizes Eric's lanky form. He's dressed in good slacks and shoes. She grins with triumph. He must have heard her and made a dash for the safety of the forest without putting on a coat and boots. Who did he think he was running away from? Probably a Gaian assassin. Her.

At the forest edge, he dares to glance over his shoulder and, recognizing her, stops suddenly and releases a hysterical laugh of relief. "*Schnucki*! Are you my Christmas present? You found me!"

She gives him a sarcastic smile and taps her own forehead to indicate the ragged scar on his temple that pulls at his eye, the scar she gave him the night he caught her stealing his files. Her smile curls into a sneer as she pulls out the Glock tucked into her jeans under her coat. "*...Welcome to your life...*"

His face tightens at her use of those song lyrics. The song she used to play when they had sex.

"I told you that the next time I saw you, I'd kill you." She pulls the slider back and lets it spring back to cock the gun.

"You can't kill me," he says with nervous bravado, eyes flicking from the Glock held loosely in her hand to her steely eyes, flashing with the flame of the glowing sky. "You still love me. How can you not?"

She can almost smell his fear among the swamp

poplars. She gives him an oily humorless smile.

"You love my brother," he stutters out. She's unsettling him. "He and I are the same, after all. And I know your fantasy ... to have us both at the same time, eh? I used to try to get him to join me in my trysts in college but he wouldn't have it. I always figured him for a smarmy little gay boy, but all he needed was the right woman, eh? And he found you, didn't he? If you kill me, that threesome will never happen, *Schnucki*—"

Her lips firm in a snarl and she raises the Glock to point straight at him. He recoils slightly and raises his arms quickly, palms facing her in submission. She catches his darting glances toward safety in the swamp forest. "Listen, think about it. I know you think I betrayed your cause, betrayed you, even..."

"*...Turn your back on mother nature...*"

"Wait!" Reciting lyrics of that song is unbalancing him, she realizes with a sardonic smile. "That time when you found my papers on the DNA-specific virus. Don't you think I wanted you to find them?" She blinks at him and he sees that he's caught her attention. She's always wondered about that; he never kept papers. "I *wanted* you to know what I was going to do. And didn't it bring down the Technocrats? Just like we wanted, eh? Achieving the third principle of Deep Ecology, *Schnucki*. I released the virus to reduce our over-populated world, paving the way for Icaria, *your* Icaria, using behavioural engineering and enclosed communities. That's been my plan all along."

"*...It's your own design ... it's your own remorse...*"

"I did it for you!"

He's growing more and more nervous. More darting glances to the darkening swamp forest. Looking for escape. Grey fibrous trunks of tall cedars catch streaks of waning sunlight.

"...For your Icaria. Your Walden Two. You've been following my plan the whole time, *Schnucki.* Everything you've done is part of my plan," he practically shrieks out. "Everything my brother has done too. Because I *know* you. I know both of you, like I know myself. I know the kind of person you are, what drives you, what you want. What you fear. And everything you've done is to my bidding! You can't stop me now!"

She shoots him in the knee.

He screams like a woman and collapses in the snow, staring at her with real fright now. Terror in his gentian blue eyes.

"...Nothing ever lasts forever..."

Bravado stripped away by intense pain. Sweat beads on his forehead as he crawls away from her on the snow, dripping blood, inching toward the cedars and poplars. Seizing in halting breaths. He pants out, "For God's sake, Monica! It's Christmas!"

She releases a wicked laugh. "Like God has anything to do with you?"

His lapis eyes rapidly blink, betraying a brief look that tells her he disagrees. Does he see himself as God? Of course he does.

"You can't...kill me..." he insists, backing away from her, dragging his injured leg, as she steps slowly forward, Glock steadily pointed at him. "Think about it, *Schnucki*...You and me, we could—" He cuts himself off at the cold fury in her eyes and releases a nervous laugh. "You're just like me, Monica," he pants out. "A fierce warrior willing to do what it takes to realize your directive. No room for sentimentality. You'd unflinchingly kill and sacrifice anything and anyone to save the environment—just like me. After all, 'the environment has no voice to defend its sovereignty'; you said that to me the first time we met, remember? That was in '42 and you said we had ten years tops to get things right. So, I did what was needed. I did what no one else had the guts to do. Call me a *Backpfeifengesicht*; but you know I'm right. I addressed Principle Four: *flourishing of human and nonhuman life requires a substantial decrease of the human population*. I removed the potential refugee problem. You have to agree, *Schnucki*, it's working splendidly—"

"For some... not so good for others," she bites out, closing in as he continues to crawl backwards in the snow, leaving a smeared trail of pink under his useless leg. She thinks of the millions his splendid little gene-specific virus killed.

His nose flares in pain and anger. "Like that really bothers you. I know you; you're not a bleeding-heart liberal. You're ruthless ... like me. We both know that asking the public doesn't work; the birth control lottery was doomed to fail. You can't ask; you can't even tell; you must *do*. It's a numbers game and you know I had to choose. That's all it was. Arbitrary choice; *someone* had to go—"

"But not your boujee friends, who are all mostly Caucasian—"

"Not all!" he pants out, still inching away from her. "Many were non-white. That's why it worked ... I played no favourites, *Schnuki*..."

"You still killed more than half the human race."

He manages a grin of victory. "Yes, exactly!" Unapologetic.

"You executed your most loyal worker..."

He erupts in a crazy laugh that rings of wild hysteria. "Ben Hardy? Out of the millions I killed, you pick that loser?" he pants out, staring at her with a look of incredulity. "That bastard abandoned me when it got tough."

A loose end with proprietary knowledge, thinks Monica. He was also one of few who figured out that Eric had purposely released the White Plague; though leaving Dodge in such a hurry pegged him, the fool. Can't have that. But did Eric have to torture them all?

Eric adds, "Hardy was a fucking coward."

"His kid isn't."

"That brat's still alive?" He stares at her. Then he suddenly understands and lets out a horse laugh. "You saved her, didn't you? You're always saving Bambi—"

She steps on his hand with a pursed-lip smile and he gasps in pain.

"Who gave you the right to play God?" she snarls out.

"I did!" he spits out through gasps of pain. "Just like you will when your time comes. You'll see..." The blue in his eyes grows dark like the deep sea. "Because the time will come when you must make that decision ... for your Icaria...for your Gaia..." He draws in a rattling breath, face sweating in pain despite the cold, as she removes her foot from his hand. Taking her move to mean she is relenting, he perks up and continues, "So, here we are now, fourteen years after you gave us just another decade to get things right; we're still in a mess, but far fewer of us. And change is in the air ... literally—" He cries out as she stomps down on his smashed knee. She sees new fear in his eyes. A kind of panic. "Come on, *Schnuki*!" His voice pleads, bravado long vanished beneath the crackling veneer of solid fear and pain. "You're ... just ... like ... me," he pants out heavily.

She takes her foot off his knee and blinks then looks up at the darkening clouds of a reproachful sky. As if considering. She looks down at his raptor face, no longer supreme and in control; more like pathetic. "You're right, Vogel." Then with a malevolent smile, "I am..." She shoots him in the chest three times in quick succession. "...Just like you. *Everybody wants to rule the world.*"

His lapis eyes go wide in surprise, then the life in them dies and he collapses. Bright pink soaks into the snow, reminding her of a strawberry slushy. She stands over him, studying his face, frozen in a grimace of terrible surprise.

"And, just like you, I will do what it takes to realize my directive, unflinchingly kill and sacrifice anything and anyone to save the environment," she adds to herself. "As for that threesome sex fantasy..." She kisses her teeth. "Already taken care of," she says with a sly grin. "Isabo's far nicer than you and I'm going home tonight. Merry Christmas, Vogel."

She turns to where she's left her horse and walks away from the corpse lying in the snow. She doesn't look back.

DECLINE

Biological and social systems are open systems, governed by nonlinear mechanisms; understanding them in mechanical terms will not work. Open systems contradict the second law of thermodynamics; they contain such a high number of variables that the flow of energy in a far-from equilibrium condition spontaneously generates self-organization. They are creative. Nature contains deep order.

Most of reality is not stable; it is full of disorder and change: smooth flow becomes turbulent around strange attractors of periodic motion. Order emerges from dissipative structures through dramatic reorganization. Chaos lies in order and order lies in chaos. Like the mythical Ouroboros, the cycle naturally follows the pattern of creative-destruction.

—Euan Tsutsumi, "The Creative-Destructive Force of Nature's Ouroboros," ICARIAN LETTERS 12 (2) June, 2061

THIRTY-TWO

FAST TRAIN FROM SCIELAB TO ICARIA 5, April 17, 2065: early afternoon

I study the rolling scrub landscape of mostly brown and blue-green through the window of the jet train that speeds from SCIELAB to downtown Icaria-5. We pass fields of wind-powered generator towers, hundreds of them in rows, arms languidly turning in the breeze. In the distance, I make out a few clear domes covering large algal ponds. Bright orange eco-droids track across the pools like little ladybeetles, adjusting pH, nutrients, and other chemicals through nano-machines.

Aside from the domes associated with SCIELAB and the wind towers, there is nothing except a fragmented mosaic of relic countryside. Vestiges of old roads, now breaking apart and overgrown by scrub. Crumbling farmhouses and barns. Fields overgrown by squat shrubs and taken over by heath. Here there hasn't been wilderness for centuries. But now the wilderness—alien and invasive—is ruthlessly taking back what humans tried to tame.

I make this trip daily and while my eyes have grown used to this familiar dreary landscape, my mind laments how it has changed from when I was a boy and I wonder if that is another reason my cousin and little brother have abandoned me for the city. There's barely any forest left. Wildfires, heat waves, disease and pests have taken most of the trees and left forlorn patches of stunted forest scrub, remnant islands of listless brown-green, struggling to keep up with an advancing silver-green heathland that is taking over the landscape like a weed and changing the soil in its favour as it does. The ericoid dwarf-shrub *Calluna vulgaris*, along with *Erica cinerea*, *Vaccinium myrtillus* and many others form a rolling patchwork of purple and silver-green shag that dominates the landscape. In some acidic gullies, *Sphagnum*—which loves carbon dioxide—crowds the moist ground in a saturated shag of yellow-green. Pale skeletons of gnarly birch trees crowd in, adding dark green to the mix. In exposed hillsides, gnarly wizened krumholz grows like curmudgeonly old men.

According to the Ecologists, the heath's unruly bog and scrub exploits disturbed environments. Poised on the edge of chaos, thriving in its created habitat, the heath balances order and chaos by self-organizing through phases of destruction and creation. Like a crafty shape-shifter.

Six thousand years ago, the moors and heath lands of western Europe and Britain were forests too. Then, the Mesolithic humans began to cut all the trees and burn the vegetation to clear the land for cultivation and grazing. Seedlings were destroyed and gave way to plants more suited to the new climate; just as they are doing here.

As the train whistles through the brooding heath, I consider that for a disturbed ecosystem, the heathland is rather beautiful. The sticky-sweet scent of Sweet Gale blossoms amid sweet clover and broom fills the warm air with an undulating tapestry of vibrant purples, pinks, and yellows that stir in a climate-warmed spring breeze. I imagine the trill of warblers amid the buzz of insects and the rustling vegetation. But it's a cruel beauty. Cruel and unrelenting for the trees.

The edge of the forest has always been humanity's home; our relationship with the forest has sustained us for millennia. Many forest people believed that trees were antennae, links between the upper and lower worlds. Like warden trees in Germany and Scandinavia, the old Norse mythic sacred tree Yggdrasil that linked upper and lower realms, has firm roots in our very survival. We've drawn nourishment, shelter and power from the forest, whether it was the thriving forest, the remnant forest, or the fossil forest. But only the thriving forest gives us the very air we breathe. Air that in many places across the globe is no longer breathable. In most Icarias, masks must be worn outside; even at SCIELAB, seventy kilometres from the city, most of my colleagues wear a mask when they go outside to check the algal vats and domed experimental stations. My gaze glances over some wind-sculpted krumholz in the heath stubble, all that is left of the trees in the landscape that races past me. And I think: *this* is why...

Over a century ago, American geographer Jared Diamond made the observation that environmental degradation, specifically deforestation, was central to the collapse of every civilization.

Bobby told me that farther north the Balsam Poplar still grows in large clone colonies, braving the drought and heat of climate change. Half a century ago they'd documented a huge clone stand of poplars, all bearing the same DNA as their ancient ancestor that dated back to the Pleistocene ice sheet melt 1.6 million years ago. These tall ungainly knobby trees once provided a kind of health shield for the boreal ecosystem through shade, soil enrichment and medicinal aerosol dispersal. Bobby tried to bring them into our enclosed Icarias, but found that the medicinal aerosols released—the oleoresins, esters and terpinoids that are anti-inflammatory, anti-bacterial, and anti-fungal—were less effective in our indoor climate. Balsam poplar evolved to thrive in a harsh climate from deep cold, up to minus thirty-seven degrees Celsius to extreme heat, up to plus thirty Celsius. Without those triggers, the tree got lazy.

A century ago, ecologist Diana Beresford-Kroeger suggested that trees have embedded in their cambium tissues the neural ability to listen, think, plan, and decide. Like many women scientists at that time, she was laughed at and her ideas—no matter how well supported—were ridiculed by the traditional scientific community. The censure didn't stop her. She went on to prove that trees have similar hormones to ours with similar effects on behaviour. Does that mean that a tree can be sad? I gaze out at the struggling trees and hope she's wrong. Or there is far too much sadness in the world right now...

Diana started looking at climate change a hundred years ago. She predicted that the Amazon would die, even if deforestation stopped. Fires and drying took care of it. The northern Boreal became our last forest. And now, it too is going to fires, drying and disease. The fine gradations of temperature, altitude and latitude first reported by Alexander von Humboldt in the 19th century have decoupled along with the melting Arctic Ocean that helped dissipate the Beaufort Gyre and the polar vortex, and muddled the Rossby waves in the upper atmosphere. Everything is out of stasis and in the chaos of transition. I wonder musingly when crocodiles will once again live at the North Pole.

Some think it all started with the Boreal fires, but I think that it all really started with that virus Eric Vogel at BioGen released ten years ago. The sad thing is most people think the White Plague started as an accident, from an infected animal or an accidental release from a lab like Uncle Ben's lab. But we know better. Janet and I pieced it together from things her father said and what Janet found out through her uncanny sleuthing. Her father knew that Eric Vogel intentionally spread the virus and I think that's why Vogel killed him and our families.

But the virus affected more than the four billion people it killed. It travelled and morphed in surprising and devastating ways. Biodiversity was impacted and some key predators destroyed, which precipitated destructive trophic cascades and the rise of pests and disease. The rising storms, drought and floods only exacerbated the destruction. Then the spikes of heat rising off the melting permafrost and methane hydrates caused famine on the land. Because land and sea are intimately connected, increasing famines on land are causing increased famine in the sea. As plankton and trees die off, less oxygen interferes with our ability to reproduce, adding to what endocrine-disrupting 'forever chemicals' were already doing to our systems. Reduced fertility. Increased miscarriages. Like a demon shade calling in its minions of destruction, a toxic soup has settled on the land and now we've retreated indoors...

Feeling the dark tendrils of solastalgia, I turn away from the window with a small gasp and check the time on my vee-pad; I'll be at my destination in twenty minutes. I cheer myself up. I have a meeting with Euan at the Enviro-Centre, which I'm excited about. Euan is a brilliant young ecologist—not much older than me, and with a sunny disposition—who has recently created the new Department of Industrial Ecology, DIE. He's been all over North-Am, sharing his habitat modeling expertise to help each Icaria deal with its own unique climate-environment issue and to help each city set up its own DIE, complete with its own Environmental Stress department that regularly tests for Human Pollutant Burdens. I'll make it to the city in time to meet and talk to Janet about Bobby's problem at school before my meeting with Euan.

Of the three of us, only I decided to remain at the Commune Farm, which eventually turned into Experimental Farm-5 and now SCIELAB. As a student I commuted to the downtown university campus for some classes but stayed at SCIELAB for others and to do my experimental work under the domes that housed enclosed ecosystems. With a major focus on algae—as both food and climate influencer—I joined a team of Gaia University researchers in the

Department of Life Support Systems, looking at the balanced needs and ecosystem services of plant communities under differing levels of carbon dioxide, temperature, humidity and light.

Functional ecosystems all come down to dynamic balance and the interrelatedness of all components in community. Checks and balances work in concert like an autopoietic self-organized organism to achieve overall functionality. When something goes off kilter, everything adjusts around it to realign the dynamic equilibrium—but always at some cost. If a keystone species changes—such as removing an apex predator—then a trophic cascade may result: a kind of overcompensation that cascades throughout the entire system and potentially destroying an entire ecosystem. My current work with algae looks at both bottom-up and top-down cascades, such as a pool in which fish, invertebrates and algae interact under the synergy of warming and eutrophication. I remember learning that too much carbon dioxide in the air causes confusion and lack of coordination in humans. This is something the transhumanists are working on under Christian Isabo—the man who designed those creepy Techno-clones—and Damien Vogel, who led the revolution. I wonder how that work is proceeding. Evolving human and machine...I find it scary but Janet is fascinated by it all.

Now, with my degree completed, I've decided to stay at SCIELAB, where my work is; where my life is, I guess. I've taken lodgings there to avoid the daily commute. Janet and Bobby left the first chance they got. Janet left the farm before it became SCIELAB to study science at school then neuroscience at the university. She got a flat in a Liv-Centre in District-7, overlooking the Don River. Schlange sent Bobby to a Care-Centre with associated Ed-Centre, Humboldt Secondary School. He'll get his own flat, probably in the same Liv-Centre as Janet's, when he turns eighteen and goes to university—if he makes it that far. I worry about him and his destructive attitude. We've all grown apart.

The image of Commander Schlange pushes itself into my memory, unbidden, as always. Even in my own mind, she's a bully. The memory comes from last year when she addressed the entire SCIELAB community in our main atrium with the intention to educate us on the rhetoric of science: "Your work here at SCIELAB is important to Icaria and to the very survival of the human race," she boomed over the microphone from her elevated position on the balcony that overlooked those of us crowding the floor. Even from that distance, her probing eyes gripped me, trapping me there like an insect. "But, make no mistake; we are all Deep Ecologists here. We practice Deep Ecology. Not ecology. The science of ecology does not ask what society is best suited to maintain a particular ecosystem. Only Deep Ecologists concern ourselves with questions aimed at the level of organic wholeness and 'Earth Wisdom.' That is our mandate. Don't confuse small science with the greater truth."

I wanted to puke at her words. Science directed by philosophy or belief is no longer objective and therefore doomed to fail. What did she really mean by 'Earth Wisdom'? I'd done my research on the ice queen. Monica Schlange studied environmental ethics with a minor in political science. Her background was mostly philosophy and politics, not science. She was a media influencer with incredible skills in propaganda on the internet. I heard that she even got a Technocrat minister jailed before the revolution. So, 'Earth Wisdom'? More like 'Schlange Wisdom,' which spelled out more accurately to 'Schlange's Way.' I recall the argument I overheard between her and Damien Vogel in her office back when SCIELAB was Commune Farm 5; about ensuring everyone was happy about 'building a world inside.' What was the ice queen's real intention? What was that lie she mentioned? *Let them grow up with a lie. They don't deserve the truth...*

As I glanced at my colleagues crowded in the large atrium that day, I kept my thoughts to myself. So did they, I noticed, briefly meeting unresponsive expressions all around me. Some understood the import of that day; it was the day Science died.

My mind returns to the dying forest screaming past the window of the train and I glance from the window to the readout on the vee-pad on my lap: the note to Janet and I from Humboldt Secondary School about Bobby's third detention this month for violence in the classroom. I sigh.

My dark thoughts dissipate as a pleasant female voice calls over the intercom: "Nadezdha Station, Terminus for District 10." I prepare to disembark; I'm at my destination.

ICARIA 5, Nadezdha Mall.
April 17, 2065: afternoon

I check the time on the vee-set on my head as I stand in the large skylit atrium of Nadezdha Mall at the entrance to the Enviro-Centre. Of course, Janet is late. I stand nervously tapping my foot beside a large island of trees and plants, some of which I helped create. I can't help comparing these stately indoor trees—Black walnut, locust, red maple—to the straggly poplars and buckthorns that dot the sad landscape I've just travelled through to get to the city. I cast my eye far down the large atrium, past the rainbow AI20 traffic droids and stout litter droids that glide along the large hallways, picking up garbage left by careless Icarians. It seems that more and more of Icaria is run by AI or droids. I even spotted one running a food stand in Darwin Mall. I still can't stomach watching the AI07 recycle droids do their job—ejecting a viscous fluid of recycling digesters that behave like an amoeba, extending pseudopods and digesting material that it engulfs then sucks into its metallic belly, later disgorged into the DIE's main recycling depot, to finally emerge as someone's nano-soup or wall-art.

I see her first, walking with long fluid steps as if to a dance tune and aiming her gaze up through the skylights at the flax flower sky. I feel a wistful smile curl my lips; it's just like Janet to dream of heaven. Her skyward glance seems to match her ambition. At a mere twenty years old, she has already snagged a research position in the university's neuroscience department in the Med-Centre in Pielou Mall. And, just like me, her work is keeping her alive and mostly sane. I take off the vee-set and wave to her.

"Hey, Leonard, you slug!" she calls across the mall's atrium. When I was a boy, I used to hate how she called me 'slug' or 'turd;' now it's become a kind of endearment that I enjoy. As she reaches me at the island of trees, she puts on a rather sheepish face. "Am I late?"

I laugh. "You're always late, Cuz; so, no, you're right on time, except—"

She pokes my arm and points to the food stand. "I'm starving! I missed lunch. Join me?"

"I can't, it's too late." I laugh and fidget nervously with the vee-set in my hand. "I have a meeting with Euan in ten minutes."

"Oh, he's Euan now, is he?" she says catlike. "Not Doctor Tsutsumi?" She studies me for a moment, eyes sparkling with curiosity. "Do you think he's going to offer you a position at DIE?"

"Don't jinx it, Cuz!" I retort then laugh nervously. It seems like the Gaians have given Euan and DIE a huge amount of support in his work to create more sustainable food sources for humanity. Much of it aimed at in vitro, enclosed production; hydroponics, cultures and the like. Oddly enough, stuff Janet's father was doing before the revolution. Two days ago, Euan found me in the city campus of the university and took me aside to talk about the work I was doing with mixed-species algal culturing over at SCIELAB. It felt like an impromptu interview. The next day—yesterday—he sent me a text, asking to meet in his office at DIE on the tenth floor of the Enviro-Centre in Nadezdha Mall.

"Don't worry, Leonard." She grabs me by the shoulders and smiles like a mischievous urchin. "You've got this."

"I really wanted to talk to you about Bobby, but we don't have time now," I begin.

She firms her lips thoughtfully and looks sad for a moment. "Bobby...The school..." I guess that she's seen the note. I know that Bobby's school troubles are another failure she takes responsibility for. She quickly cheers herself up. "When you're done, come to Pielou Mall and find me in my lab, ok? We can discuss Bobby then. But first I have to get one of your ugly noxious concoctions to satisfy my growling stomach..."

I force a smile of amusement at her half-hearted insult. "OK. Thanks, Cuz. Enjoy the algae." I give her a quick kiss on the cheek and hasten down the mall to the Enviro-Building as she heads to the Synth-Food stand to have her late lunch.

As I ride the lift to the tenth floor, I consider how each of us bears the wound of the revolution in our own way, according to our experiences and our comportment. That wound defined us. It broke something in each of us and made us all loners. Despite her outward cheerful and almost cavalier attitude, Janet is a cynical and distrustful introvert; she keeps to herself and shuns company. She's twenty-five and has never had a boyfriend or girlfriend. For my part, I have become even more hesitant and distrustful than I was as a boy. I prefer spending my time outdoors conducting my algal experiments or studying and sketching the dying trees over going to *ambrosia* parties with colleagues and friends.

Janet and I were teenagers when we first experienced the atrocities of the revolution. Bobby was only six years old when he lost his mother, watched his cousin murder a man, and was repeatedly raped by cruel smelly men. That trauma is enough to make a grown man insane, let alone a child. I understand why at age fifteen Bobby still clings to his cousin, and is perpetually angry, moody and distrustful. I've seen him push potential friends away with a surly insult. He tells me that books are his friends. He and I aren't close now. Does he blame me for not stopping that first molestation? He should; I blame myself every day...

—

Euan is waiting at the lift doors when I arrive on the tenth floor. He's dressed in dark trousers, crisp blue shirt and a white lab coat. He greets me with a beaming smile. His hair is the colour of a Storm-Petrel and in the heavy layers of a tousled wolf-cut. It hangs partly in his eyes like he's just a boy. In fact, he's only eight years older than me. But he already runs one of the most important departments of the Enviro-Centre. He wears earrings on both ears, proclaiming him a bisexual.

"Glad you could make it, Leonard," Euan says with casual friendliness, as if we've known each other as friends for a while. "Come on to my lab-office." He spins on his heels and leads me with brash steps down the large white hall to a set of glass doors at the end.

When we enter, the first thing I see is a large mural on the far wall of the whitewashed lab-office. I halt in front of a plum coloured leather sofa and arm chairs to stare at the huge mural. It depicts hundreds of peoples' faces, grading through all shades of pigment from sand to obsidian.

Euan comes beside me and looks on. "I have that up to remind me of what we used to be. How incredibly diverse we once were." He sighs and turns to me with an intense look. "Did you know that entire sub-races are now extinct thanks to that demon?" I guess he means Eric Vogel, the man who personally killed my mother after carelessly murdering four billion people. Does Euan know that Eric Vogel purposefully spread the virus? Most people still think it was accidentally released from a lab or came from some sick animal. After a long sigh, Euan turns to study the poster, umber eyes focused elsewhere. "I was twenty when the White Plague swept through Vancouver. Well, others call it the White Demon. I think that's more appropriate, given its purpose and who developed it: a demon."

So, Euan does know that Eric Vogel purposefully caused the White Plague. Makes sense; Euan is no slouch.

Euan goes on, "It took my mom, but only after my dad and I got sick. I almost died, but somehow I pulled through; I guess that proved my genetic make-up. My dad was white and I guess my mix was sufficiently white to pull me through. That taught me something, Leonard. Up to then, I realized that I was passing as white; I hadn't acknowledged my non-white heritage as important. I have lighter skin and I had my father's last name: Miller. Most people thought I was white and I let them. So, I changed to my mother's last name: Tsutsumi. And from then on, I made sure that everyone recognized me as a Japanese-Canadian. I wear my hair to accentuate that." He glances back at the mural. "In honor of those who are no longer. I do it for them."

He then turns away from the mural and gestures for me to sit down on one of the plush chairs. As I do, he sprawls on the sofa across from me with a huge grin.

"How would you like to work for DIE?"

I stare at Euan's round sanguine face in surprise. I wasn't expecting an open invitation so soon. I thought he might give me a tour and discuss all his departments like Biomimicry, Biophysics, Environmental Stress, Department of Life Support Systems, and others I don't even know about. I thought he'd ask more questions before deciding. He reminds me a little of Janet, in his apparent impetuous nature, and his cavalier façade, which I recognize hides a hidden sensitive wound—just like Janet. The poster proves that.

Euan laughs. "Leonard. I like what I see and I make my mind up fast; I don't like wasting time. I'd like us to work together in partnership: you at SCIELAB with your outside cultures and domed ecosystems and me here in the Enviro-Building at the DIE experimental and culture labs. I've got some projects in mind that would suit our two set ups perfectly."

He suddenly leans forward across the small coffee

table that hardly separates us and pushes his face close to mine, making me suddenly uncomfortable. He's too close. I can feel his breath on me and see the reflection of the lights in his earth-coloured eyes. I fight from recoiling, not wanting to appear impolite, and reason that it's likely a cultural thing with him. He just likes to be close, just like he wanted to go to a first name basis as soon as we met. Not someone keen on formalities.

Euan adopts a quiet almost-whisper, as if sharing a confidence, "DIE is a lot more than just about how to physically adapt to climate and environmental change and survive these viral pandemics with enough food and air to breathe. Of course, that's the main reason we're being supported by the Circle. But thanks to that support, we're able to explore subtle but equally existential concerns for humanity. Things to do with enclosed existence. Like living indoors with filtered air, living mostly without direct sunlight, and eating synthetic food. Of course, we think of potential nutritional deficits—easily met by supplements for Vitamin D or Vitamin B, for instance, that are made and provided in all our synthetic foods. And of course we look at the fragile balance of carbon dioxide and other gases in the air we breathe. But I'm talking about things less easy to measure and much less easy to control." He leans back, as if to make a point, and I sigh with the added space to breathe. I hadn't realized how cramped I felt until that release. As if he knows this, Euan releases a sneaky smile. "I know you've thought of that too."

I swallow reflexively and blink at him, not sure

what he's getting at.

"Your latest report on mixed algal culture experiments mentioned nonlinear feedback loops related to creative-destruction and autopoietic behaviour as part of self-organization." He grabs a vee-pad from the coffee table and coaxes out something on the screen. "Here," he points to the screen only he can see. "where you write about the complex algal communities D-1 through -12..." He reads: " '...a signature of these complex systems is that they have so many variables interacting in so many ways that they achieve creativity through nonlinear dynamics; they spontaneously organize around a balance point between stability and total dissolution into turbulence.' " He puts the vee-pad down and studies me with dark eyes the colour of coffee. "You didn't come right out and say it, Leonard—you're too clever for that—but you might as well have..."

He's talking about stable chaos! I stare at him in frozen fear and feel my heart pounding. Is he going to turn me in for spreading anti-Deep Ecology? These days Deep Ecology operates more like a cult than a philosophy; its hegemony makes the concept of stable chaos a blasphemy. I'm really not sure why; the only thing I can think of is that it doesn't align with some aspect of Icarian enclosed society and I find my thoughts returning to what Schlange said to Vogel back at Commune Farm 5: about building inside and perpetuating a lie.

Euan reaches forward and touches my hand with a reassuring smile. "Don't worry, Leonard. I mentioned it because I think you're on the right track with it and it harmonizes with my work at DIE and the long-term project I want us to collaborate on." He leans back, eyes focusing on the past. He studies a shelf of old books on the far wall before returning an intense gaze at me. "The first thing the Enviro-Centre did when it got set up right after the Gaians took over was help enclose all Icarias against the toxic outside. People had to move indoors and secure ourselves. Tornadoes, ice storms, floods and heat drove people indoors. Air pollution from residual pandemics, industrial toxins and wildfires—together with climate inversions, heatwaves, and storms—are still feeding a positive feedback system that's making it worse over time, not better. So, naturally enough, the focus has been to seal our buildings and rebuild for security, until it supposedly gets better. All as a temporary measure. But, Leonard, the Gaians aren't thinking that way anymore—if they ever did. They intend to eventually have everything enclosed with *no access* to the outside. That's their design. They're planning for permanent enclosure. I've seen the designs. Heck, my work is part of them!" He studies me, looking for a reaction.

He gets it. Despite my resolve not to show it, my expression of dismay—but not surprise—leaks out of me. This is something I've suspected for a while and my thoughts slide to the ice queen's argument with Vogel about executing Fairweather and labeling him a dystopian. I tried unsuccessfully to broach this suspicion with Janet several times. But she refused to listen, preferring to brood alone. She's overly dark about life in general and I find her isolation unhealthy. Bobby has his books and I have my outside world; Janet appears to have no outlet for her growing darkness. She's worse than Bobby, who is a tinder box of hurling anger at the world. Where does she direct hers, if not inside? It must be eating her like a virus.

Euan slides into an easy smile of victory at my reaction and nods to himself. "The plan is for full permanent enclosure by 2080, if not earlier. Think of it, Leonard; we're almost there now. Each Icaria is already divided loosely into districts with associated Undertunnel connections to malls that connect all the major centres. Most people don't go out anymore to avoid the mask-wearing and pollution on their exposed skin; the streets have become deserted, so for them it'll be an easy move—as in, no move at all. Very soon, outdoor access will be restricted to Enviro-Centre workers and researchers like you and me. They don't want anyone outside, Leonard. It's just too risky."

I nod my understanding, but I find it harsh. Janet will be angry. She still enjoys her short walks in the stunted forest of the Don Valley by her Liv-Centre in District-7.

"And that's where our study comes in, Leonard. The permanent move inside will occur in stages and we're going to use it as an ongoing experiment."

I'm intrigued. "What will we be looking for?" I think of his mention of my indirect reference to stable chaos and wonder why he did.

He draws in a long breath and suddenly rises from the sofa. He walks to a small bar where he pours himself a drink. "Want some *ambrosia*?" he asks. It's a little early to drink drug but I feel overwhelmed and nod. He brings me a clear drink, and passes it to me with an intense expression on his round face and sits back on the sofa. As I study the synthetic recreational drug that's become incredibly popular, Euan studies me with deep umber eyes, like he's measuring me. The cavalier sparkle in his eyes dims to something darkly intense and he says in a slow voice of deliberation, "I think this total move indoors will lead to the extinction of the human race. And I intend to prove it."

I stare at him, aghast, holding the drink in my hand without taking a sip. What comes out of my mouth is instinctive, "But being inside and using air scrubbers and filters and algal cultures and water purifiers has kept us from going extinct..."

"Yes, it kept us from dying during the great virus purge and the wildfires and inversions." He says, then takes a sip of *ambrosia*. "But, it's not a long-term solution, Leonard. It's a short-term band aid, based on over-simplification."

I stutter out, "You mentioned my work..."

He nods to himself as an open smile lights his round face. "I intend to use my Inverted Loop Model, which relies on concepts of stable chaos and fractal ecology, to predict the collapse of all enclosed Icarias."

My mouth gapes.

He leans back and crosses his legs with an arcane smile. After another sip, he adds pointedly, "And I want you to help me."

A long moment of silence passes between us

as I digest what he's just said. I finally blurt out, "those theories and concepts are heretical to Deep Ecology—"

"—but not to valid science." Euan studies me for a moment as my heart beat quickens. When he leans forward to make some point, I instinctively recoil. He smiles ruefully with a sigh and leans back, raising his hands in conciliation. "Today's Deep Ecology is propaganda, not science. It's a religion the Circle is using to convince us to be moles—to go along unquestioning with their agenda. I'm betting you agree with me. Your reports betray as much."

Betray? Is he blackmailing me? Is this a threat to reveal my heresy to get my buy-in to his project? Or is he just stating what's obvious to him? That I'm a closet fractal ecologist who uses heretical concepts like stable chaos to describe the world. Either way I'm wall-art.

Recognizing my discomfort, Euan leans forward again and pushes his face close to mine. "Listen, Leonard, you don't have to worry. It's not obvious to anyone except another heretic." He grins suddenly with that remark, like it's a game changer, which I suppose it is. "No one else will recognize the heresy," he reassures me. "Your words resonate with the underlying truth beneath the heresy; the Deep Ecologists are too wound up in the surficial rhetoric to really understand the underlying science." He giggles conspiratorially and finally says more gently, "I'm not threatening you, Leonard. I just want you to understand that I think the same as you and I'm a friend." He finally releases me by leaning back to let me breathe. "I want us to work together."

I take a deep breath and find myself smiling like a deep-sea diver just come up for air. For the longest time, I've felt alone in my views of ecology. Even Janet was reluctant to join into heretical discussions with me. I realize that I feel refreshed, even comforted, by this overture of Euan's.

He knows it too. He laughs with joy and raises his glass of *ambrosia* to me and I raise mine, inhaling its pleasant sweet floral vapour. We clink then take a gulp. I cough as the drug fires my throat with bright sparks of pleasure and warms me all over. We both laugh. It's obvious I don't drink much. We're both grinning like boys with the promise of great things. Together, we might navigate this challenging and dangerous road to save humanity from a self-imposed extinction.

Seized by some irreverent thought, Euan springs to his feet and slides to his bar, pulling out a container and a pipe. "*Hedon*!" he says joyfully. "You smoke it like tobacco in a pipe. It's the new rage in the inner-city these days. It's not legal yet, but it will be soon. Want to try it with me? I've been wanting to and didn't have the guts. Let's do it together!"

I really don't want to smoke this new drug, particularly since it's illegal, but I feel the rush of the ebullient mood. Noticing my hesitation, Euan gives me a reassuring smile. This feels like a kind of rite of passage, a symbol of our first heretical step toward a larger truth, the truth of Science. Something I thought I would not have a chance to practice again under this new Gaian regime of Deep Ecology. So, why not?

Euan grins conspiratorially. "Together, ok? Like our science."

I nod with renewed conviction, eager to experience something outside my normal comfort, something illegal. "Together."

Euan fills the pipe cup with *hedon* chips, lights it with a lighter from his pocket, and sucks in a mouthful of *hedon.* He pulls in a long breath then exhales, coughing out pungent yellow smoke that gives off a mild scent of burning cloves and lavender with an added pepper of cardamom. The smoke coils up from his mouth and snakes around his head and shoulders before dissipating. Euan's eyes crinkle with silent laughter as he hands me the device. "You have to breathe as deeply as you can," he says through halting breaths in a voice that strains against the stringent residue in his lungs. I take the pipe and, with eyes fixed on his laughing face, suck hard on the pipe mouth, taking in a deep inhale. I pull in acrid sharp smoke that burns inside me with a strange euphoric feeling of lightness. I cough out a pungent heat that tastes of clove and lemon.

We stare at each other, blinking simultaneously, then break out into crazy laughter. I laugh so hard, tears spring to my eyes. I have no idea why I'm laughing but I haven't felt this good in a very long time. Giggling, Euan leans on my shoulder and grabs the pipe for another inhale.

THIRTY-THREE

ICARIA 5, District-7, Care Centre,
May 9, 2066: early evening

Janet and I are making a rare visit together to see Bobby. He had just been reprimanded by the Head Principle of Humboldt Secondary School for violent behaviour and she and I coordinated our visit.

As we ride the tube-jet together to District-7, we discuss Bobby's dire situation. He's sixteen and fast becoming a problem child at both the Care-Centre and the Ed-Centre. It is all narrowing his chances at success at university and even as a Gaian citizen. While neither of us openly mentions it, I know we both fear that he will come to some disastrous end.

The fear we both share but don't express spills out of Janet in a different way. "Maybe Bobby fears not having a purpose in life to make it meaningful, of not accomplishing something worthwhile that will give him some fulfillment and a reason to live," she says. Is she talking about Bobby or herself? "We're both very alike in some ways..." she admits. Why does everything she and Bobby say appear to exclude me? As though that time back at the Corporation Farm, when I fled, broke us apart like drifting continents.

—

"I brought you some books, Bobby," Janet says when we arrive. She takes them out of the heavy bag slung over her shoulder. Both Bobby and I look over the books with curiosity. I notice that he is impressed; a good sign. I glance at Janet and she meets my eyes with a glint of hope in hers.

"They're beautiful!" Bobby says, leafing through them and smoothing his fingers over the covers.

"I hope you enjoy them," she says. "But listen, Bobby." She bends close to him. "Don't show them to anyone. Keep them hidden, all right?"

I look at her with puzzlement. So does Bobby. But I notice how this alone has made them even more tantalizing to him.

"Why, ma?" he asks. Gaia! I hate that he has taken to calling her 'ma.' I know that it makes her uncomfortable too, but she's long since stopped trying to stop him, as if resigning to her role as surrogate mother.

"Because they're frowned upon," she answers his question—and mine. "Some people are trying very hard to make them all a thing of the past," she adds. I think her wise with her advice. The Deep Ecologists have already made it known that certain literature is frowned upon. They call some of it Dystopian, the term Schlange used for the ecologist she executed in '57. The dystopian list is a varied litany of accusations, from writers being Capitalist decadents, romantic utopians, brigands, and egotists to followers of dystopian ecology. It seems that almost anything written before the revolution is fair game for them. The next step is making it law, but I'm sure that's far away from now. Still, I think Janet prudent in her advice to Bobby. Bobby's unruly behaviour has already put him on the fringes of decorum. He doesn't need anything else to place him on the outs with the Gaian establishment. Janet continues, "If you like them and you want to keep them, they're yours. I have plenty more. I hope you'll want to read them all."

He looks from her to the books he's handling very carefully then to her again, fascinated.

"For all I know, some of them may be the last copies around," she says. "These books are special, Bobby. Take them seriously. Some were written more than a hundred years ago, long before the revolution and the Gaian regime. They're real and wonderful and they paint a very different world from this one. And I think they might explain some of the things that you are confused about and troubled with. Of course, they may raise many more questions for you. I'll try to answer them for you if I can.

"You may find one book that will give you more than words—it will reach out to you and speak to you. It will pull you inside. The words will dance like the music of birds. The phrases will trickle like a cool forest brook. The words will spring out at you and at some odd moment it might seem like the reverse—that they are jumping down from your head to the book, as if you had known it all before, locked away somewhere, and it was all coming back to you. You almost knew what was going to happen next, what the people would say or do..."

Then she loses that dreamy far-away look and refocuses on Bobby. He's staring at her with awe. Nothing new, I decide. She is pretty much the light and anchor of his life. But this time I know she has touched him with something special. He opens a hardcover book, *The Overstory* by Richard Powers—a favourite of mine—and runs his hand over the pages as if trying to imbibe the magic in them from touch.

Janet glances at me and we both smile.

ICARIA 5, District-9, Outside Darwin Mall, February 17, 2070: Late evening

When I emerge, fully masked, into already crowded outside, the noise of excitement is in the dank air. I'm on my own; neither Janet nor Bobby wanted to join me. I understand Bobby's trauma but feel disappointed that Janet has refused to come. The crowds still pour out of exits from several buildings. Figures holding lit vee-sets from outstretched arms crawl like benthic creatures beneath a thick grimy sea and spill into the large open square on the old University of Toronto campus. Like an opalescent sea, the air shifts and flows as people move through it and create wakes of swirling eddies. It's the first time I've seen so many people outside in over a decade. I try to stay back but the crowd engulfs me like a shivering amoeba and pushes me forward through the suspended grime. We merge into a singular body, shimmering like bioluminescent ostracods in a night sea, as we approach our destination: the location of the book burning.

AQC informed us that the weather conditions would be excellent. I wonder at their definition of 'excellent.' We'd been given two weeks to go over the Dystopian literature list and drop off any black-listed books. Tonight is the deadline, after which anyone found harboring a black-listed book will suffer severe consequences.

In a sudden instant the centre of the square bursts into shocking flame that throws a garish green-gold light on people's faces. I smell lighter fuel through my mask as the book pyre lights up the sky. The blaze grows and licks the polluted air as black smoke coils up like an ominous snake. The crowd laughs and cheers, eyes reflecting the dancing flames that roar like an old tube-jet.

Then the frenzy begins and my heart thunders with both excitement and fear. People dance and shout. They crowd closer to the fire and feed it with books they've brought for the burning. The books fly, covers flapping outward like crazed birds, pages flailing helplessly. The fire eats them. It swallows them up and roars in victory. The paper crackles and fizzles in resistance then ignites with a dark sigh to a sudden death. Huge black ashes are thrown up high into the air by the force of the fire as a great sweltering wind hisses over the crowd. Migrating ashes float down languidly into the perimeter of the crowd, where I stand.

I catch a piece of flying paper, partly burned and read: *when heaven doth weep, doth not*—the rest is burnt. Shakespeare, I guess. From someone's cherished collection. I let the paper drop to the ground and watch with a frozen face as the Pols throw more books into the fire. People close to the fire ripple in the heat. I watch them absently, trying to remember the rest of the phrase I read. Suddenly it becomes very important. Then I notice an older woman to my right. Her face is grotesquely lit by the glowing light. She is weeping.

I think of Bobby and his prized collection, given to him by Janet in an effort to salvage his sanity. Whenever he and I talk, which isn't often, he always manages to mention how his books are his friends. His family. And each time I'm pinched with guilt. Does he prefer his books to his real family? Perhaps not Janet, but me certainly. Now his precious family is down the chute and burning in that fire.

I remember the day Janet turned things around for him. Will that all disappear now? Is he doomed, like his books, by the righteous fires of Gaia's Ecologists?

THIRTY-FOUR

ICARIA 5, District 9, Darwin Park in Darwin Mall, June 12, 2074: early afternoon

I can't believe I've done it. I just got hitched! Deborah and I just kissed after exchanging our vows in the gazebo of Darwin Park. The small wedding party stands up from their chairs and claps in celebration. A dozen or so faces smile jubilantly at us, their various work-related outfits creating a sea of bright colours from the rainbow. Every centre is represented by a colour and these days most people elect to wear their work colours everywhere, proudly proclaiming their allegiance to their workplace, which in a very important way defines them. For instance, Lisa, who works at the Department of Information Control in the Com-Centre, wears a cherry red outfit; Glen, a tube-jet driver with the IUTT at the Trans-Centre is dressed in cobalt blue; Blaine and Isha both wear the mustard yellow of the Ed-Centre. There's a lot of forest green here, I note. It makes sense; most of my friends work at the Enviro-Centre.

I glance at my new wife, beautiful in her orange Rec-Cenre work clothes and beaming at me. With me in Enviro-Centre green, she had earlier argued how our complimentary work clothes meant that we were supposed to be together. Deborah's nuyu cherry-red lips pinch with mischief as if she's just gotten away with something. It's that teasing naughty smile that captured me in the first place the first time I met her at the Leisure Unit of the Rec-Centre in Odum Mall; that impish smile reminded me of my cousin when we were young. It was Euan who got us together, by dragging me there several times and pointing her out. For some crazy reason she showed an interest in me from the start. To this day, I wonder if Euan had said something privately to her about me to encourage her.

Deborah and I giggle like children and we proceed together into the seating area beneath a canopy of black walnut, maple and beech trees as our friends approach us and clasp our hands or pat our shoulders to congratulate us.

Bobby, dressed in Enviro-Centre green like me, seizes Deborah in a bear hug, squeezing her diminutive body a little too tightly. Her eyes fly to me in minor distress, but she bears it silently and he finally lets her go. He then turns to me and grabs me with the same bear hug and smacks my back with his coarse gardener hands. He's my younger brother but he is bigger than me, with a more muscular build, shaggier hair, dyed with light blue tips, and a dimpled smile that sends girls into a tizzy.

"Way to go, Lenny!" he says a little too loudly and I wonder if he's drunk on *ambrosia* already. I inhale a combination of its sickly-sweet floral notes on his breath along with the sour smell of nano-soup. I have to fight from pushing him off me in disgust.

Euan saves me by barging past Bobby. After pushing Bobby aside, Euan greets him tersely, as if he just realized Bobby was there, then clasps my hand firmly, grinning like a superstar. I grin back like an accomplice, as Bobby retreats to the temporary bar set up near the gazebo.

Euan glances between me and Deborah. "Congratulations, you two. You make a wonderful couple. May you be healthy and freely profligate!" Then he chuckles at our shared joke. He and I had discussed and joked about the draconian offspring limits imposed by the previous Technocratic government and how they'd even resorted to a lottery, which had been disastrous. Euan told me that something like it is bound to come to Icaria though. While the White Demon had efficiently taken care of global overpopulation, now that we were all living in enclosed Icarias, limited space for a growing population would again become a factor. The little joke between Euan and I was that Deb and I should get moving fast with making babies before we are no longer permitted to and before the Department of Progenesis—the DP—instates its new rule about genetically controlled offspring. Euan's contact close to Christian Isabo at the Ed-Centre revealed that a new stipulation restricting potential parents to genetic examination and manipulation is in the works. He was told in confidence that very soon a couple won't be allowed to just have a kid the traditional way: through spontaneously and unplanned good old fashioned sex. The Icarian government doesn't care who we have sex with, whether within a marriage or not, and how often. The sin of adulteration no longer exists; many Icarians have multiple partners of both sexes in or out of marriage—itself a waning institution. Most couples now choose to co-exist, drift apart like algae in a spate, then lodge on another shore with another partner. The Icarian government actually encourages it. When it comes to children, though, the government is showing a serious tone by cracking down with controls. Euan revealed that potential parents will need to apply for permission to have a child and then submit to genetic testing to create a genetically engineered Icarian child: robust, intelligent and free of predispositions to diseases and other genetic ailments and weaknesses. A good and strong Icarian, I think sardonically, mind calling up the first line of the Isabo Creed: *I obey therefore I am strong; those who disobey are weak.*

Euan shakes Deborah's hand politely and moves off as Janet, dressed in startling Med-Centre white, takes his place. She hugs and congratulates Deborah, who giggles like a hysterical girl. Then Janet turns to me. I tense, meeting her deep green eyes with something close to fear. I look for her approval but I wish for something else from her. Some sign of jealousy?

Janet grabs me in a silent hug and I give in to her soft touch and the smell of spring flowers.

She tugs my single left earring playfully. "I never thought you'd do it, Leonard," she whispers like a conspirator in my ear before pulling back to my disappointment. "I'm so proud of you, slug!"

I return her a tremulous smile of triumph and secret longing. It's her I really want to be with. It's her I really want to have children with...

Lisa, our wedding organizer reminds us that it's time to go to the reception. Janet gives me an arcane grin then heads to the bar to join Bobby. Deborah grabs my hand and we lead our small wedding party to *Café des Fleurs* for our small reception. We walk along paving-stone pathways through the mixed forest of the 5-hectare park that Bobby helped build. I think it his crowning achievement as a landscape designer. He now works for a different department of the Enviro-Centre, maintaining the large indoor parks of all the malls in Icaria-5. He's basically a glorified park janitor. I glance back, glimpsing Janet and Bobby walking together, bent on quiet conversation.

When we reach the café, I turn again to see Bobby standing on the edge of the café patio, no longer with Janet; she's gone, replaced by an unkempt-looking man in a Work-Centre blue-green suit with matching blue-green hair. Bobby used to wear two earrings—declaring his bisexuality—but has recently taken to wearing only one on his right ear, like this Work-Centre man who looks twice Bobby's age. I catch Bobby slipping a book into the man's hand. The man, in turn, shows Bobby his vee-pad. Showing Bobby his purchase no doubt. I find my lips pursing in disapproval; I know what Bobby is doing. Now their heads bow close, foreheads almost touching, in intimate conversation, and the strange man's hand briefly brushes Bobby's cheek in a tender caress. Damn him for pimping himself at my wedding. He's peddling illicit books and himself at my wedding!

Mind numb with anger, I dumbly let Deborah lead us to our seats at the head table that faces the patio and forest. Janet suddenly appears beside me and sits down on my other side. I barely acknowledge her and watch Bobby, still on the patio, casting furtive glances around him as he takes the hand of the Work-Centre guy, and they slip into the forest.

Janet leans close to me and whispers, "I know..."

I find myself shivering with anger and whine, "Gaia! Does he have to peddle his Dystopian shit and his body right here at my wedding? Can't he?..." I trail and throw an angry glance at the seat next to Janet that will remain empty; Bobby won't be coming back. He's probably already fucking that Admin-Centre guy on the very forest bed that he'd planted.

Janet pats my hand. "I know... It sucks..."

"You mean *he sucks*!" I snarl out in a low whisper. As in he's probably sucking cock right now.

"He lives in a shitty place, Leonard. Those books earn him good credit," she whispers back. "And ... well, the other too, I suppose..." she trails with a nervous glance to the forest.

"Are you defending him?" I shrill out. Deborah turns to me, looking concerned, but I ignore her. She's probably worried my temper will spoil her wedding. I snarl out in a growling whisper, "His whoring around with older men is his business. I just wish he wouldn't ruin the sanctity of my wedding with his Dystopian book peddling crap. What if we'd invited a Pol to the wedding?"

Janet remains silent and looks straight ahead at nothing in particular.

I think what a mess Bobby has turned into. He's twenty-four years old, very attractive in a boyish way and constantly sought after by young girls, who he mostly ignores. He's in excellent physical shape, well-muscled, and at the peek of his development;

but he's wasting it all away on drugs, illicit book peddling, and promiscuous sex with older men. My mind slides to the Corporation Farm and the many times he was violently raped as a child. Raped by men who looked just that old Work-Centre guy he went into the forest with. I don't understand. Is this his way of coping with what happened? His way of making some sense of it, and getting something from it? At least he makes some revenue, as Janet pointed out. My breath shudders out of me with the memory of that first day that turned into a several months-long nightmare of molestation for the two of them. How might it have changed if I hadn't run away and left them there in the kitchen? Did Bobby ever have a chance to be normal?

Janet's hand closes over mine and squeezes.

She says nothing. She doesn't have to; she is there too. That day in the kitchen. In some ways all three of us are still there, stuck, unable to move past that sultry hot day when everything changed.

THIRTY-FIVE

ICARIA-5, District 10, Pielou Mall, Med-Centre. January 6, 2075: mid-morning

I stop at the door to Janet's lab, overhearing her laughter and the voice of a man in the back alcove behind a high bookshelf. Her laugh is coquettish and his voice deep and playful; two sounds foreign to my cousin. I can't help quietly approaching, barely seeing them standing beside a counter behind the bookshelf. They argue about serious science but the tone of their banter is flirtatious.

"...No, no, no ... look at this," he says playfully. "Remember that the brain is bidirectional, so it can receive information in while it sends signals out... Like Schrödinger's cat..."

She releases a throaty giggle. "More like Schrödinger's Ouroboros. Cats aren't that compliant. They won't suffer *Quatsch*..."

He snorts out a laugh. "True, true. Although my Gretchen was rather solicitous..."

"No doubt because you fed her copious amounts of cream, *mein Freund*. Through feedback loops, of course, eh?"

They must be having at least two conversations at the same time, I decide.

She continues, "... The viral vector helps the BMI process learn and innovate so the same cortical neurons that fire improve through the additional feedback."

He barks a sound of victory. "Yes, yes, my darling!"

Good Gaia! He might as well be ejaculating with that outcry.

He goes on in a self-pleased voice, "...And because she wasn't alive and dead at the same time, though with all that cream you'd wonder ... But, not only that; we see a kind of acceptance and binding of exterior with interior environments like..."

"...A *verdammt* bridge!" she shouts gleefully.

Good, Gaia, they're finishing each other's sentences. And she's even swearing in German! Their conversation flows like a braided river, twining and looping around the other with ease.

"*Boah*! Artificial treated as biological. Oh, darling! *Das ist erstaunlich*!"

"*Ausgezeichnet*!" she hurrahs.

I can't stand it and shuffle past the bookshelf. Both turn and smile awkwardly at me—as if they've just been caught doing something naughty. But they're only standing shoulder to shoulder, bent over a vee-com. From his deep purple suit, I can tell that he works in the Admin-Centre. He's older, very tall, with striking features that resemble a great raptor. Long prominent nose. Sensual intelligent mouth. Brilliant blue eyes that meet mine squarely. Thick grey hair rises from a high forehead like the crest of a great bird of prey. Odd, that he hasn't dyed it; most people, particularly elders, are dying their hair—often to complement their work suit. He nevertheless looks elegant and distinguished in his purple suit. No earrings to proclaim his sexual orientation either. Another oddity. He's very handsome and unnerving,

I decide.

The man straightens, eyes creasing with a kind smile and nods to me in silent greeting. Then, as he makes to leave, he brushes a hand with tender affection over Janet's arm; she responds by touching his hand lightly with hers. I find something about that subtle sensual exchange unsettling, as though I'm intruding on a tender private moment. It sets my heart thundering up my throat.

The man then nods again at me as he passes me to leave the lab. I track his disappearing figure down the hall with narrowing eyes then turn back to Janet, feeling an unruly jealously coursing through me. I find the man both threatening and familiar but can't place him. I don't like how he touched her...and how she responded. "Who's that man?"

"That's Damien Vogel, part of the Gaian Triad—"

It comes to me in a violent flash. "Janet! He's the man who—"

"No, he isn't," she cuts in firmly, knowing what I was about to say. "He's his twin brother." She smirks at my expression. "I know, I almost had a bird when he first walked into my lab two months ago."

I stare at her incredulously. "How ... I mean, how do..."

"I manage to even talk to him?" she answers for me in what I think is a far too casual tone. She tilts her head at me with a sardonic look. "Really, Leonard? You slug! He's a totally different person. Damien is actually a very nice man."

"But he called you ... *darling*!"

She chuckles and looks past me with an expression of fondness. I notice her cheeks flush slightly.

"It's just an expression he uses," she quips, gazing directly at me in challenge. "Doesn't mean anything. I'm sure he uses it on all the women he deals with. He's a bit of a flirt."

I make a noise of disgust. "More like a horny old coot," I scoff. "He's got to be at least eighty years old by now!"

"Seventy-five. And you have to admit he barely looks sixty. He's very fit."

I'd noticed that about him, especially when they were touching each other. It just feels weird to see the head of the Gaian government flirting with my cousin, a junior scientist, who is young enough to be his daughter. And it doesn't help that he looks exactly like the brute who killed Simon and was responsible for my mother's death.

"And he's teaching me German," she adds. More like German swear words, I decide. "Something I've wanted to learn since I was a kid and wanted to call out that oaf Fritz at school."

Recalling that she mentioned Vogel showing up two months ago, I fish: "How often has Vogel ... did he?"

"A few times, I guess..." she says. He came a few times in just two months! I notice that she is trying too hard to be casual about it. Or is that just me trying so hard to be casual? How'd they get so friendly?

"You know he's gay," I blurt out. I know, despite him not wearing any earrings to proclaim his orientation.

"What's that got to do with anything?" she retorts. "You sound jealous or something, Leonard. He's just interested in my work with theta rhythm feedback loops and quantum energy frequencies. It harmonizes with what they're doing at AIHV in Icaria-11 on human adaptation and evolution with AI using biological vectors." Then she adds mischievously, "And he isn't just gay. Rumours say the Triad is really a sexual threesome. Vogel, Isabo, and Schlange share more than government policy...If you get my drift." She smirks at me.

I don't say it, but I wonder. How can this man not bring back awful memories that she doesn't want to feel? He may not have killed Simon, but he looks just like the man who did. Why is she encouraging him? Is he serving some kind of therapy for her? Or has she just convinced herself that being polite with him is being a good Icarian? I decide that such an action is, in fact, smart. He's a Gaian Triad Commander, after all. One of the three most powerful people in Icaria. But why does it seem as though she actually likes him? Judging from their body language and flirtatious behaviour I'd venture that she likes him a lot. And if that's the case why does it bother me so much?

ICARIA-11, Darwin Mall, Med-Centre, AIHV of Darwin Clinic. March 12, 2075: late afternoon

Dressed in a crisp purple Admin-Centre uniform, Damien sits on a soft armchair in an outer alcove of the Med-Centre's Darwin Clinic. He crosses his legs and taps his hand on the vee-pad on his lap, willing himself to be patient. He checks the time on his vee-pad and remembers that Janet is usually late for her engagements. It's even in her file.

He brings up a concerning briefing note on his vee-pad. Sent to him two days ago, the note from Euan Tsutsumi at DIE identifies a rising infertility in several Icarias. Tsutsumi is careful not to suggest possible causes, but makes some correlations with factors to do with the enclosed nature of Icaria. Likely culprits include various environmental conditions of enclosed life from filtered air to sunlight, Icarians' heavy use of recreational drugs and their reliance on nano-synthetic foods. The note suggests that nano-products and various drugs, which are an integral part of Icarian life, may have spawned a chemical soup of endocrine disruptors contributing to infertility and may also exacerbate potential neurological disorders; the briefing note also highlights a serious increase in neurological malaise such as various forms of encephalitis, ADHD, and autism.

When Damien showed the briefing note to Christian and Monica, both vehemently agreed that the Gaian decision to instate behaviour engineering in the schools and in the progeny programs at the DP was a good idea. "What better way to keep this in check and to promote a more healthy direction for humanity," Christian argued. "The gene-therapy will greatly help," Monica added. Damien thinks it ironic that the very programs he helped put in place and actively supported by his two Triad colleagues were originally conceived by his brother for his utopia Walden Two. Eric was even going to call it Icaria. Damien lets out a long sigh. How have they come to this? They're following Eric's plan! Good Gaia! The whole thing is worrisome. All the more reason to roll out his Proteus project and get people outside again, he concludes.

His dark thoughts evaporate as Janet arrives, looking crisp in her Med-Centre white uniform and fresh like a summer breeze. Damien leaps up from the chair like a twenty-year old and laughs to himself with the realization that he is a nervous seventy-five-year old. He clasps her hand and offers, "Janet, thanks for taking time away from your work to come to Icaria-11. How do you like the city? It used to be called Montreal before the revolution and I recall it was a vibrant multi-lingual city."

She doesn't respond except to blink at him without a smile. She looks a little nervous, which he understands. So is he.

Undaunted, Damien continues, "Welcome to the Artificial Intelligence Human Vector lab." He shows her into the lab facility with an open smile. She doesn't smile back and follows him inside. He shows her various small labs and their workings. "We've talked about my lab so much and here it is, finally. What do you think?"

She says nothing, but betrays interest, eyes studying everything and mind taking inventory. She reminds him of a cat investigating a new territory, sharp eyes flitting around her, taking in possibilities and threats alike.

"We're actually part of the Darwin Clinic, which is a teaching clinic," he explains, taking her through several hallways to his private lab-office. "This is the research component of the teaching clinic." Once in his private office, he closes the door and turns to her with a nervous smile. Before they even sit down, he says eagerly, "Janet, I'm going to cut to the chase. I asked you here to offer you a position at AIHV as one of my assistants. We're so impressed with your work! It's so innovative, imaginative and creative; I can't wait to work with you. Of course, I'd expect you to move here—"

"You look just like the man who killed my father and tortured his family in front of him," she challenges in a surly voice, eyes now dark with emotion.

Damien freezes at her harsh remark, then recovers and gives her a faint smile. From their first meeting in her lab, she's been friendly, cheerful, and often playfully flirtatious. He got the impression that she was a little sweet on him, which pleased him greatly because he was a little sweet on her. She even liked that he called her his little darling and made a point of learning German from him and teasing him with new words she'd picked up. But they'd never talked about his brother. Damien thought it a taboo. Why would she bring it up now and here? "I know," he says quietly. "Except Eric had a scar on his temple. I don't."

She blinks at him. "You're right. You're not him. But you're his twin."

"I am. But, despite looking exactly the same, we couldn't be more different. I'm *not* my brother." Damien sighs inwardly. Why this sudden belligerence from her? He realizes he may have made a mistake in inviting her here like this without preparing them both. Now that he thinks of it, this was not well planned. Why did she agree to come? Surely she knew it was an interview for a position if not an outright job offer? Why else come all the way here? Has she come just to throw his offer back at him?

When he'd asked her over the vee-com to come to Icaria-11 to meet him here, she looked pleased and enthusiastic. She'd swiftly overcome her shock at his resemblance to his murdering brother the first time they met in her lab, and quickly warmed up to him. They'd easily fallen into fun banter about science and Icarian life that often had them both laughing and giggling like silly children. From the start, she never demurred with him, never treated him like a superior; she treated him as an equal, a fellow scientist—which he found so refreshing. He started looking forward to his weekly visit with her more than anything and he knows she enjoyed them too. Her clever banter, genuine laughter and relaxed demeanor are proof of that. Janet reminds him a little of Monica when she was younger, before she turned hard. Surely he isn't wrong about her liking him? But those encounters took place in Janet's habitat, where she feels comfortable. Is that what this is? Now that she's in his habitat, does he threaten with memories of the worst moment of her life? Perhaps he should have consulted Christian, who may have advised him on how to behave with a wounded animal when displaced from its habitat.

Damien brushes back his crest of greying hair with his hand and repeats, "I am *not* my brother. And I'm sorry if I remind you of him. I wish I didn't. Perhaps that's my curse. But, believe me, from the beginning, my brother and I were on separate sides of the war that brought about Icaria."

"I don't care about sides."

"You should." He seizes her arm with uncharacteristic force but just as quickly lets go, realizing his reckless impulse. He hangs his head in sheepish apology. "I'm so sorry. I'm a foolish old man sometimes and get carried away. Sit, sit, please, Janet. Let's talk." In response to her hesitation, he adds, "You're safe here."

He offers her a place on the sofa and watches her take her seat like a cat, poised to flee. Then he sits beside her, but not too close, with thoughts to clear the air. Their conversations up to now have been careful to circle away from any reference to the revolution and the terrible things that happened at both farms.

He thinks perhaps it is time to broach that topic and confesses in a gentle voice, "When I was younger, I refused to take a side, because both were polarized aspects of a larger issue, and neither was the answer for me. So, I adopted the high moral ground and took myself out of the debate altogether. I buried myself in science. But I soon realized that I only became bitter about what was happening to the environment and that I, by doing nothing, was part of it. I learned that to ensure change for the better, I had to take a stand for that better world. My beloved Christian taught me that." He exhales a long breath and studies Janet. At least she's settled a bit. He notices how she's relaxed her body a little. "What we're doing here is important for the human race. If we are going to survive on this changing Earth, we need to adapt. We need to adapt more quickly than we currently can. What we've done by creating these Icarias is buy us some time. But that's not enough. That's where you and I come in. We can do such good things, Janet. Like your father tried to do, to save humanity. Unfortunately, he was working for an unscrupulous man who wanted to cut corners and who didn't care how many people died to create his dream society. I'm offering you the chance to be your father without the subversion of politics or hidden agendas like my brother imposed on your father and others at BioGen. What BioGen did to your father and to my beloved Christian was heretical. It was criminal. I won't do what Eric did. I give you my word."

"No?" she challenges, meeting his eyes with unflinching steadiness but body still poised to run. "And yet, you've imposed curfew and restrictions on going outside."

"To keep people safe and healthy. So there is still a human race when the environment lets us go back outside."

"You're doing nothing about the heat, drought, floods and storms outside..."

"We're letting nature adapt to the changing climate, which it is doing. We've stopped virtually all our harmful and toxic emissions. No more fossil fuel extraction or emissions. We're trying to be benign. But, like I said, we must focus on staying alive for when we can go out again. Which might be soon, depending on our Proteus project..."

She says nothing but he sees evidence of her

mind working through what he'd told her about his various projects. Studying her in silence, Damien decides that Janet still simmers with a deep anger. It steams off her in her tightly held body, in how she hangs her head in apparent submission while aiming seething eyes of blistering heat, in her firm jaw and mouth poised to snarl. He's seen her laugh and smile, particularly in the company of her cousins. But she remains cool with everyone else. Only with him, it seemed that she was lowering her guard a little and let herself laugh and giggle at his silly jokes. He recognizes that she's angry at the world for being so harsh. Angry at Icaria for its unfair limitations. Angry at Icarians for their docile acceptance of it. But mostly she's angry at herself, for all that she did and didn't do. She has a right to be angry, he decides. She had to bear so much to ensure that her child-self and her child-cousins survived. His eyes grow hot as tears of sorrow and guilt threaten. How easy he had it in comparison! He is responsible for her sad history. And the history of so many others. Eric—that son of a bitch—had murdered so many human beings with his White Demon; but Damien, in forcing everyone to make hard choices during the revolution, had altered anyone who remained.

He thinks of something Tarana Burke of the #MeToo movement in the '20s said and decides to share it with Janet. "Someone once wisely said that 'as long as we are not living at our full humanity, we cannot create a world for humanity.' I created AIHV with that quest in mind. So, will you join me at AIHV, Janet?" He sweeps his arm around the lab. "You'd have your own lab to work in with full autonomy and living quarters close by. I have a wonderful project for us to work on. It involves an artificial virus that promises to permanently enhance a person's brain so they can interface directly with AIs. I'm calling it Proteus. We're thinking of creating a new species, in effect ... a human-viral-machine capable of incredible machine speed and logic, possessing human intuition, problem-solving capabilities, a spiritual conscience and the ability to correct itself; a transhuman able to evolve and change rapidly in incremental ways through its viral counterpart." At her peeked interest, he surges on with excitement. "Imagine getting sick; the virus would pick it up, diagnose the sickness using your AI and then help you fix it. You'd be an efficient self-regulating, self-correcting autopoietic system. Still a human, but so much more; more like a human community." He knows he's captured her interest. Many of their discussions have already covered this intriguing topic. "I see our body as a collection of rhythms, each dancing to its own frequency in a kind of stable chaos; I see Proteus as a kind of viral Mozart, a genetic genius capable of directing those rhythms into a wonderful synchronous symphony through the hippocampus and secondary sectors of the brain." Encouraged by a glint of keen interest in her eyes he forges on. "OK, well you know that we've set up our central AI core as an open, bottom-up system, designed to learn and continue to mature. What we envision—well, it was Christian's vision, really—is a symbiotic relationship between the developing AI core and developing humanity. Christian is designing an interface—he calls it Interact-SYM—that will transmit and receive a quantum corridor beam between the vee-com's holo-receptor and the human's retina. These quantum signals produce a long-term potentiation in the hippocampus that are somehow connected to theta rhythms involved in learning. Anyway, that's how Christian describes it; he's the transhumanist genius. So, Proteus will help us create an integrated learning machine-human community, one able to adapt both in the short-term and long-term to anything. We've been exploring the use of this intelligent virus that learns and adapts as a conduit between human brain and machine intelligence for a while. One of the things it does is help maintain the brain's plasticity to increase action potentials generated by neurons and help neurons actually evolve. Our preliminary work uses high-frequency tetanic pulses that activate a particular phase of theta rhythm in the dentate gyrus of the hippocampus." Damien opens his smile to a grin. "Think of it. Maybe soon we can live outside again, this time in harmony with Nature, even as it changes..."

"Like those Techno-clones your Christian Isabo created for BioGen?" she says, voice still sharp with sarcasm. "Because that went so well, didn't it?" She narrows her eyes at him, meeting his gaze head on. "Didn't Isabo re-engineer them to police Icaria's inner-city

Damien sighs. "You've heard about the cypols." He brushes his hand nervously along the length of his nose. "Christian is a talented robotics and bio-engineer. His vision of transhumanism is brilliant and convincing; he's even turned me into a proponent. The Techno-clone project only went south because my brother weaponized the clones. Christian designed them to withstand the rigors of climate change and increasing pollution. In that regard, he was successful." He finds his hand sweeping his hair back. "But the inner-city is a problem area. It's chaos there and too many of our officers of the law were getting killed. So, I asked Christian to design a more efficient police force. The cypols are mostly machine with a biological base for increased innovation—they are more like an efficient guard dog." He leans closer to share. "Like you, I want what's best for humanity," he says gently. "But also what's best for the environment and the planet. I don't want us to abandon one for the other. I've been a deep ecologist since I can remember; and unlike today's Deep Ecologists of the Circle, I firmly believe we can both co-exist without eliminating the other: nature and humanity. That's why I think that integrating our machine technology with our unique biology will be the answer for humanity's future, so we can eventually go back outside—equipped with adaptive abilities through genetic engineering with machine intelligence and speed—to live together not separate from our environment."

Damien studies her reaction. Her eyes tell all. Though her mouth and face and body remain reticent, her eyes have lost their guard. They light up with acceptance and promise. Curiosity has seized her in its embrace. Time to see it home. Eric would crack her open now like a nut. But Damien refuses to do that; he prefers to encourage her to open herself. He inches toward her, just enough to show intention but not to crowd her. "We can save humanity with this, Janet. This is the next step, after the revolution. I can't pretend to know how you feel about the things that happened to you and your loved ones during the revolution. Commander Schlange told me about what happened, how your family were all killed—by my brother—on your farm and how you and your cousin were abused at the Corporation Farm—"

"I killed a man to save people I loved," she blurts out then adds darkly, "But that killing resulted in a loved one being killed." She lifts her chin in desperate revolt. "So, I won't be responsible for 'saving' anyone's life again. It only gets another killed."

Unintended consequences. The bane of the engineer; Eric had taught him that. Ecologists call it life. But with her confession, he sees how it now all fits into place: her initial belligerence, her nervous reaction to a project that should have her unadulterated enthusiasm. She just confessed her deepest fear and her reason for hesitating to work with him. He sighs and thinks to take her hand but stops himself. Instead, he says gently, "We can never know all the intricacies of how all things are meshed. We can only do the best we can in that limited circumstance and let Nature take care of the rest. I know you feel responsible for that other death, but think of all the variables that created that scenario. Not just your action. Their actions. Others' actions. Nature's actions. We can't take responsibility for all that; but we can take responsibility for ourselves and I'm certain that your action that day came from a place of integrity and love. I *know* it did. Your intention was to save your cousins and that's exactly what you did. You kept them safe at great personal cost. That cost was your innocence. You gave it away to save theirs."

He watches her break and, feeling her heartache, feels compelled to break her further even though it means breaking himself along with her.

Drawing up a breath, Damien surges on, "My brother is dead, did you know? Dispatched by your guardian angel, the one your cousin calls the ice queen." He adds to her mild surprise, "she knew he called her that, thanks to her impressive surveillance, and therefore so do I, thanks to mine." He smiles with the irony then pulls in a long breath of sadness before continuing, "I killed my brother, Janet. I sanctioned her killing him, the brother I grew up with and still loved. But he was a monster; he did terrible *furchtbar* things, and would have continued, if we didn't stop him." Damien pushes out his lower lip and draws in a long sigh, looking down at his hands. "I realize now that's why I came to Canada in the first place. I followed him here, as if I knew what he might do—did...I wish to Gaia I'd stopped him sooner. That is a regret I will live with to my dying days." He draws in a ragged breath and continues, now looking directly into her beautiful eyes, "The revolution changed us all in ways I had never anticipated. Janet, there isn't a moment in my too long life I don't mourn and feel the pain of so much innocence lost to this revolution. Mine and yours. You lost your innocence that day on the farm and I'm so sorry for that, because in some way I'm responsible for it just as my brother was. Perhaps we all lost our humanity for a while, doing unspeakable things, making others do unspeakable things." He dares to lean forward, "But, Janet, my sweet darling, now it's time for life. Not saving. Just living. Time to heal. Because, that—if nothing else—is what the revolution gave us, the opportunity to heal ourselves...And be human again..."

In that moment, he realizes that he's broken her, and feels both relief and guilt as she bursts into violent sobs. He pulls her into his arms and she lets him, leaning into him for comfort as she shudders out her deep anguish. "There, there, I'm so sorry, so sorry," he repeats in a sad murmur. The saddest part of it is that her pain will never end. He knows this because she is like him. But he also senses a darkness inside her that won't leave. He prays it does not consume her. She is a fragile soul, like ice in spring. Thinking of his lost brother, Damien feels tears heat his eyes. Grateful to release them, he weeps openly for them both.

When Janet pulls away, she stares at his tearful face in surprise. Her moss-coloured eyes grow gentle and he knows that this is finally the real Janet looking at him. Raw, hurt and vulnerable, but strong, determined and curious. Something has settled for her. Perhaps her earlier belligerence came from a hidden yearning for closure. Damien isn't her enemy, yet he bears its face. He realizes too that he has been seeking her forgiveness even as she needed to forgive herself.

She meets his shy smile with one of her own and her eyes grow gentle with acceptance and relief. He almost cries out with the joy of it.

"I won't betray this trust, my darling," he says in a quiet voice, full of emotion. He dares to reach out with a trembling hand, brushing her wet cheek in a soft caress. Her eyes almost close at his touch. This time it is she embracing him and he settles into it. He lets a smile of hope light his face and says in a low whisper, "What do you think, my darling? Perhaps together, a wounded cougar and a scientist with an unlucky face can help humanity heal and be what it can be..."

THIRTY-SIX

ICARIA-5, District 9, Darwin Mall,
Café des Fleurs. March 19, 2080: noon

Janet and I are having lunch in the patio of *Café des Fleurs* surrounded by the tall maple and poplar trees and shrubs of Darwin Park. The café nestles in the heart of the mesh-enclosed 5-hectare park, complete with birds and small wildlife. The park is riddled with neat cobblestone paths that wind through it with benches to sit on and enjoy the natural setting. It is Bobby's crown achievement too, his design, I ponder with a smile, proud of my young brother. He was instrumental in scavenging many of the plants from the local heath and other Icarian ecosystems. I helped with the pond-building and others helped with the provision of trees from lab cultures.

Janet dabs a spot she's made on her crisp white Med-Centre uniform and licks her fingers after finishing her tofu burger. After wiping her hands on a serviette, she reaches for her latte. I've already finished my quinoa salad with gamagrass bread and curl my hands around my coffee cup like it's my salvation. We've paused in our conversation about my work with algal cultures at DIE and I sense with a sullen foreboding that she wishes to broach a topic with me that involves a favour.

I study her for a moment as thoughts of the past haunt me. She looks like springtime. Unruly straw-coloured hair frames her sanguine face and she holds her mouth in a quirky half smile that teases with potential mischief. She wears no earrings, suggesting she's not inviting anyone into her life; but I know she likes Vogel. She and I seldom see each other now—we're both so busy—and particularly now that she lives in Icaria-11, several hours away on the jet train. When we do meet, it's usually because she wants a favour from me. Seems like that's the only reason we meet these days. I wonder what she's after this time.

Without realizing what I'm doing, I draw on my surly mood and say what's been on my mind. "How could you go live with that Vogel?" I stroke my coffee cup as if solace can be found there. "He looks just like the man that killed Simon."

She groans at me with annoyed impatience and lashes out, "What about you, eh? You stayed in that place where we were abused by those Corporation Farm brutes. You chose to stay there, Leonard."

"Dammit, that's where I work!"

"Turd! What do you think I'm doing? Damien and I are working on a meaningful project to help—"

"Damien, eh? Not Commander Vogel? Does he still call you *darling*?" I realize that my voice simpers with sarcasm and lean both arms on the table as I push myself forward.

"So what!" Her night shade eyes flash at me with growing anger.

"I worry about you, Janet. You've never had a boyfriend or girlfriend and then when you do, he's old enough to be your grandfather."

"He's not my boyfriend!" She waves a hand in the air. "And I'm not living with him, Leonard. You're just mad that I moved to Icaria-11 and you can't see me every day!"

I hang my head with the truth and stare down at my empty cup. She's right. I miss her far more than I'm willing to admit. And when we do meet, we usually end up like this, arguing.

She leans across the table and gently places her hands on my arms. "Oh, Leonard," she says sadly, big eyes diving into mine. I inhale her scent of spring flowers. "You have a beautiful sweet wife and family now," she says in a soothing voice, looking for truce. "Your eldest, Julie, is five years old, isn't she? She's starting school and already learning the Isabo Creed. And your little two-year old, Diana, must be a handful these days," She's grinning now and I realize that I live for those grins, how her upturned mouth forms crease lines and how her eyes the colour of a mossy forest light up her face with hope for the future. She sighs out. "You don't need to hang around with me..."

"But you're family," I say too quickly. "You and Bobby. We need to stay close."

Janet looks at me funny. I realize that I've not made a good argument for closeness; despite living in the same Icaria, Bobby and I hardly see one another. We aren't close and Janet knows it. Now that he's taken to peddling illicit books, he and I don't get along. Janet sees both of us more than Bobby and I see one another. Bobby—like me—still clings to her. I suppose that will never change. Although I think Janet wishes it would. Is our refusal to release her choking her? But I can't help it; the world doesn't feel safe or right without her in it. As though her presence defines mine.

Much of what I've achieved is only the result of her encouraging presence. Although painfully insecure socially, I've become daring in my work. I've invoked the long abandoned chaos theory and apply it to my models of ecosystem behavior. The signature of chaos appeals to me, how the subtle effect of a single event has the potential to spiral into overwhelming and irrevocable change. Chaoticists call it the Butterfly Effect: sensitive dependence on initial conditions, based on the strange notion that a butterfly stirring the air in Peking today could set off a tornado in Texas next month. I recognize its hand in everything, including our behaviour. How the imperceptible mark of that initial disturbance has cascaded into a turbulent squall that still acts on the three of us. She was just my cousin, but when we were still children, Janet killed for us. Using the hunting bow Nicole gave her, she slew a man who charged at us with a knife, the same knife he'd used to kill our parents. When my brother was attacked, she flew to his aid and threw herself into a den of assault.

Then, when she pleaded for my help, I ran away.

I was just a boy, only thirteen years old. But I know better. That moment defined me. She faced fear head on, bravely pushed it aside and rose to the call; I let fear chase me away. I still hear her screams and see that face frozen in painful anguish. When she isn't in front of me, smiling to show me all is well, that terrible image creeps in.

"Leonard," Janet says gently and squeezes my arm, pulling me back to her. Forest green eyes probe inside me with an intensity that forces me to sit up. I've seen that look before; it simmers with retribution and expectation. As if she knows she clutches my soul in her hand and I'll do anything for her when she squeezes. Which she is about to do now. I know she will ask me for a favour and I fight from cringing. The last time she looked at me this way, she wanted me to use my connection with DIE to help her cut through the bureaucratic tape in getting a restricted drug, something she needed for her neurological experiments on rats. And, of course, I did my bidding.

"Julie is already gifted, isn't she?" she asks me casually.

I give her a guarded smile and nod. Why did Janet say 'already'? What's she after? Every child in Icaria, once they reach five years, surrenders to a series of intelligence tests to help determine their primary school stream in the Ed-Centre. The Isabo IITT test for Intelligence Type demonstrated that Julie is a Type 3 combination of spatial-linguistic; someone who looks at things differently. She is indeed gifted. Forgetting to be suspicious for a moment, I proudly rattle off the details, "She was one of the highest ranked five-year-olds in the Isabo IITT tests. She scored 89% and 82% on the SPAT and LOG tests."

She nods. "I'd like to run some tests on her. Use her as a test subject for our project on the virus-vector we're testing in BMI. We need someone her age and intelligence. She'd be a shoo-in. I hear she's already good with vee-coms."

There it is. That's her style; no beating around the proverbial bush. She wants my oldest daughter as a lab rat. I blink in silence and feel my heart thump with the inevitable surrender.

Ignoring my obvious discomfort, Janet forges on, "She's reached the perfect stage of development for our procedure. We're testing a new virus that basically enhances a person's brain so they can interface directly with AIs—without the need for a clunky vee-com." Then, after an infinite pause, in which both of us silently stare at the other—lurid thoughts calling up another time and another place—she adds perfunctorily, "It's not harmful, Leonard. I would never ask if there was even a chance of that. The inoculation is perfectly safe. She'll come out of it enhanced and probably the first of the very best vee-com users in all of Icaria. This will make her one of the most sought-after workers in Icaria. It's a real win-win scenario here for her, for you, and for Icaria." Then she leans over the table, clasping my arms again as if to trap them there, face glowing with a mischievous smile. "*And,*" she emphasizes, "giving Julie to the AIHV lab for testing constitutes a service that earns you a Level 1 card, Leonard." Her crooked smile opens to a victorious grin. "I know that Deborah has been nagging you to get a nicer flat in District 12, one you can only get with a Level 1 card. One with a bigger bedroom for the kids, chute service, a PCU, cleaning droids, a full AI kitchen, and top grade environmental system."

She's packaged it all up into an alluring offer.

But I know she doesn't need to, because this is just another retribution for what I failed to do thirteen years ago when I ruined both our lives by running away and turning us all into victims. Bobby too.

I sigh. I can't refuse. I nod in silence.

"Good!" She brightens, eyes gleaming like emeralds. "Schlange will be so pleased—"

Schlange! If she was going to mention anyone, I expected Vogel's name. I was ready for that insult; not this! "What? You're friends with the *ice queen*?" My voice goes shrill with reproach. Janet is far too trusting. She has always seemed somewhat naïve to me. Even when we were children, I was always the cynical one who held back, suspicious and wanting to check the evidence or details, while she charged ahead. Her impetuous nature had gotten her into trouble too many times already.

"Really, Leonard!" Janet shakes her head at me. "Schlange is the mayor of Icaria-11 and a scientist herself. Of course, she takes an interest in Damien's work. They're both Triad Commanders, after all—never mind that they share a bed. This could be ground-breaking, Leonard. And because AIHV resides in Icaria-11, Schlange sees it as important for her city. As she should."

"Since when are you chummy with the ice queen?" I repeat.

She frowns at me. "Good, Gaia, Leonard. You, slug! She looked after us. She ensured that we were safe at the farm." Her dark eyes pierce into mine and her voice rises with emotion, "She stopped them from raping me..."

Before I could, I add to myself. I still feel peevish about her charging into the washroom as the brute was about to rape Janet—just as I was about to make my move to repair my earlier act of cowardice. Instead, she dispatched him like Wonder Woman, earning Janet's awe and respect. Schlange had robbed me of that prize. She'd ensured that for the rest of my life I would wallow in the guilt of my earlier cowardice. And for that reason, I can't bear to accept any kindness from her. I still don't trust her motives. I don't think she's kind by nature; kindness from Monica Schlange only happens when it suits her agenda.

I realize with some shame that I hate Monica Schlange.

ICARIA-11, Darwin Mall, Darwin Clinic. April 12, 2080: late at night

Dressed in crisp white Med-Centre top and slacks, Janet meets me at the entrance to the clinic. She's pushing a gurney. I am carrying my sedated girl in my arms.

She picks up a vee-pad from the gurney and says peremptorily, "Put her on the gurney, Leonard."

I hesitate. Something in me doesn't want to give her up. Something in me tells me that this is wrong. But how can I say no to Janet, especially since I promised? I'm here, aren't I?...

I somehow knew that Deborah wouldn't condone this. I'd left telling her until the last moment, after I'd sedated Julie, shortly after she went to bed. I walked out of the bedroom she shared with her little sister, Julie's limp form already in my arms, and told Deborah right there in the hallway. I explained the procedure and how it would help Julie become successful and how we'd get my Level 1 card privileges for it. Deborah didn't take it well. I think she couldn't believe I would do such a thing at first; but, when it became clear that I fully intended on taking our little daughter to the Icaria-11 Med-Centre, she went crazy. At first she pleaded for me to stop. She didn't care about the Level 1 card anymore. "Please, please, Leonard! Don't do this," she'd exhorted me. When I didn't relent, she got angry and flew at me in a rage, trying to claw Julie back to her. I had to push her off me so hard, she fell to the floor. She didn't get up and I pulled Julie up over my shoulder like a sack of potatoes and left, hearing Deborah weeping on the floor and shrilling out for the entire floor of the Liv-Centre to hear: "You're an *OGRE*! And you love *her* more than me! Giving her our child! *Our child*! Let her get her own to experiment on!"...

"Put her on the gurney, Leonard," Janet repeats, growing impatient with me.

I lay my little girl down on the gurney and blink repeatedly as Janet pulls a blanket over Julie to keep her warm; she looks asleep and so calm and relaxed. So innocent.

Janet almost gruffly hands me the vee-pad and laser pen with a terse nod.

I look down at the form displayed. There's a place for me to sign.

"It's an NDA, Leonard. This is top secret and proprietary research. It can't leave the clinic."

I start to read. "What's this? What's *Prometheus*?"

"For Gaia's sake, Leonard," she says in a clipped voice, showing impatience. "Everything is top secret, OK? Now sign it and we can get started."

"OK, OK..." I sign, noticing that my hand shakes a little. Is this a mistake?...

Showing great relief, Janet takes the vee-pad from me and gives me a genuine smile. She pats my hand in terse reassurance. "It'll be okay, Leonard," she says. "Go get some sleep; We'll inoculate her tonight and I'll call you in the morning when she wakes up." Then she abruptly wheels my sleeping child down the hallway to the AIHV lab, where the procedure will take place.

Left alone in the antiseptic hall, I stand in frozen silence, feeling like I've sacrificed my five-year-old daughter to the crucible of science. It is more than that, I finally decide, and feel the incrimination of a terrible insoluble bargain. Who have I done this for? My cousin or me? This is just another in a long line of Faustian deeds I've carried out for my cousin to assuage my guilt. But the cost is too great, I suddenly conclude, even as it's too late. I stare down the hall, knowing I can't stop what I've started. The hall lights break up into a million shards as my eyes cloud with tears of guilt. What have I done to my little girl?

ICARIA-11, Darwin Mall, Darwin Clinic. April 13, 2080: early morning

"I just want you to be prepared, Leonard," Janet is saying to me as we walk down the hall toward the room where my little girl is. She looks nervous and that alarms me. She's never nervous. I walk faster and burst through the door, past a Pol dressed in black. I stop dead and take in the scene.

Vogel and Schlange stand bent over Julie's bedside like two vultures. They look on with some concern as Julie moves about in some kind of delirium. She's almost writhing with discomfort, as though she has a fever or is drugged.

I flash accusing eyes at Janet, who stands behind me. "What have you done to her!"

Janet stares at me with wide eyes, mouth open but saying nothing.

Vogel offers, "Her vitals are strong. She's just adjusting to the virus as its new host—"

"I asked *her*! Not *you*!" I shout, eyes reverting to Janet who shuffles her feet. She can't look straight at me.

"Leonard, I—don't know exactly how..." she trails, eyes almost tearing. "She was talking to herself, all confused, and arguing with herself like a schizophrenic; so we gave her some drug to calm her. Then she went into ... well *this*." The half-conscious writhing and discomfort.

"What happened to her?" I shriek, aiming accusing looks at each person there. No one says anything. My gaze lands on Schlange, looking far too calm. Overcome with rage, I shout, "Get out! Get the vee out! Everyone! Especially *you*!" I point at Schlange.

"Calm down, Leonard," Vogel says, nodding to the Pol by the door and I feel his presence right behind me. He's probably pulled out his weapon. "We gave her a sedative with ambrosia to calm her down and she's reacting to that. That's all. She was hearing voices, hallucinating. She'll calm down soon, I'm sure." Then seeing that I'm not flying into a rage, he nods to the Pol to stand down and says kindly, "We'll leave you with her for a few moments." He glances at Janet and Schlange pointedly. "Let's leave them for a bit."

They leave but the Pol stays by the door. He diffidently watches me, hand resting casually on the butt of the weapon hanging in its holster at his waist.

I find a chair and bring it close to the bed and sit beside Julie. A large bouquet of roses stands by her bedside. Its scent permeates the room with an almost cloyingly sweet aroma. I wonder who they are from as I take Julie's little hand. It seems to calm her, I think. Or is it my imagination? Tears spring to my eyes. Why did I let Janet take my little girl? For *this*? Deborah was right to call me an ogre. How could I have done this to my own daughter?

"Daddy?"

I realize that I've been looking out the window into the smog of the city and return my attention to Julie. She looks up at me with some confusion and looks a little scared.

I squeeze her little hand in mine. "It's OK, Angel. You just got sick. You went into convulsions and then into a coma. I brought you here, where Auntie Janet works. She's fixing you all up. How do you feel now?"

"Why do I hear voices, Daddy?"

"Voices? Like what?"

"Like I'm catching pieces of conversations by other people, but they sound weird. Like they're building something or tearing something down."

I blink at her, unable to respond. Gaia! She's still hallucinating.

"Daddy, I want to go home!"

I pat her hand. "I know, honey. I'll get you out of here. I promise." Fearing what they might still do if they know she's still hearing voices in her head, I lean close to her and command her quietly, "Listen, Angel, don't tell anyone about the voices, OK? If you want to go home, don't tell anyone about the voices. Not even Janet, OK? If they ask you about them tell them they're all gone. Promise?" I think to myself: we'll handle those inner voices later. Once she's home safe, once she's out of this place, we can deal with that.

"I promise, Daddy."

Then she suddenly grows agitated again and her palm goes sweaty in my hand. I watch her eyes roll up and she starts to writhe. The monitor starts to beep.

"Nurse!" I shriek. "Nurse! Help!"

A nurse charges into the room and gruffly pushes me aside. She adjusts the feed line into her arm and Julie calms down. Now she looks just asleep.

The nurse turns to me with a commanding face. "I think you should leave now."

ICARIA-11, Darwin Mall, Darwin Clinic. April 18, 2080: late morning

On the fifth day Julie finally wakes and remains in a lucid state and Janet calls me. Euan gives me leave to skip work and I go to Icaria-11.

As I approach the room in the Clinic, I hear excited

chatter among several people and stop outside the door to eavesdrop.

"Her V29 prostaglandins are abnormally high; do you know what that means?"

That sounds like Christian Isabo. What is he doing here?

"No, pray tell," Schlange drawls, voice dripping bored sarcasm.

"Did you see her score on my IITT tests? A hundred percent on all of them!"

"So, you're saying it worked?" Vogel's anxious voice. "Is that what you're saying, Christian?"

"Hmmm... not really. It's possible, but she isn't showing any signs of being able to connect with the machine intelligence. The Interac-SYM tool is a bust on her. Nothing, Damien. It could be that the sedatives and meds we're giving her to stop the fever and delirium are interfering, but I doubt it. I'm sorry."

"That's so disappointing," says Vogel. "I'm concerned about her high fevers and that delirium. Honestly, I don't think it's worth it."

"Give it time, Damien," Schlange says. "Vee, it's only been five days."

"While she was in a coma and almost died!"

Died! My heart thunders. No one told me that!

"You're such a drama queen, Damien. Sometimes I wonder if you're a clone of Eric's."

"Enough!" he blusters, clearly annoyed that she has brought up his twin brother and compared them. "I think we should hold off anymore work with Proteus. This is too dangerous for clinical trials yet. I'm shutting it down, pending more research."

"Hey, slug!" Janet taps me on the shoulder. I jump in surprise and turn. She smirks at me with a knowing look. She's just arrived from down the hall. "Are you doing what I think you're doing?"

I give her a sheepish smile. I'm about to tell her what I've overheard when she shoves past me into the room, grabbing my hand and pulling me behind her.

"Look who I found!" she announces.

The three of them straighten from their bent positions over Julie's sleeping form, and Vogel gives me a genuine smile. "Good to see you, Leonard. Come and see your daughter. She was awake a moment ago, but looks like she's fallen asleep again. Perhaps you'd like to wait for her to wake up? We'll leave the two of you alone." He indicates for them all to leave.

Janet says, "I'll stay with my cousin and his—"

"Actually," Schlange cuts in, grabbing Janet by the arm. "I have an urgent matter I'd like to talk to you about, Janet." Schlange sends a warning glance at Vogel and Isabo.

I blink and wonder what I'm witnessing. Is this some kind of power struggle? Thanks to Deborah, who keeps me informed on all matters to do with the Triad, it seems that Schlange and Isabo had a major falling out. The rumor mill has been busy speculating on the relationship of the Triad since someone at the ridiculously popular Peekaboo Show covertly documented a huge lover's tiff between Schlange and Isabo outside Peppars. She actually struck him in the face, which no doubt impacted her relationship with Vogel, who he's reportedly been lovers with since before the revolution. According to Deborah, people speculate that

Schlange now resides exclusively in her Icaria-5 residence even though she maintains her mayorship of Icaria-11. Judging from her nasty comment to Damien Vogel, I think the two original lovers have ousted her.

Janet gives me a conciliatory smile as Schlange ushers her out. It's as though Janet belongs to her. Vogel look puzzled and disconcerted. I glance from them to the door through which Janet and Schlange disappeared. Why does Janet follow her around so easily? What is Schlange's hold on her?

ICARIA-5, District 12 Liv-Centre. April 29, 2080: late morning

Julie has settled nicely and looks unaffected by her ordeal at the Icaria-11 Med-Centre. After a week of observation, Janet released her and she came home to my great relief. She's even gone back to school and acts normally. We haven't talked about those inner voices in her head, but it seems that all of that has stopped. I don't bring it up and neither does she.

Julie has been back home for close to a week when the first cases are reported in Icaria-11: a new arcane disease is spreading frighteningly fast in the Icaria-11 population. The Med-Centres are rapidly filling with patients reporting anything from memory loss and confusion to muscle spasms and heart problems. It reminds me of Julie's initial delirium, confusion and hallucinations after being inoculated with the virus. Worried that they might be connected, I try several times to contact Janet on my vee-com. She doesn't answer.

ICARIA-5, District 12 Liv-Centre.
May 2, 2080: late evening

She never answers. I start to panic. Where is she? I think of the NDA she forced me to sign.

Deborah, who is always glued to *Icaria Now*, keeps me informed of the grizzly details of the new disease. The CDC have now traced over 70% of the original cases to the Darwin Clinic in Icaria-11, people who have gone in for minor things. Others were spouses or friends, so it is very likely to have originated there. They're calling it Darwin's Disease because of it.

Some people have died already from complications; heart attacks, organ failure, other things that interfere with basic brain functions.

Deborah sits on her lounge chair facing the large wall vee-com screen. I stand by the door to the living room, having just tucked Julie in bed. We both watch the news on the large screen on the wall. Icaria has just reported that a few cases have already appeared in Icaria-5. Deborah turns to me in sudden fright. "What about Julie? She was there just before." Then she suddenly realizes. "And you too!"

Her panic is contagious. Should I be worried for Julie and me? Where is Janet? Is she OK? Surely, she didn't succumb to Darwin's Disease? Why hasn't she responded to my calls?

"Oh my vee!" Deborah's voice goes shrill like a child's. "This is just like the White Plague that got out and killed half the world!" She jerks to her feet. She races to me standing at the door to the living room and seizes me in a tight embrace. "Leonard! What should we do? It must be contagious; it's spreading so fast!" She steals a glance at the bedroom where the girls are sleeping.

At the same time, we quickly disengage. Am I contagious? Is Julie? Neither of us is suffering any signs, though Julie certainly had similar ones before at the clinic. I remember Janet explaining to me how insidiously the White Plague spread, by affecting different DNA types in different ways. Is this disease another smart virus?

ICARIA-5, District 12 Liv-Centre.
May 13, 2080: late evening

I'm so sorry, Leonard," Euan consoles me. "I only heard at supper." He faces me on my home vee-com looking sad and solicitous. "Vee, she was so young and so brilliant!"

"Thanks, Euan," I croak out and abruptly sign off my vee-com. My throat is so thick with emotion I can hardly speak. I know my eyes are red from crying. Why did Janet commit suicide? Vogel informed me this morning soon after he found her dead in her lab at the Darwin Clinic. Apparently she'd taken Miaclone, a cyclopyrrolone sedative she used on some of her test subjects that, if taken in too large amounts put you into a permanent sleep. After the initial shock this morning, I went numb for the rest of the day. By now, the numbness is turning into great loss and a simmering rage. How could such a thing happen? Why would she do such a thing? She'd always been dark. But *this* dark? Something isn't right...

There's a knock at the front door and I shut the vee-com.

Deborah opens the door. It's Bobby. He looks past her and, seeing me, he charges past her and grabs me in one of his bear hugs. It's just what I need. My eyes tear and we both cry together. Our saviour is dead...

ICARIA-11, District 9 Liv-Centre.
May 16, 2081: late evening

"How can we continue this work? It feels almost disrespectful..." Damien says. Dressed only in pajama bottoms, he sits on the living room couch, gazing forlornly at the faux fireplace, patting his elderly cat.

"Because of Janet?" Christian, dressed in the matching pajama top, sits with his naked butt beside Damien and brushes his hand gently across Damien's cheek. "You have to stop blaming yourself for her suicide, *chouchou*. There's no way that anyone could have known that this virus would escape the clinic and morph into Darwin's Disease. Gaia! We're still not even sure if it was Proteus or what it was to begin with because we haven't pinpointed its origin and how it got out. All we do know is that a number of us come in and out of the lab, handling all our Gain of Function research drugs. They're all potentially dangerous if they get out without proper procedure and do something we don't expect. Accidents do happen. But why does she blame herself? It's not logical," Christian argues in a lecture voice. He draws in a breath and gazes absently at the flickering flames of the faux fireplace. "Great Gaia, back in the days of BioGen, these kinds of accidents were happening all the time. We just kept going on for the sake of the science. In most cases, it didn't amount to that much, given a lab culture's limitations in the wild. We knew the risks. Just like now."

"But I feel so..."

"Responsible?" Christian pushes a stray lock out of Damien's eyes and gently guides it behind his ear. "You know you shouldn't feel responsible for that accident. It'll eat you alive, *chouchou*."

"Not for the accident. But for being inattentive to my little lost darling," Damien murmurs as if to himself. He pats the old cat, which purrs loudly. Damien sighs and looks up into Christian's sea-green eyes. "I should have known, Christian. She takes everything so personally. I should have kept a better eye on her. She could be so dark sometimes. Such a delicate hepatica. So sweet and bright but so ephemeral. Too easily collapsing into the darkness. No one knows how this Darwin virus got out. A broken test tube? Some contamination with clothing or other instrumentation? It couldn't be the girl." He shakes his head. "That's not logical. She's fine with Proteus. We're not even sure it's Proteus." He brings his hands to his face. "Christian, I remember Janet sharing with me her greatest fear: the unintended consequence of doing something good: saving a loved one but in doing so ensuring another loved one's death..."

Christian seizes Damien's hands from his face, startling the cat, which springs from the sofa onto the floor. Christian cups Damien's hands in his. They are rough like a gardener's and so beautifully large.

"Damien, that's the point." His hands squeeze and he fixes Damien with a steady gaze. "Why would she react with such violence? It feels like an act of guilt. Why would someone feel such guilt about an *accident*?"

Damien flashes intense eyes on him, hands still gripped inside Christian's tight clasp. "What do you mean?"

Christian looks away, shaking his head. "I'm not sure. It's just..." he trails. When his gaze returns, it gleams with a sudden thought. "Listen, *chouchou*, I came home today with some interesting news. It may be related to this. It is certainly why we must continue our work with Proteus."

Damien perks up. "What is it, darling?"

"Remember, I was doing some extra research, based on those strange findings I mentioned about Julie's V29 prostaglandins? Well, we discovered that she is unique in other ways, ways that may yet prove AI-compatible, and possibly in ways we haven't yet imagined. That she didn't take to the Interact-SYM may simply be *its* limitation, not *hers*."

"What are you saying, Christian?" His hands grow hot in Christian's grasp.

Christian's eyes sparkle like a brilliant tropical sea. "We may have discovered a new species!" He giggles with hysterical delight. "I'm tentatively calling them veemelds, because of what I think they may be capable of and because I think there are more of her..."

Damien stares at Christian, unable to speak.

Christian goes on, "And this unique genetic makeup could suggest that she may even be immune to Darwin's Disease among other things—considering that she was right there just before it got out..."

Damien blinks hard and his first thought is of Monica. Does she know about the girl? Of course she does. He thinks of her extensive surveillance system. She ran the Secret Police, for Gaia's sake. Now her Secret Pols have infiltrated every work sector of every Icaria he knows. Her spy network blankets all of Icaria, not just Icaria-11 where she is currently mayor. His thoughts slide to the number of times he found her at Julie's bedside, watching her, sometimes talking to her comatose form as if giving her instructions. Monica had spent a lot more time with the girl than anyone else—even Janet, who was supposedly in charge of her. Why did Monica take such an interest? He knew that she wasn't fond of children. Then there was the day he announced the termination of clinical trials and she pulled Janet aside... He thinks he knows why now.

Damien pulls his hands out from Christian's and places them on his lover's face. "Great Gaia, Christian! Does Monica know? About what you discovered?"

Christian cups his large hands over Damien's and frowns in thought. "I haven't shared any of this with her. But you know about..." he trails with the obvious.

"Yes. Her many eyes and ears," Damien snarls out an ill-humored smile and straightens into a stiff position, hands back to wringing themselves. "The only thing that remains to be ascertained, is what she is going to do about that knowledge." Then he thinks of what Christian said earlier and that strange exchange with Janet. He draws in a sharp breath. Maybe she already has.

"Exactly!" Christian barks with excitement, as if reading Damien's mind. He responds to Damien's sharp inhale by abruptly sliding Damien's pajama bottoms off and pushing him gruffly down on the couch. Damien barks out a laugh as Christian straddles him and their naked lower bodies touch, warm and stirring like reptiles in the heat. Leaning over Damien like a bear about to feast, Christian presses into him and pants out through excited breaths, "We must find all we can about these veemelds. They may be the key to Icaria's survival. I'd like to use AIHV to test for veemelding, *chouchou,* find out what they are capable of, then incorporate it in our offspring potential scan at the DP."

"Yes, yes!" Damien grunts out, hand diving between Christian's inner thighs to seize his prize. "Do it, *Süßer*! As for that viper, I'm guessing she knows it all! *Mein gott,* she's such a pest!"

Christian gasps out, "But you must admit, she's an awesome fuck!" He then erupts into mischievous giggle-moans to Damien's coaxing hand.

Aroused by that boyish giggle, Damien rasps out, "Not as awesome as you, *mein Süßer*!" He seizes Christian by his pajama top and pulls him down to kiss him fiercely on the mouth.

CONVALESCENCE

Contrast and paradox lie deeply embedded in nature. Just as wisdom exists in folly, action in inaction, bravery in cowardice, and ultimately order in chaos. Just as laminar flow spills into riotous tendrils only to find a uniform pattern of turbulence, stable chaos permeates everything and everyone. The spread of an epidemic. Changing populations of insects. The rise and fall of civilizations. Like fractals of a larger interconnected universe, each individual has their own cycle of creative destruction to experience before merging into a greater community of consciousness.

—Leonard Crane, "Use of an Inverted Loop Model to Predict Environmental Collapse in Enclosed Icarias," ICARIAN SCIENTIST, 136 December 2084

THIRTY-SEVEN

ICARIA 5, District 12 Live-Centre.
February 25, 2083: after supper.

It's well after supper, as usual, when I depart work and head home. Wearing my mask, I sit in the tube-jet car on its way to District 12. They've removed seating to create space and social distancing is encouraged. Only two other people are in the car with me, a man and a young woman, both wearing masks. Luckily, most of us here in the outer-city prudently follow the imposed restrictions about wearing a mask and not touching. I've heard that people in the inner-city flagrantly ignore the restrictions, unwilling to be bullied by a government infringing on their rights and freedoms. More like the freedom to get Darwin, I think scathingly.

It's been three years since Darwin Disease broke out in Icaria-11 and spread quickly to the other Icarias, including Icaria-5. The CDC described it as a neural disorder caused by the retrovirus they've named Pro-V. It initially spread through nosocomial infection—likely some kind of accidental contamination—and resulted in the current pandemic, despite full quarantine measures. The CDC describes the infection as interfering with several neurotransmitters, eventually destroying cholinergic neurons of both peripheral and central nerves. Symptoms develop from simple memory loss, related heart problems and muscle spasms to eventual dementia and death from complications. Duration of the disease from initial symptom presentation to last stages of dementia and loss of critical brain functions vary from two weeks to five months. They don't yet know the mechanism of transmission, although aerosol spread via the respiratory tract has been ruled out. They also never figured out how the disease initially got out or where exactly it came from, although lots of speculation has come out. I'm inclined to think it was another GOF research lab accident like Janet's father experienced at BioGen. Only this time, instead of crashing a wheat crop, it is crashing humanity.

The disease collapsed Icaria-11, just as Euan predicted.

For several weeks, I've been working long hours on my project with Euan at my new lab at DIE in Nadezdha Mall. We've been number-crunching the newest data on Darwin's Disease that Euan is certain will provide irrevocable proof for our Inverted Loop Model's prediction of Icaria degeneration. Despite its use of Stable Chaos Theory and Fractal Ecology—both considered Dystopian and illegal—Euan thinks it will be snatched up by the journal *Icarian Scientist*.

I tersely greet the security droid at the entrance of our apartment building. The droid is another Level-1 perk I'm not used to and feel rather uncomfortable with. The AI50 raises a copper arm in greeting and straightens its streamlined human-shaped form in attentiveness. "Hello, Mister Crane," it says in a tinny voice, cocking its head and peering at me with neon eyes, pretending to be human. "Fine evening, isn't it?"

"Yes, it is," I respond tersely and enter the building,

still uncomfortable with the idea of talking with a machine like it's a person.

As I enter our flat, I hear a loud smack and Deborah's angry shout at our eldest daughter in a slurred voice of *ambrosia* inebriation: "Julie, you virus! That's the last time you break a dish!"

I storm into the kitchen as Deborah hits my eight-year-old daughter again. Both turn to me and freeze as I surge toward them. I don't strike my drunken wife; instead, my quiet voice carries my knife-sharp rage. "Don't *ever* hit our daughter again, do you hear me?"

I bend down to hug Julie and rumple her hair. "You're OK now, my angel."

Deborah snarls, "Stop calling her an angel. She's no angel—"

I abruptly stand up, hand flying up with rage but I stop myself in time and see both mother and daughter cringe at my violent action.

Suddenly brave again, Deborah lashes out, "You're telling me how to treat our daughter? After what you did? You made her into a monster. A freak!"

"Shut up!" She's not a freak.

"When are you going to tell her? She still thinks she just fell ill that night you took her to Janet's lab. Gaia, Leonard. Janet said *jump* and you said *how high*! You sacrificed your own daughter for her—"

"Shut up!" I scream, advancing on her. I smell the reek of *ambrosia* on her breath. "You don't know what you're talking about!" I seize her gruffly by the shoulders and push her out of the kitchen with such force, she stumbles. I turn to my daughter who stares at me with scared saucer eyes. "Go to bed, Julie," I command her. Julie runs out of the room.

I let my anger simmer down by rooting in the fridge for something to eat and find leftover tofu stew, which I eat cold out of the container with a fork I find in a drawer. I wolf down several mouthfuls and throw the dish back in the fridge then wash it all down with some *delilah*—Deborah has drunk all the *ambrosia*.

I root in my pocket for my pipe and some *hedon* and put it all together, light it and take in a long inhale. I let its soporific notes coarse through me, softening the edges, cooling down the sparks, quieting down the raging voices. When I enter the living room, temper finally under control, Deborah has the large wall vee-com monitor on and is following the news on *Icaria Now*.

"Good vee, Leonard, look at this!" Deborah calls to me as if we hadn't quarrelled. "Two members of the Triad are dead! They were murdered!"

"What?" I stare at the wall screen.

Doris Croome, anchor for *Icaria Now* sits demurely behind a desk with a backdrop of gleaming towers of Icaria-11 on the screen behind her. I catch her in mid-speech: "...leaving Damien Vogel, the remaining Commander of the Triad in deep mourning. Of course, these three commanders were very close in their personal lives as well as sharing government responsibilities. They shared a penthouse in the Liv-Centre of Icaria-11's District 9. But last night, because of duties, Commander Schlange was staying in her flat in District 13 of Icaria-5. Unfortunately that place, with her inside, was bombed by an unknown assailant, likely a Dystopian terrorist. Icaria-5's Head-Pol, Wolfgang Kraken, has assured *Icaria Now* that they will catch the culprit." The image of a burly man in his forties wearing the imposing black uniform of the Pol-Centre comes on the screen. Stallion-black hair sweeps across his wide temple as he eyes the camera with a shrewd gaze. His single left earring identifies him as a heterosexual. Obviously Kraken. Croome's voice continues, "So far the Head Pol has shared no leads but it is rumoured that a Dystopian radical from Icaria-11 is responsible." The image moves to a candid head shot of Schlange, caught running with dark hair flying behind her. The shot highlights her attractive face and intense dark eyes. No earrings. The badass scar on her temple only adds to her stunning looks. Damn her beauty.

As if mocking my thought, Deborah expostulates, "Isn't she beautiful, honey? It's so sad she's gone! She was our saviour in the revolution, leading it to its final victory," she coos raptly. I think of how so many people like Deborah have succumbed to the propaganda about that ice queen. "She was so nice!" Deborah goes on. "So sad about those three, how they couldn't get along in the end. Who will they replace her with? I hope it's not that ogre Kraken from the Pol-Centre. He's a terrible man, such a brute. It's so nice to have a woman at the top..."

"...As Commander of the Gaian Army then the Gaian Secret Service, Schlange actively removed many dangerous Techno sympathizers and Dystopians from society," Croome continues in tribute. The image moves to a head shot of round-faced Isabo, looking friendly as he always did. In that shot his hair is dyed mauve and he sports earrings on both ears. Croome goes on, "It is not known why Christian Isabo was in the tube-jet station at Margalef Mall when he was struck down in cold blood by a shot to the chest at close range by a man some describe as wearing a Com-Centre suit. Both dead commanders of the Triad leave Commander Damien Vogel as sole leader of the Gaian government."

The image fades to a still shot of Damien Vogel. It's a candid shot some reporter caught of him in Darwin Park of Icaria-5 soon after the double murders. I'm stunned by how old and gaunt he looks. And he's so forlorn that I almost feel sorry for him. His grey, almost white hair looks limp and no longer crests like a great bird.

Croome's voice continues over the image of Vogel, "While Commander Vogel has declined to reveal more about his personal grief for his long-time lovers and colleagues, he did inform *Icaria Now* that he intends to place more responsibilities on the Icarian Circle of Ecologists. Whether this also means that he intends to dissolve the Triad, is unsure at this time. *Icaria Now* will keep you apprised of what that will all mean in the days to come..."

Deborah keeps watching the screen as I turn away, mind reeling with the shocking news. The ice queen and that virus Isabo are both dead. It's unbelievable. But, after my initial shock, I feel a kind of guilty *schadenfreude*. Good riddance, I think. I never liked Schlange. I never trusted her. To this day, I think she used Janet's good nature and naivety to achieve her own agenda, perverting Janet's innocent dedication to science and turning it into something political and nefarious. Janet would have insisted that Schlange saved us at the Corporation Farm and I suppose she did. But then she went on to use Janet as her lover's science project in her city of Icaria-11; almost as if Schlange had saved her for that purpose.

I hate all of them. Schlange was a sly and clever vixen and a cold-hearted killer. I still remember how she executed Janet's rapist like he was a stray dog with rabies; according to Janet Schlange also executed Eric Vogel, Schlange's former lover, like a cold assassin. Isabo was a slippery robot-lover who treated humans like lab rats to manipulate with his stupid creed and intelligence tests. And Vogel was a dirty old man who ogled Janet until he got her into his bed; I'm sure that they became lovers. I could tell she was sweet on him.

My mind slides into a dark place where I imagine all four of them on Vogel's bed, naked bodies glistening with sweat, limbs entangled. I see them writhing and sliding over one another like a pile of snakes, moaning and sighing in perverse sexual ecstasy. I can't help my imagination. It makes me want to cry and scream in anger.

I still can't believe that Janet killed herself out of grief at thinking she helped cause Darwin's Disease. That's the story: that some accident caused a virus being researched at the clinic to leak out and morph into Darwin and Janet felt responsible for the accident; but stories these days have a way of being wrong and I can't believe Janet ever being that reckless with a virulent organism. This is the kind of thing that seemed to always happen when her father Ben Hardy worked at BioGen. Bad viruses were always escaping. Like the one that caused the wheat crash in '36, before I was born. But no one committed suicide over an accident. I find my anger focusing on Vogel with an insane idea that makes more and more sense to me the more I think about it: that this is really murder. Vogel is the one who found her; it's too convenient.

What if Damien Vogel knowingly spread Darwin, by orchestrating that accident? He is the twin brother of Eric Vogel, after all: the villain who created a DNA-specific virus that wiped-out half of the human race—just to lower the population to a targeted few. Most people still think *that* was an accident too. Is that what Vogel has done again? Filtering out the weak from the strong? Icaria is in trouble, after all. There's already too many of us in these enclosed cities. The research Euan and I are conducting reveals some harsh realities: dramatically increased rate of infertility; increased neurological disorders and loss of brain function generally; increase in immune loss and immune syndromes. Did Janet find out what Vogel was doing and did he kill her, making it look like suicide, to shut her up? Now with these two murders, I wonder if he also ordered Schlange and Isabo killed for the same reason. Surely they knew if they shared a vee-dammed bed! Does that make him a Dystopian? I remember Euan revealing some things about Vogel's philosophy; some of it seemed to touch dangerously on Dystopian thought. Did the other two of the Triad finally call him out? Schlange was definitely a fanatical Deep Ecologist and despised anything Dystopian. Chaos, she practically invented the use of that term in Icaria.

I glance at Deborah, her eyes glued to the vee-com monitor, and walk back to the kitchen, fists clenched with terrible thoughts of revenge.

—

I quietly enter the large bedroom that my two daughters share. Because I surrendered my eldest daughter to science, the girls now share a large bedroom in a Level-1 Liv-Centre. It all seems rather petty considering the incidents that followed: Julie's delirium and confusion after the virus infusion that didn't really do anything except increase her cognition a bit and confuse her a lot at first. But she's alright now. No more delirium; no more voices in her head. She's a normal little girl, I say to myself. Bright and talented. But normal.

A quick glance reveals that Diana is fast asleep. Julie blinks up at me from her bed. Thankfully, she doesn't look scared of me anymore.

I approach her bed and crouch down to face her with a gentle smile. "I'm sorry I snapped at Mommy and frightened you, Angel," I offer. I stroke her honey-blonde hair "I never want to hurt you. You know that, eh?"

"What did Mommy mean about me being sick in Janet's lab, Daddy?"

I swallow down my discomfort. "She's just a bit mixed up. Don't you worry about it. I love you very much, my little Angel." I seize her in a hug then kiss her good night.

"Good night, sweet Angel."

"Good night, Daddy."

I walk out of the room with thoughts of Janet when we were little.

THIRTY-EIGHT

ICARIA 5, Nadezdha Mall, Enviro-Centre. August 15, 2085: late morning

I lean back in my chair to read some Darwin data in my new lab in DIE. Without looking, I reach out to grab another Turkish Delight, exquisitely dusted with sugar, and pop it into my mouth. Another treat from Euan.

He's been extra nice to me lately. Bringing me pastries from Ziggy's. Inviting me to join him at the Pit Ball Game finals. Buying Deborah and me the newest wall vee-com from Charlton's.

I think he actually feels bad that I'm having to deal with all the flack on our ILM paper published by the *Icarian Scientist* last December. Without my knowledge, the chiphead only put my name on it—like he knew what was going to happen. At first, the paper stirred a lot of interest and excitement among scientists and scholars throughout Icaria. I even got interviewed on *Icaria Now* and felt the flush of celebrity. Deborah was so proud of me. It sparked a renewed romance between us that had been waning since Janet's death. We both laughed at how much sex we were having. We would have made a baby if we were allowed to, but we'd reached our allotment with two girls already.

Then it all came crashing down on me. Only me. Euan quietly watched from the sidelines as everyone vilified me. It started with the Circle who decreed the paper heretical because it used precepts that touched on stable chaos. Euan's reassurance that no one would notice or understand the basis for the rhetoric no longer held water. I started to drown along with the paper. Taking their cue from the Deep Ecologists, the social scientists questioned my methods. Some accused me of fabricating the data. All the scientists who had initially called the work ground-breaking and important, suspected my motives and suggested that the study was not valid because it was fraught with bias errors. The last insult came when the *Icarian Scientist,* pressured by Circle Ecologists, eventually retracted the paper. I was devastated. My career as an ecologist would have been over right then except I was working for Euan at DIE. Of course, he kept me on. The bastard!

The problem is I can't be angry at him for long; he's just so dedicated to his science and he's so jolly and fun to be with. He's like an older brother. Not brooding like Bobby. Though, since Janet's death, Bobby has been less hostile and more friendly. He's even stopped whoring and curbed all that drinking. He still peddles illicit books, which worries me, but we see one another more often and have good conversations. Euan did apologize to me, explaining that I was a better person than him, that I'd displayed far more courage than he ever could. He congratulated me on my guts. The chiphead! I suspect that he's a Dystopian. And that's the real reason why he wished so badly for that article to be published, but also why he was so fearful of being identified with it. The Secret Pols are everywhere and may have already identified him as a likely candidate based on his use of language and other subtle triggers.

On the other hand, is it simply because he's grooming himself for a position in the Circle and can't afford to sully himself with anything remotely controversial?

ICARIA 5, Nadezdha Mall, Enviro-Centre. August 15, 2085: early afternoon

The latter turns out to be true.

Euan bursts into my lab, grinning like an urchin and holding a large bottle of amber-coloured *delilah*. He announces his new position as an Ecologist with the Circle and barks out a cry of victory. He puts down the bottle and grabs me by the shoulders, hauling me up and hugging me. Before I can even flinch, he gives me a great big smacking kiss on the mouth. Then he stumbles to a chair and pulls out the *hedon* from his shoulder bag and two pipes. I recover from his excessive show of affection, understanding that he's a little drunk already, and accept a glass of *delilah* and a pipe already smoldering with *hedon*. We drink and smoke until we both find ourselves rolling on the floor, laughing at nothing in particular. We're both wasted and not in any condition to work the rest of the day. But who am I to complain? That's my boss drooling on the floor beside me.

"You have to come with me to my first meeting in the Circle!" he says, voice slurring between giggles. "I can bring a guest and you have to come. I owe you big time, Len!"

ICARIA 5, Pielou Mall, McMillan Conference Centre. August 17, 2085: early evening

Feeling my heart race a little with excitement, I take my seat next to Euan in the auditorium, removing the vee-set from my head and placing it on my lap. We are seven rows up and the place is filling up with people. It's a kaleidoscopic sea of colours. More colour than I expected; I had somehow thought most Circle members would be from the Enviro-Centre. But I see lots of different colours. Euan and I are, of course, both in Enviro-Centre forest green. I also had no idea there were that many Circle members; then I remind myself that the Circle represents much of Icaria throughout NorthAm. They are essentially the governing body, an anonymous one.

A tall lanky man with matching purple hair and suit stands up from the audience and takes two steps up to the dais. He raises both hands to draw us to order.

Euan leans over and whispers to me, "That's the Circle Speaker, Leif Hansen."

"As you can see, we have a full agenda," says Hansen. "Check your vee-sets for the updated agenda. So, I will get on with it. We will start the meeting with opening remarks from the Circle's Chairperson." The speaker points with an open hand toward a section of the audience and steps down from the dais as a beautiful woman with midnight silky hair stands up. She looks stunning in a sleeveless floor-length blood-red dress that matches her nuyu lips. The plunging décolletage and form-hugging smart material accentuates her smooth skin and tight curves as she effortlessly glides onto the dais. I stare at her, realizing that I'm mesmerized.

Her deep red lips blaze in an electric smile as knife-sharp eyes sweep the auditorium then cut into me with a mere glance. I'm momentarily caught in those probing sapphire eyes like a fish in a net. She is so incredibly beautiful. And she knows it. Then the instant passes and her eyes sweep the crowd like she owns it. Released, I gasp out a small laugh and, embarrassed, whisper through the side of my mouth, "Vee, what's with her dress..."

Euan giggles. "I should have warned you. Her wardrobe is awesome. No regulation Centre uniform for her. She *always* dresses like that."

"Good evening," she says in a calm self-assured voice that is smooth, dark and rich like *delilah*. I find it hypnotic. "My name is Gaia..."

Euan leans into me and whispers quietly, "She's actually the mayor of Icaria-5. Mayors are, of course, anonymous to the public, even to the Centre Heads. Just like Circle members are. But we in the Circle know." He grins like a smug boy with a new game. "And, of course, she's the chairperson of the Circle!" He winks. "Which makes her..."

"...The most powerful person in Icaria," I finish for him.

He punches my shoulder. "You got it, Len!" Then he adds in a conspiratorial whisper, "Vogel's just a figurehead these days. He's just wasted away. I hear that he lives by himself in his flat in Icaria-11 with his cat and doesn't leave. He never sees anyone and seems to do nothing. *She* runs it all..."

Vogel is a broken man, I agree. Deborah and I saw a recent image of him on *Icaria Now* yesterday and he looks half dead. He must have deeply loved Isabo. How could a man kill someone he loved? Then again, I've seen what people can sacrifice for principle and self-preservation. I glance briefly at Euan who gladly sacrificed me for his cause. Is Vogel's grief tinged with guilt? Is that why he is so devastated? He and Schlange had already had a falling out when she died, so no one missed her. Good riddance. I'd feel sorry for Vogel if I didn't think he was responsible for Janet's death—whether he drove her to suicide or outright murdered her. Everyone gets their due, I think, lips firming with repressed anger. And his has come.

Gaia is saying, "...Welcome Circle members, old and new..."

Euan nudges me with his elbow. "She means me, Len!" he whispers gleefully and I can't help a smile at his naïve joy.

"We are the Circle," she proclaims, arms raised to encompass all of us here, as though we are special. "We are the Deep Ecologists upon whose shoulders lies the welfare of the world. We are Atlas reborn. We are the planners and managers to whom all the Icarias of NorthAm answer to. The mayors and the centre heads. We remain anonymous and humble, so no one may feel in debt to any one figure or group..."

More like so no one can target you, I think scathingly to myself and try not to fidget. I am a bundle of nerves. I suspect that they cemented this new ruling after the brutal murders of Triad members Schlange and Isabo a few years ago. They still haven't found the killers.

"There are no heroes in Icaria; there is no need for them. We guide without imposing..."

Tell Deborah that, I think; she wants more kids and we can't have more.

"...As positive reinforcement continues in our schools and homes, thanks to the Isabo Method, there is less of a burden on personal judgment; people find they have all the voice they need to be happy in Icaria..."

Not according to the rising numbers of Dystopians in Icaria, I think. I don't agree with behavioural engineering in the schools and I hate the Isabo Creed. It condescends and over-simplifies and reeks of social agenda and social punishment. I swallow convulsively at the sudden thought: does that make me a Dystopian?

"Because of our selective breeding and genetic modification program at the DP," Gaia continues, "only healthy prosperous children are born and raised by responsible Icarian parents and their supportive Ed-Centres."

Thanks to Euan forewarning us, Deborah and I squeaked in with our 'broadcast' seed way of making babies; Julie and Diana weren't created through the DP's genetic program. We made them through good old fashioned sex and Darwin's heritable chance. We couldn't do that now, even if we were allowed to have more children past the allowable two.

"We are creating a *Homo Deus*, a healthy Icarian who lives sustainably and well-adapted to life inside

Icaria. The family unit is open to free relationships. Free sex for everyone! No restrictions except your imagination!"

The audience around me responds with lots of cheering and some laughter. Gaia laughs lightly. A performance; I can tell.

"We encourage it all," she goes on, smiling out of the corner of her mouth, face creasing slightly with it. Even her smiles appear like a performance. "Sex is very healthy and a healthy Icarian is a good and happy Icarian."

I want to puke at her use of platitudes. She walks the dais, long crimson dress flowing behind her like a trail of fresh blood as she surveys us. I feel her eyes lightly touch me and fight from recoiling from their powerful gaze. Cold eyes the colour of an enigmatic sea lance into me as if mining my soul. She is like a witch, drawing on my energy. I feel suddenly nauseous. As if the cloying smell of disinfectant coils around me. Why do I feel like I'm back at the commune farm with Janet and Bobby? Who is this woman? She's too beautiful, I decide.

Gaia looks down for a moment, as if collecting her thoughts, but more likely to establish the dramatic pause of a skilled orator. I can almost feel everyone palpably leaning forward, caught up in what she will say next. When she does, I'm caught: "Our mandate as Deep Ecologists in the Circle of Icaria is to protect the environment at all costs; it is also our mandate to ensure that humans flourish in our built sanctuaries here, inside Icaria." She looks us all over in another long pause as if assessing each one of us. "It is a dual role we have, my fellow Circle Ecologists. We must maintain that sacred circle of inside and outside. Together yet separate."

My eyes narrow. This touches on something I've heard somewhere before. Something that tears at the frayed edges of my consciousness. Something I should know. I can't bring it to mind but it feels dark and ominous.

"...So, as Nature heals and learns outside, so we heal and learn inside, in this perfectly engineered world," she says, her liquid voice smooth like dripping honey. "In fact..." She stops walking the dais and lifts a slender arm, finger pointing up as if to the heavens. There's that dramatic pause again. "...We are already adapting to the inside. I have it on good authority that an Icarian-specific genetically adapted variant of humanity has naturally developed among us..."

The crowd hushes, followed by murmurs of excitement.

She trains her gaze over the audience then settles those soul-stripping eyes on ... *me*!

I can't help recoiling and halt my breath to keep from gasping. Those eyes... She's looking directly at me. It's just my imagination, isn't it? But then Euan glances at me too.

"What?..." he breathes out, shooting covert glances at me.

My heart pounds like thunder inside my chest as I have a sudden horrible thought. Great vee! Does she mean my little Julie?

Then she looks away and adds casually, "...*Welcome to your world*...because *we all want to rule the world...*"

I inhale sharply. Only one person has ever used those phrases: Monica Schlange. The supposedly dead Monica Schlange, whose body they never recovered. My mind reels as all the wispy tendrils of discomfort find sudden clarity. Did Schlange fake her own death and did she murder Isabo using her Black Guard, leaving Vogel a destroyed man, incapable of anything? Is that who is standing there? With aggressive neurgery and nuyu treatments it's possible. I scrutinize her more closely. I imagine the resemblance. And those knife sharp probing eyes—now a startling blue—always calculating. I know I am looking at Monica Schlange, reborn.

Gaia, the most powerful person in Icaria, is the ice queen!

GLOSSARY OF SCIENTIFIC TERMS AND EXPRESSIONS USED IN THE STORY

Aggressive Symbiosis: When two organisms engage in a symbiotic relationship wherein one of the partners directs aggression outward (exogenously) at a potential rival of the symbiotic partner. Examples abound, including the ant and acacia plant, herpes-B viruses, malaria and yellow fever. The trypanosome that causes epidemics of sleeping sickness is symbiotic with ungulates and its devastation to the human population may be the major reason that the ungulate herds of the African savanna have survived to the present. See *symbiosis* and *co-evolution.*

Ambrosia*: A synthetic recreational drug, dispensed like liquor at parties and bars.

Autopoiesis: Autoproduction. The process whereby an organization produces itself. An autonomous and self-maintaining unity which contains component-producing processes, examples being a cell, an organism, and perhaps a corporation. An autopoietic system achieves self-organization, order out of chaos. It is simultaneously producer and product.

CARifle*: Computerized Automatic Rifle; Techno-made weapon that connects with vee-set and eye-com technology; used by both Technos and Gaians during the revolution.

Chaos Theory: A field of scientific inquiry to explain unstable aperiodic behavior in deterministic nonlinear dynamical systems; a kind of order without periodicity, examples being weather, the spread of epidemics, metabolism of cells, the propagation of impulses along our nerves, changing populations of insects and birds, the rise and fall of civilizations.

Co-Evolution: A dynamic process of change, where two very different species evolve in parallel; in the case of a virus and his host, the host responds to its environment and the virus to the changing genome of the host.

Community of Intelligences*: Concept developed by Christian Isabo that recognizes that human societies and intelligences are multi-faceted and tend naturally toward hierarchy, as do other gregarious species on the planet. Isabo developed a multiple intelligence test (IITT) based on the concept of a community of intelligences; the Gaians also configured their AIs specifically to avoid an AI community of intelligences from developing.

Corporation Farm*: Large federally run experimental farms organized and managed by Canadian Enterprises and affiliated corporations.

Creative Destruction: A term taken from the work of C.S. Holling (University of Florida). A theoretical model developed by scientist, Leonard Crane, to explain the natural cycle of animate and inanimate systems. Crane's model is based on the theoretical and empirical paradigm of ecological behavior proposed by C.S. (Buzz) Holling, which recognizes ecosystems as non-linear self-organizing and continually adapting through cycles of change from expansion and prosperity to creative destruction and reorganization.

Darwin Disease*: A fatal neural disease caused by the mutation of an artificially produced retrovirus, Proteus. Proteus was designed to co-exist in a mutually symbiotic relationship with its human host to enhance cognitive AI communication. Transmitted sexually, once in non-target hosts the virus takes on the role of *aggressive symbiont* and selectively interferes with several neurotransmitters, eventually destroying cholinergic neurons of both peripheral and central nerves. Due to their genetic makeup, *veemelds* are immune.

Deep Ecology: an environmental philosophy and movement that recognizes nature's inherent value and regards humans equal and not superior to other aspects of the global ecosystem.

Delilah*: A synthetic recreational drug, dispensed like liquor at parties and bars.

Dystopian*: The term *dystopian,* coined by revolutionaries in 2056, describes any thought, philosophy or argument that is counter to the current linear order of the current Icarian regime. This includes promotion of chaos theory, stable chaos and other related theories. The term *Dystopian* is the name of a terrorist anarchist organization formed during the height of the darwin plague in response to perceived unwillingness by government to act. Dystopians took the term already in existence since 2056 as their icon to hallmark their force of destructive chaos against the sham of an "orderly" government.

Dystopian Ecology*: a branch of science that follows the ideas and precepts of pre-revolution ecology, some of which is defined by the current Gaian government as driven by dystopian philosophy.

Fractal: Fractals are complicated geometric patterns made up of the same motif repeated on ever-smaller scales. Examples include circulatory and nervous systems. Trees and mountains are other examples. Mathematician, Benoit Mandelbrot, coined the word in 1975 from the latin word *fractus*. All fractals are self-similar – that is, they look the same when examined from far away or nearby.

Fractal Ecology*: A branch of science of chaotics that uses fractals to show how a continually repeating set of organizational levels from molecules to cells and so on to ecosystems interact through functional vehicles like predation, competition, commensalism.

Gaia Hypothesis: a theory proposed by James Lovelock and Lynn Margulis that all live collectively defines and regulates the Earth for the continuance of life and likened to a vast self-regulating organism.

Gaian*: Name of radical activist/eco-terrorist group and later political organization that took power of former Canada in 2057 (with execution of incumbent Technocratic Prime Minister jlkjlk Robinson); member of said organization; adjective for concept or lkjlkj that follows the dialectic of the Gaian movement (e.g. deep ecology, far left politics and radical environmentalism); name originates from Gaia, goddess of the Earth and the belief of Earth wisdom based on the Gaia Hypothesis.

IITT Test*: Isabo Intelligence Type Test, based on multiple intelligences (MI) recognized by psycholgists of 20th century. Isabo applied MI in education and the work environment to maximize efficiency and productivity. The test ranked people Type 1-11, based on known intelligence domains.

Interact-Sym*: A device intended to permit a *veemeld* to communicate directly with the neural network of a single AI or the AI-core, via a retinal scan.

Inverted Loop Model (ILM)*: Uses Fractal Ecology and Stable Chaos Theory to predict the spread of enclosed city-specific disease (environmental disease) such as DARWIN to collapse the city. ILM demonstrates the recursive symmetry of a paradoxical world, displaying regular irregularities that coil and spiral through phases of contrast: smoothness with roughness, motion with inertia, creation with destruction. ILM proved that destruction and creation were one phenomenon, existentially linked and promoting each other as part of stable chaos.

Neurgery*: Neurgery is a procedure of nano-technology in cosmetic surgery to permanently change aspects of a human's form and structure (e.g., bone structure, fatty tissue, etc.). Often done in conjunction with *nuyu*.

Nuyu*: Nuyu is a temporary nano-technological cosmetic procedure to change superficial aspects of a person's anatomy (e.g., eye or hair colour; skin tone, facial hair, etc.). See *neurgery*.

Proteus V (PRO-V)*:an artificial virus which is expected to permanently enhance a person's brain so they can directly interface with an AI.

Provirus: A retrovirus that has integrated itself in the DNA of the host cell. The provirus remains inactive while integrated. It is passed on to the cell's offspring, which will bear proviruses in their genomes.

Retrovirus: A virus possessing a unique cellular enzyme, reverse transcriptase, which uses the viral RNA as a template to make a DNA copy, which is then incorporated into the chromosomes of the infected cell. Endogenous retroviruses (proviruses) may lie dormant inside the chromosomes, until they manifest once more. They may seek out the germ cells (eggs or sperm) and subsequently passed on from parent to offspring. See *trasposon* and *provirus*.

Stable Chaos*: A precept within *chaos theory*, which suggests that order emerges spontaneously from chaos as synchronous self-organization. Dr. Leonard Crane used this concept in his model to explain the natural cycle of creative destruction in both ecological and societal behavior. The theory proposes that every system undergoes cycles that are never quite the same each time and driven by what chaotics calls 'strange attractors' into a kind of evolving destiny of destruction and creation. The concept originated partially from the 1974 Gaia Hypothesis by Lovelock and Margulis, which proposed that the planet is a self-regulating organism. Stable chaos was first coined by Gleick in his 1989 bestseller, "Chaos", who provided an excellent example: Jupitor's Great Red Spot. "The spot is a self-organizing system, created and regulated by the same nonlinear twists that create the unpredictable turmoil around it. It is stable chaos."

Stable Chaos Theory*: Posits that every system undergoes fractal cycles that are not quite the same but with some self-similarity and driven by what chaoticists calls 'strange attractors'. The phenomenon of stable chaos is considered a kind of evolving system destiny of destruction and creation. Originally formulated by Dr. Patrick Fairweather in 2025, it was later refined by Leonard Crane and Euan Tsutsumi and applied to Icaria through ILM.

Strange Attractor: A term used among chaoticists and mathematicians, an attractor is the property of complex systems that represents the state to which the system eventually settles. Strange attractors, coined by David Ruelle, professor of theoretical physics, are attractors that consist of infinite dimensions. These fractal objects describe how order can dwell within chaos and represent the outward manifestation of organizational *autopoiesis*.

Symbiosis: In context with co-evolution, symbiosis is the state of equilibrium that results from two co-evolving organisms over a long time and many generations.

Technocracy: A form of government in which the decision-maker(s) are selected based on their expertise in a given area; any portion of a bureaucracy run by technologists. Technocracies control society or industry through an elite of technical experts. The term was initially used to signify the application of the scientific method to solving social problems.

Technocratic Government: See "technocracy"

Transposon: A movable element ("jumping gene") that can move or have its DNA copied from chromosome to chromosome and inferentially from cell to cell. Transposons may contribute to variation in all genomes. See *provirus.*

Trophic Cascade: An ecological phenomenon triggered by the addition or removal of keystone requirements that create reciprocal changes in relative populations of all trophic levels of a food chain and often resulting in dramatic changes in ecosystem structure and nutrient cycling. First described by Aldo Leopold based on his observations of overgrazing of mountain slopes by deer after human extermination of wolves, trophic cascades are powerful interactions that regulate biodiversity and healthy ecosystem functioning; they may occur as top-down, bottom-up or subsidy cascades. Trophic cascades control species composition and production of biomass, as well as interaction of plants and herbivores. Marshes and other aquatic ecosystems represent a balance of bottom-up and top-down regulated systems, with bottom-up controls including resources available such as water, nutrients and light and top-down controls being consumers and their all-important predators.

Trophic Level: The trophic level describes the position in a food web or ecological pyramid within an ecosystem at which the transfer of food (energy) takes place from one organism to another. The various levels include primary producers (autotrophs such as plants and algae) and their heterotrophic consumers, herbivores and omnivores, and their predators up to the apex predator. Decomposers (fungi, bacteria) have no assigned trophic level, operating independently to recycle energy from all levels.

Vee-com*: Quantum-operated computer that includes holographic components for 3D visuals or large or small screens. Mobile version is the vee-set (worn on the head) and vee-pad (that acts like a book or drawing/writing device).

Veemeld*: Noun: A person whose unique genetic makeup permits them to communicate directly with the AI-network through a retinal scan (*Interact-SYM*). Julie Crane (daughter of Leonard Crane and Deborah Lerner) and her daughter, Angel Woods, are capable of spontaneous communication with machines via the symbiotic virus, Proteus, inside them. Verb: the act of communicating with the AI-network via a retinal scan or through the symbiotic virus, Proteus.

Vee-pad*: See vee-com.

Vee-set*: Essentially a computer worn on the head. Along with eye-coms that neatly attach to the head, these provide recognition software and instant AI intel similar to what the Techo-clones use and more powerful than a current smart phone.

White Plague / White Demon*: DNA-based virus developed by Eric Vogel and technicians at BioGen. The virus was designed to specifically make Caucasians sick and possibly infertile, kill people with higher melanin content, and leave Techno-clones unaffected. The virus killed half of the world's population and inflicted additional impacts. The term was originally coined by a conspiracy theorist as a sarcastic pejorative, suggesting that the virus was manufactured and purposefully leaked by Technocrats with a white supremacist agenda in purposeful extermination. Other open racists embraced the term as being delivered by God to purge humanity of less pure elements.

*** a fictional term or concept created by the author, or modified or expanded from another source by the author**

GERMAN, SWEDISH (S) AND FRENCH (F) TERMS AND EXPRESSIONS USED IN TEXT

Älskling (s): Darling; sweetheart

Ausgezeichnet: Excellent

Backpfeifengesicht: Someone deserving of a face slap

betriebshedingte kündigung: Compulsory redundancy

boah: Exclamation of amazement

Chouchou (f): darling; my sweet (endearment for a person of unmatched care, love and beauty, who makes your world go 'round')

Das ist erstaunlich: That's amazing

Drecksau: Filthy swine; 'Shithead'

deutsche Gründlichkeit: German thoroughness

Furchtbar: Terrible, horrible, frightful

Guter Gott: Good God

Hase: Rabbit

jag måste ha dig nu (s): I must have you now

Jammerossi (Jammer Ossi): Complaining East German; taken from the slang terms 'Ossi' for East German and 'Wessi' for Western German. Contributed to two opposing derogatory terms: Jammerossi (complainer) used by West Germans, particularly Besserwessi types; and Besserwessi (know-it-all) used by East Germans that refers to a person from the former West Germany who behaves condescendingly towards people from the former East Germany

Kneipe: Bar or pub

Kuddelmuddel: Jumble, hodgepodge; confusion

Letzte Generation: Last Generation

Liebender Gott: Loving God

Ostalgie: Nostalgia for all things from the former DDR

Popo: One's bottom; slang term for police

Reichsbürger: Citizen of the Reich

Reichskanzers: Imperial Chancellor; head of state

Schlampe: Slut

Schnucki: Sweetie

Schnuckiputzi: Sweetie pie

Schrecklich: Dreadful, terrible, awful

Süß: sweet

Süßer (mein Süßer): Sweetie (my sweet man)

Verdammt: damn

Wende: 'turning point,' referring to the changes associated with East and West German unification

Zersetzung: A military term that means attrition or corrosion, redefined by the Stasi to describe their tactics and methods used to 'switch off' a group or individual by undermining the target's quality of life (both socially and in the workplace) and rendering them ineffective by destroying their confidence; this included gaslighting, isolation and creating conflict.

Zögerlich: hesitant

BIBLIOGRAPHY / FURTHER READING

Brinks, J.H. 1997. "Political Anti-Fascism in the German Democratic Republic." *Journal of Contemporary History* 32(2): 207-217.

Diamond, Jared. 2011. "Collapse: How Societies Choose to Survive or Fail." *Penguin.* 608pp.

Holling, C.S. 1987. "Simplifying the complex: the paradigms of ecological function and structure." *Eur. J. Oper. Rel.* 30: 139-146.

Holling, C.S. 1973. "Resilience and stability of ecological systems." *Annual Rev. Ecol. Syst.* 4: 1-23.

Holling, C.S. 1977. Myths of ecology and energy. In: Proceedings Symposium on Future Strategies for Energy Development, Oak Ridge, Tenn., 20-21 October, 1976. *Oxford University Press,* New York, N.Y.

Gibson, William. 1999. "The Science of Science Fiction." *Talk of the Nation,* Washington, D.C. National Public Radio, November 30, 1999.

Gilmore, Scott. 2016. "A Forgotten Horror Comes Roaring Back." *Maclean's Magazine.* May 30, 2016.

Gleick, James. 1989. "Chaos: Making a New Science." *Penguin/ Viking Books,* New York. 352pp.

Jackson, Lauren and Tara Godvin. 2021. "On the Path to Day X: The Return of Germany's Far Right." *The New York Times,* July 6, 2021.

Kappelt, Olaf. 1981. "Braunbuch DDR. Nazis in der DDR." Berlin.

Karavolias, Nicholas G., Wilson Horner, Modesta N. Abugu, and Sarah N. Evanega. 2021. "Application of Gene Editing for Climate Change in Agriculture." *Front. Sustain. Food Syst.* 5: 1-23.

Kennedy, Jonathan. 2023. "Pathogenesis: A History of the World in Eight Plagues." *Signal,* New York. 294pp.

Kulish, Nicholas. 2008. "A Dancer Goes Back to Her Past in Berlin." *The New York Times,* July. 5, 2008.

Loose, Ingo. 2008. "The Anti-Fascist Myth of the German Democratic Republic and its Decline after 1989." In: Michal Kopecek, ed., *Past in the Making: Historical Revisionism in Central Europe after 1989. Central European University Press.*

Luxemburg, Rosa. 1915. "The Junius Pamphlet: The Crisis in the German Social Democracy." Marxists.org.

Munteanu, N. 2016. "Water Is... The Meaning of Water." *Pixl Press,* Vancouver. 586pp.

Ng, Jimmy. 2022. "CRISPR Gene Drives: A Weapon of Mass Destruction?" Medium.com, Dec 29, 2022. Online: https://medium.com/predict/crispr-gene-drives-a-weapon-of-mass-destruction-81dcc6be4e5b

Osborne, Margaret. 2023. "Destructive 'Super Pigs' From Canada Threaten the Northern U.S." Smithsonian Magazine, February 27, 2023. Online: https://www.smithsonianmag.com/smart-news/destructive-super-pigs-from-canada-threaten-the-northern-us-180981692/

Powers, Richard. 2018. "The Overstory." *WW Norton & Company,* New York. 512pp.

Rawlence, Ben. 2022. "The Treeline." *Jonathan Cape,* London. 342pp.

Rennefanz, Sabine. 2019. "I was a teenager in East Germany when the Wall fell. Today we are still divided." *The Guardian,* November 6, 2019.

Thompson, E.P. 1980. "Notes on Exterminism: The Last Stage of Civilization, Exterminism and the Cold War." *New Left Review* 1: 121.

Wiesenthal, Simon. 1968. "Die gleiche Sprache: Erst rur Hitler-jetzt fur Ulbricht." Pressekonferenz von Simon Wiesenthal am 6. September 1968 in Wien. Eine Dokumentation der Deutschland-Berichte. Jiidisches Dokumentationszentrum, Simon Wiesenthal Centre, Vienna.

Ysselstein, Geraldine Marion. 2007. "East German Material Culture: building a collective memory." Master of Arts Thesis, University of British Columbia, April, 2007. 81pp.

www.ingramcontent.com/pod-product-compliance
Lightning Source LLC
LaVergne TN
LVHW050915080826
845145LV00001B/89

* 9 7 8 1 7 7 4 0 0 0 7 6 2 *